The Miles to Dundee

The Miles to Dundee

D. A. Ferguson

The Pentland Press
Edinburgh Cambridge Durham

© D. A. Ferguson 1993
First published in 1993 by
The Pentland Press Ltd.
1 Hutton Close
South Church
Durham

ISBN 1 85821 077 1

Typeset by Print Origination (NW) Ltd., Formby, Merseyside
Printed and bound by Antony Rowe Ltd., Chippenham, SN14 6LH

To Dorothy,
with my love as always

"Cauld winter was howling o'er moor and o'er mountain,
And wild was the surge on the dark rolling sea,
When I met, about daybreak, a bonnie young lassie,
Wha asked me the road and the miles to Dundee."

Contents

1. Pitbuddo
1850 – 1857

There were few folk about on the High Street. Apart from a barefoot bairn or two at their games, the man and woman standing at the open door of the grocer's shop, and the horse and cart drawn up nearby at the pavement's edge, the place might have been deserted. The September sunshine filtered through the overhanging branches of the beeches which long-sighted men of an earlier generation had planted on the far side of the street, dappling the pavement with a shimmering pattern of light and bringing out russet glints in the woman's shining hair. The man had one arm around her shoulder and she was doing her best to wriggle clear and not succeeding.

"Don't touch me!"

"Och, Jessie, lass, don't be daft – surely you can send me on my way with a wee kiss!"

The woman stamped her foot and her eyes were flashing. All the signals were set at danger.

"Don't you come soft soaping me, Tom Gray! You're nothing but a drunkard and a wastrel! Why I ever married you goodness only knows. Now leave me and get away up the glen with your cart – if you can see well enough to drive!"

"Och, Jessie! That was last night, just; to hear you go on, anyone would think I was out at the 'Temperance' every night."

"You were drunk, Tom Gray! That's what you were! Singing in the street like any tink' and laughing fit to burst – all the neighbours would hear you! What kind of a way is that for an honest citizen to behave?"

"Och, Jessie!"

"Och, Jessie! Och, Jessie! Is that all you can say?"

"Jessie! I've told you a hundred times what happened. I met Willie

Guthrie as I was coming up the street and, as we were passing the 'Temperance' at the time, we went in for a dram, just! That's all!''

"That's all! You should think shame of yourself for getting mixed up with that Willie Guthrie – spending siller that should go to feed and clothe your wife and bairns! Aye! Right enough! You'd better get off up the glen and fill that leather pouch of yours – I don't want you here!''

Tossing her head, Jessie wrenched herself free and fled through the shop, slamming behind her the connecting door leading into their house. Tom, a rueful expression on his open and comely countenance, scratched his head and was about to lock the shop door when, out of the corner of his eye, he saw something move behind the counter.

"What are you doing there?"

"Nothing, father!'' The boy's voice was sharpened by a feeling of apprehension and guilt.

"Well – come out and let's have a look at you! I suppose you heard all that?''

"I heard Mamma raise her voice and I came down to see if anything was wrong.''

Andrew, their first born and their only surviving son, was barely fourteen. Tall for his age and well built with a mop of fair, curly hair, he looked his father steadily in the eye.

"I saw Willie Guthrie going into the 'Temperance' as I came home for my dinner.''

No-one could remember who had coined the name "Temperance" for the town's one and only hostelry but everyone from far and near knew it as such and nobody would have thought of calling it by its real name, "The Ramsay Arms". It had a fine ring to it of which Danny Dow, the publican, was justly proud and he was forever lamenting the cruel fate that had foist upon the premises such an unjust sobriquet.

"Well!'' said Tom, "You just forget it! It's high time you cut along to school – you'll be late if you don't hurry!''

Andrew was still looking at him with the wide-set blue eyes that reminded Tom so forcibly of Jessie.

"Were you really drunk last night, father?''

"Go! – confound it – before I take the side of my hand to your lug!''

Andrew lowered his gaze and took himself off down the street where he was joined by a few others of his age making their way back to school. For his part, Tom closed the shop door behind him and locked it. He unhitched the horse's reins from the post to which they had been tied, jumped on to the driving board, and set off up the street. The cart was well laden and they went slowly, rolling slightly to the camber of the cobblestones.

Tom liked Tuesdays when he could shut the shop at midday and go away up the glen. Usually he had the cart loaded on Monday but as he had been otherwise engaged last night he had thrown things together hurriedly this morning and he hoped he had not forgotten anything. The regular rhythm of old Jenny's hoofs, combined with the warm sunshine, made him feel drowsy, but he was aroused by a great shout and was just in time to see big Geordie Milne, the farmer at Mains of Pitbuddo, drive past in his smart new gig.

"Ho, there, Tom Gray! A grand day, man!"

"It is that, Pitbuddo!" Tom waved acknowledgement.

Indeed it was a beautiful day. In fact, it had been a fine summer. The crops had ripened early and, for once, those who worked the land were well pleased. Down in the strath, the stooks of oats and barley had been cleared from the broad riverside acres; hares and the smaller creatures of the banks and hedgerows had the bare stubble to themselves and the farmers, as they surveyed the well-filled stackyards, were already dreaming of the substantial bills they would be able to draw upon the grain merchants at the market in Forfar. It would all depend of course, upon timing. Heavy yields made for a glut, and a glut meant lower prices. The fortunate ones would be those who could hold the corn, without fear of loss, until diminishing supply should force prices up again.

Here, on the braes, the hill farmers like Pitbuddo, and those whose small holdings were scattered throughout the glens, were equally pleased. They had secured a good return for the wool crop – the demand emanating from the Yorkshire buyers appeared as insatiable as ever and – when they could be persuaded to part with it – their money was good. Lambs had sold well and even the hill cattle, for which there was normally only a local market, had fetched satisfactory prices. All this was in stark contrast to the usual run of events. Life on the land was never easy. Often – especially here among the more marginal farms – it could be harsh and downright grim. In consequence, the aura of well-being that hung in the air this September day was almost palpable – something which permeated not only the countryside but also villages and towns throughout the county since each was quite inextricably dependent upon the other.

Jenny the mare had got into her stride and as they left the cobbles behind and set out on the rutted country highway stirring up thick dust on either side, Tom set to speculating upon the ways in which his neighbours in the red sandstone houses now falling away behind them would react to this new-found prosperity. The tradesmen would be eagerly looking forward to the prospect of being paid for work done over a period at farms and country houses; the shopkeepers – like himself – could anticipate an upsurge in business, as could Danny Dow at the "Temperance", while old Sam Coutts, the banker, sitting behind the green wire screen at the high counting house desk installed in one of the front rooms of his law office, would be positively euphoric. Now at last he might go rummaging in his Bill Case to dig out some of the past due paper about which his Head Office in Edinburgh had been pestering him for ages.

Doubtless he would get a few of these paid off and, as he was a crafty old devil, he might even think it worth his while to journey into Forfar on a Saturday. If he did he would probably catch some of his borrowing customers as soon as they left the market and before they had any chance to squander the proceeds of sale.

Tom's first stop was at the wayside cottage where Annie Ogilvie, the roadman's widow, lived in somewhat straitened circumstances. Her worldly wealth, a few golden guineas she kept under the mattress in the toe of an old stocking, would not last forever and Tom knew it was a question of which would run out first, the old lady or the cash. He prayed it might be the former for Annie, who was independent to a degree, would not take kindly if she became a dependent under the new Poor Law.

Annie was in the backyard feeding her hens. They supplied her with eggs; she had a couple of nanny goats that kept her in milk, butter and cheese; and, on the patch of land by the gable end of the cottage, she grew enough potatoes and curly kale to see her through the winter. She also kept bees and Tom bought, for sale in the shop, such combs of honey as were surplus to her requirements.

In consequence, her needs were small; oatmeal for porridge and bannocks; barley and a ham or knuckle bone for the black stock pot forever simmering on the hob; tea and sugar, soap and candles. On occasion, when Joe Spalding the gamekeeper could so contrive, she would get a rabbit or a hare – sometimes even a cut from a haunch of venison – but, like many of the poorer folk in town and country, she never attained the luxury of wheaten bread or butcher meat.

Annie eagerly awaited Tom's coming. She looked forward to these visits and, when she heard Tom's shout, she laid down the empty pail of poultry food and hurried round to the front door, wiping her hands upon the ample folds of her long black skirt.

Every week Tom fetched up whatever his customers in the glen had ordered on his previous visit. Today he had brought her a few ham shanks and a large bar of soap.

"Tom Gray! Tom Gray!" Annie scolded him. "Ye were to bring me a bane for the pot – naething mair. Guidsakes, man! Yon are mair like ham legs!"

"Indeed no, mistress," said Tom. "They're shanks, just – no meat on them worth speaking of!"

"Ye ken that's a lee, Tom; but I thank ye kindly for a' that. Come in ben for a cup of tea."

Tom followed her indoors. There was only one room in the cottage, sparsely furnished with a stout oaken table and two wooden chairs. A tall, old-fashioned dresser stood against the far wall in a corner of which, that nearest the hearth, was a box bed neatly made up. A fire of logs was burning in the grate and a kettle, sitting upon a trivet swung over the fire, was boiling merrily. The room was warm and smelled sweetly of southernwood. On the table were six combs of honey.

"I took these off yesterday, Tom. Ye'll be taking them back wi' ye?"

Annie Ogilvie took the kettle from the hob and infused the tea.

"They're kittle creatures, the bees," she said. "There's a new queen in the hive and like as not some will be off wi' her any day noo seeking a new hame. Sit doon, lad! Sit doon for any favour and hae your tea!"

Taking the big earthenware teapot in her hand, she poured a drop or two of the black, scalding liquid on to the fire where it hissed and evaporated in a wisp of steam. Then she filled two cups. They each stirred in two spoonfuls of sugar and a little goat's milk from the jug on the table. Tom spoke very little. He had no need; Annie Ogilvie said enough for the pair of them. Except when she went to the kirk on Sunday and for Tom's Tuesday call, she rarely had the opportunity of talking and being a naturally garrulous person she made the most of it. When his cup was drained and he rose to go Tom placed eleven shillings upon the table.

"What's this?" said the old woman, sharply. "I havena paid ye for the ham banes."

"I've allowed for that, mistress. You have six combs of honey there, so I'm due you twelve shillings. I've taken eightpence off for the ham shanks and fourpence for the soap and that's the balance on the table."

Annie suspected that Tom overpaid her for the honey and she was quite right. He would be lucky to get tenpence a comb for them and there was no finer honey produced in all the countryside.

"Thank ye, Tom Gray! Ye're a kind man!"

"Good day to you, mistress!" Tom turned away to hide his embarrassment.

When Tom got outside he found Jenny quietly cropping the wayside grass and once he was up on the box and moving off he waved goodbye. The widow woman stood and watched until they were out of sight. Just over half a mile from the cottage the glen road makes a sharp left-hand bend before rising up the steep ascent known as Cadger's Brae. It is a testing climb for man or beast. As he always did, Tom jumped down from the cart to ease the weight slightly and, with the reins in his hand, he plodded uphill at Jenny's head. They said locally that Cadger's Brae was over a mile long. It was barely that but – apart from the corner at the lower end – it ran straight and true throughout its length. At the top the glen opened out – a wide valley of woods and farmland threaded by the silver ribbon of the river. The higher slopes were awash with the royal mantle of the heather and, where the glen narrowed, up towards its head, the Grampian peaks crowded together on the skyline. It was a fair prospect at any time but with the sun beating down from a blue sky it was as intoxicating as wine and Tom found himself singing with the sheer delight of it.

In a half mile or so they turned off the highway at the ornately pillared gateway into the wooded policies of Pitbuddo House. The porter at the lodge waved as they passed.

"Aye, Tom!" he called.

"It's a rare day, Davie!" Tom raised an arm in salute and the porter, who had been cutting the triangular patches of lawn flanking the gate, laid down his scythe and turned to the task of sweeping up the cut grass.

The driveway curved gently through a thick screen of shrubbery. It was cool in the shade and skeins of midges danced up and down about Jenny's ears. Tom was bitten himself and his ineffectual swipes at the little pests succeeded in driving them off but only temporarily. Back they came a few seconds later to settle round his ears, in his hair and inside the cuffs of his shirt sleeves.

Pitbuddo House consisted of a mediaeval tower alongside which, in the previous century, Sir George's grandfather had built a compact modern residence. The entrance, reached by two flights of steps curving up on either side, looked as if it might have been transported from Charlotte Square and above the lintel of the door, carved into the stonework, was the family coat of arms and the date, "1785", in Roman numerals.

Tom drove on round to the back of the house where he expected to find the butler. This day, however, was out of the ordinary for, when he reached the cobbled courtyard, he found himself face to face with the laird himself.

"Good afternoon, Gray!" Sir George was a man of medium height, with a florid complexion and thinning hair which had once been golden but now was the colour of old straw. He had piercing blue eyes under fierce looking and extremely shaggy eyebrows and his dress would not have looked exceptional in a London club on the eve of Waterloo. Under his right arm he carried a sporting gun which he now brandished right under Tom's nose.

"Having a shoot tomorrow! Just making sure all is in order! Have you brought any whisky?"

Tom had leapt down from the cart and, although he doffed his bonnet respectfully, he stood erect and looked the laird in the eye.

"Whisky, Sir George! Why no! It has never been called for in the Pitbuddo order. Perhaps there has been some mistake."

Out of the corner of his eye Tom saw, behind Sir George, the portly figure of Mr. Cloake, the butler, and Mr. Cloake's countenance wore what could only be described as a thunderous frown. Tom smiled inwardly and hoped he was keeping his face straight. Sir George was talking again.

"Can't stomach the stuff myself! Rot gut! That's what I call it – fit only for Highland caterans and robbers! Never used to drink it in the old days. Men were men then! By God, sir, they were! We drank Rioja in the Peninsula – by the caseful. Have you ever tried it? Just as good as claret and a damn sight less expensive. When anything spiritous was called for we drank Armagnac, when we could get it, and West Indian rum when we could not. But now the new generation want nothing but this Highland firewater. Having a few guests for the shoot – fellow officers and their sons – so we had better have some whisky. I hear there's a very popular blend being marketed by some fellow down in Ayrshire."

Tom found Sir George's accent, acquired during his schooling at Eton, very difficult to follow and it took him a second or two to realise that the man was talking of John Walker, the Kilmarnock grocer who, in little more than a decade, had made a name for himself and for his whisky throughout the land.

"I can let you have a case, Sir George; I have a little in stock but, if you need it quickly, I cannot be of help, sir, until next Tuesday when I shall be in the glen once more."

"If you have it in the shop, Gray, then I shall send for it! Good day to you!"

"And to you, Sir George!"

The laird strode away and Tom was left with the butler. Mr. Cloake was an Englishman who hailed from near Ashford in Kent and ruled the staff at Pitbuddo with a rod of iron. He tried to rule Tom as well but had long since given him up as a bad job. Mr. Cloake always tried to convey the impression that he was bored to distraction with everybody and everything at Pitbuddo and that he was counting the days until he would be able to return with the family to their town house in London. It was some time before Tom, his business at Pitbuddo completed and his leather pouch weighing somewhat more heavily, turned Jenny's head back up the driveway to rejoin the main road. He pulled out his large fob watch. The time was past four o'clock and he had two farms – the Mains and another – and two crofts to visit.

In consequence it was fully six o'clock before he returned down the glen and nearly half an hour later before he passed the lodge gates at Pitbuddo and headed for the crest of the Cadger's Brae. The cart was lighter now with most of its load left behind at the various stopping places in the glen and Jenny, going at a brisk trot, was making good time. The westering sun was now out of sight behind the shoulder of Pitbuddo Hill at the entrance to the glen and the road lay in shadow.

At the lip of the brae the spreading branches of an old gnarled oak tree hung over the road. Tom was surprised the tree had not been cut back long ago. He had mentioned it to Davie Lowson at the lodge and Davie had said he would see to it. The wonder was that Sir George himself had not complained. How the coachmen could pass without having their tall hats knocked off was a mystery. Today as he approached Tom was conscious of a humming sound which for a moment he could not place. In fact, Jenny was turning slightly to the right to avoid the worst of the overhang before Tom realised that the humming, intensified to a throbbing and sustained buzzing, was coming from a large swarm of bees which had settled on the lowermost branch of the tree and now hung over the road like a menacing cloud.

In an instant, horse, cart and man were enveloped in a stinging mob of angry workers as they hastened to protect their newly flighted young queen. Tom threw up his hands to protect his face while Jenny, alarmed and terrified, and maddened by painful stings, took off in a headlong dash down the brae. The cart rocked violently to and fro on the uneven surface of the road, bucking and twisting crazily from side to side. Tom tried to fling his weight upon the brake but it was no use – he was being tossed about like a cork in a bath, and it took him all his time to remain on the driving box. Jenny's speed, aided by gravity, grew faster and faster as they hurtled on down the brae but – miraculously – the cart remained upright and they might have escaped unharmed but for the bend at the bottom and a particularly deep pot hole which buckled the left-hand wheel and wrenched it off. The cart pitched on to its side in a jack-knifing motion, the shafts shattered and broke while Jenny, suddenly freed from restriction, galloped off round the corner, trailing behind her the traces and splintered ends of wood.

As for Tom, he was catapulted clear – straight into the smooth bole of an old beech standing at the roadside. He hit the tree trunk head first with considerable force and was killed outright.

* * *

Jenny the mare, arrived home at dusk, wild eyed and in a lather of sweat, with pieces of broken harness and splintered timber trailing beside her. Andrew who was hard at work chopping sticks was first to see her as she clattered into the yard. One look was sufficient to see that she was blown but she stood quietly enough, her flanks heaving, while Andrew grabbed the short end of rein still dangling from the bit in her mouth. With his other hand he caressed her muzzle and the mare, reassured, sighed deeply.

Jessie too had heard the noise of hoofs and, with her elder daughter, Meg, at her side, came running. With a sickening sensation in the pit of her stomach Jessie took in the scene at a glance.

"Meg, dear," she said, quietly, "run away like a good lass to the Gardynes and ask Jim to come round here right away!"

Meg, who was ten, sped off at once and, together, Jessie and Andrew freed the mare from the debris. Then Andrew led her off to rub her down and to see that she was fed and watered before he tied her up in her stall. Neither he nor Jessie had spoken as neither wished to put into words the fears that assailed them. There had been an accident and from now on any news was more likely to be bad than good. They were, however, totally unprepared for just how bad the news was when it eventually came.

In a matter of minutes, and long before Andrew had finished at the stable,

Meg returned with Jim Gardyne. In addition to being close friends, the Gardynes were neighbours who lived only two doors away. Generations of the Gardyne family had served the community as soutars in the old Scottish tradition. Jim still made working boots for men, and boots and shoes for the women and bairns. When new soles or heels were needed, or when uppers required stitching, folk would call in at the cobbler's shop which occupied the room at street level at the front of the premises. Jim had been a life-long friend of Tom's and both wives, Jessie and Agnes Gardyne, were very close.

"What's all this, Jessie?"

"See for yourself, Jim. The mare's come back on her own as if chased by a pack of demons and she brought that with her."

Jessie pointed to the debris lying where they had left it on the cobblestones.

"She must have broken loose. Tom will be back directly. You'll see!"

"Jim! We can't be sure. Tom may be lying somewhere badly hurt. It looks as if the cart overturned. He may be trapped underneath."

"Jessie! Jessie! If we let our imagination run riot there's no end to the dire pictures we can paint. Let's look on the bright side!"

Jim sounded confident – much more so than he felt. He was inclined to think Jessie was right in the gloomy view she was adopting. Nevertheless his words reassured her, as was intended, and she smiled hesitantly.

"Look, Jessie! You get away in-bye with Meg. Andrew can look after you. I'll gather a few folk and go to find Tom!"

"I'm coming with you!"

Neither of them had seen Andrew come out of the stable. He spoke quietly, but from the tone of his voice, it was obvious they would have extreme difficulty trying to persuade him otherwise. Jim looked at Jessie who gave an almost imperceptible nod of the head.

"Very well, laddie! Get a coat on for it can be gey chilly at night in the glen now that autumn's here. Jessie! I'll ask Agnes to come over and keep you company. We have her aunt from Montrose biding with us just now and she can look after the bairns."

Andrew had already run off but he returned immediately wearing an old riding coat of his father's which reached only to his knees and acted as a perfectly good greatcoat.

"Come then! Let us be off! Goodbye, Jessie – and stop worrying!"

They set off within the hour, a party of six. Jim, with Andrew mounted behind him, rode a horse hired from Danny Dow at the "Temperance" and with them, but on his own chestnut gelding, rode Sandy Shirress, the builder. They carried lanterns and picked their way carefully along the darkened road. Since it was likely they would find Tom hurt to greater or less degree, Matt Lundie, the carrier, in a two-wheeled cart, not unlike Tom's had been, brought up the rear. Two of Matt's sons, lads in their early twenties, came with him.

They reached Annie Ogilvie's without incident. There was a light burning in the cottage and the old woman herself, having heard the sound of their approach, was at her door as they drew level.

"Good e'en to you, Mistress Ogilvie! It's Jim Gardyne. We're seeking Tom Gray. His mare's home without him bringing with her bits of harness and splintered wood. Did you see or hear anything?"

Annie was shocked and taken aback.

"Na! I've heard naething ava. Tom Gray was here earlier on, but I didna hear him coming back. That's nae muckle wonder, mind, for I was gey thrang maist o' the time awa' doon by the back dyke yonder ettling to nab a swarm o' bees, but they jinked me, the deils! Tom Gray's a kind man and I wadna wish ony ill to come ower him. It doesna sound good but maybe ye'll chap on the door, Jim, on your road hame for, good or ill, I wad wish to ken."

"I will that, mistress. Thank you!"

They moved on. The harvest moon had not yet risen and it was extremely dark. In fact it would have been impossible, even by the light of the lanterns, to pick up the line of the road ahead had it not been for the white dust lining the verges. Here and there where the surface of the highway was particularly stony, the horses' hoofs struck sparks off the road. The sound of their going combined with that of creaking leather, the jingle of harness, and the rumble of Matt Lundie's cart, shut out all others. It was therefore a considerable shock when they came round the bend at the foot of the Cadger's Brae and saw, in the guttering light of several lanterns and flares, a number of men standing in the middle of the road. As Jim and his party drew nearer, a big man, holding a lantern at the full extent of his upraised arm, detached himself and came towards them. As the light from the lantern fell full across his face, Jim recognised him at once.

"Pitbuddo!" he exclaimed.

"Aye sae! And wha's this?"

"Gardyne!" he said, "Jim Gardyne."

"Aye, aye. I see ye noo! If ye've come to seek Tom Gray ye needna look nor speir ony further. A sorry day it is too and a sorrier for his wife and bairns! Ye'll find Tom laid oot on the grass yonder. There isna a mark on him ither than an ugly bruise on the temple. Deid? Aye – certies! Frae the looks o' it he wad hae felt naething ava!"

The words hit Jim like a hammer blow and, in the same instant, he realised that Andrew was no longer seated behind him. He had been so taken up listening to Geordie Milne that he had failed to notice the lad slipping down from the horse's back. Alongside him Sandy Shirress, who had also been giving all his attention to the big farmer, motioned with one hand.

"Go and get him, Jim! I'll look after the horses."

Jim flung a leg over his horse's head and jumped to the ground. The ring of men parted to let him through but he took only a couple of paces before stopping short. Tom's body was stretched out on the grass verge. The flares lit up the scene in a lurid glow that cast on the bushes at the wayside long shadows looking for all the world as if they were engaged in a macabre dance. Andrew was kneeling beside his father quietly sobbing. Jim was annoyed with himself. He should have kept a proper watch over the lad and spared him this ordeal. After all, he was little more than a child. Pulling off his bonnet he moved forward and bent down to place a hand on the boy's shoulder.

"Come, Andrew! There is no more you can do. I am truly sorry, lad! I loved him too, you know."

Andrew, his eyes brimming with tears, gazed up at him. His face was devoid of all expression and the look in his eyes was one of utter desolation. Jim knew that, in this instant, Andrew was a child no longer and he grieved for that lost boyhood every bit as deeply as he grieved for Tom.

"Andrew; come now," he spoke again, softly, and this time the boy did as he was bid. As they turned away Jim could see in the flickering light that Tom's face looked peaceful and serene.

Once more the men in the centre of the road made an opening for them. Sandy Shirress and the Lundies were waiting with Pitbuddo.

"How long have you been here, Pitbuddo?"

"Ten – twal' minutes, just, afore ye. I was in toon the day wi' my gig; 'deed I saw Tom Gray in the High Street and gied him a shout in the bygaun. I had a wheen o' business to see to and I was keepit gey late. It was getting fell dark by the time I wan this far but I could see weel eneuch. I dinna mind telling ye the auld horse fair shied but I had a guid grip o' him and poued him up. It's mair than Tom was able to dae wi' his, puir lad! The mare maun hae bolted. Man! Ye should hae seen the cairt. Ye'll see it in daylicht – bits just strewn alang the road and hauf way up the brae. It didna tak' me ower lang to find Tom, nor to ken that the puir lad was past helping. Nae doobt ye'll be wishing to tak' the body hame wi' ye?"

"Aye – we'll do that."

"I'll come back doon the morn's morn and get this redd up." Pitbuddo kicked aside a piece of shattered planking and called upon some of his men to lift Tom's body and place it in the Lundies' cart. This they did gently enough while Andrew stood shivering with Jim's arm round his shoulders. There was nothing more to be done and, after bidding each other goodnight, the two parties turned about and, in opposite directions, set off for home.

Jim stopped at Annie Ogilvie's. He did not need to speak. The old woman took one look at his face and covered her own with her apron. It was much the same when they got back to town. Jim did not know how he could face Jessie and he slid from his horse as he heard her come running across the yard. When she saw his face and Andrew's tear-stained one she stopped in her tracks.

"What – happened?" she asked in a dull, listless voice.

"I think he must have been thrown out of the cart: likely he hit a tree head on. He would feel no pain, Jessie."

"Where is he?" She took a step forward towards the street where they could just see the head of Matt Lundie's horse.

"Jessie! No!" Jim stood between her and the gate.

"Get out of my way, Jim Gardyne!"

He moved aside and she went through to the street. Sandy Shirress and the Lundies bowed their heads in embarrassment and were silent.

Notwithstanding the jolting of the cart over the rough road, Tom's body remained as Pitbuddo's men had placed it and for long minutes Jessie looked down where it lay stretched full length on the wooden planks Then, she stooped and kissed the cold forehead.

"Forgive me, Tom, darling," she whispered. "Oh, please forgive me!"

She turned abruptly and, finding Andrew at her side, she fought bravely to hold back the tears.

"It'll be all right, mamma; I'll look after you." Already the boy's head was level with her chin.

"Yes, my dear. I'm sure you will." She put an arm round his shoulders. Then, turning to the men standing there, "Thank you," she said. "Thank you for all you have done."

"You have our sympathy, Jessie lass." Sandy Shirress raised his head and looked her directly in the eye.

"'Deed aye, mistress!" Matt Lundie was never a talkative man at the best of times.

"We'll take him down to Gibbie Meldrum's," said Jim.

"No!" said Jessie, vehemently, "Bring him in-bye."

"But, Jessie . . . . "

"Please do as I ask, Jim. I'm not having him carted all over the town. This is his home; he belongs here and here he'll bide. Gibbie Meldrum can come round in the morning and see to him here, just as if he had died in his own bed."

They laid him down in the parlour and Jessie shut and locked the door.

Agnes Gardyne stayed with her overnight and, in the morning, she went back to her own house taking Meg with her. Little Jemima, the baby, who had just turned three, had been ill and was being kept in bed which, in the circumstances, was a blessing. Agnes had scarcely gone before Dr. Robertson arrived and he was followed within minutes by Gibbie Meldrum who had his work completed by mid-forenoon. Gibbie's establishment proclaimed that he was in business as a joiner and undertaker. He was indeed a craftsman in wood, although many folk, tongue in cheek, described him as a boxmaker. Clock cases or coffins – it was all one to Gibbie, so they said, as each doubled for the other.

Once she was alone again, Jessie re-locked the parlour door and so it remained until the Friday morning when she endeavoured to take her mind off what was about to happen by busying herself cleaning, dusting and airing the room. Again Agnes was there to help which was just as well since Tom's Aunt Eliza – a forbidding-looking woman in black bombasine, with a seemingly endless supply of lace handkerchiefs tucked away in the small reticule she carried everywhere with her – had arrived from Dundee and would have taken charge had not Agnes, very firmly, set her down by the curtained window where she was able to look out discreetly and keep her all-seeing eye upon everything that was going on in the street.

Shortly before eleven o'clock Aunt Eliza spotted the first arrivals and, within quarter of an hour, the minister of the United Presbyterian congregation was in a position to commence the short service he was to hold for the immediate family and close friends, following which the coffin would be carried out to where the other mourners were waiting by the black-draped hearse. Apart from Jessie and Andrew, Aunt Eliza and the Gardynes, there were only seven others in the parlour – the Reverend James Black, Sandy and Jean Shirress, old Adam Kidd, the baker, and his daughter Lizzie, Gibbie Meldrum and young Charlie Tait who was employed by Tom in the shop. Charlie had kept the shop going over the past two days – but now the shutters were up and no groceries would be sold until he should re-open tomorrow.

Jessie was dry eyed and calm although, inwardly, grief weighed her down like a stone. She knew that if she once started to sob she would not be able to control herself. For the three nights Tom had lain here in this room she had hardly slept at all and there were dark circles under her eyes. Mr. Black's voice seemed to come from very far away.

"Let us pray," he said, and they bowed their heads reverently. It is doubtful if Jessie heard a word. Over and over again she castigated herself for not having wished Tom goodbye that terrible day. His voice – that of her heart's darling now gone from her forever – kept coming back to her as she knew it would continue to do so long as she lived.

"Och, Jessie, lass, don't be daft – surely you can send me on my way with a wee kiss!"

If only she had. Oh – if only she had done just that! There had been no necessity for her to berate him as she had done. The night before he had returned home merry, but not drunk; most assuredly not drunk; she knew him better than that! It was just that she had had a particularly bad day. Little Jemima had developed a hacking cough. She was having a great deal of difficulty regaining her breath and on several occasions she had been sick. They had lost their second child – a boy christened Thomas after his father –

at much the same age, carried off by the dreaded croup, and Jessie was sore afraid. She had come down to the shop at least three times that morning but Tom, who had been very busy serving customers, had made light of it.

"Don't worry, Jessie. She'll be all right. Just get Dr. Robertson to see her. He'll know what to do!"

Dr. Robertson had been late in coming, although Jessie had left a message at his house by the middle of the forenoon. He had in fact been up the glen and it was dusk before his gig drew up at the house door. By this time Tom had gone out to see Matt Lundie as he was expecting a load of provisions up from Dundee. The consignment had not arrived and it was while he was walking back home that he had met Willie Guthrie. Dr. Robertson had been reassuring.

"Keep her in bed and warm! I'll call again tomorrow. Meantime I'll make her up some medicine to ease the cough – perhaps you would be good enough to send young Andrew to fetch it."

Jessie was just beginning to relax when Meg, who had been in the back yard helping her brother to cut sticks, took a bit out of her thumb with the axe which Andrew had laid down when he went out for the medicine. Meg was screaming as though she had chopped off her thumb at the root. Certainly the cut was bleeding profusely and Jessie had difficulty in staunching the flow before tying on a bandage. In the middle of this, Jemima had another coughing fit and hardly had Jessie got her settled before Andrew was back with the medicine. So it had gone on until, at last, with the children all abed and asleep, she had seated herself, thankfully, in the rocking chair at the kitchen hearth.

It was then she heard Tom coming back. He was clearly in good humour. She could hear him singing softly to himself as he fitted the big key into the outside lock. She could hardly be blamed for rounding upon the poor man when he came through into the kitchen. She had given him a piece of her mind right enough, and she should have left it at that. But, as so often is the way, her wrath fed upon itself and intensified. To her sorrow, as she thought of it now, she had refused to speak another word to him, not only then but also when they awoke in the morning – he, alone in their big feather bed, and she, wrapped in a blanket and lying on the kitchen floor.

Vaguely she heard Mr. Black reading from St. John, Chapter fourteen – "Let not your heart be troubled: ye believe in God, believe also in me. In my Father's house are many mansions: if it were not so I would have told you . . . ."

If her conduct, excusable though it was, merited some form of punishment, surely there could be no justification for the tragedy which, in the event, had been inflicted upon them.

Mr. Black was deep into his final prayer and now Jessie was fully alert. Looking between her fingers she saw Gibbie Meldrum screwing down the lid of the coffin and opening the parlour door to admit two of his men. They blundered into a small table set rather too near to the door and knocked it over. Mr. Black's sonorous voice rose appreciably in volume and Gibbie picked up the table and set it down out of harm's way. By the time Mr. Black came to the final "Amen" Gibbie's men had departed with the coffin and Gibbie had closed the door behind them. The men filed out, Andrew going with Jim and Sandy. To Jessie, left behind with the other ladies, it was all rather unreal.

Out in the street there was a very large gathering indeed. Tom was a popular member of the community and everyone had been shocked and saddened by his tragic and untimely death. Now, with heads bowed and tall lum hats in hand, they took their places behind the hearse and its pair of glossy black horses to walk to the little burial ground outside the town beside the pre-Reformation kirk of Pitbuddo. On arrival they stood around wherever they could. Many were unable to get in at the gate and they crowded together outside the cemetery wall and did their best to hear what Mr. Black had to say.

Back at the house Jessie and Agnes had plenty to do. While Aunt Eliza, who appeared more taken up with the rigours of her journey from Dundee than with the demise of her only nephew, poured out the tale of her sufferings to Jean Shirress and Lizzie Kidd – who were a captive if not necessarily a receptive audience – Jessie spread her best lace cloth on the table and set out cups and saucers on a wooden tray. She and Agnes had to be quick for it would not be long before the other ladies, having seen their men-folk off to join the funeral procession, would be chapping at the door. When everyone was back there would be tea, a dram for the men if they so desired, scones and fruit cake. Jessie wished Aunt Eliza would stop chattering. Already she was well into her stride.

"Such a shaking! And the noise! You've never heard the like. The locomotive clatters and clangs and goes 'chuff – chuff – chuff'; the smoke and steam blow back into the carriages and, to crown it all, there are hot cinders fleeing about all over the place. It's a wonder we weren't all set on fire! What with the carriages creaking and groaning and the wheels going 'dumpity dum – dumpity dum' I can assure you it was a terrible experience. I cannot imagine how I am going to find the courage to climb aboard again to go back to Dundee."

Neither of her hearers had experienced the thrill of riding in a railway train. Indeed it was only comparatively recently that the Aberdeen Railway Company had built a branch line up the South Esk to Brechin and, in truth, Aunt Eliza's journey had been an onerous one involving three different railway companies and three changes.

"Well!" said Jean Shirress, "I have never had any necessity to travel by train but, from what you say, I fear I shall think twice about it although Her Majesty seems to enjoy it!"

"What it is to be young!" Aunt Eliza was not going to be put off, by the Queen or anyone else. "In any case they say that the Prince is not too keen. He once told the conductor that he hoped the train would travel much more slowly the next time they had occasion to use it on the way from London to Windsor! He is a wise man! I wish he would have a word with the powers that be on the Dundee and Arbroath. The speed they reached outside Carnoustie was positively frightening!"

Jessie wished with all her heart that Aunt Eliza would cease her eternal chattering but, even when the ladies began to arrive, she could still hear her above the general hum of conversation. Once the men returned the little room was crowded to capacity and Jessie was so taken up trying to see that everyone had some form of refreshment that, for the time being, she ceased to turn everything over and over in her mind.

"It's a good thing Jessie has got the Gardynes to help her," said Dr. Robertson, setting down his glass and looking somewhat askance at the teacup in the minister's hand. "Looking after the shop and the bairns too will be gey difficult. I canna think what she'll do."

"She's a good living woman, doctor," said the minister. "The Lord will provide."

"Ah well, minister, I hope you are right! Whiles I think He doesna mak' a very good job of it judging by what I see in some parts of this town – and that no so very far from here!"

Mr. Black, who was a sincere man and devout, swallowed the retort that rose to his lips. After all, Dr. Robertson was not of his flock. He was a member of the Established Church and remarks of this nature were only to be expected. He tried to move away to have a word with Mr. Coutts, the banker, but everyone was jammed in so tightly he had to stay where he was. Dr. Robertson, however, had managed to slide towards the door where Jessie was standing, teapot in hand.

"How's that bairn now, Jessie?"

"She's much better, doctor, thank you; the medicine seems to have stopped the cough."

"Capital, Jessie, capital! I'll just take a look at her before I go. No! Don't you come; it's no as if I didna ken the way. Then I'll just slip out, Jessie. Thank you, lass. Tak' good care of yourself!"

One or two people, seeing the doctor leave, decided that it was time to go and the crowd in the parlour began to thin out.

Aunt Eliza, who had not stirred from her seat at the window, was as talkative as ever but the faces of the two ladies beside her now wore rather glazed expressions.

Lizzie's father, who was very deaf, had moved across to join them.

"I was telling them of the changes I saw in Brechin yesterday!" said Aunt Eliza.

"What were you seeking?" Adam Kidd cupped a hand to his ear.

"No – not seeking! Brechin! There have been some changes since John and I left."

"Oh!" said Adam, "Brechin!"

"Yes! I've been all of seven years in Dundee."

"Ah!" said Adam, "Dundee! I thocht you said Brechin. I havena been in Dundee since I was a lad."

"No, father!" said Lizzie, shaking her head, "Mrs. Barrie's speaking about changes – aye – changes that she sees in Brechin since she left!"

"Don't worry, Lizzie, dear. My John was deaf, poor dear, before he passed on and I know how tiresome it can be. Well, as I was saying I see a big difference in the town. The new school looks very braw, and I see they've completed all these additions at the Mechanics' Institution. I mind the day they laid the foundation stone. My! That was a day of days right enough. You never saw such a carry on!"

"That's right, Mrs. Barrie – a wonderful day! Sandy and I were there too. I mind the flags in the street and the procession – twenty eighth June wasn't it, 1838 – Coronation Day!" Jean Shirress was not going to be outdone.

"Yes," said Aunt Eliza, somewhat miffed. "Were you also at the ball?"

"No."

"We were! What a marvellous occasion it was! All the county was there. What with the colours of the ladies' dresses, and their jewels and tiaras and things, and all the ribbons of the decorations worn by the men, I remember saying to John that I was quite dazzled. And then, there were the fireworks! Such a whizzing and banging. We never seem to have such festivities nowadays. I – "

Whatever else Aunt Eliza was about to say was cut off short as Sandy Shirress came up to announce that it was time he and Jean were off home. Thankfully, Jean bowed to Aunt Eliza and followed her husband to the door. It was not long before the family were left to themselves and to the tidying up that had to be done.

"Now, Jessie," said Aunt Eliza, after the children were in bed and Jessie, in a state of near exhaustion, had thrown herself down in a chair by the kitchen fire. "It is time you and I had a talk about what you are going to do!"

"Please, Aunt Eliza! No! Not just now; I've had just about as much as I can stand!"

"Now, Jessie! You must pull yourself together!"

Aunt Eliza was looking even more forbidding than usual but Jessie was past caring.

She rose to her feet, the chair legs scraping on the floor, and she clapped her hands over her ears.

"No!" she screamed, "No! No! No!"

She flung out of the kitchen and into her own room, banging the door behind her. She threw herself on the bed – the big feather bed she had shared with Tom – and at long last her reserve broke and the tears welled up. She sobbed uncontrollably until her pillow was sodden and then, throwing it away, she curled up on top of the blankets and cried herself to sleep.

* * *

Lying on his bed in the little room with the dormer window, Andrew heard his mother crying and he wished with all his heart that he could comfort her. He also heard Aunt Eliza moving about in the kitchen. Maybe she would go off soon to the bed in the girls' room normally occupied by Meg who was staying on meantime with the Gardynes. Andrew also had been crying. He was very young and he had never been to a funeral before. Any burial would have been bad enough but, when it was your own father down there in the box, the pain of it was beyond telling. All he could think of now was the hollow sound of the clods of earth falling upon the newly lowered coffin as the gravedigger shovelled the soil down in time with the minister's chant of "earth to earth – dust to dust". Andrew shut his eyes tight and put his hands over his ears to shut out the sight and sound that had haunted him ever since they had left the cemetery. Fortunately he was tired and he too fell fast asleep.

In the morning when he awoke he could still hear the earth showering down – "dust to dust – ashes to ashes" – but gradually, as the days passed and the family settled down into a new routine, the picture of the open grave, although he would always recall it with startling clarity, was inevitably pushed into the recesses of his mind.

Aunt Eliza, shaking her head over Jessie's continued refusal to talk about "her future", took herself off back home by hired carriage to Brechin and thence by the railway train she viewed with such foreboding. Meg came home from the Gardynes and little Jemima, looking pale and thin, was running about once more and playing in the yard whenever the weather, which remained remarkably mild for the time of year, allowed.

Jessie – poor Jessie – did her best to pick up the threads of life: she knew she owed it to the children and she willed herself to carry on and to remain outwardly calm when the girls, unwittingly, turned a knife in the wound when they would ask such things as –

"Where is pappa?"

"Why can't we go and see him?"

"Will he be coming home for my birthday?"

"Do you think he'll be getting fish for his tea?"

Jessie worked, at that time, harder than she could ever remember. In addition to the daily chores of running the house, cooking the meals, washing, wringing and ironing the clothes, darning socks and stockings, sewing hems and threading on buttons, she proceeded to give the house what she called its "autumn cleaning". This involved beating rugs; cleaning out cupboards, drawers and shelves; taking down curtains, washing them and putting them through the mangle, and cleaning windows and rails before putting them up again. Everything received a dusting which was more thorough than normal – if this were possible. Brass ornaments were cleaned with lemon and all the furniture was polished.

On top of all this, Jessie went over the shop books and accounts with Charlie Tait once a week and agreed the orders he wished to place with the wholesale merchants in Dundee. As they felt it essential to keep the glen customers supplied, they hired a cart from Matt Lundie to enable Charlie to continue, with Jenny's help, the Tuesday afternoon round. Once all the bills had been paid, including that rendered by Gibbie Meldrum and the cost of the hires which Jim Gardyne had arranged that awful night – the hack from Danny Dow and the outfit from Matt Lundie – there was just enough left over to ensure that the rent due to Pitbuddo Estates, the landlords, could be paid when it should fall due at the Martinmas term.

Andrew was doing well at school. He seemed to have a real flair for mathematics and Menzies Dickie, the dominie, considered him one of his star pupils. He had confided so to Jessie who had flushed with pleasure and determined she would do her utmost to see that he finished his schooling – as Tom would have wished – when, hopefully, he might go on to university at St. Andrews or Aberdeen. Tom's own father, a graduate of St. Andrews and a minister in the Relief Church, had died when Tom was only three, and he always used to say what a want this had been in his adolescent years, and how greatly he envied those of his contemporaries who could turn to their fathers for guidance and advice. His mother – Aunt Eliza's eldest sister – having died when he was born, Tom had been reared by his maternal grandmother on whose death he had inherited the grocery business. As for Jessie, she had lost both her parents at one and the same time, victims of the cholera epidemic of 1832, just a few months after her marriage to Tom, and for her part she knew full well what it was like without a mother to turn to. In consequence, Jessie felt very keenly indeed the responsibilities which now rested upon her shoulders as a surviving parent. Unusually for their day and generation, Jessie and Tom had few living relatives – Jessie had been an only child – and she felt very alone.

The fine weather continued into October and clear skies at night led to frosty mornings when the trees in the High Street were dusted with rime and the mist lay in pockets along the low-lying stubble fields of the strath. The swallows that had nested above the stable door had long since flown south while, up the glen, Charlie Tait had heard the muttering and roaring of the red deer stags at the rut.

One morning, towards the end of the month, he was in the back shop discussing the deer and their life cycle with one of Matt Lundie's sons who had just driven up in a cart laden with sugar and dried pulses. One by one, Jock Lundie pulled and dragged the sacks to the tailboard of the cart while Charlie backed up to take the weight on his shoulders. They had nearly finished when Charlie heard the bell which gave notice that a customer had come in through the shop door. Straightening up, he let the sack he was carrying slip gently down on top of the stack he was piling up in a corner of the storeroom and brushed his hands together to knock off the dust.

"I'll have to go, Jock!"

"Aye, aye – we're gey near through. I can dae the lave."

When Charlie came back into the shop, he saw to his surprise that the customer was a man he did not know. They seldom had strangers in the shop or even in the town. The man was tall and well dressed in riding breeches and cut-away brown coat with a black velvet collar. His freshly laundered neckcloth was neatly tied, his brown boots were polished and shining and, draped resplendently across his waistcoat, was a gold watch chain. In his right hand he held his hat and his riding crop which he tapped against his boot as he spoke.

"Mistress Gray, please!" His tones were a little clipped but the voice was Scottish.

"Yes. She's in the house. Who will I say is calling?"

"Major Webster," said the man, "from Brechin."

Charlie turned and took a step towards the front door. He was conscious of the fact that this Major Webster was following him but the man had an air of authority about him and Charlie did not like to ask him to wait on the far side of the counter. Jessie was black-leading the parlour grate when she heard Charlie knocking. What on earth could he be wanting at this hour of the forenoon? Nevertheless, she went to the door wiping her dirty hands on her apron. When she opened the door she saw Charlie's anxious face and, to her astonishment, a tall man standing behind him.

Oh, my goodness, she thought in alarm, it's the Major! What on earth can he be wanting? And – oh dear! What a ticket I am! She was right, too. Her hair had escaped from under her mob cap and, where she had tried to brush back a few of her golden-red locks, her fingers had left a pattern of black smudges on her forehead. Strangers would expect to see her doucely clad in widow's black but instead she was wearing the dress in which she usually did the housework – a cotton shift in faded pink which nevertheless contrived to show her comely figure to advantage and, being a degree or so too short, also displayed neat ankles, black woollen stockings and black buttoned boots. The ribbons of her apron were tied at the back in a large bow but the apron itself was soiled with the dirt from her hands where she had wiped them.

"Oh! It's Major Webster isn't it?" Jessie had never spoken to the man but like most people in town she knew the Major by sight. She stood aside and motioned him within.

"Yes, thank you mistress!" The Major brushed past Charlie Tait as if he did not exist and stood in the narrow lobby which ran the width of the house between the front door and that leading into the yard. With his riding crop he continued to beat a tattoo against his booted leg.

"Thank you, Charlie," said Jessie. "Er – this way, Major, if you please."

Charlie withdrew back into the shop, closing the door behind him while Jessie, walking before the Major, led the way into the parlour. Major Webster was conscious of the swing of her hips and the way her buttocks moved under her dress and he moistened his upper lip with the tip of his tongue. Jessie pointed to the grate, to the basket containing cloths and black lead and polish, and to the brushes lying where she had left them on the hearth.

"As you can see," she said, "you have surprised me in the middle of my forenoon's work, and I fear you must take me as you find me."

The words struck a chord atune with the Major's thoughts but he bowed acknowledgement and was silent.

"Please sit down, Major," Jessie continued. "Will you take a cup of tea?"

"Thank you, mistress, no!" The Major was looking about him at the modest furniture, at the lace antimacassars on the two high-backed armchairs, the plainly curtained window and the china ornaments on the mantelpiece. He had held the post of factor to Sir George Ramsay for close on twenty years. For this reason the townsfolk assumed he must be good at his job. Although he divided his time between the Estate office in Brechin and Pitbuddo itself, and scarcely ever condescended to visit the town where most of the feus and leases were concentrated, he was known to be a cold and hard man with a reputation for pursuing his factoring duties with a degree of ruthlessness which was foreign to the nature of his gentlemanly employer. Major Webster cleared his throat.

"Hrrm! I was distressed, mistress, as was Sir George to be sure, to learn of your sad bereavement."

"Thank you, Major; you are most kind." If Jessie was sure of anything, it was that Dick Webster had not called here this morning to commiserate with her upon Tom's death. The Major cleared his throat again, rather more noisily. He stood with his back to the door, legs planted firmly apart.

"H-H-Hrrm! Your late husband's lease of the house and shop, Mistress Gray," he said, "expires at the Martinmas term. I would not wish you to think that it will be renewed in your favour."

Jessie was aghast – her face drained of colour. She had invented one or two reasons for the factor's visit but this, the obvious one, had never so much as entered her head. In any case, Tom's will had left all his worldly goods to her.

"Expires?" she said, dully. "I understood there were still some twenty years of the lease to run!"

"Ah, yes! The lease was entered into between your late husband and the estate at Martinmas 1835 for a period of thirty-five years. You are therefore correct when you speak of a span of years but this is a maximum time – I trust you follow me, Mistress Gray – not a hard and fast determinate period of years. The lease also provides for breaks – points at which the contract may be terminated by either party at one month's notice. One of these breaks occurs at the fifteen-year point – that is to say at Martinmas in this present year of 1850. Accordingly, Mistress Gray, I am formally giving you notice to vacate the premises by the twenty-eighth day of November next, that is to say four weeks hence."

"Vacate the premises? You mean – give up the shop and leave this house?"

"That is exactly what I mean, mistress!"

"But – I have the money for the Martinmas rent; the Martinmas rent will be paid!"

Indeed it will, mistress – but not by you, I fear!"

"But – the shop is my livelihood and the house is our home. How shall we live? Where can we go? Where shall we find a roof to shelter us – and the winter coming on?"

"That is no concern of mine, mistress! But, of course, the new tenant will require to pay you for the stock, appurtenances and goodwill – that is to say if you decide to sell the business."

"Sell the business; what else can I do?"

"That is for you to decide, mistress; but I consider it likely that you will receive an offer from the new tenant!"

"The new tenant?" Jessie was repeating the factor's words now in parrot-like fashion. "Who?" she asked.

"I have no idea. There are one or two applicants but no decision has yet been made. It is unlikely, however, that it will go to – a woman!"

Jessie felt her mind reeling but she fought to keep her emotions under control.

"Major Webster!" she said, "we have been good tenants over the past fifteen years, as my late husband's family were for many years before. The property is wind and water tight and in good repair. We have not called upon the estate to put this, that and the next thing right as is sometimes the way between tenant and landlord. The household at Pitbuddo are our good customers and, so far as I am aware, they have always found the service we provide to be satisfactory. Why, then, are we being treated thus? Isn't there anything I can do to make you change your mind?"

To her surprise Jessie found that, as she talked, her despair was giving way to anger. The colour returned to her cheeks and her eyes flashed. Dick Webster looked at her afresh. She was a good looker and no mistake, especially now she was aroused.

"There is one thing maybe – " He spoke slowly and the look on his face sent a cold shiver up Jessie's spine. " – Yes! – There is one thing that might persuade me to recommend a renewal of Tom Gray's lease in his widow's favour! I need a bed in this town from time to time, Mistress Gray, and if you would – eh – co-operate, I think – no, I am sure – there would be no occasion for you to be selling the business!"

Jessie was stunned. She could not believe her ears. That such a thing could be said by the laird's factor, to her, Jessie Gray, here in her own parlour was beyond everything. She drew back her right arm and, with her open palm, she struck the man full across the mouth. Jessie was a strong woman and the blow was a heavy one, tempered only by the fact that Webster had seen it coming and was drawing back slightly. As it was he bit his own lip and drew blood.

"Maybe you will now wash out your dirty mouth and leave my house." Jessie spoke firmly and with authority. "It *is* my house, Major, until Martinmas. After that you will require to deal with your new tenant. In the meantime I shall take myself up the glen and have a word with Sir George himself. I wonder what he will say, Major, when I tell him how his factor deals with his tenants, especially when they happen to be women!" The contempt and loathing in her voice were very plain.

"It will do you no good – even supposing Sir George were misguided enough to see you," Webster's face was livid. He was dabbing at his mouth with a linen handkerchief and his eyes were like burning coals. "You may tell him what you will, I shall deny it! Which of us will he believe, do you think? His right-hand man, his man of business, his factor? Or a woman half crazed with grief over the death of her husband and the imminent loss of livelihood and home? Good day to you, mistress." With his left hand he pulled a letter from his jacket pocket and threw it down on the table. "Your formal notice to quit!" he said. "We shall inform you, in good time, as to the name of the new tenant."

"Get out!" said Jessie. "The front door is straight ahead down the lobby."

Dick Webster turned on his heel. Without another word he strode down the lobby, pulled open the front door and slammed it shut behind him.

On the following Tuesday Jessie accompanied Charlie Tait on his weekly journey up the glen. It was a cold, raw day and a thin wind shook the trees with sufficient force to loosen a leaf or two and send them spinning to the ground. Jessie had spoken to no-one regarding Dick Webster's visit and she was still in a state of emotional turmoil. Her chagrin was all the greater for the thought that Webster could think it might be possible to buy her off in such a way. Those about her, finding her withdrawn and short tempered, shook their heads and commented upon how deeply she was being affected by Tom's tragic death.

She spoke little to Charlie as they drove out of the town and when they reached Annie Ogilvie's cottage she remained on the driving box.

"And what like is your mistress noo, Charlie?"

"Not very grand, Annie; in fact she is with me the day. Sitting in the cart, just staring into the distance. Not like herself at all. She's hardly spoken a word to me all the time we've been on the road. Perhaps if you went out and spoke to her – ?"

"Na! Na! Charlie. Just leave her alane. Gin she wished to see me she wad hae come ben wi' ye. Sic a shock as yon wad fash onybody. Ye maun hae patience, Charlie loon; time'll tak' tent o't!"

"She was a wee bit more like herself, Annie, until the factor's visit last week."

"The factor! Mercy on us!" Annie Ogilvie said no more. She had a good idea as to why Jessie should have been singled out for such a call and, if she were right in her surmise, it was small wonder Jessie was keeping her own company and looking dowie and wae.

Jessie had not been near the Cadger's Brae since the day of the accident and she had no wish to see it now. Accordingly she stared fixedly at the toes of her shoes as they drove round the corner. Charlie got down to ease the load for the hill and Jenny, who was not too keen on the hired cart, made heavy weather of the climb. Jessie was glad when they reached the top of the brae; it would not be long before they would be at Pitbuddo House. Her heart was beating faster than normal and she felt nervous and keyed up. She hoped the laird would be at home: certainly the family were still in residence – Charlie was taking up an order – although any day now they would likely be leaving so that they could be installed in their London home in good time for Christmas. Suddenly she realised what a cheek she had thinking that, even if the laird did agree to see her, he would be the slightest bit interested in her petty affairs.

Jessie was seized with panic and it took every ounce of her will power to refrain from grabbing the reins from Charlie's unsuspecting hands and driving on past the lodge gates. But she steeled herself to remain calm – outwardly at least – even when they started down the long drive through the damp and encroaching shrubbery. Jessie had wondered whether she should go to the front door and ring the bell but, on second thoughts, she had decided that such forwardness might not only be unproductive but might also jeopardise her case – if she had one. Far better to pocket her pride, go to the tradesmen's door at the back and ask Mr. Cloake to arrange an interview.

When they got there one of the housemaids was coming down the steps from the kitchen door with a pail of hot water in her hand. Seeing the cart approach she set down her pail and ran back into the house. Before Charlie had brought Jenny to a halt Mr. Cloake appeared, stalking majestically down the steps, the girl at his heels. Had Jessie not been so preoccupied with her own thoughts and worries she would not have failed to notice the colour suffusing the girl's cheeks as she picked up the steaming pail and looked coyly at Charlie while making her way across the yard to the stillroom. Nor could she have missed seeing how Charlie himself blushed to the roots of his hair.

"Good day to you, Mistress Gray!" said the butler, bowing. "It is not often we have the pleasure of seeing you at Pitbuddo!"

"How do you do, Mr. Cloake." Jessie inclined her head but remained seated on the driving box. "I came up today with Charlie for a very good reason." Tom always used to say the radiance of Jessie's smile would charm the most cantankerous of men. Mr. Cloake was certainly not in that category but Jessie's smile assuredly put him in rare good humour and, although it did not quite succeed in cracking his habitual mask of pomposity, her next remark certainly did.

"A very good reason indeed," she continued, "I wish to speak with the laird!"

Mr. Cloake's jaw dropped and he came within an ace of uttering a most un-butler-like expletive: tradesmen and the like did not present themselves before the gentry unheralded and for the widow of one so to do was even more heinous.

"You – you wish to speak with Sir George?" Mr. Cloake sounded affronted and outraged. "I – I very much doubt if he will see you."

"But you will ask him – please, Mr. Cloake!" The smile had faded from her eyes and she looked hapless and forlorn. She was certainly very alluring in her adversity and Mr. Cloake, who was of a kindly disposition, felt his heart go out to her. He did, however, contrive to retain the dignity of his exalted station.

"Very well, Mistress Gray. I shall do as you request. Kindly wait here until I return." With measured and unhurried tread Mr. Cloake re-entered the house.

No sooner had he gone than there was a flurry of petticoats as the little housemaid came running from the stillroom to where Charlie stood waiting. Once again Charlie's face went a bright pink and the girl, catching sight of Jessie, hitched up her skirts and ran, giggling up the kitchen steps.

They had to wait fully five minutes before Mr. Cloake returned. His face was impassive as always and gave nothing away.

"Well, Mr. Cloake?" Jessie looked at him expectantly.

"I have spoken with Sir George. He was much taken aback – 'pretentious' – I think, was the word he used. At first he demurred but after

I had spoken to him at greater length he graciously agreed to spare you a few minutes. Let me help you down, mistress! So! Now, follow me, please!''

Never before had Jessie been inside the house of Pitbuddo and she looked about her now with considerable interest. For their part, the kitchen maids stared at the lady in the black coat and bonnet. One of them – the girl who had come looking for Charlie – whispered something to one of her companions, whereupon they both giggled and earned a frown of displeasure from Mr. Cloake and a hissed warning from Mistress Barker, the cook. At the far end of the kitchen, a short flight of steps led up to a green baize door, beyond which they passed into the spacious high-ceilinged hall where their footsteps rang out loudly upon the flagged floor.

On their left was the stairway – wide and carpeted – and, straight ahead, the door leading to the front vestibule. The afternoon light came in through long windows one on each side of the vestibule door and filtered down from a glass cupola high above the upstairs landing. With a degree of satisfaction Jessie saw the candle sconces which would light the house during the hours of darkness – no question of modern improvements here in the depth of the country. In the town it was different. The streets of Brechin had been lit by gas lamps for a number of years past and many of the better houses too. Even in their own little town a gas works had been built within the past year and most of the High Street houses now boasted a gas supply. On the right, through an open door, Jessie caught a glimpse of chintz chair covers and a small table covered with a wine-coloured tasselled cloth. A vase of autumn flowers stood on the table along with a number of silver photograph frames.

The door for which the butler was making was to the left beyond the foot of the stairway. Mr. Cloake stopped before it and knocked deferentially. Jessie heard Sir George's voice calling, "Come in!"

Signalling clearly and unmistakably that she should remain meantime where she was, Mr. Cloake opened the door with a long, sweeping motion and disappeared within. When he returned, Jessie squared her shoulders and followed him in, her head held high. The room was simply furnished. The whole of one wall was taken up by an immense bookcase, shelf after shelf stacked with old leather-bound volumes reaching up to the ceiling. On the opposite wall were two full-length portraits – one of his late Majesty King George III and the other of Wellington, the Iron Duke himself. Of family portraits there appeared to be none.

Sir George, who had been seated at a writing desk placed in the window embrasure, arose at Jessie's entrance and bowed stiffly.

"Mistress Gray, Sir George!" the butler murmured.

"Very good, Cloake: I shall ring when I require you."

Mr. Cloake bowed and, moving slowly and silently upon the thickly carpeted floor, left the room. When the door shut behind him there was a brief moment when Jessie could hear no sound other than the thudding of her heart beat and the slow ticking of a long-case clock standing against the wall to the left of the door.

"Good day to you, Mistress Gray," said Sir George. "I was distressed at your husband's sad demise. Pray accept my condolences. Capital fellow! Could do with more like him! Seen a few in my time – in my regiment, you know, back in the Peninsula – but they breed 'em soft nowadays. No back bone! Too many distractions and modern inventions – like this railroad, damn it!" Notwithstanding his clipped, somewhat staccato turn of speech, Sir George spoke gently enough and the expression in his eyes belied those fierce-looking brows. Jessie felt that, maybe, there was hope for her after all.

"You are very kind, Sir George," she said quietly, "both in the sympathy you extend and in your ready agreement to spare a moment of your time for one who comes as I do without appointment."

Sir George inclined his head, a gesture that caused the high, old-fashioned stock he was wearing to ride up towards his chin.

"Pray be seated, ma'am." He indicated a chair set at one corner of the desk.

Jessie was glad to sit; her knees felt as if they might give way at any moment. She settled her skirts about her. Sir George, resuming his own chair, regarded her steadily for a brief moment.

"I understand you have a young family, Mistress Gray; it will not be easy to bring them up and look after the shop at the same time!"

Jessie's heart turned over; clearly, the laird had no knowledge of his factor's notice of eviction.

"Maybe so, Sir George. I should, however, have liked to attempt it. Unfortunately, I am to be denied the opportunity!"

Sir George pursed his lips. He was beginning to realise the purpose behind the woman's visit and he did not relish the thought.

"Why so? Can you not afford the rent?"

"The rent is not a pressing problem, Sir George. I have the money laid aside."

"What is it, then?" he spoke rather more sharply than he had intended.

"A question of the lease, Sir George. It expires at the Martinmas term and will not be renewed!"

"You know this for certain?"

"Yes: Major Webster has served me notice to quit! That is why I am here – to appeal to your good self. Oh, Sir George! It is little a widow woman can do to protect herself and her bairns. She has no man at her side to press her case and argue for her!"

With a start Jessie realised that she was on the verge of tears and this she wished at all costs to avoid. Sir George – his face expressionless – was drumming his fingers upon the arms of his chair.

"Mistress Gray! I am truly sorry to learn of this. I doubt Dick Webster has given the matter insufficient thought. Nevertheless, he is my factor, ma'am, and – much as I would like to help you – I have always made it a rule never to interfere in the daily running of the Estate. Once started along that path, there is no going back! No, ma'am! The responsibility is Webster's and whether I like it or not, I must support him – or dismiss him – and I do not wish to do the latter for he is a competent factor, Mistress Gray, and I should be hard pressed to find a suitable replacement. I am sorry!"

Jessie nodded. She felt an aching void in the pit of her stomach. She had not really expected that the laird would overturn Webster's ruling. It had been an outside chance only, but for her own peace of mind she had had to take it. What would the laird think, she wondered, if he knew the rest of the story? Nevertheless, if she were any judge, she was quite sure that the laird would have it out with Webster and this, of course, would fuel the fire of the man's already powerful dislike of her.

She rose to her feet and bowed.

"In that case, Sir George, there is no more to be said and I shall detain you no further!"

Sir George rose to his feet and tugged at the bell pull hanging by the side of the window.

"You are young, ma'am; a strong and healthy woman! I doubt not but you will be able to turn your hand towards earning sufficient to feed and clothe your family. If, on the other hand, you fail to find work and you are in straitened circumstances, I should wish to know."

"I do not require your charity, Sir George – nor would I take it! Good day, sir!"

Jessie knew she was being ungracious but she was past caring. She reached the door before Mr. Cloake arrived. She pulled it open and swept past the astonished butler, across the hall, down the kitchen passage and out.

"Charlie!" she called.

"I'm no quite ready, Mistress Gray –" Charlie's cheery voice died in his throat at the sight of Jessie standing on the driving box of the cart, the reins in her gloved hands. A fine figure of a woman she was – upright and imperious.

"Never mind what else you have to do. I am leaving now, Charlie, and if you are not on the box this instant I go without you and you will require to walk home!"

Charlie looked at Mr. Cloake who had just reached the foot of the kitchen steps and was preparing to complete the order he had been giving to Charlie when the laird's study bell had rung. Mr. Cloake shrugged his shoulders and Charlie looked round in time to see Jessie flick the reins and set off with a lurch down the drive. He had to break into a rapid sprint to catch up and – although he still had several calls to make in the glen, including one on their good customer Mistress Milne at the Mains, who certainly did not like being kept waiting – he had little option but to allow himself to be driven down the Cadger's Brae and back into town. Jessie drove fast and the cart rocked somewhat on the brae sending Charlie into a cold sweat. They sped past the scene of last month's tragedy and were past Annie Ogilvie's in the twinkling of an eye. Once into the yard at home Jessie handed Charlie the reins and, without a word, marched off into the house slamming the door behind her.

* * *

Sam Coutts picked up the deed lying amongst the clutter on his desk. Old Sam – he was seventy-five if he was a day – was one of the outstanding local characters. Although the plate at his office door described him as a lawyer – "Samuel Coutts," it read, "Writer and Notary Public" – he had, in addition, been the Bank's agent in the town for nearly half a century. In fact, banking ran in his blood since he was related to the Coutts family in nearby Montrose, some of whom had gone south and prospered, founding kenspeckle banking houses first in Edinburgh, then in London.

He adjusted his spectacles which had a habit of sliding down to the tip of his nose.

"Now, Jessie!" he said, "Let us discuss the question of settlement. In my view, you have received a fair price, a very fair price indeed." He sat back and regarded his client over the rim of his glasses.

Jessie said nothing. She felt numb and drained of emotion. It was bad enough to have lost a husband, her livelihood and her home. She was a highly sensitive woman and had been badly scarred by the blows heaped upon her. The final insult had come when she was informed that the new tenant of the house and shop was to be none other than her *bête noir*, Willie Guthrie, the man Tom had met on the street the night before he was killed. She could not imagine a more unsuitable candidate than Willie Guthrie for the tenancy of a licensed grocery business. His fondness for work was in inverse proportion to his notable fondness for the bottle and consequently it was extremely likely that he would lie around all day sampling his own wares. Nevertheless, as Mr. Coutts said, Guthrie had met her price – the enormous figure of £549. 15s. 6d. which, to Jessie, seemed like a fortune.

The whole thing was of course another of Dick Webster's machinations since Guthrie happened to be a full cousin of his wife's. Bess Webster's family were fisher folk in Arbroath and so were the Guthries, although Willie himself had never lived within sight of the sea. Nevertheless, it was the Guthrie family lawyer in Arbroath who had negotiated with Mr. Coutts in the purchase of the business.

"A very good price." Mr. Coutts was still muttering to himself: he had felt

Jessie was asking too much but he had refrained from saying so. If Guthrie was fool enough to pay over the score that was no concern of his.

"Now, Jessie!" Mr. Coutts was again seeking to gain the benefit of his client's undivided attention.

"Yes, Mr. Coutts. I am sorry. My thoughts were far away. Pray continue."

"The price of £549. 15s. 6d. is to be paid thus:- the sum of £149. 15s. 6d. here and now in cash and the remainder by means of two bills, each for £200, the first payable twelve months hence and the second a year later. The solicitors in Arbroath sent me a bank draft for the cash portion –" he rummaged among the papers and produced something that, to Jessie, looked remarkably like a bank note.

" – Here it is!" Mr. Coutts waved the draft under Jessie's nose. "I think you should take the odds in cash, Jessie – that is to say, £49. 15s. 6d., and place the balance of £100 upon Deposit Receipt where it will earn interest for you."

Jessie nodded her agreement.

"Then," she said, "I must sit idly by and wait for the remainder. I simply do not understand this business of bills – I think we should have held out for the full purchase price to be paid now in cash."

"Then, lass, we might not have got a sale at all. Few folk can raise £500, just like that! Payment by means of bills in a series is commonplace and you need not distress yourself over it. The bills could be discounted, if you wish: that is to say, the Bank would be prepared to advance you the money involved against the security of the bills: but I hardly think you have immediate need of such a large sum and in any case the Bank would charge you interest on the advance."

"No! I certainly have no need for the money here and now but – supposing such a need does arise between now and next year – what then?"

"You can discount the bills at any time you wish."

"I see. And what would happen were I to do so only to find that, at the end of the day, Willie Guthrie is unable to pay up?"

"Jessie! Jessie! I have taken the precaution of obtaining what we term an opinion upon Mr. Guthrie from his bankers in Arbroath and I have no reason to suspect that the bills will not be honoured at maturity."

"But – I am sorry, Mr. Coutts, to keep on at this – but I have to know what my position is. Just supposing the Arbroath banker is wrong. Are these – what did you call them?"

"Opinions."

"Yes – opinions. Are they always reliable?"

"Most of the time – yes!"

"But not always?"

"Well, occasionally, we do run up a bad debt notwithstanding having had a satisfactory opinion in the first place."

"I see! Well – supposing this is a case like that. Suppose you advance me £200 and Guthrie cannot pay. Would I not be liable to refund the Bank?"

"Yes – you would: after the Bank had exhausted Guthrie's estate that is. You would then be liable to pay back the balance."

"But I might have spent the money."

"In that case, Jessie, you would indeed be in trouble."

"That is just what I was thinking, Mr. Coutts. I most certainly have no wish to seek an advance upon the bills either now or at any time in the future!"

Privately Jessie wondered how a banker like Mr. Coutts could even think of suggesting that his client might consider taking out such a loan – but Mr. Coutts was not yet finished.

"All that remains now," he said, "is to create the bills."

Once again he searched amongst the litter on his desk before unearthing two oblong pieces of paper which he handed to Jessie.

"Here they are! Perhaps you would be kind enough to read them, Jessie, and then – if you find them in order – I will show you where you must sign as the drawer."

Jessie read aloud: "Kirkton of Pitbuddo, 12th November 1850. Twelve months after date pay to me or my order the sum of two hundred pounds sterling for value received. To William Guthrie, Swan Street, Brechin."

"Now, Jessie!" How Jessie wished he would stop saying that. "Sign them, if you please, just below the word, 'received'."

Jessie did as he bade her.

"What happens now?"

"Now I send them off to the Western Bank, Arbroath, for acceptance by Mr. Guthrie."

"What does that mean?"

"Well, as you can see, these bills are addressed to Mr. Guthrie and he will then signify his acceptance of them by adding his signature."

"What if he refuses to do so?"

"In that case the bills are dishonoured by non-acceptance and the contract falls. He will not gain access to that which he has purchased until I have the bills back in my hands duly accepted."

After Jessie had gone, Sam Coutts remained deep in thought. It was not often his legal clients, or bank customers, particularly female ones, probed so thoroughly and asked so many questions. Usually they were content to do that which they were asked without question. His respect for Jessie Gray had increased enormously. It was perfectly plain that she was well able to look after herself and would not be imposed upon.

The fact that Jessie had received notice to quit had spread throughout the town like wildfire and a deep sense of outrage was felt by everyone who knew her. Charlie Tait was horrified and apprehensive. There was no guarantee that the new tenant would keep him on and he spent a very uncomfortable week before he learned that Willie Guthrie would be glad of his help. Charlie was heart sorry for the mistress. Now he understood what the factor had been about. Now he knew why Mistress Gray had accompanied him up the glen and why she had sought out the laird. It also explained their unexpected homecoming and the breakneck speed at which she had driven.

The Gardynes were shocked and incredulous. They themselves had not a great deal of room but they immediately offered to take Jessie and the children in to live with them.

"Maybe I shall have to take you up on that," she had said, "but I have a week or so yet in which to look around."

Jim Gardyne shook his head. Jessie knew as well as most people that there simply were no properties available for renting anywhere in the town. Everyone was incensed that Webster should be evicting the Grays simply to find a home and a job for a worthless cousin of his wife's. They were all loud in their condemnation and in this they were eagerly supported by the local Chartists and the rougher elements of the community. Things had got to such a pitch that, on the Sabbath after Jessie had signed the bills, the Reverend Black stood in the pulpit at the United Presbyterian church and preached from the twenty-second chapter of St. Matthew at verse twenty-one: "Then saith he unto them, Render therefore unto Caesar the things which are Caesar's; and unto God the things that are God's."

From the uncomfortable shuffling of feet and downcast looks of those around her Jessie could be in no doubt that the congregation sat rebuked. For her part, if she were conscience stricken, it was by reason of the fact that she had so much on her mind that she paid scant attention to the minister's diatribe. After the kirk scaled, she collected Meg and Jemima from the Sabbath School and hurried home to prepare their dinner. Andrew, in his first year at the Bible Class, was not home until half past one.

After they had eaten, Jessie – as had become her habit every Sunday afternoon – took the girls round to the Gardynes and then set out with Andrew along the road to the cemetery. There had been a sharp frost overnight – indeed the puddles in the road were still iced over and crackled when trodden upon. Overhead the sky was an arching dome of palest blue, except away down the strath in the west where the winter sunset was already colouring it in shades of red and gold. The leaves were nearly all down but now and again they passed a tree still decked in a glory of russet, while scarlet clusters of berries hung from all the rowans.

During the week Jessie had had a visit from old Dod Watson. Dod was a master mason who, when his services were not required at a building site by Sandy Shirress, cut, inscribed and erected gravestones. He called himself a monumental sculptor and he was a craftsman of considerable ability. The stone Jessie had ordered for Tom had been finished and set in place – so he said – and both she and Andrew were anxious to see it.

There were no other visitors at the cemetery when they got there. A pair of ravens flew croaking from the ivy-covered ruin of the old kirk as they un-latched the gate and walked across the grass in between the stones. The un-weathered granite at the head of the green plot where Tom lay was apparent even at a distance by reason of its rawness. Jessie had no time for what she considered the sickly sentimentality of the day and had steadfastly refused to countenance any references to "beloved husband" or "sorrowing wife". The stone she had chosen was a small one and it bore the simple inscription:-

"In loving memory of
Thomas Gray
1815 – 1850"

and Jessie, when she saw it in place, was well pleased. Now, with Andrew's help, she busied herself tidying the little plot, sweeping up the leaves and twigs which the winds of the past week had strewn upon it. She wished she could put flowers by the stone. Tom had always loved flowers but it was now too late in the season and there were no longer any to be had. By the time their task was finished the short winter day was drawing to a close and it would soon be dusk. They closed the gate behind them and turned back along the road. Ahead of them lights were springing up in the houses of the town and the hearth smoke was curling upwards in the still air.

"Mamma!" Andrew tugged at Jessie's sleeve. "There's something coming up behind us!"

Sure enough Jessie could hear the sound of hoofbeats, the creaking of harness and a rumble of wheels . The road to the cemetery and the ruined kirk was, in fact, the old road to Brechin which had been superseded some thirty years ago when the present macadamised and more direct highway had been constructed. Now traffic on the old road tended to be highly localised emanating in the main from the farms and small villages it served. Whatever was coming would no doubt be a farmer's gig, unusual though this might be at this time in the afternoon of a winter Sabbath. They could see the lights now – two yellow blobs swaying from side to side a couple of hundred yards on the far side of the cemetery. The driver was clearly in a hurry for the horse was moving at a spanking trot and overhauling them fast. Andrew knew they might not be easily seen in the half light so he helped his mother across the ditch as they moved off the road to avoid being run over. They need not have worried. The driver had keen eyes and had seen them. A man's voice shouted, "Whoa!" and the outfit came to a halt level with where Jessie and Andrew stood between the ditch and the adjacent hedgerow.

"Mercy on us! It's Jessie Gray and young Andrew! You're late on the road, Jessie, lass! Come on! Hop up here beside me – you too, laddie! We'll gie ye a ride hame."

Jessie had recognised the doctor's gig before he had spoken, and she smiled in relief. There was still the best part of half a mile of dark country road between them and the outskirts of the town and she had not relished the thought of meeting up with a stranger.

Dr. Robertson's gig was a large one and, like the wise man he was, he invariably employed a driver when he went out on a call. In any case, the work involved in a country practice such as his was very demanding and he had more to do than act as his own groom. Now he reached down and grasping Jessie's upstretched arm, he pulled her up and made room for her on the driving box. Meantime Andrew made his way into the open boot beside the doctor's bag and medicine case.

"Thank you, doctor. I must say we are extremely pleased to see you! Hello, Dochie! How are you?"

"Just graund, Mistress Gray although it's fell cauld up here in this weather."

"Get awa wi' ye, man!" Dr. Robertson laughed, a great rumbling guffaw that seemed to well up from deep inside him. "This Hielan' stot's aye got some grouse or other!"

Dochie, a thin wizened little man of middle years with a mournful demeanour, gave his employer what he hoped was a withering glance and, with a flick of the reins, set horse and gig into motion again.

"Aye, Jessie lass!" said the doctor, "I hear your minister was thumping his pulpit this morning – throwing in his lot with yon scoundrel, Webster, so they say. Man, Jessie! It's enough to mak' ye spew!"

Jessie was horrified. Much as she loved and respected Dr. Robertson as a physician and a friend, she could not bring herself to approve of the flippant attitude he seemed to delight in displaying towards the kirk – especially those dissenting branches which had broken away from the mother stem.

"Perhaps it needed saying, doctor," she replied a little coldly. "The text is plain enough, is it not? 'Render therefore unto Caesar the things which are Caesar's.'"

"Aye! Maybe!" The doctor sniffed. "But, Jessie, I seem to remember another bittie in that self-same chapter which says: 'Thou shalt love the Lord thy God with all thy heart and with all thy soul and with all thy mind, . . . and' – now here is the bit, Jessie – 'Thou shalt love thy neighbour as thyself.' Think on it, Jessie. Think on it!"

Jessie was silent. They were near the town now and soon the bell of the parish kirk would be ringing for Evening Worship.

"Now, Jessie!" They were all the same, Jessie thought – Mr. Coutts, Dr. Robertson – even Jim Gardyne – they all liked to lecture her – 'Now, Jessie' indeed!

"Hae ye got a place to bide yet?"

"No, doctor. I am looking about, without success so far."

"Nor are you likely to, lass – be successful that is – believe me! However, I hae a bit property at the top of the Meal Wynd – three rooms just – maist o' them gey wee. They're no in great order, mind; been vacant for a while – but at least there is no sign of damp. If they're any use to you, you're welcome! Why dinna ye tak' a daunder doon and see the place? Here's the key; it's one floor up."

Jessie burst into tears.

"Losh keep's, lassie! Dinna greet!"

Jessie wiped her streaming eyes and smiled weakly.

"Please forgive me, doctor; it's just that nothing nice has happened to me for so long." On impulse she reached across and kissed his hairy cheek.

"That is so kind of you! Yes, of course, I'll have a look, although I'm sure it would do us nicely. How much rent will you require?"

Dr. Robertson's eyes twinkled.

"Well, now, let me see. It will be high, lass! Property for renting is a scarce commodity in this town as you have found out."

Jessie's eyes clouded again and she bit her lip. The doctor would be entitled to pitch his price beyond her reach.

"Na! Na! Jessie, I'm only teasing. The rent I require is to see you and your bairns in a place of your own where neither Webster nor the laird can touch you: I want to see the glow of good health on all your cheeks and I want to see these bairns grow up in the way Tom would have wanted. For me, Jessie, that rent will be sufficient and to spare; but if it will make you more comfortable – to mak' siccar o' your independence as it were – you can pay me £5 a year, in arrears mind, the first instalment of £2. 10. 0d. to be due at Whitsunday next! Here, come on, girl! Dry your eyes."

Dr. Robertson placed an arm round her shoulders and, in his other hand, he held out a large coloured handkerchief.

Dochie had pulled the gig to a halt at Jessie's door and Andrew, already on the pavement, helped his mother climb down. Dr. Robertson stuffed his now sodden handkerchief into his greatcoat pocket and raised his hand in salute.

Jessie could not trust herself to speak. All she could muster was a pathetic-looking half smile. Then she turned and, slipping her arm into Andrew's, she allowed him to see her up the steps and in at the front door.

* * *

The year 1851 came in on a still, frosty night and to the ringing of the bell in the steeple of the parish kirk. The church stood at the widest part of the High Street, close by the market cross, directly opposite the top of the Meal Wynd and the noise of the bell reverberated through the Grays' little house, shaking the crockery on the kitchen dresser and causing all the windows to vibrate. When they first came, Jessie thought she would never get used to the noise but, gradually, they had all grown accustomed to it and the joyous ring-ing to celebrate the New Year failed to wake little Jemima, or for that matter, her big sister.

Jessie had moved within days of meeting Dr. Robertson that Sunday in mid-November. They were a little cramped, but the rooms were all of a reasonable size – "no ower wee" – said Charlie Tait who, along with Jim Gardyne, helped Jessie with the flitting. First of all Jessie had scrubbed the place until walls and floorboards gleamed like new. Then, with the men's help, she transferred from her old house waxcloth for the kitchen and carpets for the other rooms, all of which had to be cut to size and laid. After that was done the men brought up such items of furniture as she wished to retain. Clearly there was no room for all her things and she had to be quite ruthless in deciding against anything that was not strictly necessary.

She decided to allocate one room for Andrew and one room for the girls while she, herself, elected to sleep in the kitchen/living room where, for-tunately, there was a box bed built into one of the walls. Accordingly she brought with her three beds and two wardrobes together with the kitchen table and dresser, a number of chairs, including the rocking chair, and a couple of small tables. Everything surplus to this she sent, via Matt Lundie, to the saleroom in Brechin. The thing that gave her the greatest trouble was transferring and sorting out crockery, cutlery and kitchenware, together with all their clothes and personal belongings. But by dint of hard work it was all accomplished before the week's end, enabling Jessie to set about making the curtains. They settled in surprisingly quickly and, although Jessie could hardly help missing the home she had shared with her beloved Tom, the atmosphere of the little house was good and she felt reasonably happy in it. Unfortunately there was no piped water and supplies for the wash basin in the kitchen had to be carried up from the pump in the back court. The only closet was out on the landing and this they had to share with their neighbour, an old lady who had lived alone for many years and was a bit of a recluse.

Jessie was glad to see the back of a year which had dealt so harshly with her and she welcomed the new one with all her heart. Jim Gardyne came round to see her after midnight. He had a lump of coal in one hand and, in the other, a box of special biscuits baked in Forfar of which he knew Jessie was extremely fond. He shared a glass of toddy with her and a piece of Jessie's black bun. Jessie was pleased that he had come to be her first foot but his arrival on the scene at that very moment brought a host of memories flooding back for, in the days of their youth, she and Tom had often been out and about on New Year's morning going the round of their friends with Jim and Agnes. The freshness of the moment, the promise of a new beginning which she had felt so clearly when the bell rang out at midnight, had somehow been spoiled and she found herself feeling annoyed with Jim for breaking the spell.

"It's a fine wee house right enough, Jessie!" Jim stretched his legs towards the flickering flame of the fire in the kitchen grate. "I'm glad you're so cosy and comfortable!"

"We can't all live in mansions, Jim, and anyway, the place isn't all that wee! I don't know why all you folk harp on like that – you're always at it. 'Oh Jessie's snug enough in that wee place.' 'It's just what she needs – a wee corner to herself.' 'Yon wee place Jessie's got – ' 'Jessie's wee bit hoosie.' For goodness sake, Jim, why can't you all stop patronising me?"

"I'm sorry, Jessie. Of course there's nothing wrong with the house. It's just lovely." Jim's honest face wore a puzzled frown. The last thing he had wanted to do was to upset her.

"Now you're humouring me. It isn't lovely – it's a home and I'm grateful for it! Why is it that everyone is so – so mealy mouthed? Mustn't upset her! Oh no! That would never do. She's a poor widow – that's what she is. She's only a widow!"

Jessie started to sob and Jim, now thoroughly disconcerted, reached out a hand and touched her shoulder. She twitched sideways and got to her feet. Jim followed suit and together they stood on opposite sides of the fireplace looking at one another. Jessie wiped her tears with a little handkerchief.

"Jim," she said, "I'm glad you came to first foot me! I am really. It's just that – every now and then – everything seems to, kind of, overwhelm me. I'm truly sorry. Tell Agnes we'll be round first thing in the morning."

"Are you sure you'll be all right?"

"Thank you, Jim – yes!"

"Well! Goodnight then, Jessie!"

"Goodnight, Jim!" She stood on tiptoe and kissed him lightly on the cheek. Jim clapped his bonnet on his head and she heard his boots clatter on the stone treads as he made his way downstairs.

Jessie sat up for a little longer. She was angry with herself. Whatever she may have felt she had no right to take it out on Jim, especially after he had taken the trouble to come out on a bitterly cold night just to see her. She sighed and stared into the fire still burning brightly. People said you could see pictures in the fire but she could never make anything out with any clarity. She was glad of this, for you could never tell whether the pictures represented scenes past or scenes to come and she had no wish to see either.

The fire had died down considerably before Jessie stirred. She raked the coals until she was satisfied it was safe before undressing and clambering into bed.

The frost which had ushered in the New Year intensified and lasted for several weeks. February was wet and blustery but a spell of mild, spring weather in early March spread a film of green upon the grass and set the trees in the High Street into bud. Alas! a searing wind later in the month and some bitterly cold weather in April, culminating in a heavy snow storm, effectively halted all growth. The glen road was blocked for several weeks and, on the second Sunday after Easter, Jessie and Andrew were confined to the house after morning worship as the Old Brechin Road was quite impassable. During this time the older children, who had to trudge to school through the snowy streets, often came home with wet feet, and the clothes horse at the kitchen fire was invariably festooned with drying garments of one sort or another. Little Jemima could not get out to play down in the back court and she tended to get under Jessie's feet as she went about her daily chores.

Since settling down at the Meal Wynd, Jessie had begun to take in garments for repair or alteration. She had a flair for dress-making and in the past she had frequently made dresses and petticoats for herself. Now – while the children were out at school and after they had gone to bed in the evening – she spread her work out on the kitchen table and set to, cutting, snipping and sewing. She was glad the floor was covered with waxcloth and not carpeted, as this made it very much easier to sweep up threads and snippets. As more and more people became aware of the service she could provide, not only did she find the work beginning to pile up, but she also began to receive orders to make dresses out of material supplied by her customers. It was hard work, sore on the back and especially on her eyes as it was invariably rather dim in the kitchen whether she was working during the day or by candlelight. Nevertheless, she kept at it, doggedly, and in so doing avoided any necessity of encroaching upon the little bit of capital represented by the funds Mr. Coutts had lodged in her name upon Deposit Receipt at the Bank.

Andrew helped too, delivering newspapers that, on certain mornings in the week, now came up from Dundee by train to Brechin for collection by Matt Lundie. Matt then delivered the tied-up bundles to the little shop in the Meal Wynd where Jessie's neighbour, Bob Spence, sold a variety of goods including snuff and tobacco, sweets for the bairns, and toys like kites, marbles, hoops and tops. Bob was a big, kindly man who had served in the Dundee police force at the time of the "Black Band" which had so terrorised the honest citizens of the town back in the early thirties. He and Andrew were in the shop before six in the morning, waiting to tear open the bundles on Matt's arrival, after which Bob would sort the papers into three piles – one for Andrew and one for each of the other two laddies he employed on delivery duty.

Andrew's round lay at the top end of the town where, on Tuesdays and Fridays – the days the *Advertiser* was published – he had to visit most of the houses. The round was a good deal easier on Wednesdays – the day the *Courier* came out – for, although nearly everyone took the *Advertiser* which supported the Liberal government of Lord John Russell, only a few of the more well-to-do households subscribed to the rival newspaper which had definite Tory leanings.

One of the households taking the *Courier* was at the Grays' old home. Jessie, when he told her of this, felt it was just like the Guthries: they were sure to consider themselves a cut above the rest of the folk in town. Andrew did not like going to their door. The house looked so different: the curtains were always only half pulled back and more often than not the blinds were askew. He never saw anybody about the place, as was hardly surprising for Charlie Tait would not be due to arrive to open up the shop for at least another hour. But one cold morning in April he met Guthrie himself and such was the look of him that Andrew wondered whether he had been out all night, although how he had not caught his death of cold Andrew could not imagine.

Willie Guthrie was a man of medium height with brown, curly hair and eyes that were almost black. He had a face that, apart from a slightly receding chin, might once have been handsome before a surfeit of hard liquor began to take its toll. His most prominent feature, however, and one which had never failed to intrigue Andrew, was the peculiarity in his right eye, the iris of which was flecked with white. Now both eyes were bleary and the face below unshaven. His hair was dishevelled, his neck-cloth untied and his jacket and trousers were rumpled and covered with mud.

He was standing at the front door as Andrew approached and he held out a none too clean hand for the paper.

"I'll take that, lad." His voice was slurred and thick and his hand shook as he held it out. The fumes of liquor on his breath made Andrew wince.

"You're Tom Gray's lad, are ye no? Mind! You're not unlike him."

Andrew nodded and turned away leaving Guthrie fumbling with a key in the door lock. When he told his mother of his encounter Jessie merely shook her head. More and more was she becoming convinced that she would never see the money she was due.

In its issue on Tuesday 6th May the *Advertiser* carried a verbose spread about the opening by the Queen on the previous Thursday – and a fine, sunny day it had been – of Prince Albert's Great Exhibition in Hyde Park. Everyone was talking about it. The men marvelled at the breath-taking advances in scientific skill which had enabled the engineers of the day to erect this enormous glass structure – this crystal palace – which, although hard to believe, was large enough to enclose under its vast domes some of the park's mature trees.

The women on the other hand never tired of discussing the Queen herself who made up for lack of stature by the majesty of her bearing and the splendour of her appearance. It was said that she had worn a little crown on her head – for the people expected the Queen to wear a crown, although they had not expected to see the two feathers she sported in addition. It was said that the great Koh-i-Noor diamond, recently surrendered to the Crown after the annexation of the Punjab, had sparkled upon the garter ribbon she wore across her gown of pink and silver.

Dr. Robertson, who thought the whole thing a waste of money that could be put to better purpose – improving standards of health for instance, or endowing much-needed hospitals – was cutting in his remarks. He had called in at Bob Spence's for a measure or two of snuff to replenish the silver-topped box he carried in his waistcoat pocket. Andrew had just finished his round and had returned briefly to the shop, before going home for his breakfast, when the doctor came in.

"Aye, doctor," said Bob, "it's a pity ye dinna tak' the *Advertiser*, man; it's fu' to bursting wi' clavers aboot yon exhibition in London. Could ye no do wi' a copy the day? I'm sure Mistress Robertson wad like fine to read aboot it!"

Dr. Robertson was one of those who took the *Courier* and, to Andrew's amusement, he snorted in disgust.

"Ach! Haud yer wheesht, Bob! Mistress Robertson has more to do than bother herself wi' stuff like yon! In any case, it's not something I approve of – this exhibition. If you ask me they've taken a loan of him – the Prince, I mean – it's a rare opportunity for Russell and his bonny lads to air their radical doctrines and blow their trumpets for free trade!"

As the doctor finished speaking, Sandy Shirress came in for his *Advertiser*.

"What's all this about trumpets being given away free?" Sandy was a shade deaf.

Dr. Robertson glared at him.

"Ye'd better mak' an appointment, Sandy, and let me take a look at your lugs for ye're gey hard o' hearing these days! We were discussing yon drain on public money, the Prince's Great Exhibition or Russell's advertisement for liberalism! Teugh! It gars me grue!"

"It's more than that, David, surely!" Sandy picked up an *Advertiser* from the pile on the counter and paid for it.

"Aye! A monumental waste of money!"

"No, no. I mean – it's a brave gesture is it not? Hope! That's what it is. Hope for a new beginning. Europe united. Peace in our time!"

"He didna get very far – did he?"

"Maybe not – but it was a bold attempt."

"A foolish one, more like! Nae doobt he was thinkin' on yon passage in Isaiah about the leopard lying down with the kid, but I'm thinking the folk concerned don't know the Scriptures very well – the leopard was gey suspicious of the kid and the kid of the leopard!"

"Nonsense, David! The foreigners *have* come; they say there's a wheen o' foreign goods on display."

"And a prodigious amount never came! Na na, Sandy! They still mistrust the leopard, especially the Prince's Continental counter-parts. They believe this country's a hot-bed of revolutionaries; and who can blame them with the government we've got and the damned Chartists stirring up trouble all over the place!"

"Thae foreigners wad believe onything." The customer Bob Spence had been serving had left and he was eager to join in the conversation. "It's just as well they didna come, for it's scant welcome they'd get!"

"Aye! But the Prussians came." Sandy Shirress was not going to be put off " – not King what's-his-name, mind, but the Crown Prince and that would please Albert."

"They'll be able to crack awa thegither in German!" Dr. Robertson laughed. "They say the Queen's never happier than when she's at the 'sprechen sie' too! Scarce to be wondered at, I suppose, when you hae a German for a mother!"

"Well! I still say it's a pity the wider concept – the international one – has failed him."

"That's no what your precious Foreign Secretary's thinking I'll be bound!" Dr. Robertson, his eyes twinkling merrily, suddenly caught sight of Andrew who was still standing at Bob's side although he should have been off for his breakfast long ago.

"Here, laddie!" he said, "Do you ken the name o' her Majesty's Foreign Secretary?"

"Yes, sir! Lord Palmerston."

"Aye, Palmerston! Mind it well, lad! There'll come a day when folk will look at you in awe when you say, 'I remember the days when Palmerston was at the Foreign Office.' I dinna approve of his politics but he'll go down in history when men have long forgotten Russell, or Derby for that matter. He's gey auld now, of course, not far short of eighty, but – and may the Good Lord help us – we'll maybe even see him heading a government of his own some day, if he lives long enough." He paused for breath, then asked, "How's your mamma, lad?"

"She's well, thank you, sir."

"I'm glad to hear it. She'll be gey sick, though, to see your father's business going down the hill the way it is."

"She never goes past the shop now."

"Just as well!"

" 'Deed, aye!" said Bob Spence, "Maist folk gae doon the hill to Joe Mathers. I hear he's been hiring a bit cairt and a horse frae Matt Lundie and that he's gaein' up the glen on Tuesdays. The road'll be gey thrang, I'm thinking, wi' baith Joe and Charlie Tait in the glen."

"They're not, though," said Sandy Shirress. "Charlie hasn't been out for a fortnight. It will not be worth his while for all he has to sell."

Andrew knew that Guthrie was letting the business go down and so did Jessie, for poor Charlie Tait regularly unburdened himself to them. Andrew was sore afraid that when the first of the bills should fall due in November, Guthrie would not be able to pay. What such a loss as that would mean for them did not bear thinking about. Andrew had not, however, heard the latest news which now came from Dr. Robertson.

"He canna stock up without the funds to do so and he hasna got the siller. He spends most of his time up at the 'Temperance' and Charlie says he's aye dipping his hand in the till to pay for it. In fact, things have got so bad that I hear his wife and bairns are awa to bide wi' her folk in Arbroath!"

Jessie had not heard of this development and she shook her head over it when Andrew, at long last, came home for his breakfast. But all their worries and fears, which got more and more disturbing as the summer wore on, were completely dispelled by the sudden death, early in August, of Agnes Gardyne. The poor woman had awakened one night with acute stomach pains. As hour after hour went by and she was still bent double in agony, Jim – in mounting panic – sent Ella, the eldest girl, to fetch Dr. Robertson. By the time he arrived, Agnes was weak and highly fevered and, although the doctor had done what he could, his efforts were of no avail and Agnes had died the following afternoon.

Jessie did all she could to help a distraught Jim. Leaving Ella to look after her father, she kept the younger children until the funeral was over and Jim's unmarried sister, Charlotte, came up from Forfar to care for them all. Jessie, to whom Agnes had been like a sister, wondered just how much more she could take and her strong Christian faith was severely tested. Now, on Sundays, she and Andrew had company on the road to old Pitbuddo, a change in circumstances which, so far as Andrew was concerned, had little appeal since he found himself relegated to walking with Ella.

Ella was a pretty girl with fair curly hair and eyes of cornflower blue. She had a neat and trim figure under the black cotton dress she wore and she was Andrew's senior by some six months. In addition, Ella had a frank and open manner – she was a naturally outgoing girl – and, in her company, Andrew felt shy and embarrassed. When he got all tongue tied, Ella would laugh and tease him mercilessly and, to make matters worse, Andrew was painfully aware of the fact that his mother had always considered that, in the fullness of time, he and Ella would make a good match. They had, of course, known each other all their lives but they had never before been so forcibly thrown together. When they had lived as near neighbours in the High Street it had been different somehow. They had all played together – Ella and her sisters and two little brothers, and the two elder Grays. Going to and from school was the same – there was always a crowd and they never had to walk on their own. Besides, Ella looked different now; quite grown-up in fact, and this served only to deepen the extent of Andrew's shyness.

September had come again with its poignant memories for Jessie, and after a period of blustery weather during the week of the equinox, October ushered in a spell of calm, sunny days when the Sunday afternoon walk became a pleasure rather than a chore – that is to say to all but Andrew. Things came to a head one day in mid-month. Ella had stopped to pick some late flowers growing by the wayside and Jessie and Jim had drawn quite considerably ahead.

"You're awful quiet, Andy," said Ella, rising with a bunch of flowers in her hand. "Do you really not like girls?"

Andrew wished with all his heart that he could say "no". In any case he hated being called "Andy". Nevertheless, he would try not to be rude. He stared doggedly ahead as he answered, "They're all right."

"All right! Is that all? Do you like my flowers?"

"Aye – they're pretty."

"Do you think I'm pretty, Andy?"

Andrew looked as uncomfortable as he felt. He did not know what to say and, in consequence, said nothing at all.

"Andy?" Ella's query ended on a rising note. "Did you not hear me?"

"No – I mean, yes."

"Yes what? Yes, you heard me – or yes, you think I'm pretty?"

"Yes – I heard you."

"Ah! So you don't think I'm pretty! That's not very gallant of you, Andy – not gallant at all! You should always treat a lady kindly. You should say, 'Of course you are pretty, Ella,' even although, in your heart of hearts, you may think I'm ugly."

"I never said that."

"Well! Tell me you think I'm pretty!"

Andrew kicked at a heavy stone with the toe of his right boot.

"Go on, Andy, tell me!"

"Ach, Ella! Let's talk of something more interesting." Andrew was honest and straight forward if a shade less than tactful.

"More interesting indeed! I like that! What could be more interesting to a girl? Come on, Andrew Gray! Stop looking down. Look at me and not at your feet!"

Andrew lifted his head.

"That's a bit better, but you're still not looking at me properly. Look right into my eyes!"

Despite himself, Andrew raised his eyes and looked straight into Ella's. How blue they were against their milky white background.

"There!" said Ella. "Hello, Andy! Would you like to kiss me?"

Andrew looked away then. In fact he looked around in a desperate effort to find something or somebody that might free him from this dreadful embarrassment. Alas! His mother and Jim had disappeared round the next bend in the road and he was quite alone with Ella. He felt his cheeks going bright red.

"Most of the boys don't need any prompting – d'you know that, Andy? But none of them is so nice as you! I do wish you weren't so shy!" She stood on tiptoe, for Andrew was quite a bit taller, and kissed him gently, full upon the mouth. Ella turned then and, light as a kitten, she scampered off up the road leaving a bewildered and thoroughly discomfited Andrew to follow on.

Early in November they received the shattering news that Willie Guthrie had disappeared. For several days he had not been seen at the "Temperance" and Charlie Tait said he had not been in the shop for over a week. Jessie was thoroughly alarmed and went to see Mr. Coutts.

"You have every right to be worried, Jessie: I cannot do anything about the bills yet – the first one isn't due until a fortnight hence, but I must confess that I doubt whether it will be paid on presentation."

"That means I shall have lost everything." Jessie felt as if her legs would no longer support her. She sank down on the leather chair drawn up alongside the banker's desk.

"We'll cross that bridge when we come to it." Mr. Coutts tried to instill into his voice a degree of the confidence he was far from feeling. "First of all I am making some enquiries as to the rogue's whereabouts – without much success, I fear. His father and sister in Montrose say they have not seen him for over a year and of course, his wife, as you know, has gone back to her own folk in Arbroath taking the bairns with her. It's not likely Guthrie will have gone there but I await advices from the agent of the Bank."

"But," said Jessie, "He can't go and leave the shop and everything – just like that! Quite apart from the debt due to me he must owe money all over the place."

"I rather think that is what has prompted his sudden departure."

"What can we do, then?"

"Well! If the bill is dishonoured we shall go after him in full process of law."

"We shall not be the only ones," said Jessie.

"If that is the case he will probably be declared bankrupt and doubtless someone will press for sequestration."

Jessie went home full of foreboding.

On November 12th she returned to the Bank.

"Good day to you, Jessie," Mr. Coutts looked over the top of his spectacles as she came in the door.

"I came to ask whether Guthrie has paid up?"

"I see – but, Jessie, I am sorry, only you are too early."

"But this is the due date, Mr. Coutts, do you not remember? This is the 12th of November 1851 – twelve months to the day from the date of the bill."

"Oh, Jessie! I should have explained. There are what are known as 'days of grace' to be added – three in number – the bill will not be due until Saturday, and even then we shall not know the result. The document has to be presented for payment within the office of the Western Bank in Arbroath. I have already sent it to our agent in that town. He will have it presented on Saturday and will then either remit us the proceeds by Bank Draft or return the bill dishonoured by reason of non-payment. We should know the position on Tuesday morning, Jessie. Come back then!"

As Jessie had always feared, the bill was duly presented to the Western Bank and dishonoured by non-payment. It was then returned to Sam Coutts through the mail by his Bank's Arbroath agent who, before parting with it, presented it to a Notary Public to be noted for protest. Sam received the bill late on Monday afternoon. He did not relish having to face Jessie and he was glad when the waiting was over and Jessie was ushered into his office first thing on the morning of Tuesday. She saw from his face that the news was bad.

"Then it's unpaid," she said.

"I fear so – yes. That does not mean, however, that all is lost. Guthrie may yet pay up – we still have recourse against him and I propose to use an old remedy of the law to obtain the necessary warrant."

"Does that mean I shall get the money after all?"

"Not necessarily, but it means we shall have the equivalent of a decree of the Court for the amount due, together with interest and expenses and without the extra costs and delay of having to raise an action in the Courts. The legal name is 'Summary Diligence', Jessie. It is peculiar to the law of Scotland and dates back nearly two hundred years."

With that Jessie had to be content. Nevertheless, there was now no doubting the fact that she was in dire financial straits. True, she still had a nest egg at the Bank in the form of the Deposit Receipt, but £100 – although a large enough sum of money – did not represent a great deal of capital to fall back upon in case of need, so Jessie determined that she would have to work even longer hours if that were possible. Reluctantly too she bowed to the inevitable and agreed to Andrew's plea that he should be allowed to leave school and start earning.

As might have been expected, they met with considerable resistance on the part of the dominie. It was heart-breaking for Jessie to deny her only son the further schooling he would need, were he to be able to go on to University, and she was entitled to expect a sympathetic hearing from Mr. Dickie. On the contrary, Menzies Dickie was a stranger to both tact and diplomacy. He proved to be loud in his condemnation and Jessie cut short the interview. It was yet another cruel twist of the misfortune which seemed to dog her at every turn.

There was, however, a brighter side to the picture. It transpired that Sam Coutts required an apprentice at the Bank and, hearing that Andrew was to leave school at the end of the year, he offered him the post. Andrew had no hesitation in accepting and he started work in the first week of 1852, two months exactly after his fifteenth birthday.

* * *

Andrew was an apt pupil and fully justified the faith shown in him by Mr. Coutts who had, to some extent, bent the rules in making an offer of the position instead of throwing it open by public advertisement as his Head Office expected him to do. But then, Sam Coutts was a law unto himself in many things.

Andrew learned how to cast and sum up long columns of figures, a task at which he excelled. Before long he was surprising both Mr. Coutts and Donald Graham, the teller, by his ability to sum the three columns – pounds, shillings and pence – at one go, and by the ease with which he could effect, and even take a short cut, to the trickiest of interest calculations. He learned the ins and outs of the Bank's system of book-keeping, both in regard to the accounts maintained locally and those forming part of the overall account current. He read the various provisions of the Bank Act of 1845 and used this background knowledge to understand the intricacies of the note issue, that peculiar Scottish institution for the retention of which Sir Walter Scott had at one time added his weight and considerable prestige in the face of high-powered English pressure for its abolition.

Andrew attended the local note exchange and clearing house; he gained experience in the handling of cash and – above all – he applied himself to the techniques of lending in which he had in Sam Coutts a mentor second to none. By the summer of 1855 – three and a half years after joining as a raw recruit – the Bank, on Sam's recommendation, declared his apprenticeship at an end and admitted him to the permanent staff at the princely salary of £5 per annum. Andrew was now eighteen past. He was tall – a half inch or so over six feet – and broad shouldered. Such physical attributes, however, did not always commend themselves to his mother, who despaired of keeping his clothes from looking as if they had shrunk in the wash.

As Sam Coutts had predicted, Willie Guthrie, who was traced to a lodging house in Dundee, was declared notour bankrupt and the Western Bank in Arbroath, the largest creditor, applied for his sequestration. There was a long list of creditors who, with the exception of the wholesalers in Dundee, were mostly local. For this reason, and because such assets as the debtor was known to possess were contained in the house and shop, it seemed logical, when sequestration was awarded, to appoint a local man as Trustee, and the task was laid on the shoulders of Simon Bell, a young, recently qualified lawyer from Montrose, whom Sam Coutts had assumed as a partner in his legal business.

The assets did not, of course, realise their true value. Joe Mathers, whose shop at the bottom end of the High Street had picked up all the business once enjoyed by the Grays, bought most of the equipment – scales, drums, bins, knives, and so on, at a fraction of their worth and he also took the stock, of which there was practically none. Guthrie had disappeared again but his wife's lawyers in Arbroath bid for the plenishings in the house and these fetched rather better prices. Meanwhile Webster, the factor, granted a fresh lease of the property to an incomer from Aberdeen named Strath who opened up an ironmonger's business much needed in the town.

At the end of the day there had been a considerable shortfall and Simon Bell paid all creditors a dividend of two shillings and sixpence in the pound. Jessie's situation was complicated by the fact that only one of the bills was past due. The other had not yet reached maturity although there was no doubt about her right to the money under the contract of sale. After some legal wrangling, she did eventually receive the sum of £50 in full and final settlement. Once legal fees and expenses had been deducted, she was left with £41. 16s. 8d. to add to the Deposit Receipt at the Bank which still remained intact. Nevertheless, the loss was a huge one, and the enormity of it cast a shadow which darkened their lives for many months until Jessie made a determined effort and put it from her mind once and for all.

In any case, she and everyone else soon had other things to think about as the new, broadly based government headed by Lord Aberdeen slowly drifted towards war with Russia. Patriotic fervour had mounted during the early months of 1854 until, on the last day of February, came the formal declaration in which the country found itself allied to France and Turkey. A month later, a large expeditionary force set sail for an obscure peninsula in the Black Sea and the Crimean War had begun.

Great and bloody battles were fought and, although fearful stories began to percolate home concerning atrocities perpetrated by drink-enflamed Russian soldiers, the allies were in the main victorious. And then, the war seemed as if it had ground to a halt, bogged down in the siege of the naval base of Sebastopol and it seemed they might be there forever.

During the winter, conditions had been appalling, with frostbite and disease accounting for as many casualties as the enemy guns. In London, this brought about an outcry which led to the formation of a Committee of Enquiry and, early in 1855, to the fall of the government and the succession of Palmerston as Prime Minister. Out in the Crimea, Miss Nightingale and a handful of dedicated nurses laboured to alleviate the worst of the suffering while, at home, the Queen knitted woollen scarves and mittens and – in May – she stood on a dais at the Horse Guards to distribute medals on blue and yellow ribbons to veterans invalided home.

Andrew followed the war news as reported in the columns of the *Advertiser* and he loved nothing better than to listen to, and join in the eternal arguments that took place in the office and elsewhere over the strategic situation. At the end of the day, he would sometimes go out for a walk into the country with Simon Bell. Although this tended to make him late for his evening meal, it kept him out of the clutches of Ella Gardyne who had taken to calling round, ostensibly to see Meg, now a burgeoning sixteen. She had every opportunity so to do for her father, of late, had been paying more and more attention to Jessie; and Ella did not see why she, for her part, should feel inhibited in her designs.

One evening, before Andrew arrived home, Jessie had had the company of Jim and Ella for quite some time. They seemed always to have finished eating long before the meal was served in the Gray household and, although Jessie appreciated having someone of her own age to talk to, it tended to hold her back from the various chores awaiting her attention after a busy day at her sewing. For some time now, Meg had taken over much of the work involved in cooking and baking, leaving her mother free to get on with her dressmaking activities, and Meg was busy now about her pots and pans, helped by Ella and Jemima. Jim was comfortably ensconced in the rocking chair by the fire, laying forth anent the impossible conditions facing the troops in the Crimea. They were, he said, in much the same position as the ancient Britons who found themselves facing Anglo-Saxon invaders advancing behind a screen of warriors crazed by specially administered drugs – the "berserkers".

Jessie, who had heard it all before, and who had as little interest in the ancient Britons as she had in the deliberately intoxicated troops of the Russian Tsar, excused herself and hurried out of the kitchen on the pretext of seeing to Jemima's bed. To her surprise, Jim got up and followed her. As she bent to turn down the bedcover, she was even more surprised when Jim put his arms around her and clasped his hands over her stomach.

"Jim!" She straightened and stood perfectly still. "Whatever are you doing?"

"Oh, Jessie, lass! I never get the chance to see you alone – the bairns are aye in the way!"

"Well! You certainly can't see me properly in that position. Don't you think you should let me turn around?"

"Oh!" Jim released her and, slowly, she turned and faced him. She had, of course, been aware of the increasing frequency of these visits and she had intended speaking to him about it, for the last thing she wanted was that folk should start talking. But she had not been able to do so for fear of hurting him. No-one could have been a more staunch friend than Jim Gardyne had proved himself to be – ever since that awful day when Tom was killed. She herself had tried to be equally supportive when Agnes had died but it was more difficult for her with all the conflicting and more essential claims upon her time. Now she found herself looking into Jim's eyes – his kindly, blue eyes now full of concern and anxiety.

"Jessie," he said, "can't you see what I'm trying to say?"

"How can something said be seen?" Jessie knew she was being unkind – she who had shied away from hurting him – and, even although she told herself it was he who had made the first move, she hated herself for it.

"You know what I mean."

"No, Jim, I don't! What are you trying to say? Here am I, busy with the beds, and Andrew not yet home, and you follow me around like a collie dog and start manhandling me. Whatever you have to say, please hurry up and say it!"

"Jessie! I'm asking you to marry me!"

"Oh, Jim! I'm sorry! I – I had no idea."

"Then, will you? Marry me that is?"

Jessie leant forward and kissed him, gently, on the forehead.

"Dear Jim," she said. "That is something I had not thought about."

"But, Jessie! Is it not daft for you to be living by yourself in this wee house, slaving over those hems and pleats, and for me to be on my own in mine which is big enough for us both?"

"But I'm not alone, Jim. I have the children."

"So do I – and the younger ones need a mother!"

"They have Charlotte. Does Charlotte not mother them?"

"Yes, of course. She has been kindness itself – but it's not the same thing, Jessie; you know that. Besides – you wouldn't have to take in dressmaking."

"Jim, dear: you have been and still are the best friend anyone could wish for – but marriage needs more than that."

"More than that?"

"Yes, Jim. It needs love and Jim, I am not ready, at least not yet, to give you that. I still miss Tom, far, far too much. I'm sorry, Jim; truly sorry."

That evening, Jim and Ella had left before Andrew got home.

The second Wednesday in June was an important date in the local calendar. For the agricultural community – not only in the upper strath, and in the glens, but also across the North Water right up into the Howe of the Mearns – it represented the end of one stock-rearing season and the beginning of another, when the beasts that had been overwintered, cattle in the byres and sheep on the hill, and then fattened on the spring grass, were driven to the sale rings set up on Trinity Moor, a mile or so to the north of Brechin. There had been a June fair at Trinity for as long as anyone could remember and in recent years it had become one of the largest livestock auctions in the country. For three days the moor became the Mecca of farmers and graziers and, around the perimeter, hucksters and itinerant salesmen set up their stalls and travelling showmen their booths.

There was no limit to the things that could be bought at the June Fair nor to the wonders to be seen or experienced in the booths and sideshows. In consequence, wives and daughters flocked to the Moor along with their men-folk, adding an atmosphere of carnival which was roundly condemned by all but the most liberally minded of the local clergy.

Sam Coutts, in addition to being a clever lawyer and sound banker, had a keen commercial instinct that enabled him to smell out new business wherever it was to be found. Similarly, the canny foresight which inspired him to visit Forfar market of a Saturday, marked out the June Fair at Trinity as an event which a prudent banker should not miss. In the past he had always gone himself, leaving Donald Graham to cope in the office, but in this year of 1855 he felt he ought to send Andrew. It would do the lad good to get away and it would be interesting to see what he might make of it. Besides, Sam's arthritis had been bothering him sorely and he would be quite glad, on this occasion, to stay at home.

Andrew jumped at the opportunity and took himself off very early on the Wednesday morning. The day was a fine one with a light breeze out of the east and only a few, high riding, white clouds to mar the clear, blue dome of the sky where the sound of the larks singing rose and fell in rhythm with their spiralling flight. Yellow broom blazed on all the adjacent hillsides and, in the hedgerows, the scent of the briars – covered as they were with pink and white blossom – was almost overwhelming. It was just past seven o'clock when Andrew reached the Moor and, already, the place was crowded. Andrew had never previously been at the June Fair and he was staggered at the size of it all. The whole place was alive with people – men, women and bairns – and there were animals everywhere. Those that had already arrived were cor-ralled in pens where they milled about as much as the cramped conditions would allow, their eyes showing fear and distress and their voices raised in loud, protesting clamour. Of those just being brought in, some were being driven along on the hoof and others arrived shaken and jolted in the backs of carts. The smell of dung was all pervading and it behoved the throng of humanity to tread warily on grass liberally spread with droppings.

As the morning wore on, and the auctions proceeded, the cacophony of noise had to be heard to be believed. Shrill voices of children and young girls mingled with the raucous, throaty calls of salesmen peddling everything from silks and ribbons to patent medicines and cough cures and, over it all, rising and falling like a heavy sea breaking on a rocky shore, was the terrified lowing of hundreds of cattle beasts, the plaintive bleating of sheep, the neighing of horses, the barking of the shepherd's dogs and the yelping of the hucksters' curs. How the auctioneers could make themselves heard above the din was a mystery and probably explained the ridiculous and unintelligible gabble with which they plied their trade.

By mid-morning, Andrew had met a number of Bank customers who had been only too glad to hand him, for credit of their accounts, such bills as they had received in payment for sales and any cash surplus to their present requirements. All this Andrew placed in the small satchel he carried over his shoulder and, in return, he issued each customer with one of the Bank's official Current Account receipts. Most folk were now making their way towards the various refreshment tents. There they could buy mutton pies and triangular pastries called "bridies" which were filled with a mouth-watering mixture of minced beef, onions and mashed potato. Those who could not afford such luxuries could buy floury baps spread with cheese or buttery rolls from Aberdeen with a lick of jam on them. For the thirsty – and with the midday, June sunshine beating down upon them through the heavy clothing of the period there were many so afflicted – there was beer by the hogshead, lemonade in bottles, and rum and whisky for those seeking something stronger.

Avoiding the tents, and the noisy hordes around them, Andrew found a quiet spot in the shade of a clump of whin bushes. There he sat down and unwrapped the food his mother had given him before he left home – oatcakes spread with butter, a hard-boiled egg and a couple of jammy scones. There was also an apple and a flask of cold tea. Well satisfied he lay back in the sunshine and watched a lurcher bitch playing with an old shoe. No doubt she belonged to one of the many tinkers gracing the Fair with their presence. Andrew grew drowsy and woke with a start when a shadow fell across his face and he heard himself addressed by a well-known voice.

"This is whaur ye're at! I thocht ye were awa hame!"

"Pitbuddo!" said Andrew, scrambling to his feet and brushing the crumbs from his waistcoat and trousers. "I've just been eating my dinner. What can I do for you, Mr. Milne?"

"Dae, laddie? Weel noo, it's like this: an auld freen' o' mine, Archie Fettes, him that farms up Drumlithie way, has a twa year auld Shorthorn bull for sale. Man! That bull is just what I'm needing. Gin he was to run wi' the coos up at Pitbuddo we wad hae a crop o' calves the like o' which havena been seen in the glen since the laird sold up his faither's herd some thirty year syne!"

"And can you not just buy him, Mr. Milne?"

"Weel, laddie! That's just the bit. I havena got the cash. Archie's wanting twenty guineas for him! Mind you, he's worth every penny!"

"But, surely, your account balance will take care of that."

"Aye – but ye see, I havena been idle the day and the balance o' sales and purchases is no exactly in my favour!"

"I see. What is likely to be the shortfall, Mr. Milne – including the cost of the Drumlithie bull?"

"Three hundred pounds!" Pitbuddo was certainly forthright.

"Aye – but you'll be selling again in the autumn will you not?"

"Ou, aye!"

"How were you paid for the beasts you sold today?"

"Part cash, and part bills at three months."

"And how did you pay for those you bought?"

"In the same way – bills at three months."

"Well, Mr. Milne. It seems you have enough on hand in your account to cover your outgoings over the summer months. Supposing you need it all, there will be a shortfall of some £400 once all the bills, including one for the bull, mature. Will you have enough coming in from stock and crop sales to cover that and leave a margin for necessary expenses?"

"Aye."

"Well, then, Mr.Milne, just you go ahead and give Mr. Fettes a three-month bill. Mr. Coutts will want a signed statement from you specifying the sales you expect to make in the autumn and your anticipated outgoings and expenses."

"I'll dae that, laddie! Man, ye're a rare banker! Yer faither wad hae been richt prood o' ye!"

During the afternoon Andrew collected a few more credits, until, by prior arrangement, at six o'clock, he met with Mr. Low, the Bank's agent at Brechin who had come up to the fair in his gig. Mr. Low accepted the cash and documents Andrew had collected and took them back with him to his safe in Brechin. He would account to Mr. Coutts for the cash and send the documents on the following day through the mail.

"I don't know what Head Office would say about this arrangement," he said. "It's many years now since Mr. Coutts first came to Trinity." He pronounced it "Taranty", and added, "He seems to find it worthwhile. I could not put up with it, although I do not object to playing my part in this way!" He smiled and, nodding to his coachman to drive off, waved Andrew farewell.

Andrew was tired. He had left home soon after five o'clock that morning to walk the seven miles or so to Trinity and it would be gey late by the time he walked back again. Folk were beginning to drift homeward, although many remained round the stalls, playing at hoopla and throwing balls at coconuts, while the bairns cried out in glee as they rode the gaily painted hobbyhorses and clustered round the bran tubs to try their hands at the lucky dip.

The evening was a fine one although the heat of the sun had gone and the breeze seemed as if it might yet bring a haar rolling in off the North Sea. There was no need for Andrew to linger and he set off purposefully, glad to leave the noise and the smells and the crowds behind him.

Andrew saw them from a good way off. There were three of them and they were standing right in the middle of the road. It was perfectly plain to Andrew as he approached that they had no intention of moving and that they were out for trouble. Two were lads of about his own age, the third – a thin, wiry-looking fellow with long side whiskers and a face like a weasel – was older. All were in well worn, soiled working clothes and the dirt was heavily engrained on such parts of the skin as were exposed to view. Some way back, Andrew had passed a farmhouse and steading but there was no sign of any other habitation. The road was threading its way along the course of a small burn and the land rose gently on either side effectively cutting off any lateral view while ahead, at a distance of 500 yards or so, both burn and road were swallowed up in a dark patch of woodland. Andrew could do no other than press on in the hope that the trio were less menacing than they appeared at first sight. It was a forlorn hope.

" 'Ere's a fancy young gentleman and no mistake!" the older man made a mocking bow while his two companions guffawed with mirth.

"And where d'you think you're goin', my pretty young man?" He thrust his weasel-like face into Andrew's and his breath was rank with the smell of beer and onions. Involuntarily, Andrew drew back.

"Aha! 'E don't want to talk to the likes o' us 'e don't! Wot d'you think, lads! Did we ought to teach 'im a lesson?"

Andrew had not failed to notice that while the speaker stood with his hands firmly planted in his trouser pockets, each of the younger men was carrying a heavy, gnarled stick of thornwood. Gritting his teeth Andrew made to pass on. He side-stepped the older man but, as he attempted to get back into his stride, one of the youngsters stretched out a foot and tripped him. Andrew fell on his back and was partially winded. As he rolled over and tried to rise, the thin man kicked him in the ribs but, as he did so, Andrew grabbed his ankle and, pulling with all his might, he yanked the man down beside him. The man's hand went to his waistband and Andrew saw the glint of steel as he pulled out a knife. At the same moment the two younger men began to strike at him with their cudgels. Instinctively Andrew doubled up and found the thin man's head within a few inches of his own. The man's ears stood out like milk can handles and Andrew bit the nearest one as hard as he could. Andrew had strong, sharp teeth and he not only drew blood but also tore off a part of the ear. The man screamed in agony and dropped the knife as his hand flew to his mutilated ear. Andrew's hand closed over the hilt of the knife and he hurled it away. Meantime, the thin man, yelling obscenities, had got to his feet and was encouraging the others to get on with the job of finishing off their victim. But the deed had been done. Andrew had taken too many blows about the head and shoulders and he did not feel the practised hands searching through his pockets.

* * *

It seemed to Andrew that he was floating on a sea of woolly fleeces. The sensation was comforting and he allowed himself to drift along easily. Then, as if at the end of a tunnel, he saw a blurred face and he heard a voice that seemed to be calling him. He found himself rising up towards the circle of light above and, as he did so, he felt his throbbing head and the ache in his shoulders and sides. He struggled, trying his best to swim back down to the restful peace he had left behind but to no avail; the circle of light grew bigger and the pain did not go away. He realised now that he was lying on his back and, as his eyes grew accustomed to the blinding light around him, he found himself looking into the face of the most beautiful girl he had ever seen. Memory flooded back of the weasel-faced man and the ruffians who had beaten him up and he knew they must have killed him and that he was in the presence of an angel. He tried to sit up but a wave of giddiness overtook him and he slumped down again.

"Now just you lie still a little longer!" Her voice was concerned, but firm, and Andrew felt something on his forehead, cold and infinitely soothing. When he opened his eyes he saw that this guardian angel was gently dabbing his throbbing temple with a wet napkin. So far as he knew, angels had no need of water and consequently she must – he realised with a shock – be real. He sat up with a start and once again the whole world revolved around him.

"Well! That was a bit sudden! Are you sure you are all right?"

Andrew steadied himself and his eyes focussed upon hers. Grey they were with a touch of brown like a hazel nut and they were full of anxiety.

"Yes," Andrew answered slowly, "yes, I think I am. How long have I been here?"

"Not long. I was out riding and had just left the woods yonder when I heard the noise."

Andrew looked round although it hurt his neck to do so. Right enough, a black mare with side saddle was tied to a field gate at the roadside and was quite contentedly cropping the grass at her feet.

"They must have thought there were other riders behind me for they ran away – the villains – back towards Brechin and I found you lying here. It is just as well you didn't fall in the middle of the road for I could not have moved you." She was on her knees beside him, a girl of about his own age, dressed in a grey riding habit. Gathered in at the waist, it showed off her figure to perfection and Andrew thrilled to the gentle curves of it. She had a heart-shaped face and a small firm mouth under dimpled cheeks and those lovely eyes, which caused his heartbeat to leap in a most alarming manner, were shaded by a dark, silky screen of lashes. A lock of dark brown hair hung over her forehead.

"Thank you," said Andrew, "thank you very much; you bathed my head!"

"That was the least I could do. You really need proper attention. You are all covered with bruises and there are one or two nasty-looking scratches. Thank goodness you have no broken limbs!"

"They had cudgels!"

"But you must have given them as good as you got! Look at this!" Andrew winced. The girl was holding up for his inspection a piece of bloody flesh.

"It looks like a piece of an ear," she said. "You bit him? Good for you!" Her eyes sparkled.

She was certainly a remarkable girl. Most girls Andrew had ever known, including Ella Gardyne, would have swooned, or feigned swooning, at the very thought. Furthermore, he found, to his intense surprise, that he could talk to this girl easily without the embarrassment he usually felt when face to face with a young woman.

"You were out riding?" he asked.

"Yes. I often do. My uncle is the farmer at Easter Craigbeg yonder." She pointed to the farmhouse back up the road, "My aunt, who is my mother's sister, is not well and they have no family. I have any number of sisters and am not missed at home, so I have been staying here for the past four months and helping as much as I can. But I like to get away from the house at some time every day and Dulsie yonder provides the perfect answer." She nodded towards the mare who pricked her silky ears at mention of her name. "Anyway, the countryside is so lovely here with the woods and the open parkland and always in the distance the line of hills to remind me of home."

When he thought of it Andrew recognised that her voice was not of this countryside. It was softer, with a cadence to it that was altogether enchanting.

"Where is your home, then?" he asked.

"Up in Badenoch, in the Highlands. Perhaps you've never heard of Badenoch!"

"Oh yes, I have! There was the Wolf of Badenoch, was there not? A terrible man who ravished the countryside far and wide. Did he not burn down a cathedral or something?"

"Yes, Elgin! But there are no wolves in Badenoch now, either two legged or four!"

"I think they are all down here!" said Andrew, rubbing his aching shoulder.

The girl laughed.

"What happened?" she asked.

"Not much more than you saw. I live in Pitbuddo, and I was on my way home from Trinity Fair."

"And that's where these ruffians came from, I'll be bound! Uncle says there are often unsavoury characters hanging about at the time of Taranty Fair. In fact he wasn't very happy about my riding out at all today, but he's always going on about it being dangerous for a girl to be out on her own. I'm afraid I don't pay too much attention. Ever since I was a little girl I have helped with the sheep and cattle on the hill. I think I must have grown up in the saddle!"

Her eyes were sparkling and Andrew was quite overcome.

"I am sorry," he said, suddenly recollecting himself, "I have not yet effected an introduction – please forgive my bad manners. My name is Gray – Andrew Gray."

"And mine is Mary – Mary Grant. How do you do, Mr. Andrew Gray!" It was her turn to do the recollecting. "Oh!" she said, "I forgot to ask. Did they rob you?"

Andrew looked down at his waistcoat.

"Yes," he said, "My watch has gone! It was my father's." Apart from that he had not been carrying anything of value – a few coins – nothing more – and these also had been taken. Andrew began to wonder whether there had been more to his encounter with the thieves than mere chance. Perhaps the rogues had seen him while he was transacting business. What a blessing he had handed everything over to Mr. Low!

"I'm sorry about your watch, Andrew." Mary had noted Andrew's use of the past tense in referring to his father. "We had better tell the police in Brechin! They might be able to do something!"

"I doubt it. These ruffians will be up and away long before the police could hope to catch up with them."

"Even so, you should still tell them!"

Andrew looked at her with respect. It was apparent that – once she had made up her mind – Mary Grant would not be gainsaid.

"All right then. I will. I promise!"

She laughed and the sound of it was like music in his ears.

"Now!" said Andrew, "I must get up!"

"Be careful – for goodness sake!"

Andrew slowly clambered to his feet.

"I'm not so giddy now: anyway I can't sit here all night."

He took a tentative step forward, stumbled, and would have fallen but for Mary's arm round his waist steadying him.

"You can't go yet!" she said.

"But I must –" He was on the point of saying that his mother would be waiting for him. " – I'm expected home," he ended, rather abruptly.

"Well! You have all of five miles ahead of you. You can't do it, Andrew, but if you can hold on to me perhaps Dulsie can carry us both."

"Then you'll be late home and anyway it isn't safe for you to be on the road all by yourself late in the evening."

She stuck out her tongue at him.

"You men are all the same! You're just like my uncle! I'll be perfectly safe – anyway, I can look after myself!"

"Would it not be better to wait a bit? Surely someone going my way will come along with some form of transport. There were several local farmers at Trinity today. I'm surprised none of them has passed already!"

"I'm not. Most of them will be in Brechin by this time propping up the bar at the 'Northern', and when they do go home, they will take the main road."

Andrew had to admit the logic of this. The old road was all right if you were on foot as he had been, firstly because it was quicker, and secondly because it swung down into Brechin by way of Trinity Moor. On the other hand, anyone driving would be quicker going down into town and then out along the new road.

"Come on!" said Mary, "let's have no more argument. You stand there while I fetch Dulsie." Without more ado she unhitched the reins from the gate-post and brought the mare over to where Andrew stood at the edge of the road.

"Now then," she said, "if I hold you steady, do you think you can grip the pommel of the saddle and haul yourself up?"

"I can try."

"Go on, then."

Andrew heaved himself up, and with a bit of a struggle, and more help from Mary than he would have wished, he got himself astraddle the mare's shoulders.

"Now – hang on!" Mary got herself up behind him and hooked her leg over the pommel. Andrew had his fingers entwined in Dulsie's long mane and he looked round as Mary spoke to catch a glimpse of a leg that, notwithstanding the long riding boot encasing it, clearly boasted the neatest of calves and the trimmest of ankles.

"Right!" she cried. "Off we go!"

Mary was a superb horsewoman and she rode circumspectly, minimising Andrew's discomfort as much as she could. As she had forecast, they met nobody at all on the road. Fortunately the threat of haar had not materialised but, by the time they came past the old kirk of Pitbuddo, the colours of the sunset were reflected in the windows of the town up ahead.

"Where shall I take you, Andrew Gray?" Mary asked, as they drew nearer.

Andrew was in a dither of indecision. He would dearly have liked to bring Mary in to see his mother but his inherent shyness made him baulk at suggesting it. Furthermore, he was desperately anxious not to be seen sharing a horse with a girl and, in addition, he had no wish to delay Mary any longer. She was late enough already. It was high time she was off on the road home and the sooner she left the less likely she would be to ride too fast. Accordingly he made up his mind.

"This is fine, Mary."

"What? Here? We're still out in the country; do you live in a field then?"

"Of course not! But I think you should be off home before it grows any later and I can surely walk the few hundred yards left."

Mary knew very well what was troubling him and it was not in her nature to cause him any embarrassment.

"All right – if you say so."

"I certainly do."

Mary freed her leg from the pommel and slipped to the ground.

"Hold on to the pommel and to my shoulder."

Andrew eased himself down – a difficult task, especially as he was stiffer than ever after the ride.

"Dulsie and I will walk with you a bit to see you are all right."

They walked slowly and, although limping heavily, Andrew was reasonably steady on his feet. Mary felt that he would get home safely provided he did not have too far to go.

"Perhaps I should get off home, then," she said. "Goodnight, Andrew."

"Mary!" Andrew's voice had a sharpness to it that was quite out of the ordinary. "When can I see you again?"

"Shall we say, perhaps, when you have fully recovered?"

"I'll be fit again in a day or two."

"Fit enough to walk over to Craigbeg?"

"Yes!"

"Why don't we wait until next week, Andrew! What about Saturday? Five o'clock at the field gate."

"Right! Next Saturday at five!" Andrew felt like singing to let the entire world share in his happiness.

Mary re-mounted and turned Dulsie round to face back the way they had come.

"Thank you, Mary. Thank you for being a guardian angel – and to a stranger too! I don't know what I should have done without you."

They waved goodbye, and Andrew stood watching until Dulsie, going at a brisk trot, had borne her precious burden away round the first corner and out of sight. As he limped up the High Street, the parish clock was striking ten.

Next morning Jessie called early at the Bank to let Mr. Coutts know what had happened and that she was keeping Andrew at home. She had asked Dr. Robertson to call and see him and she would be guided by what he had to say. Sam Coutts shared Jessie's distress but was considerably reassured to learn that there had been no loss to the bank by reason of the attack. Jessie was to be sure that Andrew was quite fit before she allowed him to return to work. Meantime he would write to Mr. Low advising him of what had occurred and asking him to report the matter to the police.

"Jessie," he said, "it's just another pointer to the fact that we need a constable stationed here in Pitbuddo."

Dr. Robertson came about midday, and gave Andrew a thorough examination.

"Well, well," he said, "it's not so much the broken bones – or in this case the lack of such – that worries me. Broken bones will aye mend. It's this surfeit of bruises and contusions which could spell internal injuries and that would not be good. However, I think you're in the clear, lad, and that's a blessing! Just you take care for a couple of days and you'll be right as rain. Don't go back to the Bank until Monday – old Coutts will just have to do without you. Probably do him good to have to work a bittie harder – take his mind off his arthritis! How did you enjoy Taranty? There'll be a wheen sair heids the day – of that you may be sure! Jessie, woman!"

"Yes, doctor." Jessie came hurrying in.

"Jessie! He'll do."

"Nothing broken?"

"Nothing outside anyway – and I'm pretty sure nothing inside either. I'll make up some embrocation to be rubbed on the worst of these bruises so perhaps you'll send one of the lassies up for it."

And with that, he was gone.

Andrew made a rapid recovery. When he arrived at the Bank on Monday morning Sam Coutts made no reference whatsoever either to his injuries or to his absence sick. Instead he was waiting for him with a paper in his hand.

"What is all this about?" was all his greeting.

"I don't know, Mr. Coutts. What is it?"

"It's a statement – that's what it is: I had Milne of Mains of Pitbuddo in on Saturday and he left this!"

Andrew smiled and explained what had passed between him and Mr. Milne at Trinity. Sam Coutts nodded.

"Fine I know, lad," he said, "but it would have saved me from looking a bit foolish had you thought to let me know beforehand. You could have written me a note. I don't mind you coming to an arrangement with a customer – it shows initiative and you are sensible enough not to do anything rash – but, if you do arrange something, you must always make a note of it and keep the rest of us informed! Now – are you feeling better?"

Andrew was annoyed with himself. He had been brought up in the belief that pride goes before a fall and he knew now that he had been presumptuous in thinking how well he had done, business-wise, at Trinity. In chastened and sober mood he went over the business he had transacted and Sam Coutts listened attentively. He had been right to give the lad the opportunity of going by himself: he had made a good job of it and Sam was well pleased. The credits had all come through from Brechin and the branch deposits were showing a healthy increase. Similarly, all the various instruments of exchange had been safely lodged in the Bill Case until such time as the customers concerned should call. Some would leave them lying there until maturity while others would seek to discount them for immediate cash which would, of course, boost the overall level of advances.

On Tuesday they received the news that the police had recovered what they believed might be Andrew's watch. A gang of thieves had been caught red handed as they tried to rob a jeweller's shop in Montrose. One of them had in his possession a watch which answered the description provided. It was being sent up to Brechin and Andrew was asked to call at the police office to identify it. His joy at this unexpected turn of events was tempered by the restlessness assailing him over the length of time that must elapse before his next meeting with Mary Grant. This was only Tuesday and Saturday was such a long way off. He began to count the hours and the minutes until he should see her again.

Jessie noticed a change in her first born that she could not quite place. Andrew had not said how he had come back on Wednesday evening and Jessie assumed he had walked, albeit with considerable difficulty. Meg was a little more sceptical. On Tuesday evening, while Jessie was putting Jemima to bed and she and Andrew were alone in the kitchen – Meg washing the supper dishes and Andrew sitting reading the *Advertiser* – she voiced her suspicions.

"You know what I think, Andrew?"

"What about?"

"You know what about – about your – your adventure on your way home from Trinity."

"What about it?"

"Well! You had some horrid scratches and they had all been cleaned up – I think there was a girl involved." It was a shot in the dark but it proved a winner. Andrew blushed scarlet to the roots of his hair.

"Oh!" cried Meg, clapping her hands, "There was! There was! Oh Andrew! Who is she? Not Ella I'll be bound."

Andrew realised it would be useless to protest.

"Wheesht!" he hissed, "Don't tell mother."

"Why ever not? You're eighteen now and it's only natural! Mother won't jump down your throat."

"It's not that: she pins her faith upon Ella Gardyne and I don't want to upset her."

"Don't be silly: anyway, we haven't seen much of the Gardynes this while back. They don't even go out along the road on Sundays." Meg wrinkled her nose. "I wonder why? There was a time when they were never away from here."

"Och! It's only ten days or so, Meg. They'll be back – never fear – Ella will not give up all that easily!"

Meg laughed; but before she could pursue the question of Andrew's mysterious girl, their mother returned to the kitchen and, notwithstanding the fact that she was smarting with curiosity, Meg was loyal enough to Andrew to drop the subject.

Jessie looked from one to the other of them.

"Have you two been quarrelling?"

"No!" Their expostulation was almost in unison.

"Well – you look peculiar, certainly Andrew does: you're all red in the face!"

"It's the heat, mother," said Andrew. "It's a hot day, you know, and it's like a furnace in here."

"Be glad it is," Jessie snapped. "There's nothing worse than a cold house." Then, turning to Meg, she continued, "Have you not finished those dishes yet? Goodness knows what the pair of you have been up to: there's something going on between you. Now – out of my way, Andrew, and let me in to dry these plates! Meg looks as if she'll be all night at it if I don't help!"

Later that evening Andrew announced that he was going out for a breath of air and Meg, saying that she had a book to return to one of her school friends, got ready to accompany him. Jessie laid down the garment she was stitching and regarded them somewhat quizzically – but she said nothing.

"Well then – who is she?" Meg asked as soon as they were out the door.

"Her name is Mary Grant and she lives with her uncle and aunt at Easter Craigbeg near Trinity."

Meg was kind enough not to laugh at the soft expression on her brother's face.

"She must really be quite something to have taken you by storm, Andrew Gray."

"She's all that – oh, Meg! She – she's wonderful."

It was not so very difficult for Meg to interpret the expression in his eyes.

"Tell me about her," she said, gently.

* * *

The police sergeant at Brechin closed the leather-bound volume in which Andrew had appended his signature to the entry recording the discovery, identification and uplifting by the owner, of a gold watch found in the possession of one Edmund Stacey, vagrant, of no fixed address, apprehended on Friday 15th June 1855 while endeavouring to break into the safe of Mr. James Lunan, jeweller, at his premises in the High Street of Montrose. From the description afforded by the police, it seemed that only one of Andrew's assailants had been involved. Four men had been arrested – three of them middle aged, stout and well known to the police in Dundee. The fourth – the one carrying Andrew's watch, was young, well built and English. Clearly the weasel-faced man and one of his companions were still at large. Andrew was asked whether he wished to bring charges against the prisoner but he declined. He had recovered his father's watch and this was all that mattered. Besides – despite the fact that the weasel-faced man had pulled a knife against him – he had no wish to have to give evidence in court when the matter of the mutilated ear would surely receive that which, in his view, would be unwelcome attention. Andrew thanked the sergeant and went out into Clerk Street where the sunshine was positively blinding after the dinginess within.

Being Saturday afternoon the town was busy. Mr. Coutts had let him leave the Bank early and he had been fortunate in securing a drive into Brechin on one of Matt Lundie's carts. He walked up past the Northern Hotel and over the four way intersection at the foot of Trinity Road. There, on the corner of Southesk Street, was a small shop similar no doubt to that of Mr. Lunan in Montrose which the ruffians had tried to rob. Andrew stopped to look in the window. In the centre was displayed a collection of watches and chains, flanked on either side by a small stand – one laden with heavy, rather ugly necklaces and the other with rings. Right at the back, however, almost hidden behind a tray of clasps and bangles, was a beautiful little brooch – oval in shape and convex by the look of it. It bore the design of a woman's head in white against a brown background. A bell rang as Andrew opened the door. There was no other customer in the shop and the jeweller himself was standing behind the counter polishing a silver tray which he laid down as Andrew came in.

"I saw a brooch in the window – oval shaped, brown and white."

"Ah, yes! The cameo one."

"Is that what they are called? I didn't know. How much is it?"

The jeweller reached over the interior screen at the back of the window; he took the brooch out and laid it on the counter. It was even prettier than Andrew had imagined. Worn by Mary it would look perfectly lovely!

"Is this the one?" the jeweller asked.

"Yes."

"Ah! let me see now," the jeweller pursed his lips and turned the brooch over in his fingers.

"This is the last of its kind that I have – an expensive line, imported from the continent – and I doubt if we shall have any more until this dreadful war is over. They sell at £3 17s. 6d."

Andrew's heart fell, but he contrived to look unperturbed. That was more than half his annual salary. His mother would be horrified if she knew that the thought of buying it had even entered his head. On the other hand he had known from the first that it would be expensive and he had overcome his initial scruples. Expense did not enter in to it so far as Mary was concerned. She had been his guardian angel and he was in love with her. Of that he had no doubt whatsoever. Anyway – what was the cost of a brooch compared with the service Mary had rendered him while he was lying unconscious at the roadside?

"Thank you, I'll have it," he said. He pulled out the eighteenth-century leather purse that had been his father's and counted out the cash – three King

William sovereigns and a half sovereign of George III, plus four of the beautiful new Queen Victoria florins minted for the first time only six years ago. The jeweller put the cash in the till, wrote out a receipt and handed it to Andrew with his change – a groat and two pennies. He wrapped the brooch carefully and Andrew put it away safely in his waistcoat pocket. When he emerged into the street and started off up Trinity Road, his step was light and he was whistling merrily under his breath.

Trinity Moor looked very different from the scene it had presented during the previous week. The stock pens had nearly all been dismantled and the booths and side shows were gone. Only the lacerated turf, and the mess they had left behind, bore evidence to all the livestock that had come and gone here at the time of the Fair. Behind him Andrew could see the roof tops of the thirteenth-century cathedral and the conical peak of the mediaeval round tower near by, but the town itself was largely hidden, nestling as it did in the fold of ground above the great elbow bend in the river, which was the reason for its foundation in the first place, back in the mists of pre-history. Ahead, the main Aberdeen highway continued over the moor towards the ridge of high ground in Stracathro parish marking the edge of the river system of the North Esk, while eastwards, the land sloped gently towards the salt flats of the Montrose basin, a couthy countryside of farms and tree-lined fields.

At the edge of the moor, the old road to Pitbuddo left the main thoroughfare, branching off in a generally westerly direction towards the hills. The finger post at the junction read:

"Craigbeg, 2 miles
Kirkton of Pitbuddo, 7 miles"

and, as Andrew turned off to follow in the direction indicated by the pointing wooden finger, he exulted in the beauty of the panorama spread out before him under the June sun. In the main, it was a symphony in green, ranging from the almost black shade of the conifers through the semi-dark hue of the deciduous trees to the greyish green of the partially cut hayfields, the mid-green of the acres where the root crops were about to flower, the bright green of the unripe barley and oats and the emerald of the pasture land. Far ahead the land rose in a series of ridges towards the hills, themselves a patchwork of green, the hills whose bastions sheltered the long glens that probed like inquisitive fingers deep into the rib cage of the Grampians. Andrew could see the high peaks clustered about the head of Glen Esk with, beyond, a glimpse of late snow still clinging to the ridge of distant Lochnagar, as it did on the summits of Dreish and Mayar away to the west of Glen Clova.

Close to him now was the farm of Easter Craigbeg, red sandstone house, built within the past fifteen years or so, round cart shed, neat steading – stable block, byre and dairy – and empty stackyard. A row of cottages, also stone built and slated, stood back at a distance of a hundred yards or so and there, one or two of the farmhands were busy in their potato patches earthing up the growing shaws. Around the house and steading, however, there was nobody to be seen. The whole place looked well cared for and this was in keeping with what Andrew had ascertained after some judicious enquiry. Mary had not said the name of her uncle but this also Andrew had discovered and the proof lay before him now, stamped on the iron plates affixed to the farm carts:

"John Pattullo, Easter Craigbeg."

Close by the farm a number of cross-bred stirks, probably twenty or so, occupied a roadside field and, opposite them, in a field bordering the burn, where ducks waddled among the reeds and buttercups, was a herd of some fifteen Shorthorn cows, many with calves at foot. Poultry were scratching in the straw littered ground of the stackyard and the air was loud with the cooing of pigeons ranged on the ledges of a nearby dovecot. Clearly Pattullo was a good farmer who used his land well and kept his place neat and orderly.

Mary was waiting for him at the gate. She must have walked down for there was no sign of Dulsie. She was wearing a blue summer dress edged with white, and Andrew thought he had never seen anyone look prettier.

"Hello, Andrew!"

"Hello, Mary!"

"How have you been? You are looking much better."

"Oh! I'm fine – doctor says there is no injury and the bruises no longer hurt. You got home safely?"

"Yes. It didn't take me long but Uncle John was worried. I told him I had been so enjoying the evening I had forgotten all about the time – and that was the truth!"

Andrew laughed.

"Where would you like to go?" he asked.

"Let me show you my favourite place." She slipped her arm through Andrew's and, side by side, they walked down the road.

At the bottom of the hill, a little path led into the wood through a thicket of hazel and birch. Under the spreading branches of the smooth-boled beeches, the bare earth was littered with last year's spent kernels and it was pleasantly cool in the shade. At a point where the path divided round the stump of a long-fallen tree, Mary turned off through a screen of broom, which she parted to show Andrew the way into a small grassy clearing edged on two sides with elm, whose higher branches formed the canopy, and the leafy basal shoots the sides, of a perfect natural arbour. The wood ended here and the far side of the arbour was in fact part of the long hawthorn hedge surrounding the adjacent field. A tree trunk lying across the clearing provided a seat from which it was possible to look out over the top of the hedge far and away to the distant hills.

"Isn't it lovely!" said Mary, pulling Andrew down to sit beside her on the log. They sat silently for a spell enjoying the beauty of the scene and their own company. After a while Andrew began telling her about his family, their life in the town, and his time in the Bank. For her part, Mary told him about her home in Badenoch, of the tinker clans who came in the summer time to mend pots and pans and fish in the Spey for river pearls to decorate the exquisite jewellery they fashioned out of such unlikely items as cast-away kitchen forks and spoons. As Mary talked, Andrew remembered the cameo brooch. He took it from his pocket and held it out.

"Mary," he said, "this is a little thing I got in Brechin and I would like you to have it."

"Something for me? Oh Andrew! There was no need for you to bring me anything: but how lovely! What is it?"

"Open it and see."

Mary undid the seals and opened the packet. Inside was a little blue box with a hinged lid secured by a gilt clasp. She opened the box and cried out in delight at the sight of the cameo.

"Oh, Andrew! It is really lovely; I've always wanted one." Mary lifted the brooch and held it in her slim fingers. "Put it on for me! Here!" She pointed to the neck of her dress at the cleavage of her breasts. Andrew took the brooch, opened it carefully, and with exaggerated care, considerable embarrassment and shaking fingers, he pinned it in place where Mary wished it to go. As he straightened up, Mary leaned forward and kissed him on the lips. The thrill and excitement of it ran through Andrew like a shock wave. Her hair brushed his forehead and the delicate perfume she wore was in his nostrils. The touch of her body upon his triggered off all his pent-up emotion and he responded to her kiss avidly, almost roughly. His arms were around her, crushing her until she gasped for breath. At last they drew apart and regarded each other with wonder and a certain amount of awe.

"I'm sorry, Mary! Did I hurt you?"

"Of course not, silly! But perhaps we shouldn't do it too often lest we get carried away."

Andrew was not quite sure of her exact meaning but he nodded.

"No. I suppose not. Maybe once more though!"

Mary laughed and hugged him again. Side by side, they lay on their backs on the grass talking until the setting sun told them it was time to part. Hand in hand they walked back through the wood to the road. At a corner, some fifty yards or so below the farm which was hidden from their view by a screen of trees, they kissed and parted, agreeing to meet again on the following Saturday. Andrew swung off back the way they had come and Mary made her way up to the farmhouse. John Pattullo was in the yard when she came in.

"Ye're late hame the nicht, lass: your aunt's been speiring for ye this while syne and I maun confess I was a wee thing anxious when I saw the mare still in her stall."

"I was out for a walk, uncle: it's a lovely evening: I'll go to her right away!"

Kate Pattullo had been a comely woman before chronic debilitating illness had stricken her down shortly after her marriage. Bedridden for the past two years, she was now as thin as a shadow, her eyes deep sunken and her cheeks fallen in. Mary's heart went out to her as it always did, and she was cross with herself for staying out so late, selfishly enjoying herself, while her poor aunt had need of her.

"I'm sorry, Aunt Kate. I had no idea it was so late – these long June evenings are so deceptive and it was so beautiful outside."

"I'm sure it was, Mary: but if I am any judge, it was not just the beauty of the June gloaming in Strathmore that kept you. There's colour in your cheeks, lass, that I've not seen since you came down from Badenoch and a look in your eyes that tells its own story. Who is he, Mary my dear?"

Mary knelt by the bed and cupped her hands round her aunt's.

"You're a wonderful lady, Aunt Kate: nothing misses you! I don't know how you do it. You're right of course!" And she told her aunt about Andrew, how they had met and how marvellous he was, but they talked together now in the language they shared from their upbringing in Badenoch, for it was much more descriptive and had shades of meaning that could not be rendered into English. As they talked, Mary saw to her aunt's toilet and got her ready for the night. She had nearly completed the task when John Pattullo appeared in the doorway.

"Gudesakes!" he exclaimed. "Wad ye credit the wye o't – a richt pair of teuchters! I dinna ken what ye're on aboot but I'm thinking it maun be something gey by-ordinar '." He was a big man with smooth, highly coloured cheeks that shone as if they had been specially polished.

"You're right there, John Pattullo – it is indeed something out of the ordinary." She told him what she and Mary had been discussing. "I've said to Mary that she must bring the lad in and introduce him."

"A banker, d'ye say?"

"That's right, uncle."

"Weel – I dinna hae muckle time for bankers. They're a'body's freend when it suits them and they're oot for mair business; then, when ye least expect it, they pu' the rug oot frae under your feet and lat ye dree awa' on your ain."

"I'm sure Andrew's not like that, Uncle John."

John Pattullo smiled.

"Maybe no," he said, "if ye say't!"

It was past midnight before Mary got to her own room and shut the door. She was very glad indeed that she had taken the precaution of arranging with

Willie Smith, the grieve, to have Dulsie fed and settled down for the night. She undid the clasp of the cameo and laid it down on her dressing table with extra care. When she was ready for bed, and she knelt down to say her prayers, she had something to add that was new and very exciting.

At about the same time, five miles away in the Kirkton of Pitbuddo, Andrew had just arrived home.

"Is that you, Andrew?" Jessie's voice called softly from the kitchen.

"Yes, mother. I'm a little later: it's been such a beautiful evening." He opened the kitchen door and went in to sit by his mother who had not long gone to bed. This seemed as good a time as any to tell her about Mary and another hour passed before he too climbed into bed and was immediately fast asleep.

Jessie lay awake, all that they had been talking about going round and round in her mind. She had been greatly worried that Andrew had taken so long to come back from Brechin, especially after what had happened to him on the previous occasion. He had said he would not be back in time for supper, but she had not expected he would be quite so late. She had, of course, already put two and two together and had been reasonably sure that there was a girl somewhere in the background. Of course she did not mind that it was not Ella Gardyne. She could not imagine what had given them all that idea. Ella was a nice enough girl, but Jessie would never have chosen her as the ideal daughter-in-law. Oh! How she hoped she would like this Mary Grant and that Mary would like her.

She sounded like a nice girl but, of course, Andrew would be seeing her through rose-tinted glasses as it were and it could be that his judgement was faulty. They would have to wait and see. Andrew had said that when he met Mary next Saturday he would try to arrange a day when he would bring her home for tea. There would have to be a deal of tidying up done before then. It was all very difficult since Meg seemed to have gone all starry-eyed over young Joe Shirress – eldest son of Sandy and Jean – and spent much of her time mooning about as if in a kind of trance. Thank goodness Jemima was still a child and quite uncomplicated. Jessie heard the parish clock strike three. Sunday was a busy day – kirk, sabbath school, bible class and the long walk out the Brechin road. It was a day in which she required all her reserves of strength: day of rest indeed! Mercifully, she fell asleep at last ere the clock struck four.

When Andrew and Mary met the following Saturday they went straight to the farmhouse. John Pattullo was out seeing to the cattle and Mary took Andrew up to her aunt's room where she had set a table for tea. After introductions, she left Andrew and her aunt together, talking, while she busied herself in the kitchen. Andrew was distressed to see how ill Mistress Pattullo appeared to be. She looked so frail that Andrew found himself speaking almost in a whisper and he had to force himself to speak up. For all her obvious weakness, however, Kate Pattullo kept up an animated conversation, and when Mary returned with a laden tray, it was to find the two of them laughing together as if they were old acquaintances. When John Pattullo came in and joined them, Mary – with Andrew's help in fetching things up from the kitchen – served the meal.

John Pattullo found Andrew easy to get on with and to the relief of the two women he was on his best behaviour and did not make any controversial remarks about the banking profession. After grace had been said, Mary made sure that her aunt had everything she required. Kate took the tray Mary had prepared and held it on her knee, but Andrew saw that she hardly ate anything at all.

In common with Mary and her uncle, however, Andrew did full justice to the excellent fare provided. Mary had made a stew of chicken with carrot and turnip from the farmhouse garden, and new potatoes dug that morning. When that was cleared away, Mary brought in a bowl of fresh strawberries she herself had picked and a jug of cream from the dairy. Kate Pattullo had a few of the strawberries and she shared in the cups of strong tea with which they washed it all down. When they had finished, John Pattullo excused himself and went off downstairs and out, while Andrew helped Mary to clear up and to wash and dry the dishes. They went upstairs again afterwards so that Andrew might bid Mistress Pattullo goodnight.

"I have enjoyed meeting you, Andrew. As you can see, I am not exactly in the way of meeting people or of seeing new faces. Thank you, Mary my dear, for bringing Andrew to see me."

"Goodnight, Mistress Pattullo. I have enjoyed it too."

Outside they walked down the hill and along the road as far as the field gate. They stood there for fully five minutes, pressed together in a tight embrace. One long final kiss and then – for each of them – there began the interminable wait until Saturday should come round again.

But time runs inexorably on, even for the young, and sooner than they had dared hoped, it was Saturday again. Jessie was flustered, more than she had been for a long time – and certainly more than she had thought possible. Andrew had arranged that Mary would ride over on Dulsie and, at Meg's request, Joe Shirress had agreed to make a stall available for the mare in the stable at his father's yard. Joe was easy going and likeable. At twenty-four he was much older than Andrew and considerably older than Meg, but both he and Meg appeared to be besotted, one with the other, as were Andrew and Mary. Andrew was to wait for Mary at Old Pitbuddo and their trysting time had been fixed for four o'clock.

Jessie had insisted that Meg should stop in all day and help with all the hundred and one things that needed doing. In the event, Meg baked scones and a cake, while Jessie packed away her dress-making paraphernalia – her cutting scissors and her tape measures, her pins and needles and thimbles, her reels of thread and all her bits of materials, the partly completed dresses and the garments in process of, or awaiting alteration. That done, and with Jemima's help, she dusted and polished until she had the kitchen looking as spick and span as it was possible to be. Then she sent Jemima round to the manse to ask whether it would be possible to have some flowers for decoration as she was having friends in for a meal and would like to brighten the room up a bit. Mr. and Mrs. Black were always saying that any of the congregation who wished were welcome to have cut flowers from the manse garden. The garden was a large one and it was quite impossible for them to use all that they produced.

It was not long before Jemima returned with a bunch of roses that was almost bigger than she was, even though, at seven – nearly eight – she was tall for her age. She had not seen Mr. Black who was busy preparing what she called his "semmon", but Mrs. Black had cut the flowers for her and wrapped the ends in thick, brown paper so that Jemima could carry them without having her hands pricked by the thorns. Soon, Jessie had them arranged in an old china bowl and the scent of them filled the house. Then Jessie set the table. She laid out the lace cloth last out on the day of the funeral, silver cutlery she had not seen for many a year, and the best china. She put out the new strawberry jam, made the previous day, and she rolled the butter, both fresh and salted, into neat rounds which she set out on two small plates. There was a crusty loaf, a speciality of the Kidd's bakery, and a plate of treacle scones to supplement those that Meg had turned out of the oven. Meg was to make a fish pie – a favourite of Andrew's – but, although all was prepared, this would not have to go into the oven until the last minute. By quarter to three, when Andrew left for the old Brechin Road, Jessie pronounced herself satisfied. She sent Meg and Jemima to get themselves dressed while she changed out of her working clothes into a black silk dress which, although she had made it herself, was cut on the most modern lines with a very full skirt, a fashion that had become all the rage following the recent State visit of the Empress Eugenie and her husband, Napoleon III. She combed and pinned her tawny hair and arranged it as attractively as she could beneath a black lace mutch.

When Meg and Jemima returned to the kitchen, all spruced up, Jessie sent Meg back again to pin up her dress. No daughter of hers, she said, would appear in public décolleté. Meg made a face, but went cheerfully enough and returned a few minutes later sufficiently covered to meet her mother's requirements.

Andrew stopped just short of Old Pitbuddo, at a bend in the road under a rowan tree in full blossom. The fine weather was still holding, although some high cirrus, gathering in the west, might be the portent of rain to come. For the umpteenth time that afternoon, he consulted his watch. Ten to four – he was still early. But he was sure he heard hoofbeats. Maybe Mary was also ahead of time. He was right, and the sound was coming nearer. Pulling off his hat, he stepped into the middle of the road. Round the corner came a farmhand leading a plough horse on a rope halter. He nodded to Andrew as he passed.

"Aye!" he said. "It's a fine day!"

It was five past four when Mary rode up at a canter.

"Whoa!" she cried, pulling Dulsie up as gently as she could. Her smile was radiant as she slid from the mare's back into Andrew's arms.

"Let me look at you!" said Andrew, holding her at arm's length.

"Inspection, is it?" said she with a grimace. "Making sure I'm fit to meet the Grays?"

"No! No!" Andrew was horrified. "I just want to see how lovely you are!"

She was wearing a russet-coloured dress, with ruched waistband, which Andrew thought was most attractive, and he saw, under the hemline, that she wore short boots of dark brown leather. He kissed her again and she made no further comment. Then, with Mary leading Dulsie by the bridle, the three of them, man, woman and mare, set off towards the town.

The Shirress property was right at the beginning of town as they entered and Joe was in the yard waiting for them. He smiled broadly and shook Mary's hand.

"Miss Mary Grant," said Andrew, "Mr. Joe Shirress – a good friend."

"Hello, Mr. Shirress!"

"How do you do, Miss Grant?"

It did not take long to have Dulsie safely stabled and to walk from the Shirress yard to the little house at the top of Meal Wynd. Andrew was as nervous as a kitten when he opened the door and ushered Mary in.

"So this is Mary!" A smiling Jessie came forward to greet her. "Come in, my dear. Andrew! Away you go into the kitchen and help your sisters while I see to Mary."

Andrew did what he was told while Jessie led the way into the girls' bedroom. To her intense relief she liked what she saw of this girl. She was pretty: of that there was no doubt; there was a frank and open look in those very attractive eyes; she dressed well, and when she spoke, the soft cadences of her voice were really quite captivating. Small wonder Andrew had been bowled over. If Mary turned out to be half as nice as these first impressions, Jessie would be well pleased indeed.

And so it turned out. Once the initial shyness wore off, it soon became apparent that Mary and Meg would get on well together. Jemima of course had no inhibitions. She gave Mary a gap-toothed grin, showed her all her treasures and elicited her aid in starting a cat's cradle. After supper, Mary helped Meg with the dishes while Jessie got Jemima ready for bed. Andrew watched the two girls, chattering together as if they had known each other for ages, and, in fact, they were much too absorbed in what they were saying to pay any attention to him. All too soon it was time for Mary to go.

"Thank you very much, Mistress Gray. It was most kind of you to invite me." Jessie smiled and took both the girl's hands in hers.

"It's been lovely having you, my dear. Come again – as often as you wish. Take care on that long road home; I don't like the thought of you riding alone."

"Don't worry, mother," said Andrew, "I shall be with her!"

"Well! Both of you take care then! Goodnight, Mary!"

"Goodnight, Mistress Gray."

They went downstairs and into the High Street. It was a cool evening, the cloud cover having thickened appreciably since late afternoon, and Andrew was anxious lest Mary, in her thin summer dress, should feel too cold. There were several folk about and he felt curious looks directed towards them. At the Shirress yard, Mary led Dulsie from her stall and they set out for Craigbeg. It was very late indeed before Andrew got home again.

Over the rest of the summer and into the autumn, the pattern of life remained very similar. The road between Pitbuddo and Craigbeg never got any shorter and Andrew wore out more than one pair of boots. The first time this occurred, he had no option but to visit Jim Gardyne's establishment. His worst fears were justified for, when he opened the door of Jim's cobblers shop, he found himself face to face with Ella.

"Well!" said she. "You're a stranger! Fancy you coming here! Has your lady friend deserted you?"

"I came to see your father, Ella: I have a pair of boots to be mended."

"Well – he's not here! He's out: I'm looking after the shop. It was the same yesterday, and the day before, and the day before that – as it will be tomorrow, and the next day and the next!" Her eyes filled with tears and she started to weep.

Andrew, taken by surprise, was not quite sure what to do but, before he could make any move, Ella flung herself upon him, burying her wet face in the folds of his jacket and sobbing convulsively. Andrew put an arm round her shoulders and stroked the hair on the back of her head. In a minute or so, the sobbing gradually slowed and Ella drew a long juddering breath. She pulled away from him.

"I'm s-sorry," she said, "I c-couldn't help myself."

"Ella! What's the matter? What's happened?"

"Oh! Nothing – really: I suppose it's just me – but I can't help feeling the way I do."

"The way you do?" Andrew wished with all his heart that he had never got himself into this. He should have stayed well away.

"Yes – you see, father is never home these days. He's always up at your old house with that woman, Strath. I think he's going to marry her."

"Oh!" Andrew felt a great wave of relief. Right enough, there had been some rumour in the town to the effect that Jim Gardyne was setting his cap at the ironmonger's daughter. Caroline Strath was a thin, rather ascetic-looking spinster. Although hardly in the first flush of youth, she was not unattractive, when she smiled, and it was said that she had smiled more often since coming to Pitbuddo than she had ever done in her life previously. Some said her parents had long ago given up hope of marrying her off, but others hinted that she had not been devoid of suitors when they lived in Aberdeen and it had to be borne in mind that the family's arrival in Pitbuddo had been, to say the least, sudden and unexpected.

"She has wrapped him round her little finger!" It was clear that Ella would give no quarter.

"You don't like her, then?"

"No! I do not! In the first place he's old enough to be her father and, in the second place, we are happy with Aunt Charlotte and we don't need another woman in the house!"

"I'm sorry you feel hurt, Ella, really I am, but your father will be lonely – just like my own mother – and it could be that the lady will make him a good wife."

"If it's a wife he wants, he needn't look further than my aunt."

"Ella! You know it doesn't always work out like that."

Ella stamped her foot.

"You don't care if I feel hurt, Andrew Gray! You would hardly speak a word to me at any time, and yet – if we are to believe what everybody in the town is talking about – you seem to have plenty to say to that high and mighty looking lady with the horse!"

There was not much Andrew could say to that and he did not try.

"Ella!" he said, "Can I leave these boots?"

"Oh – I suppose so! If old Casanova Gardyne deigns to attend to normal business, they should be ready for you in a couple of days."

Andrew gulped. He had never heard Ella, nor anyone else of his acquaintance, use such words when speaking of their elders.

"Good day to you, Ella!"

"And – 'good day to you' – " she mimicked, "Mr. Gray!"

Jessie had been surprised when Andrew told her of what Ella had said regarding Jim and Caroline Strath. She was very fond of Jim – but not, she felt sure, fond enough to have married him. But she did not like the Strath woman, and she was upset to think that Jim had become infatuated with her. In some ways she blamed herself for being quite so blunt with him that day when he surprised her in the girls' bedroom. It was her fault. She had driven him into the woman's emaciated arms. And yet – it had had to be said – so long as he was happy, Jessie would be content.

It was now mid-September, a time that Jessie dreaded. This year was worse than usual for, while Jessie recalled the grief-stricken weeks that had followed Tom's fatal accident, five years ago, the townspeople, in common with their countrymen generally, were celebrating the long-awaited fall of Sebastopol. Surely now the war would soon be over. It had been a difficult summer in the Crimea. In June, both Miss Nightingale and the elderly commander-in-chief, Lord Raglan, had gone down with fever. Miss Nightingale had recovered but Lord Raglan did not, and he went to join the man who had started it all, the unfortunate Nicholas I, Tsar of all the Russias, who had died back in March. To the Queen's intense irritation, the capture of the fortress on Malakoff Hill which had caused the Russians to abandon Sebastapol was effected, not by her brave British soldiers, but by the poilus of Louis Napoleon.

Andrew spent most of his spare time with Mary and, with her able tuition and Dulsie's co-operation, he acquired a new skill and became proficient on horseback.

In the early days of 1856, two events took place which brought Andrew's world tumbling about his ears. In the opening days of January, Kate Pattullo died. The funeral took place in Brechin on a bitterly cold afternoon of driving rain which, every now and again, was whipped into a frenzy by a gusty north-westerly howling down out of the glens. Much to the consternation of the minister, and the male members of the family, Mary had insisted upon accompanying the hearse to the graveyard. It was, she said, the least she could do for an aunt she had loved very dearly. Andrew went along to pay his respects and to convey, on behalf of his mother, condolences to John Pattullo. Hardly had the ground settled over the lair where they had laid Kate to rest than Mary received an urgent message telling her that her father was seriously ill and she had to hurry home to Badenoch – a difficult journey at any time, but doubly so in the depth of winter.

The first Andrew knew of this was when he received a letter telling him the news. It was, in fact, the first time he had seen Mary's handwriting and, when he arrived home one evening to find a letter awaiting him, he did not know who it was from until he had broken the seal. When he realised what it was, he excused himself and took the letter to read it in the seclusion of his own room.

Lagganeinich,
by Kingussie,
Inverness-shire.
24th January 1856.

"Dearest Andrew,
        After I saw you at Aunt Kate's funeral, I had less than a fortnight with Uncle John at Craigbeg before I received an

urgent message requesting my immediate return home as my dear pappa was seriously ill and like to die. I had no time to let you know and although I asked Uncle John to get a message to you, I rather fear, knowing how reluctant he is to put pen to paper, that he will not have got beyond the stage of thinking of doing so.

"I had a terrible journey. Uncle John took me into Brechin where I got the train to the junction with the Aberdeen line at Bridge of Dun. There, I had to wait on the cold platform for over an hour before the train for Aberdeen came in. They said it had been held up somewhere down the line. I thought I would miss my connection at Aberdeen but, fortunately, I got a cab right away at Guild Street which took me to the new Great North of Scotland terminus at Waterloo Quay in sufficient time. Like Bridge of Dun, there is nothing at Waterloo Quay but a platform. They are, however, building a passenger depot and they say it may be ready by the spring. The railway stops at Huntly and, as by this time it was late in the afternoon, there was nothing for it but to seek accommodation in the local hotel."

Andrew envisaged it all: she would be like a waif in a storm and his heart went out to her.

"The hotel was old and draughty and the bed was a little damp, but they gave me a good supper and, although I was worrying all the time about pappa, I suppose I must have been very tired, for I slept well enough. It was still dark when they knocked at my door with a pitcher of hot water. In fact it remained so throughout breakfast, and while we were boarding the coach for Inverness which I took as far as Keith. Here, I had to wait for another coach coming up from Banff which would take me on to Strathspey. By good fortune, it was a lovely day and the sunshine and the blue sky almost made me forget my sadness. It was evening when we reached Kingussie. One of my brothers – Alasdair – was there to meet me with the dreadful news that our poor, dear pappa had died at three o'clock in the afternoon and I was too late. Poor Mamma is heart broken and I shall have to stay with her – at least for the present. Uncle John will just have to manage by himself meantime. He did that for long enough when Aunt Kate was alive, so he should not be too discomfited. My sisters are here, of course, but they spend their time weeping and grieving for pappa, and are not much use. I grieve too, but life must go on and there is work to be done.

"I miss you so very much. Please give my love to your mother and to Meg, and give 'Mima a kiss from me.

"Ever, dearest Andrew, your loving,
Mary Grant"

Letter writing was not one of Andrew's most noted accomplishments but he buckled to with a will and had his reply completed in time to catch the next morning's post. There ensued a long period when the high peaks of existence, so far as Andrew was concerned, were the days when he returned home to find another letter in Mary's handwriting awaiting him. Winter merged almost imperceptibly into spring.

On 30th March the war in the Crimea ended in a peace treaty which the Queen, deprived of a great British victory, averred stuck in her throat. Soon, the trees were in blossom and the hillsides stained yellow with broom and, suddenly, it was June again and time for Trinity Fair which, this year, coincided with a great review at Aldershot when the Queen, riding a horse called Alma, sat in the midst of the returned veterans from the Crimea. They were bearded and weatherbeaten, their knapsacks on their backs and their uniforms worn and soiled. In Pitbuddo, they read about it in the columns of the *Advertiser* and they discussed the Queen's striking costume of scarlet tunic and navy blue skirt with piping of white, and a sash of crimson and gold to match the band of her round felt hat that was bedecked with a plume of white and scarlet.

And all this time Andrew fretted as it seemed that Mary was likely to remain in Badenoch for ever.

In fact Mary did not return to Craigbeg until August of the following year. She came down by train – this time Dulsie travelled with her instead of being sent on afterwards on her own. By this time also, the Great North of Scotland line had been extended to Keith and this eased the journey a little.

On the Saturday following Mary's return to Craigbeg, Andrew felt that he had run every inch of the way. When he reached the edge of the wood – their wood – he felt his heart was beating fast enough to choke him. As he emerged from the trees and could look up over the fields to the farm, he saw her at the gate, and he forced himself to slow down. He had no wish to arrive so greatly out of breath as to be unable to speak coherently. He need not have worried. Mary ran to meet him and they spent the next few minutes alternately hugging and then standing back at arms' length to look at each other in delight.

Mary was in the russet dress she had worn on the day she had come for the first time to the house at the top of the Meal Wynd and the cameo brooch was pinned on her bosom. She looked with approval upon Andrew's new suit – he had gone specially to Brechin to have it made – but she was not quite so sure about the beard which, if the truth be known, had only recently made its appearance. Mary preferred to see men clean shaven but in this she knew she was on a losing streak. The returned veterans from the Crimea had set the fashion and young men everywhere abandoned their razors and vied with one another to emulate the soldiers who had been to Russia and had survived to tell the tale.

When they reached Mary's special arbour, they found it a little overgrown. They had to force their way through the unyielding broom and there were signs of a fox's den in the bank under the hawthorn hedge.

"You've been away far too long," said Andrew. He took Mary in his arms. His lips found hers and she responded eagerly to his kiss. Slowly they sank down on the grass and rolled together in a tight embrace. All the waiting and longing of the lonely months of separation welled up within them and they could contain themselves no longer. In the euphoria of their togetherness, they made love, a new and marvellous experience for each of them. Mary was making little moaning noises and, for a moment, Andrew hesitated; but Mary held him even more strongly and their joy was complete. Their passion spent, they lay quietly in each other's arms.

The light was beginning to fail and it grew colder in the arbour. They tidied themselves as best they could and walked up the road in the August gloaming. There had been so much they had meant to say; each had so much to tell after such a long separation – but this could come later. They had shared a moment of complete fulfilment in which speech was quite super-fluous. Andrew saw Mary safely into the house before setting out in the darkness on the long road home.

In the days that followed, there was many an occasion when Mary was assailed by nagging doubts regarding that rapturous first meeting with Andrew on her return from her prolonged sojourn in Badenoch. She had of course been properly brought up; she had been taught to keep herself to herself – after all, irregular intercourse was a form of adultery and a carnal sin. The more she thought about it, the more she realised that she must be very wicked indeed because – and this was the stark truth of it – she had no regrets. She knew she was deeply in love with Andrew and there was no more to be said. The little whispering murmur of conscience, however, continued to niggle from time to time.

At subsequent meetings, they were more circumspect and they caught up at last with all the news each had to tell. Mary was happy to meet Jessie again and Jemima had given her a rapturous welcome. She was now nearly ten and, to her great joy, Mary commented upon how tall she had grown. Like Andrew, Jemima had fair curly hair. She was a particularly attractive child obviously destined to turn not a few male heads when she grew up. Meg, on the other hand, had hair with tawny overtones just like her mother's. Mary did not see much of her, however, as Meg was now officially engaged to Joe Shirress and it was expected that the wedding would take place this side of New Year.

One Saturday in mid-October Andrew suggested that they should walk down to Brechin as the afternoons were growing short and there was no longer much enjoyment to be gained by hanging about outdoors. It was pleasant in the town, walking arm in arm under the yellow light of the gas street lamps. They stopped to look at the merchandise displayed in the shop windows and they spent an hour or so in a little tea shop in Swan Street where, so Andrew had been told, they served potato scones that were quite out of the ordinary. Right enough, when the serving girl brought them their cup of tea, she also placed upon the table a plateful of the most mouth-watering potato scones either of them had ever seen. They were as thin as thin could be, still warm from the girdle and positively dripping with butter. Both ate far too many and they laughed as they saw how the melted butter had run down their faces. Andrew dabbed Mary's chin clean with a serviette while she, with considerably hilarity, did her best to clean the greasy streaks from the curly hairs of Andrew's beard.

It was very dark when they left the lights behind and trudged homewards over Trinity Moor. When they reached the farmhouse, the light streaming out from the back door showed them a horse and trap neither recognised standing in the yard. They stood at the corner of the house but their parting kiss was interrupted as John Pattullo came out the back door.

"Oh – there you are, lass. I hoped ye micht be hame early. My sister Jean and her man are ben the hoose. I didna ken they were coming but perhaps ye'd mak' them a cup o' tea and gie them a bite to eat. It'll be gey late ere they win hame to Edzell!"

"Of course, Uncle John!" Mary stood on tiptoe and kissed Andrew on the forehead.

"Gude nicht, Andra, lad!" John Pattullo called.

"Good night, Mr. Pattullo."

The following Saturday, just on twelve noon, a hired carriage drew up at Easter Craigbeg. Mary heard the crunch of the wheels on the gravel and, when she looked out the window, she saw to her astonishment and delight that the man alighting at their door was none other than her brother, Alasdair. Mary was outside like a flash just as the cabby was handing down Alasdair's valise. Hearing the rushing footsteps, Alasdair turned around, letting the case drop to the ground. He lifted Mary off her feet, kissing her with brotherly affection.

Breathless as she was, Mary's voice was far from steady.

"Oh!" she gasped, "This is just lovely! But what . . . . what are you doing here?"

"Wait now!" he said, setting her down, "while I pay the cabby."

The cab driver pocketed his fare, touched a hand to the billycock hat on his head, and flicked the reins over the horse's back. Mary led the way indoors.

It seemed that Alasdair had been in Edinburgh on business and that, on the spur of the moment, he had decided to break his homeward journey in Forfarshire so that he might see Mary. He did not have to be back in Badenoch until Monday evening so he could stay a couple of nights if it would not be too much trouble for the folk at Craigbeg!

"Of course, it is all right!" Mary was horrified that he should even think otherwise. Alasdair had always been her favourite brother. He had taken over the farm and small estate of Lagganeinich after the death of their father and was likely to make a good job of it. He was a big, loose-framed, tall man with thick black hair parted in the middle, long side whiskers and, what Mary termed, a "Crimea" beard. He had dark kindly eyes and he was Mary's junior by some eighteen months.

John Pattullo found Alasdair good company and, while Mary tidied up after the midday meal and busied herself getting the spare room ready, he took the young man on a quick tour of the farm and was much impressed with his depth of knowledge on agricultural matters. In fact, Alasdair was pleased to have this opportunity of talking to a low country farmer and he aired with John Pattullo his long held view that calves bred and over-wintered in the Highlands should be sent south in early spring to be finished on lowland pastures instead of continuing to be held indoors until such time as the grass should have started into growth in the Highland glens which, in an average year, could be anything up to six weeks later. The afternoon was well spent before Mary caught up with them in the well-filled stackyard.

"Now, Uncle John," she said, slipping an arm into that of her brother, "it's my turn to monopolise this man! After all, he is my brother and I am sure he is just bursting with family news. Come on, Alasdair *a'ghraidh*, it's time you stretched those long legs and if we don't go now it will be dark."

"Aye – certies!" Her uncle had pulled out his watch and was examining it ruefully. "Awa' wi' ye, then; oor clavers will keep." He went off to the byre to prepare for the evening milking while Mary led Alasdair down the road. As they went, she told him about Andrew and said that Alasdair would of course meet him quite shortly. In fact, here was the gate which was their trysting place.

There was no sign of Andrew, however, so they went on into the wood. On this occasion Mary kept to the path that ran round the far edge of the arbour to a stile set in a gap in the thorn hedge. The sky was clear and there was no wind. It would go to frost later. They paused at the stile and looked out over the darkening stubble towards the distant line of the hills. A smoky blue haze filled all the hollows.

"It's so quiet," said Mary, "almost as if the land lies exhausted waiting for the winter."

"That's right. Resting and enjoying a brief interlude of peace."

Mary looked somewhat anxiously at the rapidly fading daylight.

"Let's go back to the gate," she said. "Surely Andrew will be there by now."

Behind them in the wood an owl hooted and a pheasant called its jarring alarm cry. They walked back towards the road.

"It's good land, Mary; rich and productive, not like the stony acres and black heather of the north."

"Alasdair Grant! I do believe you're jealous!"

"Nonsense, girl!"

"Oh – but you are! I can see it in your eyes."

"You can't possibly. It's too dark."

"Well, in your face, then! What I can see of it under all that hair!"

He lunged towards her playfully and she slipped away and, half running, went on up the path. Alasdair caught her at the edge of the wood and she put up a hand and tugged his beard.

"Ouch!" He pulled her hair the way he used to do when they played together as children. Mary laughed happily and grasped his right arm in both of hers. She reached up and kissed him softly on the cheek.

"It's so lovely to be together again," she said.

"My own, dear Mary," said Alasdair.

Side by side, they swung back up the road in the gathering dusk. Andrew was not waiting at the gate and Alasdair could see that Mary was now worried lest something had gone wrong.

"I don't think there is anything to worry about," he said. "He has probably been kept late at the bank; it would not be surprising in the current financial climate."

"Do you think so?"

"I'm sure of it, *mo leannain*, he'll be all right; just working hard trying to keep the bank on an even keel!"

Mary nodded.

"Yes," she said, "I'm sure you're right."

As Alasdair said, Saturday November 7th had been a busy day at the Bank. The whole year had been far from easy. On the surface of things, trade was expanding at an ever increasing rate and, although these boom conditions had operated on a global scale, the effect was most keenly felt in the more industrialised nations, particularly in the United States where the inevitable effects of over trading had sparked off a series of bankruptcies to such extent that the banks had been forced to suspend payment, thereby causing embarrassment to merchants in this country who of course failed to receive payment for goods shipped.

Prior to this, so far as this country was concerned, the impending crisis had been masked to some degree by the trouble in India. And very severe trouble it was. In early spring, sections of the vaunted Indian Army had mutinied and the trouble spread like a contagious disease until, by late June, the native troops were in open mutiny throughout the subcontinent.

It was therefore a worried and irritable Sam Coutts who greeted Andrew first thing in the morning. He threw the *Advertiser* down on Andrew's desk and pointed with his forefinger to a couple of disturbing items on the business page. The first was a report by the newspaper's Manchester correspondent who, under the heading:

"Bank Rejects Lifeline Plea"

reported that the Bank of England, contrary to the expectations of the business community, had turned a deaf ear upon urgent calls for assistance submitted by two well-known banking houses in the north of England.

The second item was in similar vein; but its impact so far as they were concerned was even more alarming.

"DUBIETY OVER BANKERS' BOOKS-GLASGOW SHOCKED BY RUMOURS OF LIQUIDITY CRISIS AT TWO OF THE CITY'S PRINCIPAL BANKS.

"Glasgow, Friday November 6th: It is reported that the Western Bank of Scotland, one of the largest in the land, is in difficulties once more. Readers may recall that this Glasgow-based banking house, only ten years ago, had recourse to assistance from the central banking authorities. On the present occasion, however, the Bank of England has declined to come to its aid and we understand that loans received from banking correspondents in Edinburgh and Glasgow have already been swallowed up; and that the Edinburgh banks have expressed themselves as unwilling to render any further support.
"The outlook seems bleak for the Western Bank and, if rumours are to be believed, for other banking houses in the city..."

Andrew looked up. Sam Coutts lifted the newspaper off the desk and folded it neatly.

"Well," he barked, "what do you think of that?"

"I think the situation must be very critical."

"That certainly!" Sam Coutts had removed his spectacles and had begun polishing them with the large silk handkerchief he carried in his jacket pocket. "It should also be a lesson to all of us who call ourselves bankers. The Western Bank, Andrew lad, has ignored first principles. They say its lending is concentrated in a small number of borrowers many of whom are also shareholders! And – what is worse – it has consistently failed to keep adequate readily realisable reserves. I cannot see that it can possibly weather the storm!"

"The paper mentions other Glasgow banks."

"Aye," said Donald Graham who had been listening to the conversation, "the City of Glasgow probably. Maybe even the Union."

"One thing is sure," Sam Coutts had finished operations on his glasses and was setting off back to his room. "We are like to be inundated this morning. If I know anything at all about the good folk of Pitbuddo, they'll all be clamouring at the counter withdrawing their money lest our Bank too is dragged down in the impending storm!"

"Surely they would be daft to do so with interest rates at such a peak." Andrew had spent the last week making the adjustments necessary as the Bank of England discount rate jumped in a series of leaps which had taken it from six to nine per cent.

"Don't you believe it," Donald Graham snorted. "The *Advertiser* has yet another report which Mr. Coutts did not mention. It seems that only yesterday a couple of the big London bill brokers went under. It's a crisis, lad, and we're in for a busy day as Mr. Coutts said!"

"Just as well you've plenty notes," Andrew grinned. "You'll need them all!"

"I doubt if I will: they'll probably demand payment in coin of the realm."

He was correct on both scores. All morning there were long queues at the counter as many of the douce and canny folk of Pitbuddo withdrew their savings and insisted on receiving the cash in specie rather than in Bank notes which might not, in the event, be honoured. As a consequence, it was late before Andrew was able to leave the office.

When, at last, he was free to go, Andrew was glad to get into the fresh air and forget all the talk of calamity and disaster. The afternoon was wearing on but the sun was still lighting the hills away to the west and the golden autumnal light lifted his spirits as he strode out along the road past Old Pitbuddo. It was after four o'clock when he reached the wood and could see ahead to the field gate and to Easter Craigbeg at the top of the hill.

He stopped to look; but Mary was not anywhere in the vicinity of the gate. He hardly expected to see her. He was much too late. The best thing would be to walk up to the farm. Mary would probably be in the stable seeing to Dulsie. Just then, he heard the sound of voices. Two people were coming through the wood on the path that came from the arbour. Why he did so he could not afterwards explain, for it was not in his nature to be secretive, but – before whoever was coming came into sight – he moved silently over the grass verge until he was hidden by a thick, prickly curtain of holly.

It was growing remarkably dark and it was not easy to see too far ahead. However, as Andrew watched, two people came out on to the road, a man and a woman. The man was farthest away and he could not see his face. That did not matter, for Andrew had eyes for one thing only; and what he saw filled his entire being with shock severe as a physical blow. The woman was Mary. Of that there was no doubt. He heard that lovely cascading laugh that seemed to wrap itself round his heart strings, and then, not only was she hanging on the arm of this man whoever he might be, but – as Andrew watched in horrified suspense – she also threw herself upon him and kissed him. Quite clearly he heard the man's voice, "My own dear Mary!"

Andrew's world collapsed around him. This, then, was his reward for being late. What an idiot he had been to imagine that he was the only man in her life. She probably had half a dozen, and took them all, in turn, into her arbour in the wood. The thought was unworthy of him but of course he was still in a state of stupefaction. He felt an overwhelming sense of disgust and stood as if rooted to the spot. He must have stayed there for fully half an hour before, numb with misery as well as cold, he moved slowly up the road. The normally welcoming lights in the windows at Easter Craigbeg now appeared bleak, almost repelling. There was nobody to be seen, either around the house or the steading, which was just as well. He was soon past and heading for Trinity Moor. It occurred to him that he might possibly meet Mary's lover on the road but there was no way in which he would recognise him if he did. His mind was in a turmoil – his thoughts gyrating round and round. Below now were the warm lights of Brechin and he came in to the town down Trinity Road, past the shop where he had bought the cameo brooch and into Clerk Street.

The bar at the Northern Hotel was full and the air heavy with the smell of tobacco smoke and beer. Some men in working clothes standing at the corner of the bar, tradesmen possibly or loom hands from one of the linen mills, made way for the tall, well-dressed young man pushing his way in from the door. Andrew ordered a dram of whisky and drank it without pause. He was not used to liquor and the harsh bite of the spirit tore at his throat and brought tears to his eyes. Making a supreme effort, he managed not to cough. The whisky warmed him and took some of the sting from his heart. He ordered a second but, this time, he sipped the liquor slowly, letting it trickle over his tongue before he swallowed.

"Ye're no often in here, laddie – in fact, I canna mind seein' ye afore."

Andrew looked round. The speaker was an elderly man dressed in grey waistcoat and moleskin trousers. He took a drink from his beer mug and, with the back of one hand, wiped the froth from his upper lip.

"No," Andrew replied, "I'm not often in Brechin."

"Ye dinna hae the look o' a country loon."

Andrew did not reply. There had been something about the man's eyes that intrigued him and, on looking more closely, he had suddenly realised that the man had only one good eye. The other was opaque and probably sightless. The only other man Andrew had seen with one odd eye was that arch enemy of the family – Willie Guthrie. And, with that thought, there came to him over the years his mother's voice saying, "You were drunk, Tom Gray – that's what you were!" And then the almost forgotten voice of his long dead father, "Och, Jessie!" What? – he asked himself – what do you think you are about, Andrew Gray? Andrew pushed his half finished glass from him and turned away. He heard the man say, "Ye dinna need to gang away, lad. If I'm no gude eneuch for ye, I'll haud my wheesht. Aye, certies!"

Andrew shouldered his way through the throng and out into the cold street. Taking the main road, he set off at a brisk pace and reached Pitbuddo early enough to cause Jessie to wonder what was wrong.

Andrew did his utmost to put the whole unhappy affair as far from his mind as possible and, in this, he was aided by the developing financial crisis. Monday was a day of pandemonium and mounting panic, culminating in the news that the Western Bank had suspended payment. Fortunately the news did not reach Pitbuddo until the Bank was closed for business.

Sam Coutts shook his head.

"You see, Andrew," he said, "it doesn't always pay to try to outdo your neighbours. On the surface, the Western Bank appeared to fill all the criteria that could be wished for in a successful bank. It had a strong capital base spread over 1,300 shareholders, and it has always been vigorous and innovative in the extreme. Look at the extent of its branch system – over 100 offices spread all over Scotland, and each one attracting valuable deposits."

Donald Graham nodded his head. "Aye," he said, "and look at its note circulation – the highest in Scotland!"

"Will it be able to continue?" Andrew looked from one to the other.

"I doubt it." So far as Sam Coutts was concerned, this would likely be the end of the road for the Western Bank. It had very nearly failed on at least three occasions but this time was rather different. "They say they are up to the hilt in the American produce market. Na, na, Andrew! Folk blame the banks whiles for being over conservative but you'll find, as you go on, that the world has little time for an imprudent banker."

The following day, Tuesday November 10th, the City of Glasgow Bank suspended payment and the Glasgow business community was thrown into a state of near hysteria. Fears were expressed as to the stability of the Union Bank, even as Donald Graham had predicted, and the situation was grim enough to persuade the authorities to maintain troops under arms.

On Wednesday 11th, when Andrew arrived at the office, Sam Coutts was waiting for him, a letter in hand.

"Ah, Andrew!" he said. "Marching orders!"

"Mr. Coutts?"

"Here! Read this!" Sam Coutts thrust the letter into Andrew's hands. It was from Head Office, and addressed:

"Saml Coutts, Esqr.,
Agent,
Pitbuddo. 10th Novr 1857.

Dear Sir,

In view of the pressure of business occasioned by the lamentable failure of the Western Bank of Scotland, and the suspension of payment today by the City of Glasgow Bank, we are transferring Mr. Andrew Gray of your staff to our Dundee office with immediate effect and at his existing rate of remuneration. Kindly be good enough to release him in order that he may report to Mr. Petrie, our Agent there, with the minimum of delay.

Mr. Gray should, in due course, submit, through Mr. Petrie for our consideration, a note of the expenses incurred in travelling from Pitbuddo.

We have in view to write you in the course of the next few days regarding a replacement for Mr. Gray.

I have the honour to be, Sir,
Your most obedient servant,

James Henley,
Superintendent of Branches."

"What do they think we are going to do here?" Sam Coutts was distinctly displeased as well he might be. "If I am any judge, they are not likely to hurry over this matter of a replacement. As like as not, I'll be asked to recruit and train once more. Frankly, Andrew, I am growing too old for that! It's high time they found a new agent at Pitbuddo."

Donald Graham looked at Andrew with a solemn face and Andrew had difficulty not laughing. This was a constant threat of Sam's and nobody took him seriously any more.

"But – I'll be sorry to lose you, lad! You've been a great help to us here – an asset, just. Now then! I'm afraid you'll have to get yourself off home and pack your things. If I were you, I'd arrange to catch the train at Brechin tomorrow morning. It will get you into Dundee by mid-afternoon and you can report to Petrie on Friday morning! You may have to put up in an hotel until you find suitable lodgings. If so – be sure and charge the additional cost."

"My father's aunt lives in Dundee. Probably I can bide with her."

Sam Coutts went off to pen a letter of introduction for Andrew to take with him for Mr. Petrie in Dundee and Andrew was left to talk the matter over with Donald Graham.

"Do you know where to find the Bank in Dundee?"

"No – but even if I were told it wouldn't mean anything to me. I've never been in Dundee." Andrew did not add that he had likewise never been in Montrose, nor Forfar, nor Arbroath.

"Well – it's an easy enough town to get to know; the river on one side, wharves and docks and warehouses, and Dundee Law on the other, with streets going up like steeple-jacks! The Bank office is in Reform Street – you can't miss it!"

Andrew's mind was whirling. In the first place, he was still smarting over what he took to be Mary's deceit and he was anxious to find out the identity of the other man. But, to some extent, the awful feeling of desolation he had experienced at sight of Mary kissing someone else had been softened to a degree by the new sense of excitement at the thought of going away, with all that this would entail.

He wondered what his mother would do without him. He was, after all, the man of the house and his mother would now be on her own with the two girls. Even that was liable to change when Meg got married. As for himself, he did not particularly relish the thought of lodging with Aunt Eliza, always supposing she accepted him. However, it was probably to be preferred to strange lodgings in a strange town.

When he got home with the sealed letter given to him by Sam Coutts, Jessie was surprised to see him. She was even more surprised when he told her his news. She fussed about seeing that he had shirts and socks and underclothes and she sent him out to buy a valise of sorts to hold them all. It was, she told herself, inevitable that Andrew should leave home. No matter how greatly she would miss him, she wished with all her heart for his success in life and in the career to which chance had led him. In this, there could be no advancement for him so long as he remained in Pitbuddo – of that she was quite sure – but she had hoped that, when the time should come for him to move on, he might have been sent a little nearer home, to Brechin maybe, or even Montrose. For Dundee was so big. It must, she thought, be twice the size of Brechin, and it was so far away, maybe twenty miles.

Poor Jessie! She was wrong on both counts. Dundee, with some 65,000 people, was between fourteen and fifteen times the size of Brechin and the distance between the two was nearer thirty miles than twenty.

Jessie knew that Andrew would not be able to see Mary before he left, and it was on the tip of her tongue to ask him whether he would have time to write her. On reflection, however, she did not do so for, if the truth be told, she was a shade disturbed over his early return last Saturday. He had hardly spoken when he came in, despite the fact that Meg and Joe Shirress were in the kitchen. He looked surly and he smelled of drink. Not only was this highly unusual, it also pointed to the fact that whoever he had been with, it had not been Mary. He had merely grunted goodnight, and had gone off immediately to his own room.

All day Sunday he had behaved like a bear with a sore head and, at one stage during the evening, Jessie had completely lost her temper when an argument, that had been grumbling along between him and Meg for most of the afternoon, suddenly flared into a full blown row. It seemed to Jessie that her first born was in dire need of being sorted out and it could be that this move to Dundee would do just that. Whether Andrew would sit down and write to Mary or not, Jessie got pen and paper and, somewhat laboriously, she wrote a long letter to Aunt Eliza for Andrew to take with him. When Jemima came home from school, she was inclined to be tearful at the news of Andrew's imminent departure, but she brightened up when Andrew promised to write to her and to tell her all about Dundee.

All too soon it was Thursday morning and time for Andrew to go. He kissed his mother and Meg, wiped Jemima's tear-stained face, picked up his valise and stumbled downstairs. Outside, it was barely light and a chilly wind with a smirr of rain in it was gusting up the Meal Wynd. Andrew had arranged with Matt Lundie for a lift into Brechin and, when he reached the carrier's yard, he joined another three travellers already seated in the coach.

"We canna bide here a' day waiting for you, Andra! Hurry up!" Matt's son, Jock, was already on the driving box. He grinned cheerfully as Andrew flung his valise into the boot and clambered aboard Without more ado, Jock picked up the reins, and they were off, lumbering out of the yard and into the High Street. It was still not full daylight and only a few folk were abroad braving the November wind and rain. The houses of Pitbuddo fell away behind them and were soon out of sight.

Alasdair Grant left Craigbeg on the Monday morning and, although Mary was sad to see him go, she had to confess to a twinge of conscience in that she had been enjoying her brother's company while poor Andrew had been working at the Bank and cooling his heels in Pitbuddo until they should meet again at the end of the week. Once she got the farmhouse tidied up after Alasdair's visit and Dulsie properly exercised and groomed, she would write and let Andrew know how she and Alasdair had waited for him and how disappointed she had been at not having the opportunity of introducing him to this brother of hers whose visit had been so unexpected. Probably it would be better to delay writing until the middle of the week for, by that time, she would know definitely whether Uncle John would be going into Brechin on Saturday as he indicated he might. In this case, he could give her a lift and she could meet Andrew in the teashop which would be so much more suitable now that the weather had turned wintry. She sang happily to herself as she pulled the sheets off Alasdair's bed.

On Thursday morning she settled down to write. It had been a joy, she wrote, seeing Alasdair again but she assured Andrew that this would be as nothing in comparison with the delight she would feel when he was with her once more this coming Saturday. She added the suggestion that they should meet at the teashop in Brechin rather than at the field gate.

She sealed and directed the letter, stamped it, and handed it after the mid-day meal to Willie Smith, the grieve at the farm, who had said he would be going into Brechin that afternoon and that he would post it for her there. The remainder of the day passed without incident and she was in the act of draining a pot of potatoes for the evening meal when she heard John Pattullo coming in. He kicked the mud off his boots and came into the kitchen to wash his hands.

"Ye didna tell me young Andra was awa' to Dundee!" he said, rolling up his sleeves.

Mary nearly dropped the pot but she recovered herself and set it down on the stove.

"Who told you that?"

"I've just this minute heard it frae young Jock Lundie, the carrier. He was here wi' a load o' cattle feed frae Brechin and he said that, first thing this morning, he had ta'en Andra in to Brechin to catch a train for Dundee. He was carrying a muckle valise and it seems that, wi' a' this stramash aboot the Glasgow banks, Andra's been sent to work in Dundee. Ye'll miss him, lass! I'm thinking he'll no be able to walk a' the way frae Dundee on a Saturday!"

Mary could not believe her ears. If Andrew had been sent to Dundee – and she had no reason to doubt her uncle's story – why had he not let her know? Maybe he had written and the letter was still to come. That was it! It had no doubt been a sudden move – all part and parcel of this financial crisis which she did not begin to understand, although Alasdair had spent enough time talking about it during the weekend. She would just have to wait, however impatiently, until such time as she might get Andrew's letter. What a blessing she had written to him! Mrs. Gray would re-direct it to wherever he was staying in Dundee and he should get it quite quickly. From then on, Mary eagerly awaited a letter with a Dundee postmark and every day she was disappointed.

What she did not know was that the letter she had entrusted to Willie Smith had never been posted. Willie had not, after all, gone into Brechin. Instead he had gone to look at some stirks a neighbouring farmer intended taking to market the following week; and he had passed Mary's letter on to old Joe Macdonald, the travelling draper, who happened to have called while they were having their midday meal. Joe said he would be going straight to Brechin and he undertook to put the letter in the post.

When he reached Brechin, however, Joe called at a number of houses on Trinity Road on his way into town and he quite forgot about the letter in his pocket. By the time he got as far as Clerk Street he was beginning to feel the need for a dram or two to sustain him and accordingly, he made his way into the tap room of the Northern Hotel. The bar was busy and it was warm indoors; so warm that Joe divested himself of his outdoor coat. He folded it up and laid it beside him on a bench, where he found a vacant seat alongside a youngish man with a shepherd's crook in one hand and a white-faced collie bitch lying at his feet, her head on his boots and the rest of her tucked neatly in under the seat. As Joe put down his coat, the envelope containing Mary's letter slid out of the pocket and landed on the floor at the collie's nose.

She was feeling fed up and ill done by. Her master had just bought himself another pint of ale and she knew she would have to lie where she was until he had drunk it. But here, at her feet, was something upon which she might vent her spleen. She retreated under the bench and by the time she had finished with it, there was nothing recognisable left of Mary's letter. Neither her master, nor the old man at his side, had taken any notice of what she was about.

His pint finished, the shepherd rose to his feet and left the bar, his collie bitch padding along behind him. Old Joe remained where he was except for regular visits to the bar to have his glass replenished; and by the time he made a rather unsteady exit he would not have noticed a mail sack lying under the bench, far less the chewed up remains of a single letter. In the event he did, of course, remember the letter and the fact that he had forgotten to post it. He searched in his pockets, found nothing and assumed that the envelope must have fallen out somewhere along the line. He was not unduly worried for if this were indeed the explanation, someone would be sure to have found it and popped it into the nearest pillar box.

When Saturday came and Mary still had not heard from Andrew, she grew somewhat apprehensive. But, by the time it got to the following Thursday – a full week after Andrew had been seen boarding the train for Dundee – she was distressed beyond measure. She thought about it in every possible way but she could not arrive at any likely explanation.

In normal circumstances she would still have had a number of choices as to what to do next. She could write again, or she could make enquiries from Jessie, or from Meg. However, she was now almost certain that she was in the condition the Queen called "enceinte". In seventeen years of marriage, the Queen had undergone this experience nine times. To Mary, however, it was all quite novel and, in the present circumstances, most disturbing. The last thing she now wanted was to take any action which might look as if she were running after Andrew in an effort to force him to face up to his responsibilities. She would rather die than that. What? Oh, what was the right thing to do? She could just imagine what kind of reception she might get at Lagganeinich were she to go home and tell her mother and sisters that she was going to have a baby.

As the days stretched into weeks, Mary grew more and more miserable.

She was trapped and there was no way out. December brought in a spell of clear weather, sunny days and frosty nights and Mary found a degree of escape cantering over the stubble and occasionally letting Dulsie have her head in a full and glorious gallop. Darkness fell early, of course, and one afternoon, as she rode Dulsie back to the farm at a gentle walk, they were coming round the corner of the steading when a barn owl, its breast and the undersides of its wings ghostly white in the gathering dusk, flitted past Dulsie's nose like an enormous moth. Dulsie shied violently and unseated Mary, who was pitched headlong on to the cobbles of the yard. Mary was shocked and bruised, but she did not appear to be badly hurt. She picked herself up and, getting hold of Dulsie's bridle with one hand, she stroked and caressed the mare with the other, soothing and calming her.

That evening, Mary felt unwell and went early to bed. During the night, she awoke in some pain and discovered she was bleeding profusely. After a while, when the flow of blood had abated, she did her best to tidy things up. This took a long time; principally because she wished at all costs to avoid disturbing Uncle John. When she finally got back to bed she lay and shivered from exhaustion and cold. In the morning, when John Pattullo came downstairs, Mary was not up. He made his own breakfast and ate it and there was still no sign of her. This had never occurred before in all the time that Mary had stayed at Easter Craigbeg – either when Kate had been alive or more recently. There must be something wrong. Perhaps Mary was ill. He went up to see and knocked on her door. There was no reply.

2. Dundee
1857 – 1861

The shock to Aunt Eliza's system that Thursday afternoon in November was threefold. First, when she opened the door and found the tall, good-looking and bearded young stranger standing on her doorstep; second, when she discovered that this was none other than her great nephew, Andrew Gray; and third, when it transpired that the young man had been sent to work in Dundee and hoped to lodge with her here in William Street. It had quite upset her routine, but she had welcomed the laddie and she did her best to make him feel at home. She spent the rest of the day getting the spare room ready for him. They supped at six o'clock, somewhat frugally as Aunt Eliza did not normally have much to eat of an evening, and she had not expected a visitor. On the Friday morning, however, she gave him a good breakfast, and detailed instructions upon how to go, before Andrew took himself off to find Reform Street and Mr. Petrie.

The Bank's Dundee branch occupied a fine modern office in a thoroughfare which Andrew, in his first letter home, described as grand and impressive. It was, in fact, wide and spacious and lined on either side by prestigious new buildings. At the southern end, at the far side of the junction with the High Street, was the Town House with its pillars and steeple – built in the time of George II and recently renovated – while, at the top of the street, at its northern end, was the magnificent facade of the High School with its Doric portico, reminiscent of the Parthenon, and its double-columned gateway. Dundonians were justly proud of Reform Street, representing as it did a huge improvement from the derelict appearance they remembered of old when the area was one of dismal back courts lying between the crowded Overgate and the equally crowded Howff, or parish burying ground, and traversed by the Scouring Burn into which folk had been apt to throw rubbish of every sort. The burn, now piped and hidden from sight, ran underneath the Bank's vaults and Andrew was to learn, in due course and from bitter experience that, in time of flood, the pipe was unable to cope.

A messenger, who looked not unlike Gibbie Meldrum dressed for a funeral, ushered Andrew into the somewhat august presence of Mr. Petrie, the Bank's Agent, a thick-necked man with a face rather like a bulldog and a deep, gruff voice. Petrie had little to say to this country boy from the glens, who had been wished upon him by Head Office, and he passed the lad quickly into the care of Mr. Morgan, the Accountant, who supervised the sizeable staff and kept each one of them under his watchful and all-seeing eyes.

Henry Morgan was a dapper little man who dressed in a style fashionable in King William's time. Stiff, folded stock below high stand-up collar, narrow-waisted, swallow-tailed jacket and close-fitting trousers that showed off his ankles and calves. His greying hair was brushed forward above his ears and forehead, and in the pocket of his high-collared waistcoat he carried a snuffbox from which he helped himself at frequent intervals throughout the day, blowing his nose loudly thereafter into a large red handkerchief which he kept tucked up the sleeve of his jacket.

For all that, Morgan was a competent banker who was to teach Andrew a very great deal especially, as time went on, the intricacies of financing overseas trading transactions. On that Friday morning, however, the work to which Andrew was allotted was of a much more routine and mundane nature. As the banks, two days earlier, had agreed to accept Western Bank notes, these had been flooding in over the counters to be exchanged or lodged in deposit, with the result that the tellers and ledger-keepers were inundated with work and needed all the assistance they could get. In addition, many former customers of the Western Bank, now in voluntary liquidation, and a number of City of Glasgow Bank customers – deprived of banking services for their everyday needs – sought to establish new connections with the surviving banks of issue, causing further congestion at the counters and a huge accumulation of vouchers and unposted book-keeping entries behind the scenes.

Andrew, in consequence, had no time to weary. He revelled in all the new experiences which crowded upon him one after another. It helped to blur the thought of Mary and, while he succeeded in putting this right to the back of his mind, he knew, without manner of doubt, that whatsoever he might do, or wheresoever he might go, he would never be able to erase the memory altogether. He knew also that he was quite incapable of loving anyone the way he had loved and – despite everything – would always love Mary.

On his first weekend, and on many succeeding ones, Andrew tramped all over the city until he had the geography of the place firmly in his mind. It was, of course, much as Donald Graham had said that day in Pitbuddo, the river, the law and the streets between. The waterside intrigued him, probably because he had been brought up in the depths of the country, and he never tired of walking along Dock Street and viewing the shipping – steam boats and sailing vessels, ocean-going traders, whalers plying to Greenland and the Baltic, coastal packets and small fishing craft. Andrew knew them all and could soon recognise individual ships by their rigging or other distinctive feature. He was fascinated also by the markets – the green-market at the foot of Crichton Street, where the traders' stalls crowded round the disused, arched and turreted Custom House, and to the east of it, towards the bottom of Castle Street, the modern, well watered, clean but smelly fishmarket. In that vicinity too was the Royal Arch, erected just over thirteen years earlier to commemorate the landing at Dundee of the Queen and Prince Albert.

Further west, beyond the foot of Union Street, was Craig Pier, the terminal of the Fife ferry operated by the Scottish Central Railway Company. This was another of Andrew's favourite spots and he would often stand here, watching the steam ferry boat berthing. Once safely tied up at the quay, down would come the gangplank, and the passengers would disembark to hurry off up the pier into the city. Behind came the horses and carts, sometimes sheep and cattle with their drovers, and often a red shafted handcart, emblazoned with a crown and bearing Her Majesty's mails from the little sub-office at Newport to the General Post Office in Dundee.

It was not long before Andrew felt that he had adapted to the city life and could almost call himself at home in Dundee. At work, the intense pressure of the first few weeks abated considerably and, when the City of Glasgow Bank re-opened its doors one morning in December, Mr. Morgan felt that the crisis was over. That was the day upon which, at the farm of Easter Craigbeg, Dulsie the mare shied and threw her rider.

When John Pattullo knocked upon Mary's door for the second time, he thought he heard a sound but he couldn't be sure. Now, thoroughly alarmed, he turned the handle and pushed the door open. The dawn was only just beginning to lighten the eastern sky and the room was in darkness. His ears had not deceived him. There were indeed muffled sounds coming from the bed. He went downstairs and returned with a lighted candle. Mary was in bed, the clothes heaped untidily about her and she was mumbling incoherently. The big farmer placed his large calloused hand upon her smooth forehead. It was burning hot: the poor girl was fevered. He would have to send for the doctor. He went out to seek Willie Smith.

The Smiths were at their breakfast and when John Pattullo knocked, the grieve got up and opened the door.

"Is Bessie there, Willie?"

"Aye – surely – come in!"

Willie Smith had been up and about for some three hours attending to the milking and to the usual morning chores about the farm. In fact, he had newly come back. His wife, Bessie, was a kindly woman of middle years, plain and buxom.

"Mercy on us!" she said, "it's Mr. Pattullo himsel'! Man! Ye look as if ye'd seen a ghaist!"

"It's Mary." John Pattullo explained what had happened and Bessie Smith, grabbing a shawl from a chair by the dresser accompanied him to the door.

"Awa' into Brechin!" she called to her husband. "As quick as ye can. Go to Dr. Smeaton and tell him he's wanted at Easter Craigbeg. Hurry, man!"

In a trice, the cottage was deserted, the bowls of porridge still steaming on the table. Bessie went straight to the farmhouse with John Pattullo while her husband saddled the gelding and trotted off along the road to Trinity. John Pattullo showed Bessie the door of Mary's room and left her to go in by herself. There was plenty of work to be done outside and he might as well get on with it.

Bessie straightened out the bedding and bathed Mary's hot, damp forehead. There was not much else she could do. It was now daylight – the clear, cold light of a December morning. Bessie blew out the candle and drew the shawl closer about her. It was cold in the room and every now and then Mary had a tremendous fit of shivering – violent enough as nearly to scare Bessie out of her wits. She went down to the kitchen to search for a hot-water bottle. When she returned carrying an earthenware pig wrapped in a towel, Mary was lying quietly and her eyes were open.

"Hello, Bessie! How kind of you to come. I think I have caught a fever."

"Ye're shiverin' wi' cauld, lassie. Here! Tak' this! It'll warm ye up. Seein' ye're awake noo, I'll awa' and get ye a cup o' tea."

The tea when it came was hot and sweet and Mary, head cradled in Bessie's arm, did her best to drink it. Halfway through, however, she was seized with yet another terrible bout of shivering. When it was over, she lay back while Bessie dabbed at the blankets and quilt where the spilled tea had left a brown stain. It was after ten o'clock. Willie should be back soon. If only Dr. Smeaton would hurry. She heard John Pattullo moving about in the kitchen and, looking to satisfy herself that Mary was lying peacefully, she went downstairs yet again.

John Pattullo had a steaming cup of tea in his hand.

"What dae ye think it is?" he asked. "There was naething wrang wi' her yestreen."

"It's a fever. The doctor will ken."

"Aye – he'll be here directly."

Bessie poured herself a cup and they sat in silence by the kitchen fire. In ten minutes or so they heard the sound of hoofs and went to the door as Willie rode into the yard.

"I saw the doctor. He'll come as speedily as he can. Hoo is she?"

"Nae better and nae waur."

Bessie returned upstairs and John Pattullo went out with Willie who was leading the gelding back to the stable. The two men were still working in the yard when Dr. Smeaton came, just short of midday, driving himself in a light gig.

"Upstairs!" John Pattullo called.

"Right!" Dr. Smeaton, a heavily built man in his thirties, climbed down, lifted his bag and went into the house. He threw off his heavy driving coat and laid it on a chair in the kitchen. Bessie met him at the head of the stairs.

"In here, doctor."

"Thanks, Bessie. I'll manage fine."

"Is there anything ye'll be needin' doctor?"

"I'll give you a shout, Bessie, if there should be. Meantime – perhaps you'd be kind enough to wait downstairs."

"Aye, doctor."

Bessie took herself off to the kitchen and Dr. Smeaton entered the bedroom and closed the door behind him. Mary knew him well, for it was he who attended to Kate in her last years and she had always got on well with him.

"Well, Mary lass! It's not like you to be on the sick list – let's take a look, shall we?"

Mary smiled weakly.

"Hello, doctor. This is quite ridiculous."

"Maybe aye – and maybe no! Did the fever just suddenly start? Were you all right last night?"

"Yes .... only ...."

"Only what?"

"Well – I had a fall yesterday afternoon. It was almost dark. Dulsie shied at a barn owl and threw me."

"Where was this?"

"Out in the steading. I fell on the cobbles but I was not hurt – bruised only – but ...." She told him of what had occurred in the night.

Dr. Smeaton's examination was thorough and prolonged. Before starting, he called upon Bessie to put the kettle on the boil, fetch him hot water and have more ready should he want it. When Bessie brought the water he poured about half of it into the basin on the washstand and proceeded to scrub his hands and arms. After the examination was over, he called for fresh water and repeated the process.

"You know what happened in the night?"

"Yes."

"Do you want to tell me about it?"

"No."

"Very well, then. I'm afraid it's not all away and the bruising has in all probability set up an infection which accounts for the fever. But never mind! With care and attention we should have you as right as rain before much longer. Does Bessie Smith know?

"Good gracious – no!"

"That's all right. She'll be none the wiser, but I should like her to stay here over the next few days to look after you. Now! This is what we are going to do . . . . ''

It was well past one o'clock before Dr. Smeaton came downstairs. The men had joined Bessie in the kitchen.

"Will ye tak' a bite, doctor? It maun be weel past your dinner time."

"No, thank you, Mr. Pattullo. I have other calls to make. Your niece has a severe fever but I have given her something which should bring the temperature down. Meantime I should be grateful, Willie," he addressed the grieve, "if you would permit Bessie to stay in the house to see that Mary is all right. She'll not need much. Just keep her as warm as you can. Give her plenty to drink but no food whatsoever, you understand, and see that she has these medicaments in the quantities written on the labels and at the times stated. Can you manage that, Bessie?"

Bessie had a look at the labels and nodded. It was all perfectly clear.

"Very well, then. I shall be back tomorrow, but should there be any marked deterioration in her condition – should she get worse instead of better – send for me at once!"

With that, he was gone.

Mary remained in the grip of the fever all that day and throughout the night but it had abated slightly by the time Dr. Smeaton called in the morning, and the dreadful bouts of shivering had all but ceased. On the following day, Dr. Smeaton found his patient sitting up and much more like her former self, although pale and obviously very weak. He asked but one question.

"Clear now?"

"I think so."

"Good! Let us see – Bessie!"

When he was finished and drying his hands he looked down at her lying exhausted, her eyes closed. She seemed very young and very vulnerable.

"Mary."

"Yes, doctor." Mary stirred and opened her eyes.

"For better or for worse, it is as though it had never been."

Mary's eyes clouded and she bit her lip.

"I see." Her voice had a hollow note. "Thank you."

Dr. Smeaton pressed her hand and a fat teardrop gathered at the corner of her eye and splashed on to the pillow. Her cup of misery was complete.

From that day on Mary's health rapidly improved and by the following

Monday she was well enough to consider going home for Christmas. John Pattullo grunted. Only papists and piskies took special note of Christmas. For everyone else, Christmas was a working day just like any other. He had always known they were queer-like folk up in Badenoch but, for all that, he put no obstacles in Mary's way. She had had a rough time in recent weeks what with yon Andrew Gray going off to Dundee without as much as a word and then that frightening fever. Where she had picked that up was a mystery as great as the fact that she did not appear to have passed it on to anyone else. Maybe, of course, it was working away within them – perish the thought.

When the time came for her to leave, John Pattullo drove her into Brechin in the gig while Willie Smith rode Dulsie and saw her safely loaded into one of the railway company's horse boxes – a performance to which the mare was growing quite accustomed. At Lagganeinich, her mother fussed over her: she was so pale: what was the matter? Had she been ill?

"Oh Mamma! Please stop fussing! I am quite all right. It is the journey, you know, and this time it seemed particularly trying. I'll be perfectly well after I've had a night's sleep and one or two good Lagganeinich meals!"

It had been her other brother, Lachlan, who had met her at Kingussie, Alasdair having been busy showing a solicitor friend, who had come up from Edinburgh, something of the estate. She heard him now as he came striding through the hallway into the little sitting room their mother had made her own.

"Mary, dear!" Alasdair picked her up and kissed her. "How are you? You look pale. Are you all right?"

She very nearly stamped her foot – Alasdair was at it too.

"So this is the beautiful sister I've heard so much about. Good evening, Miss Grant."

Mary had been so taken up by Alasdair's impetuous arrival that she had quite failed to notice the dark young man who had come in with him. He was slightly built and of medium height, his most striking features being the jet black hair and the dark flashing eyes which seemed to dance with merriment as you looked at them. Deep set eyes they were under twin black scimitars, one of which was raised quizzically as he spoke. He had a finely chiselled nose, a closely shaven chin and a rather full mouth and he was bowing before her like an eighteenth-century gentleman in the minuet.

"Oh" said Alasdair, "I haven't introduced you. My sister Mary. Mr. Robin Cargill."

"At your service, Miss Grant. Robin Cargill. C-a-r-g-i-l-l. Hard 'g' and accent on the second syllable – Writer to the Signet!"

"How do you do, Mr. Cargill? That is more a Forfarshire name than an Edinburgh one, is it not?"

"But yes, dear lady. You have the rights of it. Most of my family, like St Peter himself, are fishermen, and 'red lichties': the young men catch the haddies out in the grim North Sea; the old men wind the lines, bait the hooks and set the catch out on the racks above the smoking oaken chips; while the women – sturdy women – pack the finished smokies in creels and sell them in the streets of Dundee. Yes, Miss Grant, that is what we Cargills have done for generations past and they will no doubt continue so to do, so long as there is a sound keel left in the harbour of Arbroath!" He was an eloquent young man, Mr. Robin Cargill.

"And yet, sir, you, chose to follow a different path and a landward one?"

"Ah yes, alas! I was not cut out to be a fisherman. The very sight of a boat is sufficient to make me sick. I dread the rail journey between Edinburgh and Arbroath for the two salt water crossings. I thank God that the one between Ferryport and Broughty is short enough but even there I can be most violently sick. Ugh! Forgive me, I pray. This is hardly drawing room talk!"

"Robin is my solicitor, Mary, and an extremely good one too!" – Robin tut-tutted at this and shook his black locks – "He is the junior partner in the firm of Colville, Carrington & Cargill, sometimes irreverently known as the three 'Cs' or 'Yes, Yes, Yes'."

For the first time in many weeks Mary's laugh cascaded out and she felt happy and more relaxed than she had been for a long time. As for Robin Cargill, his heart missed a beat and his elegantly clad knees turned to jelly.

In the days that followed, Mary and Robin were thrown together on many occasions. They went riding up Glen Feshie and round by the Thieves Road to Loch an Eilean, where the wind had formed the ice into long slats that rubbed against each other with a clacking noise like a mill wheel going round or roof slates rattling in a gale. They rode through the deep forest of Rothiemurcus on a soft carpet of pine needles and one day they reached as far as Lochan Uaine in the Pass of Ryvoan where the water, in Mary's words, was as green as a fairy's cloak. To the south, behind Loch Morlich, early winter snow capped the summit of Cairngorm and filled the great corrie that led the eye round to Ben Mac Dhui and the dark cleft of the Lairig Ghru. Mary pointed out all the peaks and gave them their Gaelic names while Robin sat on his horse absolutely enthralled. During the evenings, after they had eaten and Mistress Grant had taken herself off to bed, Mary and her sisters took it in turns to tidy away the supper things, while the men settled down at the cards, tobacco jar and whisky decanter ready to hand on the table. Robin loved a game of cards and he was in his element when on a winning streak and able to collect a gold sovereign or two from his companions.

"To hazard a wager on the cards!" he exclaimed, "is to live life to the full! Treading the knife edge, Mary, my girl! The danger! The panic and the palpitations! And then – oh then! Success! Such exhilaration!"

Mary laughed, but shook her head.

"Och, Robin!" she scolded. "No good ever came out of gambling. Ill gotten gains bring nothing but trouble."

"Ach, Mary!" Lachlan Grant was always inclined to be seriously minded. "You sound just like one of the Kingussie ministers."

"She's right, of course!" cried Robin, "my grandmother called the cards the 'deil's books' – and wasn't the nine of diamonds known as the 'curse of Scotland'? Beware, Lachlan my boy, lest the rascally Lowland lawyer lead you down the slippery slope to eternal damnation!"

To some extent Andrew felt himself a prisoner in Dundee. It was not that he disliked the city. Far from it; he found it pleasant and exhilarating. The busy streets, the jostling crowd, the traffic with all its clatter and din, and the many shops whose windows displayed a wealth of merchandise unheard of in Brechin or Pitbuddo. The office he found stimulating with a stir and bustle such as he had never known; and, although the financial crisis had led to a plethora of work involving long hours and late finishing day after day, he had never been one to shirk either work or responsibility, and he had risen to the challenge.

Moreover, much as he had confessed to misgivings over lodging with Aunt Eliza, he found this too working out entirely satisfactorily, although he did occasionally baulk at the clockwork-like precision with which she kept house.

The trouble was that Pitbuddo might have been on the moon, so difficult was it for him to get there in the limited time available. Any visit would have to be of short duration, arriving late on Saturday, leaving again about midday on Sunday, a time scale which hardly justified the railway fare, especially in relation to his extremely modest income. Early on, he had decided that he would confine his visits to once in every four or five weeks. He had, however, been working late for several Saturdays running and in the end had decided to postpone his first trip home until December 26th, the date of Meg's wedding to Joe Shirress. They finished work early on the afternoon of Friday – Christmas Day – in time to let Andrew catch the last train for Brechin. Once he arrived home, he found himself caught up in the wedding preparations and he had no time to pursue any of the enquiries he was intent on making.

The following day he had the task of giving the bride away. Meg looked positively radiant with the winter sunshine lighting the russet in her hair; while Joe Shirress, dressed in his Sunday best, gazed rapturously upon her in thoroughly besotted fashion. Seated beside his mother in the front pew of the United Presbyterian Church, Andrew, his whole being a-glow with pleasure to be taking his proper place as head of the family, felt more completely at ease than for many weeks past.

Across the aisle, Sandy and Jean Shirress were also very obviously enjoying the occasion, delighted that their long-standing friendship with

Jessie should be strengthened in this way. The Reverend Mr. Black excelled himself and even Dr. Robertson had to admit to finding no single fault with the service and that, for a staunch member of the Established Church, was praise indeed.

The reception was held at the "Temperance", Jessie having eventually relented sufficiently to allow Sandy and Jean to share in the cost and, although the newly married couple drove off in the early evening in a carriage which Joe had hired from Danny Dow, it was close on eleven o'clock before the party finally broke up and the Grays could walk home to Meal Wynd.

Next morning, Andrew accompanied his mother to church but he had to leave immediately afterwards for Brechin to catch the afternoon train back to Dundee. Before he left he promised that he would do his best to come home again as soon as possible.

Up at Lagganeinich, Christmas Day weather was mild with patchy sunshine, and Robin Cargill's poetic soul exulted within him – the tonic quality of the Highland air, the scent of the birch and pine, the blazing log fires in the house and – something he could never have found in Arbroath or Edinburgh – the festive Christmas board. Mistress Grant and the girls had done wonders and Robin ate more than his fill. A rich venison broth was followed by succulent roast goose, and a bramble and apple pie with thick cream liberally laced with brandy. When darkness fell, they gathered round the piano in the drawing room and Robin was intrigued by the lovely voices of the girls as they all joined in singing the popular ballads of the day. Best of all, however, were the songs in the old Gaelic tongue sung, without accompaniment, by Alasdair in his rich baritone, and by Mary whose sweet soprano voice, Robin thought, would charm the birds out of the trees. Together, Alasdair and Mary sang a sixteenth-century song about a mountain in Lochaber, followed by a much more modern one written, they said, by a Sutherland man called Robert Mackay, telling of one of his native glens, and set to a lovely haunting melody that made Robin's heart yearn – for what he was not quite sure – but at the back of his mind he wondered whether it was for the established togetherness of family life such as he, whose mother had died when he was only six years old, had never really experienced. When Mary sang alone, however, he knew he had never before heard such clear liquid notes. Robin was no great musician but he could not fail to recognise the fine tonal quality of the singing. Again – it was a song of longing and after the last quivering note had died away, he asked Mary what it was about, but she merely shook her head and, excusing herself, left the room and rushed upstairs. In the privacy of her own room, she buried her wet face in her pillow.

She knew she should not have sung it, for it was a song of love and that only served to bring back the hurt, the awful desolation; and she saw again the fair curly hair and the honest kindly eyes. Despite everything, she loved him so dearly – he who had taken her and, without a single word, had left her to get on with it. Andrew! Oh, Andrew! She had not only failed to hold him but she had also lost his child. The sound of singing swelled up from below. Alasdair was giving full value to Duncan Ban Macintyre's great pibroch in song about Ben Doran: she ought to go back down – mustn't appear all bleary eyed. She splashed some cold water on her eyes and dried them. Down in the kitchen she picked up a basketful of birch logs and took it with her to the drawing room. The splendour of the mighty song cheered her and drove away – for the time being at least – the doubts and fears churning around in her mind. The song had completed the full circle and Alasdair's resonant voice was ringing in the slow measured beat of the *urlar* the floor, or base upon which every pibroch is built up –

> *"An t-urram thar gach beinn aig Beinn Dorainn,*
> *Na chunnaic mi fo'n ghrein, 's i bu bhoidhche leam,*
> *Monadh fada reidh, cuil am faighteadh feidh*
> *Soilleireachd an t-sleibh bha mi sonrachadh."*

When the last syllable died away there was no sound in the drawing room but the crackle and spit of the birch logs in the grate. Then Robin broke the silence crying incongruously, "Bravo, Alasdair! A song of songs! What is it all about?"

"It is about Duncan Ban's beloved Ben Doran – a mountain in his native Glen Orchy. He speaks of its splendour, unparalleled under the sun and, of course, he speaks, as he always does, of the deer on the slopes and his happiness there."

"That is very akin to my own feelings here at Lagganeinich." While he spoke, Robin looked directly at Mary, who lowered her eyes under his frank and open regard.

"Like Duncan Ban, Edinburgh hems me in, week after week, month after month, year after year, until lo! – as if the fairy queen had waved her magic wand over my head – I am transported to paradise in the Highlands – to a Ben Doran of my own, here in Badenoch with all you wonderful people. Mary! You promised to show me the Christmas stars shining over Cairngorm – come on – let us go and look out from the front door! Pray excuse us, Mistress Grant – we shall be back directly: the night is but young: the decanter is by no means empty, and there is much music and song in this talented family of yours yet to come out!" His laugh was infectious. To her surprise, Mary heard her own laughter bubbling up, and despite herself, she placed a hand in the crook of Robin's left arm and allowed herself to be led out through the panelled hall where the mounted and antlered heads of red deer stags – trophies of long forgotten days on the hill – looked down on them as they passed into the porch and opened the massive oaken front door.

On Hogmanay, the village children came guising – some with blackened faces and some with masks – just as they used to do in Arbroath when Robin was a boy, only here, their chants were in Gaelic and all Robin understood were their shouts of *"tapadh leibh"* – "thank you" – when they received their gifts of fruit and nuts. At midnight, Alasdair opened the front door to let 1857 – with its legacy of mutiny and financial crisis – out, and the brave New Year, in.

"Bliadhna mhath ur!" the Grants cried, and the men kissed each one of the ladies. Before they could raise their glasses to toast 1858, there was a great hammering at the door and when Alasdair went to fling it open, there on the threshold was Padraig Mor, who occupied the position of factor and overseer on the small estate. He was a large man, as his name implied, and he seemed to fill the doorway. He had long black hair under a round blue bonnet, bushy side whiskers and warm brown eyes. In one hand he held a bundle of firewood and, in the other, a full bottle of whisky.

"Bliadhna mhath ur, Lagganeinich!" he roared.

"And a Happy New Year to you too, Patrick," said Alasdair, determined to steer the proceedings back into English for Robin's sake. "Come in, man – come in! And welcome! A timeous first-foot indeed! You'll have a dram." It was a statement, not a question.

"Well now, Lagganeinich, I might be persuaded. Thank you!" Then, raising his glass, he roared, *"Slainte!* – Good health and happiness to all here!"

"Slainte gu dearbh, a'Phadraig!"

Mary had decided that she would not go back to Easter Craigbeg. It held too many memories for her – of Kate who was dead, and of Andrew who might be dead also for all she knew. In any case, Uncle John no longer needed her about the place whereas, from what she had seen since she had been at home, Lagganeinich did. Nevertheless, she felt that she owed it to Uncle John to return, however briefly, to explain matters to him and, as she had travelled home before Christmas very lightly, to pack up the remainder of her things. On their way back from church in Kingussie on the Sunday after New Year, Mary announced her intention of leaving the following morning. Robin was delighted for, he said, he too must leave soon since he was expected back in Edinburgh by the middle of the week and they might as well go together. This suited Mary admirably as it meant that she would have company nearly all the way.

There was only one thing troubling Mary – the fact that she had not advised Uncle John of her coming – but she could pick up a cab at Brechin and he would be sure to be at home. Accordingly, in the morning, before it was light, Alasdair drove them into Kingussie in time to catch the morning coach for Grantown and Keith. The weather was still open and reasonably mild so that they made good time on the road and reached the railhead at

Keith a full half hour before the Aberdeen train was due to depart. Throughout the coach journey Robin was strangely quiet and his unusual reticence made Mary nervous to the extent that she found herself prattling away upon any subject that happened to come into her head. Robin gave every appearance of listening attentively but, by the time they had got to Craigellachie, Mary was sure that he had not heard the half of it, which was probably just as well.

A bare half dozen travellers boarded the train at Keith with the result that Robin and Mary got a carriage to themselves. They sat, one on each side of the door, facing each other and, as the train jolted down the line towards Huntly, Robin leant forward.

"Mary Grant!" he said, "Will you marry me?"

Mary stared at him: the noise of the carriage wheels echoed his voice. Marry me, they said, marry me . . . marry me . . . marry me.

"Mary, dear, lovely girl! Do you hear me? I am asking you to marry me. I'm not a great match, I know, for you can have your pick of Highland lairds – aye, and of Lowland ones too for that matter – and I am just a junior partner in one of the scores of legal firms in the city of Edinburgh. Yet I have some worldly goods, sufficient I think to keep you in some degree of comfort. But, you say, we have known each other for less than three weeks. What do you think you are about, Robin Cargill? Aha! say I, love transcends the puny ineffectuality we humans call time. Love does not require to develop and mature like good malt whisky. Love is an instantaneous thing – no wonder the ancients likened it to a wound from Cupid's arrow – and the same old fellow has implanted his barb right here in my heart. I love you, Mary – more than I ever thought possible to love any living soul. Please will you marry me?"

It does not fall to many young girls to receive a proposal such as that – most aspiring swains being inarticulate in the extreme. After Robin had spoken, Mary remained silent while he regarded her with an expression of rapt adoration.

Marry me . . . marry me . . . marry me – the wheels rapped it out over and over again. Robin was a dear soul and she had grown fond of him in the short time they had known each other but – and it was such a massive "but" – he wasn't Andrew Gray, and she could never love him the way she had loved, and would, she knew, always love, Andrew. But Andrew had probably married some girl in Dundee by now. Even if he hadn't and was still foot loose and fancy free, he had clearly forgotten all about poor Mary Grant. When she thought about it she felt she could not really face living at Lagganeinich. She had never got on particularly well with her sisters and she was not likely to do so now. Nor could she ever go back to live at Easter Craigbeg. You're homeless, Mary Grant, she said to herself, condemned to wander round and round like a ship without a rudder. Perhaps this was the answer – marriage to Robin and a home in Edinburgh far from Lagganeinich and Easter Craigbeg. As the train rattled on down Strathisla to meet the Deveron near Rothiemay, Mary leant forward and kissed Robin gently.

"Yes, Robin, dear," she breathed. "Oh yes! I shall marry you!"

"Mary, my darling!" He knew he should have taken her in his arms but he was diffident still. Instead, he reached forward and took her hands in his. For once, Robin Cargill was bereft of speech. He simply looked at Mary in wonder and a degree of awe while outside the carriage windows the short winter day drew to a close. His ecstasy was cut short by the train's arrival at Huntly, where station staff clambered aboard to light the oil lamps in the carriages. Before they left, the carriage filled up and by the time the train reached Inverurie, every available seat had been taken. The country folk smiled indulgently at the young couple now sitting side by side – backs to the engine to avoid the very real hazard of cinders in the eye – and holding hands. At the Aberdeen terminus at Waterloo Quay they waited fully twenty minutes for a cab but, when their turn came, and Robin had thrown up the luggage and they had climbed in, Robin pulled out his gold watch. It was just past five o'clock.

"Faur are ye gaein'?"

"Golden Square, cabby, number thirteen."

Mary looked at him.

"Golden Square?" she asked. "What are we going to do there?"

"Get married, my dear," said Robin, "I don't think it would be a good idea to marry in church: with the reading of the banns on consecutive Sundays and so on, it would take far too long: and then, we would have to tell our respective families and invite all sorts of friends and relations and far out cousins you and I have never heard of. No! I don't think that is the way for us."

"But . . . " said Mary, "what else can we do?"

"We can acknowledge each other before witnesses, my girl, and that – according to the law of Scotland – constitutes legal, unassailable marriage!"

Out the cab window, Mary could see the Guild Street depot of the Scottish North-Eastern Railway – the new title of the "Aberdeen" following its amal-gamation eighteen months earlier with the Scottish Midland Junction Rail-way. The thought crossed her mind that she should by rights be down there, seeking a south-bound train, but she brushed it aside.

"Before witnesses," she said. "How do we find suitable witnesses?"

"No trouble whatsoever! Mr. Robin Cargill will wave his magic wand and 'Hey Presto!' witnesses will appear!"

"Robin! Be serious – the step we are proposing to take is one of great mag-nitude and I for one have no wish to declare – what did you call it?"

"Acknowledgment!" cried Robin.

"Yes – to declare acknowledgment before anyone who just happens along.

You might as well drag a couple of hard-drinking fish porters out of one of the quayside hostelries!"

Robin grinned and squeezed her arm.

"It will be all right, my darling! Just you wait and see."

The carriage made heavy weather of the Bridge Street brae, at the top of which the cabby turned left into Union Street. In no time at all they were in Golden Square where they stopped before an imposing granite-framed doorway. The light from the gas lamp at the pavement's edge showed the number, "13", etched upon the fanlight. At the side of the door there was a sizeable brass plate and, once they had alighted and paid the cabby and were going up the wide steps of Caithness flagstone, Mary could see the inscription which read –

"Leiper and Collie, Advocates
H. R. Leiper, J. Leiper, R. P. Stronach, A. Q. Collie."

"Now!" said Robin, as they went through the door into the vestibule, "Let us hope my good friend, Quentin, is at home. He was at college with me at St. Andrews – a rare fellow, Quentin – a man of taste and excellent wit. His late father was a brother-in-law of old Leiper's and, after he had qualified, young Quentin came home to Aberdeen – a great loss to the south, I assure you!"

" May I be of assistance, sir?"

Robin found himself addressed by a tall thin man in a buff coloured tail-coat who appeared to be the Hall Porter.

"Yes, thank you. We wish to see Mr. Quentin Collie; my name is Cargill – Robin Cargill."

"One minute, sir, if you please!" He banged a bell that stood upon his high-topped desk by the door. It was answered by a much younger man, similarly dressed, who listened attentively to what the Hall Porter had to say before disappearing again back the way he had come. In a few minutes, a door at the back of the lobby was thrown open and a short, rather plump young man, soberly attired in grey trousers and immaculately tailored black jacket, burst upon them.

"Robin, my dear fellow! How good to see you! Come in! Come in! You look well – it must be the attractive company you are keeping!"

"Hello, Quentin! Mary! This is Mr. Quentin Collie. Quentin! Miss Mary Grant."

"Welcome to Golden Square, Miss Grant! But – let us not stand out here any longer: let me escort you, ma'am, to the little box I am pleased to call my office."

The room to which he led them was a typical lawyer's den. There was a desk, littered with papers, and three horse-hair chairs – one behind the desk and two for visitors. Bundles of Title Deeds, all tied up in red tape, were stacked on a table drawn up alongside a wall cupboard, through the open door of which the visitors could see, ranged along the shelves, a score or more black, tin deed boxes. Quentin motioned towards the chairs. Mary had the impression that he was all prepared to enter into lengthy reminiscences of their college days but Robin cut across the small talk and came straight to the point.

"Mary and I wish to be married, Quentin, by plighting our troth before witnesses and, since we are here in Bon Accord, this metropolis of the north, it occurred to me that we couldn't do better than to appear before you – always supposing that you agree – and one of your colleagues. Will you set this up for us, Quentin? And would you be kind enough, thereafter, to prepare a Marriage Contract and see to all the other formalities?"

"Well!" said Quentin, "Here is surprise indeed! Of course, I shall do these things for you, Robin – for a fat fee!" he added smiling, "But – when do you wish the – ah – ceremony to take place?"

"Now, Quentin! Instanter! Without further delay! Immediately! At once! Forthwith!"

"Robin! Robin!" cried Mary. "You sound as though you wish the matter concluded before you have time to change your mind!"

"Never let it be said, dearest heart! Come! Let us prepare for the nuptials!"

"I should hope so too!" Mary laughed. "Never, I think, did a maiden prepare herself for marriage vows so hurriedly and with no time whatever spent upon her toilette. I must look a perfect ticket."

"Nonsense, girl, you are ravishing as always!"

Mary was not quite sure as to the truth of that. Never, in all her dreams, had she ever imagined that she would give herself in marriage in a dingy solicitor's office – an unromantic sort of place at the best of times, its unsuitability compounded now by its being in a state which the good folk back home would call a *"bourach"* – a state she herself must surely be in after a day's travel by coach and rail from Badenoch. She did, however, demand that she be permitted to retire to tidy herself up and Quentin, leaping to his feet, showed her to a small and rather smelly closet at the end of a passage which was all that his establishment had to offer.

They made their declarations – Robin and Mary – before witnesses – and, so far as Mary was concerned, before God – in the fashion peculiar to the law of Scotland, Robin having assured Quentin that they had both resided within the country for the past twenty-one days. There, at Aberdeen, they took each other for man and wife, on Monday, the 4th day of January 1858, before these witnesses – first Alexander Quentin Collie, Advocate, and second, Ronald Polson Stronach, Advocate, both of Messrs Leiper & Collie, Advocates, Golden Square, Aberdeen. There remained only the matter of a ring and Robin solved this, temporarily, by removing his own signet ring and placing it on Mary's finger. It was of course much too large but she doubled her slim finger into her palm and so held it in place. First thing in the morning, Robin promised, they would repair to a jeweller and purchase a proper wedding ring. Despite herself, the very thought brought back to Mary the memory of the cameo brooch she carried in the little jewel case stowed away in the travelling bag she had carried with her from Badenoch.

They said their farewells to Quentin and to Ronald Stronach and took a cab to the Lemon Tree Hotel where they secured a room for the night, partook of a modest supper enhanced by a bottle of excellent claret, and retired early.

Their room was narrow and cramped, the large brass bedstead taking up most the available floor space. A dormer window gave a view of the neighbouring courtyard dimly lit by one spluttering gas lamp and Robin banged his head on the coom ceiling as he endeavoured to look out. Immediately under the window there was a small wash stand. A single chair and a wall press comprised the only other items of note in the room. There was no wardrobe and only one small oval-shaped mirror pinned to the wall at the side of the door. Above the bed was a heavily framed painting of an old woman kneeling in prayer before a stone altar in a high-ceilinged church.

The room was cold and they were glad to cling together in comparative warmth under the bedclothes. Robin's arms tightened about her and his lips were upon her forehead, her cheeks, her smooth white neck and shoulders, her firm rounded breasts; and she found herself responding eagerly in the proximity of his embrace. His lips were travelling upward again, meeting hers in an urgency he had never believed possible. Strongly his mouth pressed down upon Mary's and their first true kiss was ecstatic and long.

The chill of the room was long forgotten for Robin, in his unbridled passion, was probably rougher than he imagined. Nevertheless, Mary gave herself freely to this new-found husband who, afterwards, cradled her head in his arms in an embrace which in its infinite tenderness was the very antithesis of his earlier masculine arousal.

Robin Cargill counted himself the most favoured man in all Scotland to have secured such a wife as Mary – a woman in a thousand, bright, quick witted and intelligent, beautiful beyond all possible telling, gentle, sweet and true. Mary, for her part, kept her thoughts firmly in check. What young woman would not warm to Robin's gay impetuosity, his dark dancing eyes, his infectious laughter, his tender loving kindness?

Strangely, after such a day, they both slept soundly in each other's arms.

After breakfast next morning, Mary seated herself in a chair in the lobby while Robin paid the bill and made arrangements for a porter to bring down their bags. The hotel was busy and there were many people, both staff and guests, passing back and forward. Mary appraised them all keenly and wondered at the individual circumstances that had brought each of them here. Suddenly she stiffened and her heart missed a beat. A dark-haired young woman had just come down the stairs. She was dressed in an outdoor cloak, the collar of which was pulled up over her ears.

As she passed directly under one of the gas lamps supported on brackets mounted on the wall, the hair under the rim of her bonnet glinted like sunlight on copper. At the same instant, the young woman caught sight of Mary and recognition leapt into her eyes.

"Mary!" she cried. "How lovely to see you!"

Mary got to her feet as the girl rushed forward and embraced her.

"Meg Gray!" she exclaimed.

"Meg Shirress now!" Meg corrected. "Joe and I were married by the Reverend Mr. Black a week past on Saturday. Joe had business to see to in Aberdeen, so I came too! What are you doing here?"

"Well!" Mary said, "I too am here with my husband. We were married yesterday. Robin is over at the office paying the bill. You'll meet him in a minute or two if you have time to wait."

Meg was shattered: so Andrew had been right after all. Meg had eventually worried the truth out of her brother but had refused to believe that Mary had deceived him.

"Oh!" she said, rather lamely, and then – before she realised what she was saying – added, "it must have been Robin that Andrew saw with you that day in the wood at Craigbeg!"

"What day was that?"

"I don't know – one Saturday – it was early in November, I think."

"That wasn't Robin! I've only known him for three weeks or so and the only young man I ever saw at Craigbeg, apart from Andrew, was my brother, Alasdair, who arrived unexpectedly that Saturday. He and I went for a walk together in the afternoon. We waited for Andrew in the place where I usually met him but he did not turn up. I wrote him afterwards but got no reply." Tears sprang to her eyes and she pulled a handkerchief from her reticule.

It was Meg's turn to feel stunned. When Robin arrived, swinging along jauntily, he found both girls ashen faced but each protested that he must be imagining it. How could they – two young newly wed girls – be other than well, happy and excited? He left it at that – but, later in the day, as they went on the long, weary journey to Edinburgh by rail and water, Mary's long silences made him wonder anew what had happened that morning when she met Meg Shirress at the Lemon Tree. But whatever he may have thought, he could never have guessed at the awful ache in Mary's heart or at the yearning after the unattainable that was tearing her apart.

As for Meg, she vowed that she would not tell Andrew that which she had learned this morning. How lucky she was to have dear, uncomplicated Joe. How utterly forlorn, by comparison, were Andrew and Mary.

One Saturday in February, Andrew set out once again for Pitbuddo. The station at Brechin was busy but he hurried out and was making his way up Southesk Street, head bowed against a strongish wind blowing out of the northwest, when he accidentally bumped into a man walking in the opposite direction.

"I beg your pardon," Andrew drew to one side. "I'm afraid I was not looking where I was going."

"Gudesakes!" said the man. "It is Mr. Gray!"

Andrew, looking more closely felt an unaccountable embarrassment.

"Oh!" he said. "It's you, Willie. How are you?"

Willie Smith, grieve at Easter Craigbeg, was regarding him with a very slightly bleary eye. Willie had had a drink or two and, while he was by no means the worse of it, he had clearly had sufficient to loosen his tongue and curb his inhibitions.

"I'm fine, laddie! just fine: but what aboot you? Man! I dinna ken what you were daein' letting sic a braw lassie as Mary Grant slip through your fingers. I thoucht ye had mair sense. And she that fond o' ye!"

"It was no fault of mine, Willie: I saw her one day at Craigbeg with another man: that was that: I know when I'm not wanted!"

"Dinna be daft, man! She never saw a man at Craigbeg ither than yoursel' – unless . . . I wonder . . . maybe ye saw her yon day when her brother cried in on his way hame to the Hielands. Ach! but ye're ower late noo; ye've lost her and that's a fact. She's got hersel' wedded to a lawyer chiel doon in Edinburgh."

Andrew felt a cold sensation in the pit of his stomach. If all this were true and he had no reason to doubt it, he had been stupid in the extreme. What kind of lover was he who would immediately jump to the conclusion that his heart's darling was deceiving him? Surely, Mary had deserved more of him than that. Her brother? What a fool he had been. And now – now he had lost her forever.

He muttered a somewhat incoherent goodbye, and walked slowly away. Willie Smith took off his hat, scratched his head, and stood for a moment watching his retreating figure.

The gulls standing all along the wall of the railway pier took off in a beating of wings and a raucous screaming. Andrew, who had been sitting enjoying the warm April sunshine, looked up. One of the porters had just thrown a plateful of scraps into the water and the gulls were fighting as each tried to grab more than what might be described as a fair share. Andrew watched them – herring gulls in the main, with one or two black backs among them and a sprinkling of immature birds in their speckled plumage. As suddenly as it had begun, the screaming died away and the gulls, whether they had been successful in their foraging or not, flew back to land on the wall. Slowly, they folded their wings until next time.

Andrew liked to come here under the eye of the signal station maintained by Her Majesty's Coastguard in the ancient square tower which was all that remained of the once large and strong fortress of Broughty – one of the ancestral homes of the Grays. Not only could he watch the ever changing water but he could also, as at Craig Pier in Dundee, watch the coming and going of the boats at this other ferry which formed the vital link in the rail journey from Edinburgh to destinations north of the Tay. Less than a mile away, across the narrows, lay the southern terminus of the Edinburgh, Perth and Dundee Railway and, on this side, at the head of the pier, a branch line ran back to join the main Dundee and Arbroath railway at the Broughty Ferry depot. In fact, a train was due at any minute because, across the water, Andrew could see the puffs of smoke from the locomotive of the train from Edinburgh, as it backed its carriages down the ramp until they came to rest against the buffers, to stand adjacent to the gangplank of the steamboat tied up at the Ferryport pier. Behind him a piercing whistle announced the imminent arrival of the connecting train coming down the short branch line from the main Broughty Ferry depot.

Andrew crossed the railway and walked along the front, following the widening river out towards the links at Monifieth and the bents and sand dunes of Buddon that stand with their feet in the creaming tides of the North Sea. Andrew felt refreshed and invigorated. It was Saturday afternoon and it was April. The fury of the winter gales had long since died away and now there was only a hint of a breeze blowing in with the making tide. Daffodils nodded their lovely heads in the gardens of the neat villas – many of them newly built – which he passed on his way and once, but only once, he heard the call of a cuckoo.

Andrew liked Saturday when he could get away from the stuffiness of the office. For the past few months, he had been assigned to what Mr. Morgan called the "jute" desk, a new but extremely active side of the branch business. Since mediaeval times, Dundee had held pre-eminence in the realm of textiles. Spinning and weaving were in the blood of the people – distaff and wheel, warp and weft. In the sixteenth century, the town had been the centre of the Scottish woollen trade and had sizeable exports of cloth and, in particular, of bonnets. After the union, the home industry lost out against the heavily subsidised English staple with the result that, although Dundee continued to produce the famous knitted bonnets and plaidings – the latter dyed in Holland and exported throughout Europe – local manufacturers had turned more and more towards linen, produced from flax, the bulk of which was imported from Russia by way of the Baltic. The Dundee mills specialised in coarse material such as Osnaburgs, sheeting, duck, sail canvas, sacks and bagging. Recently, however, the war with Russia had cut off supplies of flax. With disaster staring them in the face, the mill owners did not know where to turn. The effect upon Dundee would have been catastrophic but for one of those lucky chances, or acts of Divine intervention, call it what you will – that have so often occurred throughout history.

Around about the turn of the century, a linen manufacturer in Dundee named William Anderson had received a parcel of a previously unknown fibre which had been sent to London by the East India Company. Anderson tested this "Indian grass" for strength but it proved dry, brittle and much too weak to produce an acceptable yarn. Fifty years on, however, at the time of the Crimean War, further experiments were instructed in an effort to find a substitute for the unobtainable flax and – this time – the "Indian grass" did not disappoint. It was William Taylor of the Ruthven Mill who discovered that all that was needed to make jute malleable was a good soaking in whale oil, a commodity of which as a principal whaling port, Dundee had a ready and constant supply. In consequence, the spinners and weavers of Dundee went over more or less *en masse* to jute imported into the Tay direct from Bengal. In the process they also rejuvenated the whaling industry which had gone into notable decline following the introduction of gas lighting in place of the old-fashioned oil lamp.

This then was the exciting new development which had led Mr. Morgan at the bank to set up the jute desk. Here, Andrew learned about and was soon dealing competently with such things as Bills of Lading, Warehouse Warrants, Produce Receipts, Delivery Orders and so on. It was intriguing work and Andrew had no time to weary. Fortunately, the continuing unrest in India did not interrupt the flow of raw jute into Dundee. Shipments continued on a fairly regular basis notwithstanding the turmoil and the horrific talks of massacre and bloodshed percolating home. Indian place names like Cawnpore and Lucknow became household words such as Sebastopol and Scutari had been a few years back and, as 1857 had drawn to a close, the public learned with dismay of the death from dysentery of General Havelock. In the high places it was at last being understood that the Mutiny represented an out and out rejection by the Indian people of the manner in which Britain had sought to rule, not by the Civil Service, nor even by the armed forces, but by officials – many of doubtful integrity – of a trading corporation – the East India Company.

Andrew and his colleagues had argued interminably over the Indian question but today, as he walked in the April sunshine, his thoughts were far removed from the troubles of the subcontinent and the Dundee jute men. Beyond the new villas by the water front, a few folk were out on the links with golf clubs. There was no proper course here but keen golfers were wont to use the area for practice and it behoved pedestrians and bystanders to keep a sharp look-out for any wayward ball. Andrew recognised one of the players as a customer of the Bank who had been pointed out to him by Mr. Morgan.

"Look, Mr. Gray!" the accountant had said, in hushed and respectful tones, "do you see the gentleman being shown in to Mr. Petrie?"

Andrew nodded. He saw Petrie at the door of his room, ushering in a short, stockily built man of middle years with a rather florid complexion.

"That is Mr. Henry Caldwell of R. J. Caldwell & Son of the Baltic

Mill – mark it well, lad! Henry Caldwell is sole proprietor now following the death last year of his grandfather, old 'R.J.' Baltic is not one of the largest mills but it more than holds its own: besides Henry Caldwell is an ambitious man and they say he has plans for extension. Be that as it may, the firm is one of our best connections and Mr. Caldwell himself is usually amongst our largest depositors. So – when Caldwells whistle, my lad – or the Baltic people demand attention of any sort – you jump to it – understand?''

Today, Henry Caldwell appeared to be alone, engaged in striking ball after ball with a wooden-headed club. He was dressed in a dark green jacket, buttoned from top to bottom, and trousers of a light sandy colour. On his head was firmly clamped a round peaked hat of the sort worn by country gentlemen but rarely seen in town. When he spotted Mr. Caldwell, Andrew had been making his way over the links with a view to crossing the railway line and returning to Broughty Ferry by the road. When he reached the track, Andrew noticed that a train was signalled in the "up" direction. Because of a slight rise and a curve beyond, it was not possible to see an approaching train but there was no sound of one coming. No doubt it was still well down the line – probably just leaving the depot at Monifieth. There were no boundary fences. Andrew walked up over the loose stones, stepped over the rails, and climbed the short incline to the road. Just then he heard the screech of a whistle and, from the sound of the oncoming train, which grew rapidly louder, it was very plain that, whatever it might be, most probably a local from Arbroath, it was travelling at considerable speed.

In Andrew's mind afterwards the next few minutes were all a blur and he could never be sure at which precise moment he heard the cry. At all events, the noise was loud and urgent enough to make him turn when, to his absolute horror, he saw a man sprawled across the railway track right in the path of the oncoming train. Andrew recognised the green jacket and the light-coloured trousers. It was Henry Caldwell, his bag of clubs lying beside him. He must have finished his practice and followed Andrew over the railway. Andrew jumped down to the edge of the track.

"Get up!" he yelled. "There's a train coming!"

Henry Caldwell lay perfectly still. Perhaps he was unconscious. He had most likely tripped and knocked himself out on one of the rails. The train was now very near. Andrew still could not see it, but he could feel the vibration. There seemed to be a void in the pit of his stomach. He clambered up the verge and grasped Henry Caldwell by the shoulders. He could now see the train. It was barely fifty yards away and coming on fast. Henry Caldwell was heavy and it was as much as Andrew could do to lift him and drag him clear. At the last minute, with the train rushing towards them, Caldwell's left boot stuck on the rail. Frantically, Andrew tugged but the boot seemed to be stuck fast. The ground beneath was now shaking as if an earthquake had struck and Andrew could feel the heat from the locomotive's firebox. Stretching across, Andrew made one last desperate effort and the boot came free. Pulling with all his might Andrew, with the inert body of Henry Caldwell clutched to him, rolled over and clear just as the locomotive thundered past. When the pounding of the wheels died away Andrew sat up.

"Gudesakes!" said a voice that sounded to Andrew as if it came from miles away. "It's Mr. Caldwell! If it hadna been for ye, laddie, there wad hae been gey little left o' him!" The owner of the voice took a large pinch of snuff from a box in his waistcoat pocket, settled it in a heap at the base of his left thumb, and applied some to each nostril in turn. The sneeze, when it came, made a noise almost as fearsome as that of the train and Mr. Caldwell, whom Andrew had tried to make as comfortable as possible, stirred and opened his eyes. With some difficulty he focussed upon the taker of snuff – a little fellow dressed in the garb of a coachman.

"Did you get me out of that, Joseph?" Henry Caldwell rubbed the side of his head and tried to sit up.

"Na, na, Mr. Caldwell! No me: I didna see ye. It was the young gentleman here. He stood in the wey o' the train and pu'ed ye clear: I doobt ye had a fa'! I was waiting in the carriage yonder ..." – he pointed with his whip towards the road – "... when I heard a' the stramash!"

Mr. Caldwell succeeded in sitting upright.

"Thank you, very much, young sir! It seems I owe my life to you. I saw the train signalled and I heard it coming. I tripped over a sleeper – probably I was hurrying too much – and that is the last thing I remember. I must have hit my head on the rail and knocked myself out. It was a blessing you were there! What is your name, lad? Have I seen you somewhere before?"

"Andrew Gray, sir! I work in the Bank in Dundee – perhaps you have seen me at Reform Street."

"Ye ... s!" Caldwell struggled to his feet and shook Andrew by the hand. "That is indeed where I have seen you! The Bank is fortunate if there are many like you amongst its servants! Here is my card, sir! Henry Caldwell, of R. J. Caldwell & Son. I'd like to talk some more with you at a more propitious time and in a more suitable place. My home address is on the card. Suppose you call next Saturday afternoon, say about three o'clock. Meantime, if Joseph here will give me his arm, I think I can just about hirple back to the coach – you haven't moved it, Joseph, have you?"

Andrew mumbled something, a trifle incoherently, and responded to Mr. Caldwell's courteous bow. Leaning heavily on the little coachman's arm, Henry Caldwell slowly made his way back up to the road. Andrew looked back at the railway. Down the line the shining metals disappeared over the crest of the hill and round the corner whereas, in the other direction – that taken by the local in its headlong dash towards Broughty Ferry and Dundee – the long straight stretched away into the distance. About fifty yards away –

thrown clear of the rails – Mr. Caldwell's golf bag lay in a crumpled heap but, of the clubs themselves, only a few broken and shattered sticks remained scattered about the line. Andrew felt weak at the knees; his stomach heaved, and he was painfully and violently sick.

On the following Saturday, at three in the afternoon, Andrew presented himself at "Riga Lodge", the Caldwell home – a rather palatial-looking dwelling standing high above the water at West Ferry. A driveway led past the coach-house and stables to the main door. There, a manservant answered the bell and ushered Andrew in through a wide vestibule full of pot plants, and fragrant with the scent of white narcissi. On each side of the door, like a golden tapestry, a bank of cut daffodils vied with the spring sunshine coming in through the open windows. In the hall beyond, Henry Caldwell came forward, holding out his hand in greeting. He was still limping heavily and there was a fresh linen bandage on his head.

"Come away, young man! Come away! Glad to see you: let me introduce you to my family."

He led the way into a bright and airy drawing room. A coal fire was burning in the grate under a high marble mantlepiece, on top of which was a large and ornate ormolu clock flanked by matching vases – all standing upon low pedestals topped with blue velvet cushioning and all encased in glass. There were chintz-covered chairs and two delightful little antique tables, each bearing an assortment of ornaments. On the walls were a number of paintings, and a series of etchings, depicting Italian city scenes, hung by the bell-pull at the fire-place. The principal feature of the room, however, was the large window set in the end wall and giving an almost panoramic view up the river. There was the town – its spires and tall mill chimneys ranged under the bare, slightly tilted summit of the Law and beyond, the flat shore of the Carse of Gowrie, the distant blue line of the Sidlaw Hills and, across the wide inner firth, the scarp of Norman's Law. Nearer to hand, the lighthouse tower on the Fife side of the narrows was a startling white against the green hillside of Scotscraig.

Close by the window was a large, round table covered with white damask and set for tea. Two ladies – one elderly and one little more than a girl – were seated there and Andrew bowed as his host introduced him.

"Aunt 'Tina! Vicky! This is the young hero who saved my life! Mr. Andrew Gray, banker in Dundee – my aunt, Miss Clementina Farmiloe, and my only child, Victoria Caldwell."

Miss Farmiloe was a plump, rosy-cheeked old lady whose grey ringlets and Grecian-style dress echoed a fashion long forgotten. For one of her years, her voice was remarkably highly pitched but it was nevertheless well modulated and unmistakably English. She waved a stubby, much be-ringed hand at the empty chair by her side and bade Andrew be seated.

Victoria Caldwell was pretty. She looked up at Andrew through a fringe of

lashes and gave him a smile that was an odd mixture of nervousness and co-
quetry.

Miss Farmiloe dispensed tea from a Queen Anne silver service and, after
all the cups had been filled, she poured fresh hot water into the pot from the
kettle on its stand above a small oil lamp. On the table were scones newly out
of the oven, butter, strawberry jam and several plates of cakes. Once the
initial formalities were over, Miss Farmiloe demanded to hear all about the
incident on the railway line. She had always thought it a dangerous and
foolhardy practice to cross the tracks and she had warned Henry against it.
But there! That was the way of the world, men being such heedless creatures
and stubborn to boot – and, of them all, she vowed her nephew Henry was
quite the worst. The railway line ran at the bottom of their property and he
thought nothing of crossing over to get down to the waterside. Oh, for the
days of the stagecoach and real horses, not iron ones that belch out smoke
and fumes like repulsive dragons and go at a speed both excessive and
frightening! Had Andrew heard how their windows rattled whenever a train
passes on the line below? If not, one would be sure to oblige at any moment
now! When she at last drew breath, Andrew was able to ask his host how he
was keeping now that a week had passed since the day of the accident.

"Apart from my nerve, which is shattered, and this wretchedly painful
foot . . . " – he pointed to his left leg – " . . . I think I have fully recovered. My
aunt is right, of course: we are fools, and irresponsible ones at that, to
attempt to cross the railway line other than by the bridges provided! Maybe
one of these days the railway companies will get round to fencing off their
property to keep idiots like us off!"

Andrew felt some responsibility for the state of Mr. Caldwell's foot. He
had had to tug so strenuously, it was small wonder the foot had suffered. It
must have been very severely wrenched and twisted.

"You lost your golf clubs," he said, "they were smashed by the train."

"I know. That is what would have happened to me!"

Henry Caldwell liked this lad. He was quiet and efficient, extremely well
set up and he had an excellent manner and address. On Monday morning
Henry Caldwell had had a word with Petrie who expressed himself as well
satisfied with Andrew's performance since joining his staff. Clearly, Petrie
expected the lad to do well in the Bank. Caldwell, however, had other plans.
He had no sons to manage the Baltic Mill after he had gone and, for some
time now, he had been concerned at the lack of any obvious successor from
amongst his own office staff. They were all very well in their way, but they
were pedestrian in the extreme, working along firmly established lines
without any flair or indeed aptitude for innovation. Even the switch to jute
had largely passed them by. They still thought of themselves as clerks and
managers in the office of a linen mill and their horizons were bounded by the
price of flax F.O.B. out of Riga, Tallinn or Kronstadt. They thought in

roubles rather than rupees and for all they knew, or cared, Chittagong and Dacca might be suburbs of Calcutta. To a man like Henry Caldwell, whose ambition it was to raise the Baltic Mill to a position of some eminence in Dundee, it was all very discouraging.

He had thought of trying to arrange a merger with another of the smaller mills but none of these was exactly suitable and, in any case, he fought shy of the diminution of authority that was bound to arise as a consequence. Perhaps, then, this young man might be the solution. He would watch the lad carefully and, if he proved as good as first appearances would indicate, it might be possible to tempt him away from the Bank.

After tea Henry Caldwell suggested that Andrew might like a walk in the garden. With his bad foot he begged to be excused but he was sure Andrew would not object to being shown around by Vicky. Taking a parasol to protect herself from the sun, which was growing quite warm as the season advanced, Vicky, manipulating her crinoline dress through the narrow door of a conservatory, led the way out to a terrace overlooking the river. Her dress was of peach-coloured muslin which set off her pink and white complexion and fair hair parted in the middle. Round her shoulders, notwithstanding the warmth of the day, she had gathered a brightly patterned Paisley shawl. A wooden fence ran the length of the terrace beyond which the ground fell away abruptly. A path, edged with boxwood, wound down through the shrubbery to a lawn with formal flower beds lying adjacent to the railway. Once again there was no boundary fence.

It soon became apparent from Vicky's conversation that she had led a very sheltered, even secluded life. Her mother had died when she was born; her father had not remarried and she had been brought up, first by her grandmother and then by Aunt 'Tina who, upon old Mrs. Caldwell's death, had sold up her home in Surrey to come to "Riga Lodge" to look after her nephew. All her life, Vicky had been surrounded by grown-ups and, since she had been privately educated – her grandfather had insisted on employing a governess instead of sending her to school – she had been deprived of company of her own age. All this was very apparent in her old-fashioned ways, the rather stilted nature of her conversation, and her general naivety. She had got on rather better with her grandfather, who had treated her more like a grown-up than any of the others, and she had been heart-broken last year when the old man died.

Vicky was a gentle creature and Andrew – who deemed her much more brittle and delicate than she really was – felt drawn to her, principally because of the desire to shield and protect her, poor innocent child that she was – and probably too because of her china blue eyes. In consequence he was delighted when, on taking his leave of the family, Henry Caldwell suggested that he might care to come again, next week, and have dinner with them.

Aunt Eliza was sceptical.

"She sounds too good to be true!" was her comment. "How old is the child anyhow?"

"I don't know, aunt – I should think about seventeen – no more."

"Hm! Not much older than little Jemima!"

"Oh, come aunt! 'Mima's only eleven!"

"Well! Be careful, Andrew Gray! The Caldwells move in a different world from that to which you are accustomed. Don't you let them take advantage of you! Remember! That kind will drop you at a moment's notice if they think your usefulness to them is at an end."

Nevertheless – and notwithstanding Aunt Eliza's gloomy prognostication – Andrew's friendship with Vicky Caldwell continued to flourish. On summer Saturdays they would picnic out on the lawn or have Joseph drive them down to the sands at Carnoustie. When autumn came and the leaves began to fall, they went for brisk walks along the shore or up by the woods of Forthill. Vicky, who was forever afraid of catching a chill – a fear instilled by Miss Farmiloe – wrapped up well and took care not to walk too far lest it overtax her strength. Andrew pandered to her every whim and helped her take cuttings from the hedgerows – sprays of rowan and clippings of briar – which she later painted in watercolours, bringing out the russets and the browns and the bright red of the berries and hips. Andrew found her conversation limited, however. He had not read the novels of Jane Austen nor did he know a great deal about the modern European composers whose works – particularly the two concertos of the now deceased Frederic Francois Chopin – Vicky delighted in playing for him upon the piano. But Henry Caldwell had a wide circle of influential friends – many of them merchants or professional people in Dundee – and when company of this nature was present, the conversation was wide ranging and stimulating. On these occasions, Andrew's contributions were such as to confirm Caldwell's initial opinion that this was the right young man for him.

On Sundays Andrew stayed decorously at home and escorted Aunt Eliza to morning and evening worship. Meantime his work at the Bank continued to provide the stimulus he needed to keep his mind alert and active, and, with the increased responsibility, there came – at last – a modest increase in his annual emolument from £5 to £7. 10s. 0d. Every six weeks or so, he endeavoured to make the journey to Pitbuddo to see his mother. Jessie kept fit and well – busy as always with her dressmaking in which Jemima was beginning to be of very considerable help. Usually, when Andrew was at home, Meg and Joe Shirress, who had a house in the High Street close to the Gray's original home, would come round for tea. Meg could always be relied upon to give her brother all the news of the day – "clavers" her mother called it. Away back at the beginning of the year, Meg had, of course, passed on to Jessie, and to Andrew, the news that Mary had married a lawyer and was living in Edinburgh. She had said no more. Jessie had been sorely disappointed, for she had grown very fond of Mary and had looked forward to having her as a daughter-in-law. Now – from what Andrew told them – he seemed to be setting his cap at some whey-faced lassie whose people seemed to have more money than sense. But Andrew was now twenty-two past and, although she hoped he might yet find a more spirited sounding girl, Jessie realised that he was unlikely to remain a bachelor forever.

In the New Year, towards the end of January, in the city of Berlin, the Princess Royal – with much difficulty and a breech delivery – gave birth to a boy who was christened Wilhelm. The baby's left arm was dislocated and both he and his mother narrowly escaped with their lives. Then, towards the end of April, the awful Indian Mutiny came to an end at last, the rule of the East India Company having been officially terminated during the previous summer. Meantime, there was war, yet again, in Europe when Louis Napoleon unleashed his armies in what he was pleased to see as a kind of crusade designed to free Italy from Austrian rule. At home, in mid-June, Lord Derby's government was defeated on a vote of confidence and back came Palmerston. Throughout this month, the Franco-Austrian war raged unabated through a series of fierce and bloody battles, culminating in the French triumph at Solferino, the Peace of Villafranca, the subsequent dismay of the Italian states and the inevitable rise of Guiseppe Garibaldi.

In Dundee, the only news that mattered was, first, the good news from India, and second, the return of Palmerston. One Saturday in July, when Andrew called as usual at "Riga Lodge", Henry Caldwell ushered him into his study. He came straight to the point.

"Andrew!" he said, "you've learned much about the jute trade since you came to Dundee. Ten years ago, almost nobody in Dundee had even heard of jute. If my grandfather had been told that within two decades of his death, the Baltic Mill would not be producing a single yard of linen, he would have dismissed the matter as the haverings of a lunatic. But war intervened. Obeying the dictates of their leaders, the great nations tried to tear each other apart. Forget the cause. It is immaterial in the present context. Like all wars it was remote from the people and benefited nobody, least of all the Russian farmer up in the north, looking at his fields of flax which can no longer command the premium prices formerly obtained on the export market. Poor devil! He was as far removed from the Crimea as we were but, unlike us, he had no 'Indian grass' at which to clutch to avert disaster!"

"You don't think jute is just a temporary phase? I mean – flax imports are on the increase again and you can put linen to more uses than jute!"

"Temporary phase? – no! Flax imports up again – yes! But the flax coming in, and likely to come in, will just about keep the other east coast mills going. We in Dundee have the whale oil and it is we who have built up the expertise with the 'Indian grass'. Believe me, Andrew! We are only at the beginning of the jute saga – it has a long way to go and I for one mean to take advantage of

the great opportunity that awaits us! You say jute has only limited applica-
tion but, ten years ago, who would have thought it would have replaced linen
over such a wide spread of goods? There is a piece of undeveloped land
adjacent to the Baltic Mill. I bought it some time ago as I thought it might
come in useful one day. That day, Andrew, has arrived. As you know, I have
been worried over the situation in India. We were lucky. Supplies of jute
were only minimally curtailed by reason of the Mutiny but now – now that
conditions throughout the subcontinent have returned to normal – I plan to
build an extension which will more than double the capacity of the mill.

"War cut off our supplies of flax, and war – or even civil unrest, in days to
come, could well cut off supplies of yet another valuable raw product and,
when this happens, I want the Baltic Mill to be ready and able to step in!"

"I don't think I follow you, sir!"

"Think, Andrew! What about the thread mills in Paisley and the spinners
and weavers down in Lancashire?"

"Cotton?"

"Yes, lad, cotton! They are secure enough today, the cotton manufacturers, but how long will it last? Where do they get their basic supplies?"

"America."

"Aye – America! And if I read the signs correctly, all is not perfect peace
in the land of the free. If there should be a hitch in America's exports of raw
cotton – think of the boost this would give to our sales of manufactured
jute!"

Andrew nodded. It was true that the newspapers were full of reports from
the United States indicating growing friction between the industrialised states
of the north with their free labour market and the agricultural south which
relied almost entirely upon slave labour. Already had been rioting, if
not insurrection, in Kansas between the slavers and the abolitionists whose
cause had been espoused by the extraordinary Connecticut Yankee, John
Brown; and all indications pointed to the fact that the tinder was so dry that
the merest spark could, at any moment, set off a terrible conflagration.

"You could be right," said Andrew, "that man Brown seems set on stirring
up trouble."

"I should be willing to wager upon it." Henry Caldwell, who had been
pacing up and down the small room, stopped and turned to face the younger
man.

"For all these reasons, therefore," he continued, "I should like you to
come and work with me at the Baltic Mill. Having no son to follow after
me – and no suitable candidate from out of my existing staff – I have been
anxious for some time to find a young man of character and ability who could
be trained up so that – in the fullness of time – he could take over from me.
The work will be hard and demanding – I have no time for slackers. It will

call for initiative and a subjugation of personal affairs to those of the firm which must, in every case, come first – even over any demands which might be placed upon you by my dear daughter. You will be well rewarded. What do you say?"

Andrew was completely taken aback. He had never in all his dreams contemplated receiving an offer such as this. It was an opportunity not to be missed. He could not refuse.

"I ... I don't know what to say. I would require to give notice to the Bank."

"Official notice – yes. I may say I have had a word unofficially with Petrie. He objected very strongly indeed to my seeking to take you away from the Bank – spoke highly of you – said you were the best young man he had been sent for many a long day. However, he also said he would not stand in your way if you wish to go! How much do they pay you at the Bank?"

Andrew told him.

"Ugh!" Henry Caldwell's face expressed his disgust. "How can they expect to retain quality at such a derisory level of remuneration? With Baltic you'll get £25 per annum to start with, plus a bonus should results merit it after the firm's year ends."

Andrew was quite staggered. This was almost double the salary Donald Graham, the teller at Pitbuddo, was paid, and Graham was fifty if he was a day.

"I should be happy to play a part in Baltic's expansion, Mr. Caldwell, and I am deeply honoured that you should deem me worthy of such responsibility!"

"Good man!" cried Caldwell, gripping Andrew firmly by the hand. "Come, lad! Let us find the others. This calls for a celebration!"

Mr. Petrie was not surprised when, on Monday morning, Andrew asked to see him. Nevertheless, he assumed his customary glowering look.

"Well?" he barked.

"I wish to tender my resignation, sir!"

"What!" Mr. Petrie roared. "Leave the Bank?"

"Yes, sir! Mr. Henry Caldwell has offered me a position in R. J. Caldwell & Son which I wish to accept. I shall, of course, write a formal letter, Mr. Petrie, but I did not wish to do so before speaking with you."

Petrie relaxed and permitted a slight – but only slight – easing in the severity of his expression.

"I had heard something of it. Very well. I hope you'll not regret it. I see no reason why you should. Henry Caldwell is a shrewd man – one of the best in the business and you should do well." He coughed. "I ... we ... shall be sorry to lose you." Then, glowering once more, he rapped out – "You'll work out your notice, mind, four weeks clear!"

"Yes, sir! Thank you, sir!"

Andrew retreated to search out Mr. Morgan and give him his news before he could be called in to hear it from Mr. Petrie. Mr. Morgan was very excited and he thumped Andrew on the back.

"Well done, my lad! I must have trained you well! Right! I shall now have to get someone on to that desk with you, and this very morning, so that you can start showing him what to do!"

That evening, Andrew wrote a long letter to his mother. When she read it, Jessie was worried. The Bank job provided security such as neither she, nor Tom when he was alive, had ever experienced; and she earnestly hoped Andrew was right in throwing this away. To her, it seemed that he was much too dependent upon the goodwill of one man – this Henry Caldwell. Supposing Caldwell were to die before Andrew was properly established? What would he do then? He probably would not be able to carry on at the mill – what was it called – yes, Baltic Mill. If that happened he would be out of a job like poor Charlie Tait. He would not be likely to get back into the Bank. The more she thought about it, the more she worried. What kind of a man was this Henry Caldwell anyway? So far as Andrew was concerned, he seemed to be on a pedestal and beyond reproach. When he snapped his fingers, Andrew went running. He even fawned at the feet of his precious daughter who worried lest she caught a chill and who lolled about on chintz-covered chairs reading Jane Austen, playing Chopin and painting rose hips. Doubtless she had never made a bed in her life, nor laid a fire, nor scrubbed a floor, nor boiled an egg far less made a meal. And if she used a needle at all it would probably only be on an embroidery frame. Jessie determined that she would try to see Mr. Coutts next time she was in the Bank. Maybe he could write Andrew, or write to this Mr. Petrie in Dundee, and try to have the decision reversed.

But Sam Coutts had shaken his head.

"I'm sorry, Jessie. I really couldn't write to Petrie, who must have given his consent, and it is not really for me to advise Andrew in this matter. I do know this, however, and maybe this will calm your fears, lassie. Petrie is a very sound banker, a very sound banker indeed, and if he says this man Caldwell is one of the best, you may rest assured that this is so!"

With that, Jessie had to be content, but she continued to have her doubts as to the suitability of being so dependent upon the whim of one of the wealthy Dundee manufacturers. The fact that Meg thought Andrew had done the right thing did nothing to ease her concern. Meg had always supported Andrew in whatever he did and Jessie had not looked to her for an unbiased view. Perhaps, however, Meg had a point when she drew attention to the fact that Jessie herself was heavily dependent upon the goodwill of one man in the shape of Dr. Robertson. Nevertheless, Jessie had been quick to protest that this was altogether different, the relationship being that of a kindly landlord and a tenant who paid her rent promptly whenever it fell due. In any case, Meg had other things to occupy her attention since the birth of Jessie's first grandchild was imminent and, in fact, overdue. Jemima was most excited and kept pestering her mother with all sorts of questions.

Andrew's final week in the service of the Bank came to an end at last. On the Saturday morning, he was a prey to many emotions, and he was genuinely distressed at taking leave of his colleagues, and especially at bidding farewell to Mr. Morgan whose sound advice and practical guidance he had come to appreciate so greatly. Mr. Petrie shook hands and permitted himself a wry smile at the thought that, as from Monday, he might have to rush to do his former junior's bidding.

Andrew had his overnight bag with him and he hurried to the Dock Street terminus of the Dundee and Arbroath on his way home to Pitbuddo. As the train picked up speed beyond the Stannergate, he kept a sharp look-out and, there – right enough – was Vicky on the lawn at "Riga Lodge" – a bunch of roses in one hand and a little lace handkerchief, which she waved, in the other. Andrew responded with a wide grin and a wave of his arm. Then the train was past and slowing down for the halt at West Ferry. It was past five o'clock by the time he reached Brechin, but he got a cab at the depot and was in Pitbuddo within the hour. Before he had time to take his travelling coat off, Jessie and Jemima hurried him round to see Meg and Joe and their baby girl born earlier in the week.

"Isn't she like Joe?" Meg said, holding the babe out for inspection.

"Good gracious – yes!" said Andrew, sinning his immortal soul and wondering how on earth his normally sensible sister could see any semblance at all between this little scrap, with her red puckered face and fair downy head, and the large heavy and be-whiskered face of Joe Shirress.

"Have you decided upon a name?"

"Yes. We are going to call her Jean after Joe's mother. Will you come to the baptism?"

"Of course! When will that be?"

"Probably in the autumn: maybe you'll be too busy then being a jute manufacturer!" Meg saw Jessie nodding her head and she wished she had not said that – it only added fuel to her mother's indignation that these Caldwells were patronising her son. Rapidly she changed the subject.

"Would you like to hold her?" Meg offered the babe to her brother who immediately backed off in alarm. They all laughed and Jemima clapped her hands in delight.

"Coward!" she cried. "Fancy Andrew Gray being feart of a wee baby!"

"Come on!" said Meg, "Fold your arm so that you make a kind of cradle – that's right! Hold her tightly now!"

Somewhat gingerly, to loud guffaws from the baby's father and helpless giggles from Jemima, Andrew did as he was instructed. The bundle in his arms felt as if it contained more clothing than flesh and blood, but it was warm and noticeably damp. He was glad when, after a decent interval, he was able to hand baby Jean back to Meg.

Once they had returned to the house in the Meal Wynd, and had eaten and seen Jemima off to bed, Andrew and Jessie talked far into the night. Andrew pooh-poohed the notion that he was being patronised, but he did concede it was only natural for Jessie to worry lest – having burned his boats – it should eventually transpire that he had made the wrong decision. The talk did some good, however, since Andrew was able to convey to his mother some of the sense of excitement surrounding the recent development of the jute industry in Dundee, and indeed, the necessity to ensure that the Baltic Mill should have the capacity to meet the increased demand which Henry Caldwell felt was just round the corner. Clearly, Andrew already knew a great deal about the industry – it was not going to be a case of starting from scratch – and Jessie felt reassured to some degree. Unfortunately she could not say the same in regard to her son's matrimonial prospects. He still seemed besotted with this Vicky girl. She sounded the absolute antithesis of Mary but maybe she was not quite so precious as Andrew made her out to be. She would just have to hope so. Now that Andrew had accepted employment with Caldwell there was little likelihood that he could escape from leading the man's daughter to the altar. That night, Jessie found it difficult to get to sleep.

In the morning she was tired and irritable. Mr. Black's sermon was duller than usual and, if it were possible, even longer, and she very nearly dozed off in the middle of it. In the afternoon, when she walked out to old Pitbuddo with Andrew and Jemima, she felt tired and weary and although, on their return, they went to see Meg and Joe and baby Jean, she cut short her visit and went home by herself. Andrew left early next morning and reached Dundee in time to meet Mr. Caldwell at the Baltic Mill at noon as they had previously arranged.

In the ensuing weeks and months, Andrew put his theoretical knowledge of the jute industry to practical purpose. New experiences – one after another – crowded on top of him and often he felt well nigh overwhelmed. But he rose to the challenge as Henry Caldwell had no doubt he would, and – at the end of six months – he began to feel that he understood most of what was going on around him. The Baltic Mill occupied a prominent position just off Dens Road. It was built in the form of a letter "E", the spinning mill occupying the middle stroke and the remainder housing the looms. Alongside – complete with coal bunkers, ash-pit and tall chimney – were the furnace and boiler-house providing the steam that drove the machines. The store – where the bales of raw jute and the barrels of whale oil were stacked after being hauled up in carts from the docks – was situated at the entrance to the spinning mill while, at the back of the long weaving shed were the offices and workshops, the finishing room, stock room and despatch department.

To begin with, Andrew took badly to the smell of grease and whale oil but, above all, it was the noise which took most getting used to – the whirring of the spinning frames, the rumbling of the great bobbins as the shifters moved them, loaded or empty, the clattering of the looms, the whiz and thud of the huge shuttles, and the constant hiss of escaping steam which made the atmosphere hot as a greenhouse. Over it all were the raucous voices of the overseers, shouting to make themselves heard above the din, and the screeching and foul language of the Irish women who seemed to form the major part of the work force.

Andrew spent time on the shop floor, following the entire process from the opening of the bales to the final weighing and despatch. The mill's principal product was gunny, sold either as sheets, or made up into sacks and bagging. Some material of finer quality was turned out and sold to the ship chandlers and tent makers, a side of the business Henry Caldwell was anxious to expand. Andrew was able to see for himself the various stoppages that could, and did, occur, leading to down time and loss of production. There were unpleasant days in the spinning mill attending to the tubs where the raw jute was steeped in oil before being dried and spun; back-breaking days working alongside the shifters and days in the weaving sheds looking after the looms, tying broken threads, freeing jammed shuttles, and inspecting the finished gunny, or canvas, before it went to the balers and sorters.

He served time in the workshops, and in the boiler house, and finally he graduated to the warehouse and the despatch room, after which he had to begin all over again in the office with its multifarious tasks. He learned the importance of securing the correct supply of raw material; it had to be regular and sufficient – never too little nor, and this was even worse, too much. Henry Caldwell introduced him to the brokers who imported the fibre and on-sold it to the various mills. This was a side of the business Andrew knew reasonably well from his days on the jute desk at the Bank – indeed many of the brokers were already known to him and this made it very much easier than might otherwise have been the case. Days were spent on the sales desk, learning about existing customers, vetting prospective ones and looking at ways and means of drumming up new business although, without the extra capacity, this had to be done with some care. The general accounting procedures presented no difficulty for one used to cash books, journals and ledgers. In fact, in several instances, Andrew was able to make constructive and worth-while suggestions. These were received kindly enough by the clerical staff but, although accepted by Adam Sturrock, the office manager, who was a crusty, middle-aged bachelor, it was abundantly plain that he did not relish this young upstart trying to teach him his own business, and

Andrew was quick to realise that, while he had maybe not made an enemy, he could certainly not regard old Sturrock as a friend.

Meantime, the extension to the mill had been going on apace and it was now confidently expected that the work would be completed in another two months or so – that is to say at the end of March 1860. Henry Caldwell was beside himself with excitement. He determined to make a big splash and so he arranged for an official opening to take place, timed for mid-May, for which he sought the services of no less a person that the Member of Parliament for Oxford, the Chancellor of the Exchequer, Mr. William Ewart Gladstone, who declined, but nominated in his place a junior minister from the Treasury, with whom Henry Caldwell had no option but to be content. To Andrew, fell the task of setting it all up and his days were filled from morning till late of an evening, confirming Aunt Eliza in her frequently repeated view that the Caldwells were simply taking a loan of him.

Wednesday 16th May 1860, the day of the official opening of the fine new extension to the Baltic Mill, was a day long remembered in Dundee. For Andrew, it represented the culmination of weeks of hard work, arranging the programme, sending out invitations, working out seating plans – having a care to orders of precedence – ordering the food and drink, and arranging for service. Henry Caldwell had drawn up the guest list, but this apart, Andrew had been given a free hand, and he had made an excellent job of it.

The new building was situated to the north of the existing mill, alongside the boiler-room, and a platform, with seating for all the guests, and a canopy lest it should rain, had been erected in the courtyard facing the heavy double doors of the new mill, across which was stretched a red, white and blue ribbon. On the wall, to the right of the doors, and covered by a velvet cloth, was a brass plate recording the event, and drawn up alongside, dazzling the eye, was the band of the local detachment of the Volunteer Force, all spick and span in their new uniforms, instruments gleaming in the sun. In a marquee, on a piece of open ground, adjacent to the extension, the caterers were busy putting the finishing touches to the food and the refreshments that had been set out on long tables.

Even although he had organised it himself, when the guests began to gather and the hum of conversation swelled, Andrew was amazed at this great gathering of dignitaries and persons of note. He had asked his mother to come to Dundee for the occasion, but she had declined, saying it was no place for her as there would be too many of the great ones present and, certainly, the roll-call was impressive. There was the Lord Provost in his robes, the civic chain of office round his neck; the Lord Lieutenant, all uniform and medals; and a number of ministers representing the churches in the vicinity of the mill. There were representatives from the nine incorporated trades, a score of rival manufacturers and their wives, and a number of merchants and brokers. The Rector of the High School was there together with the editors of the *Advertiser* and the *Courier*. The business profession was out in force – Mr. Petrie from the Bank together with the Chief Managers of the two indigenous banks, the Eastern in the Seagate and the Dundee Banking Company in Castle Street. Charles Scrimgeour, the Caldwell's stockbroker, arrived in company with Mr. Horsburgh of Messrs Morton, Sime & Horsburgh, the firm's solicitors and, close behind, came the Dundee manager of the North British and Mercantile Insurance Company, the General Managers of the local railways, the Chairman of the Harbour Commissioners, the Ferrymaster, and the Chief of Police.

Pride of place, however, if not of precedence, went to the architect who had drawn up such tasteful and practical plans, to the senior partner of the Dundee firm who had been entrusted with the building contract, and to the little Yorkshireman who had travelled up from Keighley to represent the manufacturer of the new looms which incorporated all the very latest in textile machinery design.

In a circle round the edge of the platform stood the mill hands in their working clothes. Many of the men, and a number of the women too, smoked short-stemmed clay pipes with which they pointed at any of the dignitaries they happened to recognise. At last the band struck up a rousing military march and the workers swayed to and fro in rhythm to the beat of the big drum.

At eleven o'clock prompt, Henry Caldwell, resplendent in dark blue tail coat and trousers of lighter shade, and wearing a magnificent tile hat, appeared in the open space by the door. At his side was Vicky in a pink crinoline gown edged with white, her fair hair hidden under a dainty bonnet of similar hue, trimmed with white rosettes. They were accompanied by the representative of Her Majesty's Government and by the Reverend Aeneas Whamond, Minister of St. Roque's parish church in the Seagate – that attended by the Caldwell family over many generations. His black gown and Geneva bands contrasted sharply with the bright colours around him.

At a signal from Andrew, the band fell silent and, in the expectant hush, Henry Caldwell introduced the gentleman from London and asked him if he would be so kind as to perform the opening ceremony.

Stepping forward, Palmerston's aspiring young statesman delivered the speech prepared for him by his personal secretary at the Treasury. It was a political speech emphasising the government's commitment to see trade, and particularly overseas trade, flourishing unimpeded; congratulating Dundee in general and the Baltic Mill in particular, for their perspicacity in turning to this relatively new Indian fibre which, he was sure, would revolutionise and revitalise the textile industry, and place Dundee right in the forefront of Britain's productive and export capacity. It was his earnest hope that R. J. Caldwell & Son – proprietor, management and workforce – would continue to prosper, and he had the utmost pleasure in declaring this new extension to the Baltic Mill, open. May it prove as fine a manufactory as the original building! So saying he seized the shining pair of scissors which Vicky handed him and, with a flourish, cut the tape. At the same moment, and to the great amusement of the workers, the doors swung open as if by magic and, when the cord was pulled, unveiling the brass plate, the band struck up "Rule Britannia". When the last stirring notes had died away, the Reverend Whamond held up his hand to still the renewed buzz of conversation.

"Let us pray," he intoned, and the heads of all were bowed. It was a long prayer. Andrew who was seated towards the front of the platform, looked at his watch and started timing it. A full ten minutes were to elapse before, to the relief of all, the minister pronounced the "amen." Then – it only remained for the five-year-old grand-daughter of the senior overseer to play her part. Clutching a bouquet of lilac and lily of the valley, the little girl was shoved forward by her excited mother. She remembered to drop a curtsey but almost forgot to present the flowers. Vicky came to the rescue and, blushing becomingly, she took the flowers from the child's hot sticky hand and thanked her for performing her task so prettily and well. There was a roll of drums and, as the band played the opening bars of the National Anthem, the crowd stood to attention, and a few voices commenced singing,

> " . . . happy and glorious,
> Long to reign over us,
> God save the Queen!"

The Caldwells, with the two ministers – the minister of the Gospel and the minister of the Crown – moved towards the marquee, the workforce dispersed back to their spinning frames and their looms, and Andrew endeavoured to guide the remainder of the guests, in some semblance of order, towards the refreshments. It was hot in the big tent and noisy – the clatter of cutlery and plates, and the sound of hundreds of voices all talking at once. Andrew sought out Vicky and found her still at her father's side, the bouquet in her hands.

"First class show, Caldwell!" The speaker was a solid, well-dressed man who happened to be the owner of one of the largest mills in the town. "Hope you'll get your money back! Danger is, of course, that increased supply will force prices down – eh what?"

"I think not, Sir David! In fact I doubt whether supply will be able to keep up with demand in a year or two's time."

"I certainly hope so, Caldwell. Pray God you are right!"

"Who was that?" Andrew asked as the other moved away.

"Sir David Baxter."

"Oh!"

"I *am* right, you know! The demand is only just beginning. Thank goodness we are now poised to take advantage of it!"

Andrew nodded. He had heard it all before but he had great respect for
Henry Caldwell's judgment and it did seem that events in America were
moving towards some form of a show down. Last October, the John Brown
man – with a view to arming slaves – had gone the length of attacking a
federal arsenal in Virginia called Harper's Ferry. He had, of course, been
captured, tried and executed, but already the abolitionists had made a martyr
of him; his soul, they said, was marching on. Neither Henry Caldwell nor
Andrew knew it, of course, but, on the very day that the extension to the
Baltic Mill was opened in Dundee, the United States National Republican
Convention, meeting in Chicago, chose as their Presidential candidate for the
forthcoming election, the dour lawyer son of a throughother pioneer farmer
from Kentucky and an illegitimate hillbilly girl from Virginia, a man named
Abraham Lincoln.

Amongst all the guests in the marquee, Henry Caldwell was in great
demand. One after another, his guests came up seeking to attract his
attention. Andrew whispered something in Vicky's ear. She blushed scarlet,
moved the bouquet to her left hand and with the other clung heavily to
Andrew's arm. As best he could, Andrew led her out of the marquee into the
fresh air and the sunshine. The platform, which ten minutes earlier had been
thronged with people, was now deserted, and they sat down in the front
row.

"Well?" Andrew asked.

"Oh, Andrew, my very dearest!" Vicky simpered, "I shall . . . I shall marry
you!"

Andrew Gray and Victoria Caldwell were married in Dundee, in St.
Roque's parish church, on Saturday October 6th 1860. The Reverend
Aeneas Whamond officiated and Jessie, who sat in the front pew, with Meg
and Jemima at her side, felt her heart turn over within her as the minister
pronounced them to be man and wife.

" . . . whom God hath joined together,
let no man put asunder."

The words beat a tattoo in her head and Meg had to nudge her into aware-
ness that it was time for her to rise and follow the bridal party into the vestry
to sign the register. Henry Caldwell bowed as she preceded him through the
door at the back of the church.

Jessie and Jemima, with Meg and Joe, and Joe's parents, had travelled that
morning from Pitbuddo. Baby Jean had been left in the caring hands of one
of Jean Shirress's unmarried sisters. Neither of the Grays had been in a train
before and the experience, for Jessie, was terrifying, and for Jemima, wonderful. Jessie had not yet met the Caldwells and her first sight of them had
been as they came down the aisle at the commencement of the service, the

bride, veiled, leaning on her father's arm. Henry Caldwell looked pleasant enough; he had – Jessie thought – kindly grey eyes, and he had inclined his head courteously towards her as he took his seat in the adjacent pew across the aisle beside the ridiculously garbed old dame, with the ringlets peeping from her ancient bonnet, who must be Miss Farmiloe. Of Vicky, she had no sight at all under the bridal veil.

Andrew had been at her for months asking her either to come down to Dundee so that she and Vicky might meet, or to arrange a suitable day when he might bring Vicky up to meet the family at Pitbuddo. Stubbornly, Jessie had refused to do either, and the more Meg pressed her to make up her mind, one way or the other, the more off-putting she had become. In her mind, there was no question of her having to inconvenience herself by making the journey to Dundee – but, even although it went sorely against the grain of her inherently hospitable nature, neither would she contemplate having the Caldwell girl to stay with them at the Meal Wynd. It would seem like a rabbit hutch to a girl brought up in a mansion and she had no intention of giving the girl an opportunity of looking down her nose at Andrew's modest home circumstances. And so, the day of the wedding had come without the meeting of families for which Andrew had hoped. For Jessie, it was better thus – here at least she had the support of her family and friends, for Henry Caldwell had been most insistent that Mistress Gray should let him have a list of *all* the relations and friends to whom she would wish invitations sent. In this respect, at least, Jessie had pocketed her pride, and her list – modest by comparison with the army of guests invited by the Caldwells – included, apart from immediate family, Jim Gardyne and his second wife, Caroline, who had been born Strath, Ella, who wept throughout the service, the Reverend and Mrs. Black, Lizzie Kidd, Dr. and Mrs. Robertson, Mr. and Mrs. Sam Coutts, and Charlie Tait, whose eyes had been round with wonder ever since leaving Pitbuddo. Andrew had also asked that an invitation be sent to Mr. Morgan and his wife, and he had been pleased to see them seated in church alongside the Robertsons. The only other person Jessie would have wished to be present was old Annie Ogilvie but she was now very infirm and, although she still managed to look after herself, she no longer stirred far from her cottage near the foot of the Cadger's Brae.

In the vestry Andrew kissed his mother and introduced Vicky to her. Jessie kissed the girl's alabaster-like cheek. Pretty enough, Jessie thought, but cold and lacking in expression – almost like a doll – and her voice? Jessie searched for a way to describe the toneless tinkling of it. She was very small – not much taller than Jemima. Oh! What a let down after that gorgeous girl, Mary Grant!

"Ah, Mistress Gray! I am so pleased to meet you at last!" Henry Caldwell held out his hand and his grey eyes were smiling. His handshake was strong and firm. He continued talking, but Jessie was not really listening. The beadle had thrown open the vestry door and the organ – "the kist o' whistles" as the old United Secession die-hards in the United Presbyterian congregation used to say – began hammering out the late Mr. Mendelssohn's "Wedding March". Henry Caldwell offered Jessie his arm and she walked with him down the aisle behind the bride and groom.

Joseph was waiting at the door and saw them safely into Mr. Caldwell's carriage, which was drawn up at the head of a long line of coaches stretching along the Seagate and across Commercial Street up into the High Street. Many were private, belonging to guests, but Henry Caldwell assured Jessie that, among them, was a fair proportion of cabs, so the Pitbuddo contingent would find transport easily enough. Joseph waited silently until, at last, Miss Farmiloe, puffing and red with exertion, emerged from the church. He helped her clamber aboard and took his seat on the driving box.

"It is so *hot* for October!" she said and Jessie all but started at the high pitch of her voice. "You must be Andrew's mother. How are you, dear?"

Jessie forced herself to smile; she did not like being called "dear" – especially by complete strangers.

"How do you do, Miss Farmiloe," she said.

The coach jerked into motion and Jessie settled back against the seat. She had no need to make polite conversation; Miss Farmiloe talked non-stop. Joseph carried on up Blackscroft and along towards the Stannergate. He drove at a fair pace, and it was not long before the horses slowed as they took the strain on the short hill leading up to the gates of "Riga Lodge". As they approached, the empty bridal coach was coming out and turning back towards Dundee. The coachman raised a hand to Joseph as he passed.

So this was the Caldwell mansion. How glad Jessie was that she had not let Andrew bring Vicky to the Meal Wynd. Joseph drew up at the door. Henry Caldwell helped the ladies alight whereupon Miss Farmiloe took Jessie away, crying over her shoulder to the effect that they would join Henry later down at the marquee. A young stableboy took over the reins from Joseph and drove the carriage back along the drive to the coach-house. Meantime, Joseph stationed himself at the end of the terrace and, as other coaches began to arrive, he directed the guests down the path to the lawn where the marquee stood waiting. There was still some bloom in the rose beds and, at the entrance to the tent, the gardeners had placed tubs of chrysanthemums that made a glorious riot of colour. In due course, the bridal party and all the guests were seated. The Reverend Whamond said a long and somewhat obscure grace and the wedding "feast", as Dr. Robertson described it, began. He and Mrs. Robertson were sitting with the Morgans opposite Jessie and Jemima, and the Shirress family.

"Aye well!" Dr. Robertson pushed his cleared plate slightly to one side and leant back. "I made a great mistake, it seems, following in the path of

Hippocrates! I doubt learning and skill are at a discount – there's mair siller to be made at the weaving!"

"Wheesht, David!" said Mrs. Robertson, looking highly embarrassed.

"Ach! Dinna fash yersel', lassie: Jessie agrees wi' me – is that not so, Jessie, my girl?"

Jessie smiled. Dr. Robertson could always be relied on to cut things down to size. Now, he beamed upon them as each, in turn, finished eating.

"Aye – certes!" he cried, "'a' their weel filled kytes belyve are bent like drums.'"

"David!"

"Ach, woman!" Dr. Robertson growled. "Naebody's listening and, if they were, I doobt they'd be nane the wiser – yon Farmiloe woman, for instance, she wadna ken her kyte frae her neb!"

They all laughed. Fortunately, for Sarah Robertson's peace of mind, Henry Caldwell had risen to his feet and was proposing a toast to the bride and groom. In a brief, but adequate speech, Andrew replied: he ended by thanking, firstly, Henry Caldwell for the magnificent reception here at "Riga Lodge" and secondly, each one of the guests for coming to see him so happily married. Jessie, finding Dr. Robertson's eye upon her, mustered a rather weak smile. She was very glad when the bride and groom, having changed out of their wedding finery, left – and it was all over. She had arranged that she and Jemima would stay with Aunt Eliza until Monday morning and Henry Caldwell, having heard of this, insisted that Joseph should drive them all the way from "Riga Lodge" to William Street. The remainder of the Pitbuddo guests had no difficulty finding cabs. Most of them had secured hotel rooms, and Meg had made sure that Charlie Tait came along with her and Joe. On Monday morning, the train to Brechin was unusually crowded.

On the Wednesday of the following week, Robin and Mary Cargill were finishing breakfast in the ground floor flat they occupied in Heriot Row. Outside the window, the trees in Queen Street gardens were a glorious golden red in the smoky city haze. Robin had the *Scotsman* in his hand and was busily engaged in reading the various notices.

"I see someone from Pitbuddo has been married in Dundee," he exclaimed, "Gray! Was that not the name of the girl we met that day at the Lemon Tree in Aberdeen?"

"Yes – that's right," said Mary, trying her best to sound perfectly normal.

"Could be her brother, I suppose," said Robin. "Married a girl, Caldwell. That must be one of the Caldwells of the Baltic Mill. If it is – he's done all right. The Caldwells must be amongst the wealthiest of the Dundee manufacturers!" He folded the paper and laid it down on the table. "Well, my dearest one! I'm late. I must go! Goodbye, my love – take care!"

Mary watched him swinging along the street, in his grey office suit, tall black hat on his head. When he reached the corner and turned up Howe Street, he stopped and waved. Mary, standing at the window, waved back. She hurried to the breakfast table and picked up the paper. There it was –

> "Gray – Caldwell
>   At St. Roque's Parish Church, Dundee, on Saturday 6th October 1860, by the Rev. Aeneas Whamond, B.D., Andrew, son of the late Thomas Gray and of Mrs. Jessica Gray, Meal Wynd, Pitbuddo, Forfarshire, to Victoria, only daughter of Mr. Henry Caldwell and the late Mrs. Annabella Caldwell, 'Riga Lodge', West Ferry, by Dundee."

For many minutes Mary stood with the paper in her hand. She hoped Andrew would be happy. She was lucky. Robin was a dear soul and the kindest of husbands.

Henry Caldwell had warned Andrew that he might find Vicky shy and sensitive. She had been a delicate child, and he had bowed to his own father's contention that it would be best for her to be spared the rough and tumble of school, and have the benefit of private tuition at home. Henry Caldwell realised now, he said, that it would have been better had Vicky been allowed to enjoy the companionship of other children where she would have had to stand up for herself. In the same vein, the poor girl had also lacked the company of mature women to counsel and guide her in the growing-up process. True, there had been Aunt Tina and the governess – but both were spinsters who had themselves led sheltered lives.

"Be patient with her, Andrew," Henry Caldwell had said. "And, above all, be gentle!"

Often and often, in the course of the brief honeymoon they spent at Moulin in the Perthshire highlands, did Andrew find these words returning to help smooth the little ripples which seemed to arise from time to time to ruffle the surface of the joy experienced in looking after his fragile, almost ethereal wife. When they were driving away from "Riga Lodge" to catch the train that was to take them to Perth, where he had booked a room for the weekend at the Salutation Hotel, it occurred to him that he had never really kissed Vicky in the way he and Mary had done so often in those carefree days at Craigbeg. In fact, he had seldom had his arm around her and whenever he attempted so to do she had shied away from him.

Their room at the "Salutation" was spacious, although a trifle chilly. But the huge double bed looked comfortable and Andrew had every hope that, once they turned in for the night, they would be warm enough.

"Look at that bed!" he cried. "What a size! I reckon we could play hide and seek in it! Never mind! We can snuggle up together and keep each other cosy."

Vicky did not reply; and when Andrew turned to look at her, he saw to his alarm, that she was standing on the threshold of the room, quietly sobbing.

He took a step towards her and put an arm round her shoulders.

"Vicky, dear Vicky," he said. "Whatever is wrong?"

She wrenched herself away from him, dabbed at her eyes with a tiny, lace-frilled handkerchief, and spoke – jerkily – through sobs.

"It's just that I . . . I'm frightened. I have never shared a bed with anyone before – not even Aunt Tina – and . . . and . . . now I am expected to sleep with a . . . a man!"

"Great heavens, girl! Not just a man. I'm your husband – remember?" Andrew had spoken more sharply than he intended and Vicky's sobs intensified.

He tried again. "Come, dearest," he said, "this is our wedding night. A time to be happy – not miserable. Let me dry those tears!" He took out his own handkerchief and gently wiped her cheeks. This time, Vicky did not draw back from him. She even permitted him to kiss her, which he did, again gently, on the lips.

"I'll tell you what!" he said, "I'll go downstairs and check again on those train times to Birnam and, while I'm away, you could get yourself into your nightdress and be in bed before I'm back."

Vicky felt a great sense of relief. One hurdle at least had been overcome, although it was, if the truth be told, a very minor one not to be compared with that which still lay ahead. Nevertheless, she was grateful for small mercies. She nodded her head and as soon as the door closed behind her husband's retreating back, she busied herself unbuttoning, unhooking and unlacing.

Ten minutes later when Andrew returned, he found her sitting bolt upright at the extreme edge of the bed, one white hand clutching her nightdress firmly about her bosom. She regarded him round eyed as he commenced undressing.

Andrew recalled Henry Caldwell's words. "Be patient with her . . . be patient . . . be patient."

He climbed in on the opposite side of the bed, blew out the lamp and lay back against the pillows.

"Goodnight, my dear. Sleep well." He turned towards her and although he held out his arms he found she was quite out of reach. In due course he sensed that she had lowered herself between the sheets. If patience were indeed a virtue, Andrew, as he dropped off to sleep, considered that he must be sporting a very bright halo indeed.

When he awoke in the morning, Vicky was still asleep. She was still lying over on her side of the bed, one arm stretched out on the coverlet, her person decently hidden by the high-necked nightgown. She looked so young, so innocent, and his heart went out to her. He vowed once again that he would exercise all the patience in the world but, at the same time, he made up his mind that he would do his utmost to teach her how wonderful it could be when a man and a woman should come together in loving, glorious union.

He knew of course that this could not be hurried but he was confident that, once Vicky should overcome her initial shyness, they would be able to share completely in the bliss of marital love. And so the days – and the nights – of their honeymoon progressed. The October sunshine was warm and bright and they walked in the woods below Baledmund House and on the winding road through the fields the innkeeper called the "garden of Atholl", down to the thickly wooded banks of the Tummel where they watched an angler land a late-running salmon. One day Andrew suggested they might walk over the hill into Strathtay and come back by hired coach but Vicky protested that this would be much too far for her. He could not expect a lady to range the hills like any gamekeeper! Instead they took a coach to Killiecrankie where Vicky shuddered at the sight of the awful rocks at the Soldier's Leap.

"There you are," she said, "that is what we might have been faced with on the way to Strathtay!" In vain did Andrew protest that the hill walk he had envisaged was a relatively short and gentle one. Clearly, the pleasures of the countryside were not for Mistress Victoria Gray.

In the evenings, they sat side by side in the cosy sitting room of the old coaching inn, watching the flickering flames of the log fire in the wide hearth and talking of the new home awaiting them in Dundee. Andrew had taken a modern semi-detached villa in a relatively new street running down off the Perth Road, a short distance to the west of the Sinderins. Compared with his mother's little home in Pitbuddo, the house was a positive palace and they had furnished it tastefully. To Vicky, however, the house seemed ridiculously small and she wondered how she would ever get used to the cramped conditions and singular lack of space. There were no other guests at the inn and, in their discussions round the fireside, Andrew's enthusiasm tended to wane in the face of Vicky's constant harping upon the little house's lack of the amenity to which she was accustomed. On their last evening, after Vicky had retired to their room to prepare for bed, Andrew went out into the yard for a breath of air. It was a clear, but moonless night, turning to frost, and the stars in the great arch of the sky throbbed in brilliant pinpoints of light. The air was heavy with the sweetish smell of cow dung and nothing broke the stillness of the night but the splashing of the burn and the sound of the animals moving in their stalls in the range of stables and byres round at the back of the main building. Suddenly, an owl hooted from somewhere on the far side of the road, probably from among the ruins of the ancient Black Castle, and from up in the Baledmund woods came the unmistakable cry of a vixen. For a few minutes, Andrew stood quietly, just outwith the pool of yellow light streaming from the windows of the inn. A shooting star flashed across the southern sky and seemed to plunge earthwards over the long summit of Dunfallandy Hill across the valley. Tomorrow, they would be home, and he wished with all his heart that Vicky was looking forward to it as much as he was. Maybe she would come to love the place – after all, a girl's first home of her own should be something special. But, in the morning, as they sat in the coach taking them down the valley to the railhead at Birnam, she reverted to the subject yet again.

"I do hope it will be all right, Andrew: it is so *small*."

"Of course it will be, my dearest; in any case, you and I couldn't live in a house the size of 'Riga Lodge'; we would rattle about like dice in a box!"

At Birnam, the station platform – pride of the Perth and Dunkeld Railway – was very busy. There seemed to be a number of English people about – probably guests from some of the large houses in the area on their way south from the shooting. Quite a few had dogs and there was clearly a sprinkling of maids and servants, all carrying large food hampers to sustain their employers on the long and tedious journey home.

When the train – in the livery of the Scottish North-Eastern Railway – came in from Perth, the passengers alighting from it were almost swept away in the frantic rush for seats. Andrew shielded Vicky as best he could and he managed to secure a couple of seats in a carriage which was otherwise fully occupied. The train set off immediately, following the course of the Tay through the glorious colours of the Murthly woods and down over the boundary line of the Highland fault to the cleared arable fields of Strathmore and the main line at Stanley Junction. Andrew and Vicky sat silent, listening – Andrew with some amusement – to the loud and strident voices of their travelling companions as they relived some of their experiences of the past few weeks.

Perth General Station was quite the largest railway depot either Andrew or Vicky had ever seen. On their way north, Andrew had marvelled at its size but, on that day, it had been reasonably quiet. Today, it was thronged with people, all jostling and pushing and shoving. Porters were everywhere, opening doors, rushing up with empty barrows, or pushing laden ones. Workers in the uniform of Her Majesty's Post Office were sorting mail bags and throwing them around in and out of the luggage vans. Locomotives belched out smoke, or hissed, as steam escaped from valves and cylinders. The noise was quite appalling – or so Vicky thought. There were, of course, few stations like Perth General. Here – the Scottish North-Eastern from Aberdeen; the Scottish Central from Larbert; the Edinburgh, Perth and Dundee from Ladybank; and the Dundee and Perth – all came together. From the platforms at Perth General, it was possible to travel to every point which had so far been reached by the rapidly expanding railway system for, at Aberdeen, there was the Great North of Scotland; at Larbert, the Caledonian connecting to Glasgow and the west, and to Carlisle and the south; while at Edinburgh, the North British gave access to Berwick, and the Borders.

After the packed train from Birnam, the run through the Carse of Gowrie to the Dundee depot at Yeaman Shore was pleasant, swift and peaceful. Between Inchture and Longforgan, Andrew pointed out to Vicky the great square keep of Castle Huntly, another ancient stronghold of the Grays, but Vicky was agog with disinterest. It was really most irritating that Andrew should keep ramming all this nonsense about the Grays down her throat. It was bad enough him going on all the time about Broughty Castle but that there should be another one here in the carse was too bad – especially when she could not very well retaliate. "Riga Lodge" was grand in its way but it wasn't a "Caldwell Castle"! She was still in a somewhat petulant mood when the cab deposited them at the door of No. 2 Strawberry Hill. The maid Andrew had engaged opened the door to them and stood aside to let them in. It was quite amazing, Andrew thought, what could be accomplished on his new princely salary. The girl, Moira, was the daughter of one of the shifters at Baltic Mill. She was barely fifteen and for sixpence a week and her keep, her mother, Sarah O'Flaherty, had jumped at the opportunity of unloading one of her brood of seven daughters.

"Sure, I couldn't be saying who the girl's father was at all, but she is a good girl, Moira, and will not be slow at the learning. Miss Victoria will be well pleased wit' her and when her own babies are born – as pray God they will be – she will find Moira of even more help! God knows she's had practice enough wit' mine!"

Henry Caldwell had arranged to let Moira into the house that morning and, despite the strangeness of these grand surroundings – huge by comparison with the single end in which she and her sisters had grown up – and the stiff uniform she had been given to wear, Moira gave every impression that she would indeed settle down very quickly.

It was an extremely pleasant house. From the oriel window in the upstairs drawing room, and from the smaller one in their bedroom next door, they could look down the steeply sloping street to the grassy parkland of Magdalen Yard Green, the line of the Perth railway and the river. They could see the Fife shore all the way from Newport pier to the braes of Balmerino and, facing east as they did, they had the full benefit of the morning sun. As they stood at the bedroom window on their first evening home, even Vicky had to admit that maybe, after all, it might not be so bad living in a little house in town so long as she had such a view to lift her spirits. She said as much to Andrew and his own heart lifted within him as he, very gently, kissed her on the forehead.

The warm glow Vicky had experienced at this new appreciation of her very own home remained with her when she got to bed and, for the first time she did not demur, nor did she push him away, when Andrew gathered her in his arms. In fact, she found the experience quite pleasurable and she had the strangest sensation that her body was actually responding to the proximity of this man who was her wedded husband.

And Andrew, on the nights that followed, when Vicky snuggled close in his embrace, found it more than difficult to exercise the restraint he knew to be essential. It was a slow build-up and one which cost him dear. For every night on which she lay in his arms, there were a dozen when she would have none of him, when she would turn and lie – back to back – and as far apart as their normal-sized mattress would allow. Nevertheless, Andrew's determination to hurry slowly had a modicum of success and gradually, on those occasions when she spurned him not, she came to answer the urgent quest of his lips in kisses which, for all their rarity, lacked nothing for fervour.

Then, as Andrew had hoped, had prayed might happen, there came the night when Vicky found the way to complete satisfaction. Instinctively, she knew the way ahead and she followed blindly along a path towards an unbelievable climax. It was something she had never dreamed of, an event of magnitude beyond all telling but not, alas, without a degree of pain which, to Andrew's overwhelming dismay, had caused her to cry out. In the midst of exultation she was assailed by doubts and fears that she would never really recover from the bruising she knew she must have suffered.

Afterwards, when they drew apart and Andrew would have lain close to comfort her with soft caress, she turned her back on him, curled herself into a ball, and – to his extreme consternation – he heard her sobbing as she had done that first night in Perth. He tried to calm her with soothing words but to no avail. In the end, she cried herself to sleep and, in the morning, refused point blank to discuss the matter.

After that it was very many days before she would allow Andrew to cuddle her again and many more before they kissed with any degree of passion. And that was the extent of their love making, for Vicky had assured herself that any joy and rapture she might have found in their physical union, was far outweighed by what she saw as indignity and pain.

In the early days of the Grays' marriage, great and far-reaching events took place in the world. In the United States, the Republican candidate in the Presidential election was, by a very clear majority, elected sixteenth President, and the shadow of coming events loomed darkly over America. Hardly had Mr. Lincoln got to Washington before, on 20th December, South Carolina seceded from the Union, to be followed, in January 1861, by six other southern states. Late in February, these seceding states formed a Confederacy under the Presidency of one Jefferson Davis and, in April, the militant south opened fire upon Federal troops at Fort Sumter in the harbour of Charleston, South Carolina. Lincoln retaliated by calling for volunteers to maintain the union by war. The war between the states – the long-drawn-out and exceptionally bloody war where brother fought brother – had begun.

As the year drew to a close, here at home, in the blue room at Windsor Castle, the Prince Consort, Albert of Saxe Coburg Gotha, Queen Victoria's "dearest dearest dear", died from typhoid at the age of forty-two, plunging the Queen, the Court and the nation into the deepest mourning.

3. United States
1865

Charlie Tait closed the big leather-bound ledger with a thump and moved it over to the side of his high sloping desk. He settled his new spectacles more securely upon the bridge of his nose as he commenced summing the columns of figures he had just extracted. When he had finished and he had drawn two lines with the heavy ebony roller he used as a ruler, he "tut-tutted" to himself at the magnitude of the final summation. Picking up the sheet of accounting paper, he slid off his stool and walked through the office where the clerks who laboured day in, day out under his eagle eye bent diligently over their figures as he passed. At the far end of the office, he paused before a door half glazed in opaque glass alongside which, affixed to the left of the door handle, Andrew's name was displayed upon a brass plate. Charlie Tait knocked, turned the handle, and walked in.

To Charlie, the Grays – mother and son – were everything in the world. Jessie had kept him on after Tom had been killed, and now he worked for Andrew here at the Baltic Mill; and come hell or high water he would continue to serve him to the best of his ability so long as was humanly possible. Charlie Tait knew full well, of course, that his ultimate boss was Henry Caldwell but, so far as Charlie was concerned, the owner of the mill was of minor significance. His boss was Andrew Gray – and don't let anyone forget it!

It was now nearly five years since Andrew, on the day of his wedding, had asked Charlie to come and work with him at the mill. Charlie, who had been out of work for a very long time, had jumped at the opportunity. He had not, of course, been given much time to think about it; Andrew had other things on his mind that day, and it had not been possible for Charlie to talk to him as he should have wished, for there was a world of difference between the grocer's shop in Pitbuddo and the thrumming activity of a modern jute mill in Dundee. He had not really been trained for office work, and Andrew had said the opening available for him at the Baltic Mill was in a clerking capacity.

Nevertheless, Charlie had started work on the morning of Andrew's return from his honeymoon. Truly, these days had been the most exciting ones in Charlie's life up till then. The city itself had been a positive eye opener; it was so big – bigger even than Brechin which, until then, Charlie had always thought of as the hub of the universe. At the beginning it had not been easy. He had found lodging readily enough with the widowed mother of one of the young lads in the office. She had originally come from Tannadice, and was pleased to have someone from her own part of the country lodging with her in the little rented flat off the Hilltown where she stayed with two unmarried sons. The office work proved more difficult than he had expected but after a slow start he had rapidly gained in confidence until Andrew began to wonder how he had ever managed without Charlie's able assistance. Henry Caldwell too had been delighted with the performance of Andrew's protégé from the Forfarshire countryside and, when Adam Sturrock retired at the end of 1863, the natural successor in the post of chief clerk – indeed the one and only choice – had been Charlie Tait.

Charlie had thriven on the increased responsibility and in the autumn of that year he had married Ellen Spalding who had waited for him so long – ever since they had first met when she had been one of Lady Ramsay's housemaids at Pitbuddo. Together they had set up home in a main door flat in one of the newly built tenement blocks in Albert Street close by Stobswell.

This morning, when Charlie entered Andrew's room, he found that Andrew had company in the form of Henry Caldwell himself, who was pacing up and down with a letter in his hand.

"Ah, Charlie!" said Andrew, "Have you brought the figures?"

"I have that – and ye'll no be best pleased." Charlie handed over the paper he was carrying and Henry Caldwell stopped in mid-stride to peer at it over his son-in-law's shoulder.

"Just as I thought!" he exclaimed, "You're sure the figures are accurate, Tait?"

"Weel, Mr. Caldwell! Gin ye've ony doobts, come awa' ben wi' me and tak' them oot for yersel'!"

Henry Caldwell laughed, and the dour expression Charlie had adopted relaxed a shade.

Andrew was worried. The figures showed that approximately seventy five per cent of the total sums due to the firm by debtors was made up by one outstanding balance – that on account of Underwood, Ward & Langley, their agents in Richmond, Virginia. Normally the firm's debtors were expected to settle their accounts on a monthly basis. R. J. Caldwell & Son insisted upon this as a prerequisite before they would accept any new account. However, there had been many hiccoughs during the years of the American Civil War and, while remittances from their agents had tended to be sporadic, payments had usually evened themselves out in such a way that accounts were settled, on average, on a ten-weekly pattern.

The American business had, of course, been very profitable, the demand for gunny and sacking from each of the protagonists having escalated with each succeeding year. In consequence there had been a general upsurge in business, particularly in sail canvas and the finer quality weaves, aided of course by the drastic contraction in the production of cotton as the Lancashire mills became deprived of one of their principal sources of supply. To some extent, the shortage of American cotton had been made up by increased imports from the east, but this took time to establish, and the gap caused by the virtual cessation of exports from the embattled and devastated southern states was never wholly filled.

Wisely, Henry Caldwell had dealt, not with individual customers, but through agents – the Richmond firm in the case of the Confederacy and, for the North, the firm of Isaacs & Zoller, of Philadelphia and New York. However, in the nine weeks or so which had elapsed since the surrender of General Lee at Appomatox, and the murder of President Lincoln at Ford's Theatre in Washington, whereas Isaacs & Zoller had continued to pay on a regular basis, only one payment had been received from the agents in Richmond, and that was at least six weeks ago.

Henry Caldwell tapped the letter he was holding.

"This is from Underwoods," he said, "a circular letter. It speaks for itself – you can all read it – but clearly, they must be working under very great difficulties. What do they say? Yes – here it is. 'Exceptional conditions – our agency only one of many pressing the various merchants to settle their accounts – same all over the south – those with best chance of obtaining settlement are the suppliers who are able to station themselves upon their debtors' doorsteps until payment is received – for us, this is not physically possible – regret'... and so on. Here! See for yourselves!" He handed the letter to Andrew.

"Aweel!" said Charlie Tait, "We ken noo! Thae foreigners are a' the same; ye canna trust them an inch! And we're ower far awa' to dae onything aboot it."

"We'll certainly not get paid by sitting back and waiting for our money!" Henry Caldwell had recommenced his restless pacing. Back and forwards he strode, deep in thought yet fully conscious that the eyes of both the others were upon him. Suddenly, he stopped and whirled round to face Andrew at his desk.

"I have it!" he cried, smiting his left palm with the clenched fist of his other hand, "We'll take the law into our own hands. You, Andrew! You will go to America just as soon as you can get a passage! Find out from Underwoods just who it is that owes us, and then – be they few or be they many – you can camp in their yards until they pay you!"

Andrew had wondered about this, and he was delighted that the idea had been put forward by Henry Caldwell in the first place. It would make it much easier for him when it came to telling Vicky that he would be away from home for so long. It was now the middle of June and, supposing he got a passage sometime towards the end of the month, it might be possible – depending upon the success of his mission – to be home in time for New Year. Meantime, he would have plenty to do both in the office and at home at Strawberry Hill. He would also have to fit in visits to Aunt Eliza and to Pitbuddo.

His mother, when he told her of his projected mission, was thrilled at his news. It would do Andrew a power of good to be away from the insipid and insufferable Vicky for a month or two – that house of theirs in Dundee was so neat and tidy as to be un-natural. There was nothing out of place – not even a book or a newspaper lying about as might be expected were a normal woman running the house. The girl, Moira, provided a link with the real world of flesh and blood but, in the presence of her mistress, even Moira was speechless and subdued. Andrew might just as well be away from home. Jessie had long ago despaired of the arrival of any Gray grandchildren but she consoled herself with the knowledge that Meg seemed set to supply her with a steady stream of Shirress bairns.

Andrew was fortunate. He secured passage on the steamship *City of Baltimore* of the Liverpool, New York and Philadelphia Line, sailing from the Mersey with a cargo of wool from Yorkshire. The vessel was due to sail on Wednesday 12th July and Andrew was informed that he would be expected to board by 1.45 p.m. that day at the very latest. When the time came for him to leave home, Vicky was tearful. She clung to the lapels of his coat and buried her wet face on his chest. She had sulked for several days when Andrew first told her of his impending journey. How heartless – she said – heartless and inconsiderate, that was what he was, even to contemplate leaving her like this. The fact that the whole exercise had been planned by her own father seemed to carry no weight at all. She had railed at him for a good half hour before flying upstairs where she locked herself in their bedroom and refused to come out.

They had not had such a bad tiff since the day Charlie and Ellen Tait came for supper. She had demurred from the start about having them. It was quite ridiculous that Andrew should expect her to entertain this, that and the next person just because they happened to work for him at the mill. She had never met either of the Taits and, really, she had no wish to do so. Why not invite Mistress O'Flaherty and a few of the other shifters! In the end, however, Andrew had managed to win her over and, when the day came and the Taits arrived, dressed in their Sabbath best, Vicky contrived to preside over the formalities as if she had been Miss Farmiloe herself. There was, however, one important difference. Whereas her aunt would have maintained a never-ending flow of small talk, Vicky hardly opened her mouth.

The effect upon Charlie was disastrous and, as his embarrassment increased, his stories grew more and more preposterous and his country accent thickened by the minute. It was a difficult evening, but nothing like so gruelling an experience for Andrew as the tantrum to which Vicky subjected him once the Taits had left and they were alone in the drawing room while Moira cleared up. Never again, Vicky declared! How could he have been so insensitive as to inflict such awful people on her. They were so *common* — especially the man – such stories! Vicky vowed it had been as much as she could do to refrain from covering her ears! Andrew was greatly perturbed. It upset him to see darling Vicky so patently unhappy, and it equally hurt that she could view one of his oldest friends with such obvious distaste. He did, of course, point out that Charlie's was the speech of the Forfarshire countryside and, if it was common, it was because it was common to all in Pitbuddo! Vicky was not mollified and averred that to her ears it sounded little different from the accents to be heard in the Overgate or Thorter Row. When Andrew protested, she ran upstairs slamming the door behind her.

And now, she was giving a repeat performance. When she did emerge, red-eyed and woeful, it was to announce that Andrew need not expect her to stay on in this mean little house all by herself. In vain did Andrew point out that she would not be alone so long as she still had Moira. Vicky would not listen to anything he said. After several days of this, it had been decided that they would shut up the house at Strawberry Hill and that she and Moira would go to her father at "Riga Lodge" while Andrew was away. It was there that he parted from her before Joseph drove him to Dundee to catch the train for Perth and, eventually, Carlisle and Liverpool.

City of Baltimore was new. Launched at Birkenhead last autumn, she had joined the Atlantic fleet just before Easter and her captain, a jovial and spare man who had first seen the light of day fifty years earlier at Barrow-in-Furness, just up the Lancastrian coast, was proud of her ability to complete the crossing in just under ten days.

When Andrew stepped aboard, Captain Parkin was standing at the head of the gangplank awaiting the arrival of the pilot to see them safely out of the Mersey.

"You been in Philadelphia before, Mr. Gray?"

"No," said Andrew, "this is my first visit to America."

"Well – you'll like it! Philadelphia, I mean. 'City of brotherly love' they call it. Maybe it was once, and maybe it will be again some day, but for the past five years even the good folk of Philadelphia have shown no love for their brethren south of the Mason-Dixon line! William Penn must be turning in his grave like a top! Glad to have you with us, sir! Hope you'll be comfortable: the steward here will show you to your cabin – Wilfrid!"

"Follow me, sir!" The steward, Wilfrid, was a small sharp-featured sailor who reminded Andrew forcibly of a weasel-faced man who had beaten him up many years ago on the Brechin road near Craigbeg.

"This way, sir!" Andrew, carrying his valise which he had deliberately kept as light as possible, followed the steward along a narrow passage and down a companion-way to a small but pleasant cabin which had been allocated for his use. It was a hot day, and the porthole was open, letting in such air as there was. Andrew looked out and saw that the surface of the water lay at roughly the same level as the floor of the cabin. It looked oily and dirty and it slapped about the vessel's hull with a choppy motion, born of the tide and the movement of other ships, rather than the wind. In the cabin was a narrow bunk, a small table fixed to the bulkhead, a wooden chair and a hanging cupboard. An oil lamp swung on chains hanging from the ceiling and the wooden floor-boards had been scrubbed smooth and clean.

Andrew stowed his valise under the bunk and returned to the upper deck. There would be plenty of time later to unpack his things. While he had been below, the pilot had come aboard and the seamen were paying out the lines as they cast off from the quayside. Andrew saw now that his cabin must be on the right hand side of the ship – named starboard since, in ancient times before the invention of the rudder, this was the side on which the "steering" oar was located. Black smoke was pouring from *City of Baltimore*'s tall stack as the skipper bellowed down the voice-tube and the vessel nosed slowly out from the quay and turned into the channel. Andrew looked at his watch. It was exactly ten minutes past two o'clock. Over on the port beam fresh new building was in course in the Birkenhead yards where tall cranes stood silhouetted against the green hills of the Wirral. Nearer to hand, on the starboard quarter, the waterfront of Liverpool – with its quays and warehouses and streets of squalid cabins where the Irish immigrants had congregated following the potato famines of the 'forties – slipped away astern. As the vessel gathered speed, the breeze whipped into Andrew's face and set his blood tingling. Truly it was good to be alive on a day such as this, with all the broad Atlantic reaching away ahead. They were close to the mouth of the river by now, approaching the open water of the Irish Sea with, away to the southwest, the mountains of North Wales, blue in the summer haze.

It was next morning before they felt for the first time the long swell of the ocean that caused *City of Baltimore* to develop a very definite roll which did Andrew no good at all. In fact, he did not finish the breakfast which, up till then, he had been thoroughly enjoying and, although he was not physically sick, he nevertheless felt unwell enough to wish he were safely back on dry land. He lay down on his bunk with his eyes shut and felt somewhat less queasy. Most of that day, however, Andrew remained in his cabin and, although the ship continued to roll, he grew accustomed to the motion and he had no more trouble.

In fact, Andrew began to thoroughly enjoy himself. Had he stopped to think about it he might, in time, have come to realise that part of his elation could be set down to his freedom from Vicky's insidiously negative personality. He did, however, feel that shipboard life agreed very well with him and he revelled in the experience. The only other passengers aboard were an elderly Welsh couple – a Methodist minister and his wife who hardly ventured a foot beyond the threshold of their cabin other than at meal times. In consequence, Andrew was accorded much more freedom than that normally enjoyed by fare-paying passengers and he was permitted to wander at will all over the ship. He was even allowed on the bridge and here he spent long hours with Captain Parkin and his officers discussing winds and tides and navigation generally. He learned how to use a sextant and plot the ship's position and he listened avidly to Will Parkin's marvellous repertoire as he whiled away the hours recounting some of the ups and downs of his maritime career.

The passengers took their meals in the officers' mess-room where Captain Parkin, or in his absence on the bridge, the First Officer, presided, sitting at the head of the table. On the wall behind, above the open port hole, a portrait of the Queen in her widow's weeds looked sorrowfully down upon the assembled company. Captain Parkin had been a naval officer and had served with the fleet during the Crimean campaign. Retiring with the rank of Lieutenant-Commander, he had little difficulty in obtaining a berth in the expanding Atlantic fleet operated by the Liverpool, New York and Philadelphia Line, where he had not long to wait before getting his own command. With such a background it was not surprising that he ran the mess like a naval wardroom and every evening, after dinner, he saw to it that glasses were raised with all due formality and a toast drunk for the health of Her Majesty. This irked the Reverend John Meredith who most strenuously disapproved of strong liquor and who deemed the whole business to smack of heathenish practices. Captain Parkin was a reasonable man. Mr. Meredith and his wife could drink lime juice, he said, if they liked not real liquor, but – and he was adamant in this – stand up they would whether they liked it or not! Mr. Meredith got his own back by drawing out his grace before meals to quite unreasonable proportions.

When the Merediths had retired for the night, Andrew and Captain Parkin would sit on at the table playing backgammon – a game to which the captain appeared to be completely addicted – a decanter of whisky at their elbow. Later, on deck, Andrew loved to feel the wind in his hair as the ship ploughed steadily onwards towards the fading afterglow of the summer night. The creaming bow wave folded back in a shimmer of phosphorescence and the shipboard sounds, stilled from their daytime clamour, were clear and easily recognisable. The good weather had held and always the bowl of the night sky was filled with stars from horizon to horizon.

On the eighth day out of Liverpool, Captain Parkin reckoned that they were now less than twenty-four hours off the continent of North America close to Cape May, which lies at the entrance to Delaware Bay. Up on the bridge, Captain Parkin pointed it out to Andrew on the chart. For the first time since leaving the Mersey it was a dull morning with only an occasional blink of sunshine and, away to the south, fine on the port bow, were some high towers of cumulo nimbus – sure sign of an advancing storm. There was no sign whatsoever of land but, looking at the chart, Andrew could see how the wide channel of the mighty Delaware River swept round in a sickle-shaped curve separating the states of Delaware and Pennsylvania, on the west side, from New Jersey on the east. At its widest point, just in from the ocean, the bay measured some twenty-five miles across; and the distance by water, from the entrance, to the city of Philadelphia would be approximately 140 miles. The proportions of this land were truly immense when measured against a British yardstick.

It was shortly after ten o'clock by Andrew's watch when they sighted the other ship. At the look-out's shout, Captain Parkin put his glass to one eye.

"Aye, aye!" he cried, "I have it! Too far away to make her out properly. Coming up fast though!"

With the naked eye, Andrew could see nothing, even when Captain Parkin indicated a point on the southern horizon. When he was handed an eyeglass, however, he had more success although, even then, it was not easy to make the vessel out as she lay low in the water against the leaden sky. Even the faint smudge of smoke tended to merge into the background.

Whatever she was, the steamer clearly had an excellent turn of speed and was gaining on them fast. Glass still at his eye, the captain continued to hold her in sight. He moved towards the speaking tube.

"God damn it!" he exclaimed.

At the same moment, there was a loud noise which Andrew took to be a peal of thunder. But it happened again, and this time Andrew realised that the sound was that of an explosion. Not only that but, out over the starboard bow at a distance of a mere one hundred yards or so, a great column of water rose into the air. Andrew found the First Officer standing at his side.

"What's going on?" Andrew asked.

"I think we're being fired upon!" The First Officer was scanning the on-coming vessel. "She's run up a string of signals. Sounds like a gunboat that hasn't heard the war is over! Nevertheless, I reckon the skipper will heave to or risk being blown out of the water!"

Together, they moved to where the captain was standing. He had already called upon the engineer to stop his engines.

"Damned privateer!" Captain Parkin's expression was as thunderous as the southern sky. "Fired warning shots, then signalled – 'Heave to – am coming aboard.' Impudent devil!"

As her screws ceased turning, *City of Baltimore* lost way and tended to wallow in the strong swell running under her keel. They could now see the other vessel clearly. Long and low – she looked what she was – an armed merchantman. At her masthead – in addition to a string of signal flags – and from her stern, she flew the saltire flag of the Confederacy. Several guns mounted forward of the bridge and the single one at her stern, were trained upon *City of Baltimore*, the black shadows of their muzzles grim with menace. Across the intervening stretch of water, Andrew read, in large letters at her bow, the name – *Shenandoah*. There were few people on either side of the Atlantic who had not heard of *Shenandoah*, one of a band of southern privateers – *Alabama, Talahassee, Nashville* – merchantmen of around 1,000 tons, many of them built in English yards. Throughout the war years, they harried the Federal sea lanes destroying a considerable tonnage of shipping, Federal and foreign alike, along with military stores and valuable war supplies.

At a distance of 100 yards or so from *City of Baltimore*, the privateer swung a few degrees to port to come broadside on. As she did so and cut her engines, Andrew could see those menacing guns swivelling round to maintain their bearing. Across the water they could hear calls and commands and the creak of davits as a boat was lowered and manned. The officers and crew of the British ship watched with unsmiling faces while the oars rose and fell driving the small boat towards them at considerable speed. As she came alongside, a sailor in her bows rose to his feet and made contact with his boathook. Captain Parkin had left the bridge and was standing at the rail as, one by one, the boat party clambered up the ladder and swung aboard. A dozen men in all, each was armed with a pistol and a wicked-looking cutlass. Their leader was a tall man in frayed naval uniform topped by a peak cap that sat awkwardly upon long and rather unkempt hair. His face was bronzed by the sun and wind, his long bushy beard blanched with constant exposure to the salt air. Under shaggy overgrown brows, a pair of sharp, light-blue eyes looked around and came to rest upon Captain Parkin.

"Good day, sir!" He spoke in a slow, almost slurred drawl. "Cap'n Waddell of the Confederate Ship *Shenandoah* at your service!" He touched the peak of his cap in salute.

"My name – is Parkin," the other said coldly. "And if you wish to be of service to me, sir, you and your bully boys here may remove yourselves from my ship and cease threatening me with your presence and your guns!"

"Where y'all bound, Cap'n Parkin?"

"That's no concern of yours! Get off my ship!"

"Oh, come now, Cap'n! Seems to me you're a mite screwed up! D'y'all aim to throw us off?"

The Confederate sailors around him – a villainous-looking bunch – loosened the pistols in their belts and laughed.

"Now, Cap'n Parkin! Are you going to tell me nice and quiet without any more trouble – where y'all goin' and what y'all totin' aboard, man!"

"Steamship *City of Baltimore* out of Liverpool, bound for Philadelphia with a cargo of wool."

Captain Waddell's blue eyes never left the other man's face. With his left hand, he signalled to one of his companions, a small, thick-set man with a cast in one eye. Apart from his cotton trousers, which were tattered and frayed at the ankles, he looked every inch a petty officer. Taking two of the sailors with him, he began turning back the cargo hatches.

"Well?" asked Captain Waddell.

"He's right, sir! Nothing but goddam wool!"

"Wool!" said Captain Waddell appreciatively, "Wool to clothe the Yankee army! Military stores, sir!" He turned to Captain Parkin. "Vital war supplies! Sir! I have no option but to commandeer your vessel and her cargo!"

"What!" Captain Parkin was beside himself with rage. "This is piracy!"

"No, sir! It ain't – it's war!"

"But – good God, man! The war has been over for several months!" At last, realisation began to dawn upon him. Quite probably *Shenandoah* had not made a landfall for long enough. She doubtless carried an adequate reserve of fuel, but even if she did have to stock up her bunkers, she most likely used some secluded southern anchorage where supplies could be dumped to be picked up as and when required.

Captain Waddell was roaring with laughter.

"Now, now, Cap'n – you surely don't expect me to fall for that one. That's what they all say!"

"Don't be a fool, man: it happens to be true: General Lee surrendered in April at a place in Maryland called Appomatox, and Lincoln's dead, assassinated at a theatre performance in Washington!"

"That last I could just believe! He has his enemies – aye and bitter ones at that – even among the goddam Yankees. As for the General – no, sir! Robert E. Lee will die rather than yield! Now, Cap'n! I reckon we've just about talked long enough. You will lower your boats, sir, and take off passengers and crew – every living soul of them. And you will do so now, Cap'n, or by God, sir, I'll blow you and your ship to hell!"

Eye to eye, the two captains stared at each other for fully half a minute. Captain Parkin was first to turn away: he was at the other's mercy and he had no option but to give the required order. At that precise moment, the storm broke and Waddell's laughter was lost in the noise of the thunder. *City of Baltimore* carried six lifeboats – three on each side – and they were soon in the water tossing violently in the rough sea that had suddenly sprung up before the gusting wind accompanying the storm. It was so dark that it was no longer possible to make out *Shenandoah* and her guns except when the whole scene was illuminated in the vivid, shimmering flashes of lightning. To Andrew, it all seemed like a fantasy – the privateer's guns, her shaggy, laughing commander, and the American sailors waving their cutlasses at the scared figures of the Merediths, who had been sent for, and were now scurrying along the deck like frightened rabbits, each clutching a large travelling bag. As best he could, Andrew helped Mistress Meredith to the rail and took her bag while the old lady put her trembling hands to the ropes of the swaying ladder. Her descent to the waiting arms of a crew member in the boat below was neither easy nor fast, but she was down at last, doing her best to keep her voluminous skirts from ballooning out around her in the wind and lashing rain. Her husband followed rather more quickly and Andrew passed down their bags. He just had time to go to his cabin and throw as much of his gear as he could into his own valise before returning to seek a berth for himself. When he reached the rail it was to find that everyone had gone except for Captain Parkin and the boarding party from the privateer. Andrew threw his valise down into one of the boats and stood for a moment at the head of the ladder.

"Now, Cap'n – if you please!" The Confederate skipper motioned with his hand to the head of the ladder.

"And if I don't please?"

"Then, sir, I can't be responsible for your safety."

"Well – I don't choose to go. My place, as always, is with my ship!"

"Come now, Cap'n – spare us the heroics! When I get back aboard *Shenandoah* there, her guns – every single one of them – will be opened up. Make no mistake, Cap'n Parkin, I aim to sink your ship and send your cargo of wool for the Yankees down to the bottom with her. Now! Will you please go?"

"Get off my ship, damned pirate that you are, and take your scum with you!"

The petty officer drew his cutlass and raised it in a threatening gesture. Captain Waddell turned on him.

"Put that goddam sword away!"

"Aye, aye, sir!" The petty officer lowered his arm.

"Well! Cap'n Parkin, sir: y'all have it your own way!" Captain Waddell turned on his heel and ordered his men over the side. As he followed the last man down he touched his hat and smiled sardonically.

"You're a foolish man, Cap'n Parkin, sir: but you sure are a brave one!"

Captain Parkin glared at his retreating figure. With grim foreboding, the noise of the storm notwithstanding, Andrew had heard the conversation out. He knew that nothing would persuade the privateer captain to stay his hand. Likewise, there was nothing he could say which might persuade Will Parkin to leave his doomed ship. Andrew had grown to respect and like this

Englishman and he knew that, whatever the cost, he must do something to save him from himself. There was one thing – and one thing only – which might just conceivably work. Will Parkin was a lightly built man of medium height – and he was fifty years old. Andrew was tall, strong and on the right side of thirty.

The captain was staring out over the rail, watching, while the boarding party regained their boat and pushed off. God damn it, he thought – one of his own boats was still lying alongside.

"Shove off, damn you!" he cried.

"Aye, aye, sir!"

Thank God, the First Officer had made to obey the order. Captain Parkin turned from the rail and found himself face to face with Andrew.   "My God, Gray! Are you still here? Get off the ship, man! There's not much time left!"

"Captain!" said Andrew, "See yonder!" He pointed behind him to his right.

Will Parkin reacted as Andrew had hoped he might. He turned slightly to look in the direction indicated, bringing his head round at forty-five degrees to his left. Acting at lightning speed, Andrew brought his right arm swinging round and, with all the force he could muster, he hit the other man with bunched fist right on the point of the chin. The older man was felled like an ox at the slaughter and, before he could regain his senses, Andrew, straining every muscle, picked him up and, hitching the inert body over his shoulder, he slowly negotiated the ladder. At his hoarse shout, the First Officer brought his boat back alongside.

"Captain fell!" Andrew gasped. "Hit his head. Here! Take him! Carefully now!"

Hands reached up and Captain Parkin was lowered gently into the boat. The storm had abated somewhat and the First Officer could see the other boats some distance off now, down wind. He steered towards them while the sailors strained at the oars as they strove to drive the heavily laden boat over what was still a very turbulent sea which, every now and again, threatened to capsize them as it lashed out in frenzy, drenching them all in ice cold water. They could see both ships quite clearly. *Shenandoah* – having winched up her boat following the return of the boarding party – was manoeuvring so as to maintain her station broadside on to *City of Baltimore*. Suddenly, and with shattering din, she opened fire. Andrew, who had been slumped on a thwart trying to regain his breath, sat up and stared. He could see the yellow flash and the black puff of smoke as each gun loosed its missile, and he could see the gaping holes torn in the *City of Baltimore's* side. The guns were dead on target. Her destruction was inevitable and did not take long. She went down stern first, tilting until her bows were at a crazy angle and then, sliding – almost gracefully – backwards under the surface. *Shenandoah* was already turning, moving off at maximum speed on a southeasterly bearing.

The storm seemed to be closing in again and, in the gathering gloom, the long low outline of the privateer rapidly disappeared from sight. Even when the lightning lit up the ocean, it was impossible to make out the other boats, so high were the seas all around them. The rain and the sea enveloped them all and the noise of the thunder was well nigh incessant. Andrew was conscious that Captain Parkin was stirring where he lay in a wet heap in the bottom of the boat and his eyes were upon him, cold and unfriendly. It might well have been better for him had he been allowed to go down with his ship. His ordeal would have been over by now. As it was, it seemed to Andrew that he had condemned the captain to share in what promised to be a long agonising death lying in wait for them all.

Andrew had not thought it possible that they could survive – especially when the storm closed round them again in all its fury. Huge green seas reached up and all but enveloped the small boat. The wind shrieked, whipping away everything on board that was in any way loose; caps, scarves, light bags – all were plucked up and whirled away into the driving spray. Every now and then a wave would break ahead of them, curling over on itself before bearing down in a snarling white foam to smother the boat from stem to stern and wet them through and through. With a shudder the boat would sit for a split second, poised delicately on the crest of the wave, until gravity sent her plunging down the far side to wallow momentarily in the trough beyond. And all the time, as the rain poured down, the inky blackness of day turned to night was lit by the incessant flashing of the lightning and filled with the incredible noise of the thunder.

Andrew calculated that a full hour passed before the storm lifted slightly. Gradually the darkness grew less intense, the rain eased, and the thunder no longer cracked above them in unison with the flash of the lightning. The wind too slackened off and with it the seas dropped, although it was quite some time before there was any visibility in excess of a few hundred yards or so. By then, patches of blue sky were showing and occasional shafts of sunlight were dancing off the surface of the water, restricting their vision even further. When, at, last, they did manage to scan the seas around them, they could see another four of the steamer's boats. Of the fifth, however, there was no sign and they all feared it must have capsized and sunk, for it seemed unlikely that one boat out of six could be driven far out of sight of all the others.

From being drenched and cold, they became unpleasantly hot as the sun grew stronger and they steamed uncomfortably in their wet clothing. But worse by far was the thirst that now afflicted them, rendering it necessary for strict rationing of the meagre supply contained in the cask with which the boat was equipped. It made them all realise how much better employed they would have been had they set about collecting some of the rainwater that had sluiced down upon them at the height of the storm. Captain Parkin, on his recovery, had reassumed command, which was not difficult seeing that all the occupants of the boat, with the single exception of Andrew, were members of his own crew. After that first baleful glance, the Captain studiously avoided Andrew's eyes and no further words were spoken between them. The Captain had the First Officer organise the boat's company into watches and those not on duty endeavoured, as best they could, to get some sleep. The sun went down; night closed about them and still, in all that stretch of ocean, there had been sign of neither land nor shipping.

Andrew had newly fallen asleep when he felt a hand on his shoulder and the First Officer's voice at his ear telling him that his spell of watch duty had arrived. It was pitch black – the complete and utter darkness presaging the dawn. A couple of seamen were on duty with him sitting hunched on a thwart peering into the curtain of darkness. The sound of the sea, loud and constant though it was, could not drive out entirely the little noises inside the boat – the sound of men turning in a confined space, their grunts and their snores. Was it his imagination, Andrew wondered, or was the darkness less intense than it had been? He sat on, trying not to let his eyes close as they so dearly wished to do. Unfortunately, the more he peered around him, the more his eyelids grew heavy and tended to flutter. But he found he was now able to see beyond the confines of his own mind. He could make out the forms of the men on watch with him and the huddled shapes of the others in the boat. And then – suddenly – he could distinguish, first the sea, and then the sky where a luminous quality was spreading up from the far horizon.

The sunrise, when it came, was superb. The eastern sky was like a skein of shot silk, pulsating with light in all the many hues of orange and yellow and gold. Then, behind them, the sun came up out of the sea, first a segment peeping over the horizon, then a half circle and, finally, the full glorious disc, its level rays sparkling over the water. At the same moment, there was a cry from one of the seamen. He was pointing ahead.

"Sail ho!" he cried.

Andrew turned and looked in the direction of the man's outstretched arm. How right he was! But – unbelievably – there was not just one sail, but a considerable number, all bunched in fairly tight formation, about half a mile or so away.

The others in the boat, roused by the man's hoarse shout, were sitting up and rubbing their cramped limbs.

"Fishing boats from the shape of them – looks like an entire fleet! Making this way – thank God! All of you! Wave! Wave whatever you can – and shout – shout like hell!" Captain Parkin stripped off his shirt, tied it by the sleeves to an oar and raised it aloft. They shouted and they bellowed as best they could with throats parched and cracked with exposure to the salt-laden atmosphere. All were now shirtless as they waved to attract attention. The fishing fleet was sailing on a southeasterly bearing which would take it past the boats away out to their left and, since there was still a heavy sea running, the small boats would not easily be spotted from the decks of the sailing vessels. Despair once again descended upon Andrew like a black cloud. The nearest boat was now close enough to enable them to see small figures hurrying to and fro. They made one last desperate effort.

"Now!" cried the Captain. "Let us all shout together when I give the signal. Shout 'ahoy!' when I drop my hand."

"Ahoy!" they yelled. "Ahoy! Ahoy! Ahoy!"

They saw a figure on the fishing boat looking in their direction and they waved furiously and continued shouting. They thought they saw the fisherman pointing and certainly he was being joined by others of the crew for there was now a knot of men standing at the rail. As they looked, they saw the boat's sail come round as her skipper altered course to point directly at them. With the light wind blowing full on her starboard quarter the fishing boat came on at good speed. The other vessels in the fleet had also turned and were coming up fast behind her.

In little over three quarters of an hour, the survivors from the steamship *City of Baltimore* found themselves safely aboard two American fishing ketches sailing, on a northwesterly bearing, which – or so the First Officer said – ought to take them to a landfall on the far side of Delaware Bay. The full complement of Andrew's boat, with the Captain and First Officer, and that of the four other boats Andrew had seen at dawn, had all been picked up by the fishing fleet, after which it had been decided that, while the bulk of the fleet would sail on towards the fishing grounds, two of their number would return to port to put the survivors ashore and to alert the coastguard to look out for the missing boat. The First Officer took a gloomy view of the prospect of its being found – an opinion shared by Andrew, sadly, especially as the Merediths were amongst those missing.

Captain Parkin had gone aft to join the fishing boat skipper in the wheel house, leaving Andrew and the First Officer in the well of the ketch with the others. They could see land now, a long low shoreline. Because of the direction of the wind they could only keep a steady course by dint of tacking to and fro with the result that the coast was sometimes out on the port quarter and at others on the port bow. But, gradually, they drew nearer and Andrew could make out white houses and trees against a background of green. Then, the sails went over and once more the ketch stood off the land. This time, however, as the sails filled and the coast fell away astern, Andrew could see that they had cleared a major headland, beyond which was a cluster of buildings and a fair sized harbour. It seemed that this was where they were heading, for the skipper stayed only a short time on the new tack before going about yet again on a course set directly for the harbour mouth.

"Where do you think we are?"

The First Officer shook his head,

"I don't know, Mr. Gray. I don't know at all but we must be somewhere on the far side of Delaware Bay."

"This is our home port, mister!" One of the fishermen had overheard them. "And here's where you limeys will land; Lewes, Delaware! A mighty old town, mister, the oldest in the state, older than Philadelphia, older even than New York City. They say the first settlers came from Holland; reckon they must have been fishermen back home, for the folks in Lewes have been dragging the sea ever since!"

There were several vessels in the harbour – fishing boats principally and one or two that looked like coastal traders. The quayside was busy and the survivors from *City of Baltimore* found they had to pick their way carefully round stacks of fish boxes and piles of ropes and nets. Horses stood by patiently while carts were emptied and filled and the smell of fish emanating from the open doors of the wooden sheds lining the pierhead was quite overpowering in the heat and strong sunlight. The skipper of the fishing ketch led them to the Customs House, a wooden-walled building where the stars and stripes of the United States hung limply from a white painted flagpole.

Inside, it was extremely hot and stuffy and, until such time as Captain Parkin, in company with the fishing boat skipper and a uniformed customs officer returned to join them, they had to cool their heels for what seemed like hours in the cramped space of a very small waiting room. The two Americans shook hands with the Captain and left – the skipper to return to his boat and the customs man to go back to his own office.

"Right!" said the Captain. "Pay attention! Before we do anything further, each one of us has now got to go through the formalities laid down by Federal regulations governing the entry of aliens into the United States. We shall form up in lines and proceed, one by one, through that door from which you have just seen me emerge. Each man, after being dealt with, will return to this chamber to await further orders. I shall lead off, followed by Mr. Gray. The First Officer will remain until last to ensure that the exercise is carried through in an orderly and shipshape fashion.

"I have also to tell you that, so far, we have no news of the occupants of our missing boat but the United States coastguard has been alerted and as soon as there is any news you will be advised. I have registered an official complaint regarding the conduct of the privateer, *Shenandoah*, and I have put the authorities here on notice that a claim for compensation will be lodged at the first opportunity.

"After formalities have been completed, Mr. Gray will be free to leave. I understand that a coach will depart at three o'clock this afternoon for Dover, the capital of the state, whence it will be possible to proceed on to Philadelphia by steamer. So far as the rest of us are concerned, arrangements are being made for us to be picked up here and transferred by sea to Philadelphia to await passage home. It is unlikely that the necessary transport will arrive for a day or two and, in the interval, accommodation is being made available for us in the hall of the Baptist Church here."

The Customs Officer, now cast unusually in the role of an immigration official, was pleasant and polite. He dealt expeditiously with Captain Parkin, and with Andrew, who felt it possible that the good temper now displayed might become somewhat frayed by the time the First Officer's turn should be reached. Back in the waiting room, Andrew took his leave of the ship's officers and crew, then, picking up his valise, he stepped out into the sunshine where the heat struck him like a physical blow. To his surprise, he saw the slight figure of Captain Parkin waiting for him at the top of the steps.

"Goodbye, Mr. Gray!" said the Captain, holding out his hand. "I should not be standing here had it not been for you, although – as I am sure you are aware – a captain's place is with his ship!"

"I think not!" said Andrew, clasping the Captain's hand in his. "A captain's place must surely be with those living souls over whom he has been put in authority – certainly not with any inanimate and doomed object such as *City of Baltimore* was in the surrounding circumstances. I am afraid, sir, that in my book, any other interpretation is arrant nonsense. You were of considerable use to us all in the boats and your men are relying upon you now to see them safely home. You will not, I know, disappoint them for you are a man I have grown to respect and admire, which is one reason why I had to endeavour to save you from yourself. Most of all, however, I acted on behalf of a lady and two little girls in Blundellsands about whom you have told me so much. Goodbye, Captain Parkin – and thank you!"

It was stiflingly hot on the coach between Lewes and Dover. The sun had burned off most of the surface water left behind by the storm and, on the driest stretches of the highway, the horses' hoofs and the wheels of the carriage had stirred the dust up into a reddish cloud that came in even through the closed windows, settled on everything and everybody, and made them all cough. Where sufficient moisture remained to lay the dust, Andrew had glimpses of pastures where cattle lay in whatever shade they could find, of white farm houses whose wooden walls looked clinker built, and long red barns with roofs resembling the tent tops of covered wagons. The coach service was efficient, however, and they reached Dover, a pleasant country town centred upon a delightful green, in the early evening. There, they drew up in the shade cast by four shapely maples standing outside the City Hotel directly across the green from the State Capitol. At the hotel Andrew secured a room for the night and thankfully sponged down. He was, he found, completely exhausted and, without bothering to eat, he lay down upon the bed and was asleep on the instant.

In the morning he did justice to an ample breakfast of bacon and scrambled eggs before taking another coach back to the coast at Port Mahon, six miles away. Here he boarded the steamer which took him up the narrowing river, first to Wilmington, and then to Philadelphia itself, where he disembarked at Penn's Landing and found his way to the Keystone Hotel.

Next day he presented himself at the offices of Messrs Isaacs & Zoller, Caldwell's agents in Philadelphia, where he was well received by the junior partner, Mr. Jake Isaacs. He stayed there the better part of an hour and after he left, Jake Isaacs stood at his office window and watched as Andrew walked down the steps and made his way past Independence Hall into Walnut Street. The clock, under the graceful spire of the tower, showed the time to be fifteen minutes past the hour of noon. There was not a breath of air in the office for Jake had ensured that every window was securely closed to keep out the almost torrid heat; for it was hot – very hot indeed – even for mid-July, close on ninety degrees in the shade, and Jake mopped his streaming brow with the large red handkerchief he carried in the sleeve of his jacket. A footstep sounded behind him and he looked over his shoulder to see his partner, Pete Zoller, coming round the end of his desk.

"Who was that?" Zoller asked.

"A young man from Scotland – from R. J. Caldwell & Son of Dundee." Jake returned to his desk and consulted a card, "Name of Gray – Andrew Gray."

"What did he want? Our relationship with Caldwells is regular, is it not? And cordial!"

"Yes, yes – of course! Said he aimed to do some travelling here in the States and that he had arranged for his mail to be sent care of this office. He will keep us advised of his whereabouts so that we may forward it to him from time to time. But, principally, he was looking for advice. Seems he was aboard that English ship that was sunk last week by the goddam *Shenandoah*. I guess you've seen the press reports."

"Yeah! Survivors picked up by some fishing boats and put ashore on the Delaware side near Dover. Captain said there had been six boats in all but only five are accounted for. Coastguard still on the alert but chance of finding other survivors must now be slim. The 'reb' skipper, the son-of-a-bitch, refused to believe that the war is over! If he goes on sinking foreign ships going about their lawful business there will be one hell of a compensation claim for the lawyers in Washington to unravel!"

"And – if the claims are upheld – one hell of a bill for Uncle Sam!" Jake shook his head. "Times are hard, Pete."

"Yeah! And likely to get harder. What did he want to know?"

"Asked us to recommend a good law firm."

"What did you say?"

"Well – what d'you think? I recommended Vic!"

"Great! But what does he want with the law?"

"I don't know, but I can guess; I reckon Caldwells have been supplying the 'rebs' with material for sandbags or whatever and have gotten themselves a few bad debts! Like as not young Gray's come over to put the screw on them. Probably anxious to know just how much pressure he can use and still remain within the law! Seemed a nice young fella!"

Jake Isaacs was partly correct. Andrew was looking for guidance on American mercantile law, particularly that relating to contract and the sale of goods. But most importantly, he sought enlightenment as to the legal position of the southern states which, of course, had not been re-admitted to the Union even though the war was over and done with. Now – he was seated in another stuffy office in an atmosphere which reminded him of the bakehouse in Pitbuddo. Facing him, across a desk identical to that of old Sam Coutts, sat Mr. Victor Zoller, son of Pete and a junior partner in the highly reputable and respectable firm of Ledger, Marks & Lindenbaum, attorneys at law in Philadelphia. Vic Zoller was a man of around Andrew's own age, small, dapper and clean shaven apart from a rim of black beard round the lower part of his chin. With his curling black hair, and disproportionately large nose, he reminded Andrew of photographs he had seen of the rising conservative politician, Benjamin Disraeli. Andrew found the atmosphere in the office well nigh unbearable but Vic Zoller's suit of heavy broadcloth, his rather flamboyant necktie and sprigged waistcoat, not to mention his thick woollen socks and heavy elastic-sided boots, seemed to insulate him from the heat in much the same way as an African tribesman wraps up his nudity in thick woollen blanket or animal skin kaross to find protection from the midday sun. Vic Zoller looked as cool and as comfortable as Andrew was hot and bothered.

Nevertheless, he proved himself to be not only a pleasant young man but also a most helpful one. From what he had to say it seemed that the letter of the law was not so very different – contract and sale of goods being regulated along very similar lines to those with which Andrew was accustomed. So far as the status of the former Confederate States was concerned, however, the picture was blurred and far from clear. President Johnson was doing his utmost to re-establish both Union, and State government. This is what Lincoln would have wished and, in this, the President had the wholehearted support of the democrats but not that of the die-hard members of his own Republican Party, who were opposed to what they regarded as leniency towards rebels – albeit defeated ones. Conditions in the south, Vic Zoller said, were somewhat chaotic. The freed slaves – none of whom had any experience of fending for themselves – wandered aimlessly from place to place looking for work and finding none. Some of them went on the rampage, looting stores – especially where stocks of liquor were involved – and generally terrorising law-abiding citizens, negro and white alike. Worst of all, according to Vic, were the chancers and adventurers, the so-called carpet-baggers, many of them from the north, who sought political and material gain for themselves by promoting the advancement of former slaves to key positions in local and state government. Andrew would require, he said, to take things as he found them, and improvise if necessary. There really was no knowing what he might find. Communications? Again – this was difficult to assess. So far as he knew, the rail links had been largely restored – mostly by the Federal military to assist them in the movement of troops while the war was still in progress.

Altogether, it had proved a worthwhile interview and, when he rose to go, Andrew expressed his warmest thanks.

"Where are you putting up, Mr. Gray?" Vic asked.

"At the 'Keystone'."

"Ah yes! At the corner of second and Arch is it not?"

"That's right!"

"Comfortable?"

"Very!"

"But no dining room?"

"No."

"Well, then, Mr. Gray. Should you be free to do so, would you care to dine with me this evening?"

"I should like that very much – but, really, that is much too kind of you."

"Not at all. I shall be delighted. Shall we say six o'clock? I shall call for you at the 'Keystone'."

When he got back to the hotel, Andrew divested himself of his sodden shirt, socks and underclothes. He sponged himself down with tepid water from the ewer on the washstand and towelled himself dry. His best quality suiting, tailored to perfection for him in Dundee, looked limp and shapeless. Tomorrow, he vowed, he would endeavour to purchase something lighter and more suited to this extraordinary climate, which reminded him of nothing so much as Sir George Ramsay's hothouses at Pitbuddo where, as a boy accompanying his father on his weekly visit up the glen, he had once been taken by Charlie Tait's father-in-law.

Vic Zoller was as good as his word. At six o'clock precisely he appeared in the hotel lobby, a smart and handsome figure, his fancy sprigged waistcoat suitably enhanced by a heavy gold watch chain falling across it in two loops. In his hand, he carried a shiny, wide-brimmed top hat.

"Well, Mr. Gray!" he called as Andrew hurried forward to meet him, "I hope you have a good appetite!"

Outside it was still hot, although not quite the oven-like heat suffered earlier in the day; but it was pleasant enough on the broad side-walk and, as they went, Vic Zoller never ceased talking as he pointed out landmarks of historical interest.

They ate at the City Tavern – one of the oldest eating places in Philadelphia and one that gave every appearance of having been left largely untouched since colonial times. Long oaken tables with benches to match, made by the early settlers back in the seventeenth century, occupied most of the dining room where costumed waiters who, to Andrew's eyes, might have come straight from a lonely conventicle in the hills surprised by Claverhouse and his dragoons, trod the well-worn floor planks. Andrew assumed these were properly nailed to the joists although, to the casual observer, they appeared to run up hill and down and, by no stretch of the imagination could be considered level.

They had a fish soup, thick and creamy, full of clams and onions and diced potato, made to a popular New England recipe and almost a meal in itself had Andrew not been surprisingly hungry. For the main course there was baked ham, skinned and scored and rubbed all over with mustard and sugar, into which cloves had been stuck like pins into a cushion. It was served with succotash – Vic said it was an old Indian dish – a concoction that combined what he called Lima beans with kernels of maize. It all tasted quite delicious and Andrew had little room left for dessert – a delightful mixture of apples and cider and cream. The meal was washed down with some very tolerable *vin rouge de Bordeaux* and, while they smoked their after dinner cigars, they sipped bumper measures of an Armagnac which, after some deliberation and *tête-à-tête* with the waiter, Vic had ordered with considerable flourish.

When, in the cool of the evening, they took leave of one another on the steps of the hotel, Andrew felt he had known Vic for a very long time. One thing was certain, and that was that he now had one very good friend here in America. Throughout the meal the conversation had ranged far and wide and Andrew had succeeded in drawing Vic out, especially as regards the kind of conditions he might expect to find in the devastated south.

"If there is one piece of advice I would give you beyond all others," Vic had said, cradling his brandy glass in both hands, "I guess it is this. If you see there is no way in which your debtor is likely to be able to raise ready cash, look for collateral of some sort to secure the debt. And – looking to the way interest rates have moved in this country – the best collateral you are likely to find might take the form of real estate or at least a mortgage over land or property. Provided you check out that your man is likely to be able to meet the interest payments, you can sit back in bonnie Scotland and watch the dollars roll in!"

"But how can I – a foreigner, a stranger in your country – know whether or not some trader in, say, South Carolina would be good for his commitments? And how could I be expected to know anything about property values?"

"Gee! I don't know! You are the banker, are you not? Me! I'm just a simple guy, practising law!"

"Well of course, at home I would rely on a banker's opinion as to a man's worth and I should probably ask him – or a local lawyer – regarding property values."

"Then, why not here?"

"I don't know any bankers."

"But I do! At least, I have a sound banker here in Philadelphia who knows his fellows up and down the land. And he knows which of them can be trusted and which to avoid like the plague for you see, Andrew, some of these country bankers are very small – very small indeed – and much under-capitalised. No! All you have to do is find out the name of the banker and let me know. I'll do the rest and pass back to you an opinion upon which you may stake your life!"

Andrew stayed in Philadelphia for several days. He had himself measured for a lightweight linen suit which turned out perfectly at first fitting – and he saw the sights. He visited Independence Hall and saw the famed liberty bell that was rung when the great "Declaration" was signed; then, in the hot sunshine, he walked back along Walnut and up Second Street as far as Christ Church where he stood in the old burial ground by the grave of Benjamin Franklin. He also set aside a considerable amount of his time in writing – in the comparative coolness of his hotel room – the first letters home since his arrival in America.

To Vicky, he sent his love and affection and the assurance of how greatly he was missing her. But even as the words flowed on to the paper from his pen he found himself assailed with more doubts than he had ever previously experienced. The truth was that he had not really missed Vicky at all. In fact, he had scarcely thought of her since leaving Liverpool, whereas he had often and often longed to see his mother and family at Pitbuddo and his companions and associates at the Baltic Mill.

To Jessie, he wrote enthusiastically regarding all his experiences both on the voyage over the Atlantic and now here in the United States. As in his letter to Vicky, he glossed over the affair with the *Shenandoah*. No doubt the story would eventually be headlined in the British press but meantime Andrew wrote merely that *City of Baltimore* had been taken by a Confederate privateer and that they had been landed at an obscure fishing port in Delaware. She would, he thought, like it here in Philadelphia, although she might find the heat trying and the food – he described in some detail the meal he had eaten at the City Tavern – unusual.

To Jemima, he described the city itself; the shady streets, all laid out on a gridiron pattern and not running higgledy piggledy like the streets of a Scottish burgh town, and all with peculiar names – those going north-south numbered consecutively from the Delaware River westwards and those running east-west named, many of them, after forest trees such as pine, spruce, locust, walnut, chestnut, filbert. He told her about Independence Hall, its red brick glowing as if newly laid, although put down 120 years earlier. Built to act as the colonial capital of Pennsylvania, it was now a national shrine since it was here the Continental Congress met to ratify the Articles of Confederation, to commission the Virginian planter, George Washington, as commander-in-chief and to sign, first, the Declaration of Independence and then, the Constitution of the United States. Andrew knew how Jemima would adore the romance of it all and he did his utmost to embellish the story as best he could. He wrote also of his visit to Christ Church which – "would you believe it, was founded in the same year as the Bank of Scotland!"

To Meg, he was more forthcoming regarding the act of piracy which had cost the Merediths and the others in the lost boat their lives. He knew that, although Meg loved to gossip, the full story of his adventures following the encounter with the *Shenandoah* was safe in her keeping and might help her calm his mother's natural anxiety when the story, which would no doubt be blown up as to be almost unrecognisable, should appear in the papers at home.

Lastly, he wrote a business-like letter to Henry Caldwell advising him of the sinking of *City of Baltimore* and his subsequent journey to Philadelphia, telling him of the arrangements he had made for his mail to be forwarded to him by Isaacs & Zoller and for the vetting of their debtors through the good offices of Vic. Very shortly, he wrote, he would be leaving for Richmond and he would write further after he got there.

When the morning of his departure came, Andrew settled his bill at the Keystone, where the bellman hailed a cab that drove him along Market Street, over the busy intersection with Broad Street and westwards across the bridge spanning the Schuylkill, Philadelphia's other and smaller river, to the 30th Street railroad depot. There, he boarded the train for Washington that pulled out promptly at ten o'clock. The journey was uneventful. As far as Wilmington, it was familiar territory for Andrew, since it was a question of retracing by land, the journey he had previously made when sailing up the Delaware from Port Mahon. Thereafter it had been all new ground – first the Maryland state line and then the train rumbling slowly across the long long bridge over the wide flood of the Susquehanna. It was slow going again over the multiplicity of points at the huge marshalling yards of Baltimore and it was after two in the afternoon before the train pulled in to Washington.

The Richmond train was scheduled to depart at two-thirty and, although there was sufficient time to make the connection, there was little to spare. As the train jolted out over the Potomac and into Virginia, Andrew could see, across the river, the huge marble dome of the capitol building and he marvelled as many have done before and since at the proximity of the Federal capital to that which, until recently, had been enemy soil. Somehow, it made it easier to understand how, at an early stage in the war, so many of the citizens of Washington – gentlemen and their ladies, their innocent belief in the invincibility of the Federal forces not yet shattered – had driven out from their Georgetown homes to view, from their carriages, the war at first hand. The occasion was that of the first battle at Manassas Junction in July 1861. True – the viewing had turned sour on them in mid-afternoon when their troops under Irwin McDowell, mistaking the Confederate reinforcements for their own, subsequently panicked and fled, leaving the little creek of Bull Run strewn with their dead, their wounded, their arms, ammunition and baggage. It was incredible to think that all this had taken place only four short years ago.

Although Andrew did not quite know what he expected to see here in the south, there was little – to outward appearances at least – to distinguish the Virginian countryside from that he had earlier seen in Delaware and Maryland. For mile after mile there was little to be seen on either side of the tracks but scrub with, here and there, a muddy creek crossed by a trestle bridge. Occasionally, the scrubby woodland thinned out to reveal farms, grazing cattle, homesteads and barns very similar to those he had first seen in rural Delaware. If Andrew had expected to see a vast acreage devoted to the cultivation of the famous Virginian tobacco, he was doomed to disappointment. In fact, from what he could see of rural Virginia, it might just as readily have been Strathmore under a hotter sun and a bluer sky. It was a different story, however, when the train reached Fredericksburg, fifty miles or so from Washington.

Here, the scars of war were all too apparent, as well they might be looking to the number of times the Federal army had attempted to force the heavily defended Rappahannock river. Fredericksburg itself had been destroyed in the fighting of December 1862; four months later it was the turn of Chancellorsville, a few miles to the west; and, in the summer of 1864, just over a year ago, great and bloody battles had been fought at Wilderness, some eighteen miles to the west, and at the courthouse of Spotsylvania ten miles or so to the south.

It was much the same at Richmond. The capital of the Confederacy had held out until the end and had not, in fact, been evacuated until the beginning of April – just four months previously. As the evacuation proceeded and the Federal troops under General Ulysses S. Grant marched in, a severe fire broke out and almost razed the city to the ground. The area round the rail depot had been particularly seriously damaged and, although much of the rubble had been cleared away, the scene was still largely one of devastation with wooden sheds and shanties of every description acting as temporary housing, offices, and stores.

Descending from the train, Andrew picked his way across the tracks to what looked as if, before the fire, might have been the carriage entrance. There were a number of carriages to be seen with carts of every description.

"Y'all lookin' for a cab?" The voice brought back vivid memories but, on this occasion the speaker was no privateer skipper, nor any sort of officer for that matter. Andrew saw a small, snub-nosed man with matted sandy hair and a straggly wisp of beard. He had shifty eyes that seemed to dart in every direction.

"Over there!" The man pointed to Andrew's left where about a dozen negroes, who clearly had nothing better to do, were lounging against a low wall. As Andrew turned to look, he felt – too late – the man's hand at his breast pocket. In the same instant, there was a sharp pain in his right wrist and a wrenching sensation as his valise was torn from his grasp. Before Andrew quite realised what was happening, the man, stuffing Andrew's wallet into his pocket and clutching the stolen case in his other hand, ducked under the tail-board of the nearest cart and vanished from sight.

Out of the corner of his eye, Andrew saw one of the negroes – a tall fellow, he must have been seven feet if he was an inch, and built to match – detach himself from the group at the wall and take to his heels in pursuit of the thief who was dodging in and out of the traffic as he made off across the square. Andrew roused himself.

"Thief!" he bellowed, "stop thief!" He too made off in the same direction.

The negro was fast, and with his easy loping stride, he rapidly gained on the other. Andrew, puffing somewhat as the heavy meals he had eaten in Philadelphia, coming on top of the restriction of shipboard, took their toll, was left a good way behind. He was conscious that few people seemed to be taking any notice of their little drama. The truth was that most of the citizens of Richmond had seen far too much in the past five years to pay any attention to a petty thief making off with a careless traveller's bag. He was probably a goddam Yankee anyway and already they were growing to detest the sight of strangers, most of whom turned out to be carpet-baggers or other unwanted visitors.

Andrew saw that the chase had turned into a street running at right angles to the one he was in. As he rounded the corner, he still had the two men in sight, the negro now right at the other man's back. Just then, Andrew heard the sound of two shots and he saw both the thief and the negro pitch forward on their faces. When, panting with the heat and the exertion, he at last drew level, the two men – the puny white one and the tall muscular negro – were still lying where they had fallen. By their heads, pools of blood were spreading over the side-walk and into the gutter. Bending over them, a smoking Colt revolver in his right hand, was a heavily bearded man in a blue uniform. With his free hand he tipped his peaked cap to the back of his head and kicked Andrew's valise with his toe.

"This yours, mister?" he asked, pushing his gun into the holster at his belt.

"Yes, it is," said Andrew, swallowing hard. "He took my wallet as well – but – surely you've shot him! He's hurt! And so is the other fellow who was trying to catch him!"

The man bent forward again and jerked loose Andrew's wallet from the thief's dirty jerkin.

"This it?"

"Yes" Andrew took the wallet and returned it to his inside pocket.

"Good! I guess you could say they're hurt." He laughed, "Man! they're dead, both of them – they won't go troublin' no-one again!"

Andrew paled under his suntan.

"You take what's yours, mister, and keep goin'. They're only scum!" He placed a toe under the thief's side and rolled him over on to his back. The sightless eyes stared horribly and seemed to bore right into Andrew's. "White trash!" The man spat noisily. "And this – " he poked at the negro's buttocks with his boot " – means one good for nothing nigger less!"

"He was trying to help me!" Andrew's indignation was mounting and he had difficulty in controlling his temper. "Anyway – I thought you fought a war to set them free!"

By this time, a crowd of onlookers had gathered. There was some angry muttering, and Andrew heard more than one voice growling, "nigger lover!" in menacing tones. It was not difficult to reach a decision as to his next move. He picked up his valise, turned on his heel and marched back the way he had come. To his immense relief the ring of onlookers parted to let him pass. Up at the intersection, he hailed a passing cab and, once he was safely ensconsed in the last available room at the Belle Isle Hotel, he did not venture abroad again that night.

In the morning, his first port of call was a large wooden shed on 9th Street being utilised as temporary office accommodation by Underwood, Ward & Langley. In a little room, not much bigger than an average-sized coal cellar, he was interviewed by two of the partners who introduced themselves as Paul Underwood and John J. Langley. They were pleased that R. J. Caldwell & Son had taken note of what they had written in their circular letter. So far, Caldwells were the first of their British customers to send over a representative. Admittedly, Caldwells had more to lose than most – nevertheless they deemed it highly commendable that someone should have taken the trouble to come all the way to Richmond – and at such a difficult time. They sympathised with Andrew over his experience on leaving the railroad depot. Alas! This was all that could be expected when the people of this proud state, and indeed of all the south, had to suffer the indignity of occupation by Federal troops. Most of these behaved correctly, of course, but there were bad apples in every barrel.

"You see, Mr. Gray," John Langley, a dapper little man and a Virginian through and through – his middle name was Jefferson – warmed to his theme, "the black man in the south is worse off now than ever he was in the bad old days of slavery!"

"But – " Andrew demurred." – Surely there has been considerable restoration of basic human rights?"

"Yes – if you care to put it that way. But, I wonder. Who do you think had the most dignity? One of those guys you saw hanging about the railroad depot or a trusted servant in the old days? O.K.! Those blacks at the depot are free men whereas the old servant would be a slave owned by his master; but – believe me, Mr. Gray – he was his own man in every other aspect and, as near as makes no odds, a member of the family!"

"John's right!" Paul Underwood entered the conversation for the first time. Paul was the junior partner, his grandfather having started the business back at the turn of the century. "Freedom is all very well but no-one was prepared for it – least of all, the blacks. Now official Washington policy seems to do nothing but seek their glorification. That's what sticks in everyone's gullet and gives some folk – especially the poor whites – an excuse to go the other way and indulge in a spot of nigger baiting."

"What about the big owners – the plantation bosses?"

"Well, Mr.Gray, that's something else!" said Langley. "You'll find that the plantation owners, the professional men, all of us whom you might class as the southern 'establishment', are still in a state of shock, not only at having lost the war but also by reason of the fact that our slaves, many of them trusted companions since our childhood days, folk whom we regarded as affectionate and loyal members of the household, nearly all ran away when the end came."

"Yeah!" Paul Underwood nodded vigorously; "some ran towards the Yankee soldiers; some fled before them, but – they ran away! It was their 'Day of Jubilee' and those who desperately wanted to stay behind – and this applied to the great majority, for only a few had bad masters – even they left. Why? Well – a lot of them, when asked, said the same thing.

"'Why we goin'? Well! If we don't leave now, how we ever goin' to know that we're free!'

"Then, Mr.Gray, on the heels of the decamping purposeless slaves, what did we get? Why! We got these goddam Yankee missionaries who compounded our problems, immense as they are in every field, social, economic and humane!"

After all that, Andrew felt he had best not muddy the waters any further so he refrained from making any mention of his brush with Captain Waddell and the *Shenandoah*

Once they got down to business, John Langley produced a list of the customers to whom they had onsold goods imported from Caldwells. Unfortunately, these were many rather than few and they were widespread geographically. Although the amount outstanding averaged out fairly evenly across the board, there were two relatively large sums due – one by a firm in Tennessee and another, which was by far the biggest, by a concern in Austin, Texas, which rejoiced under the name of "Lone Star Trading Post". Having expressed his thanks Andrew bore the list back to his hotel room and, with his American atlas open before him on the table, he went over it in detail, memorising as much as he could and mapping out the best route to follow.

Before leaving Richmond, Andrew obtained from Underwoods, firstly, letters of introduction to all the customers concerned and, secondly, assignations of all the debts in favour of R. J. Caldwell & Son. This had taken some time since preparation of the necessary deeds necessitated involving Underwood's lawyers who, like every law firm in town, were already inundated with work. While he waited with some impatience, he wrote to Vic Zoller, as a result of which he received, a few days later, a note authenticated by Vic's bankers in Philadelphia, naming the banks of known integrity and strength in the towns and cities which Andrew had listed. Accordingly, it was well into August before Andrew was able to turn his back upon the once proud capital of the Confederacy where the human dregs of war roamed aimlessly among the charred timbers, ruined masonry, and burnt-out buildings.

In the ensuing weeks Andrew travelled all over the south, or so it seemed, sitting in trains, sailing in river boats, jolting along in coaches over poorly surfaced, dusty, country roads and riding horse after horse until he was saddle sore and infinitely weary. Many a time did he have occasion to think of Mary Grant and Dulsie, and bless her for passing on to him a modicum of her equestrian skill. Without such a grounding he would have been absolutely stuck in this country where coaching services rarely extended beyond the principal arterial turnpikes and where minor roads were frequently little better than tracks following the old winding Indian trails.

He found he was thinking a great deal about Mary these days; and over and over again, it occurred to him that he had never been truly happy since she had gone out of his life, and he out of hers. He often wondered whether she was truly happy with her lawyer husband. No doubt she was; and no doubt she would now be surrounded by a brood of children. If so, she would no longer have much time for riding. She would miss that – for she had never been happier than when setting Dulsie at a fence or wall, or when careering along at a full gallop, her long hair streaming out behind her like a pennant.

It was mid-September when Andrew reached Atlanta and he stayed in the city only long enough to collect a bill at three months currency in payment of a debt due by a firm of sack manufacturers. The "approved" banker pronounced them good for such an acceptance; consequently, Andrew lodged the bill with them and thankfully moved up state towards the blue haze of the southern Appalachians and the Tennessee border. The old Indian trails converged here at Chattanooga where the Tennessee River bends under the immense escarpment of Look-out Mountain. And at Chattanooga, Andrew picked up letters from home sent on from Isaacs & Zoller in Philadelphia in response to a note he had despatched to them some ten days earlier.

He opened Henry Caldwell's letter first, a concise, business-like epistle commenting, in the first place, upon the *Shenandoah* affair, news of which had appeared in the press early in August. Now he had noticed a report in the *Scotsman* and in the *Advertiser* to the effect that the Foreign Secretary, Earl Russell, was proposing to the Americans that a commission be set up to deal with claims for reparation respecting the Confederate privateer, *Alabama*, which had been sunk off Cherbourg in June of the previous year by the United States corvette *Kearsage*. If successful, it would no doubt also attend to claims in respect of the other privateers, including the *Shenandoah*.

Business at home was, he wrote, good and, with buoyant markets and a full order book, the Baltic Mill was working to capacity, although the strain upon working capital – eaten into as it was by reason of non-payment of the American debt – was making Charlie Tait's life a misery. Nevertheless, they had received only the previous day the first remittance from Isaacs & Zoller, and Henry Caldwell was fulsome in his praise for the good work Andrew was so obviously doing in trying and difficult circumstances. Henry Caldwell did not say how much had been remitted but, considering the relatively small total received by way of cash or sight drafts, Andrew felt it could not have been very substantial. Once the earlier bills should mature in November, however, it would be a very different story. He laughed to himself as he thought of the eulogy this could be calculated to produce.

The smile faded from his face, however, as he read on. Henry Caldwell, as was ever his wont, never mixed business and personal matters. On this occasion, his personal note was brief and succinct. It contained the sad news of the sudden death, in the last week of August, of Miss Farmiloe. They missed her deeply and her passing was very sincerely mourned. Vicky, poor girl, had been quite desolate and indeed had, herself, been quite ill ever since.

Desolate or not, ill or recovered, Vicky had found the strength to pen Andrew a few lines on paper framed with a thick edging of black. He could not *imagine*, she wrote, how deeply this sad news had affected her. As he knew she was of a *delicate* constitution and she had so loved her aunt. It had all been too much for her and she had taken to her own bed as she felt *quite quite* ill. When was Andrew coming home? His place was beside his wife – especially as she was ailing so badly – and not far away in America, gadding about all over the place. She quite omitted to ask whether Andrew himself was well: nor did she remember to send her love or marital greetings.

There was only one letter from Pitbuddo, from Meg, who was pregnant again but cheerful as ever. All in the family were fit and well and, as always, sent their love.

The second largest of the debts on Andrew's list was due by a firm called "Racoon Mountain Depot" – R.M.D. for short – who had an address in Main Street, Chattanooga. They had no ready cash, nor were they in any position to accept a bill or even a meaningful series of bills. This was a case where Vic Zoller's advice could be put to the test. Andrew demanded collateral. At first, the R.M.D. spokesman professed that this was impossible but, after some legal pressure, an offer was made of a mortgage, to the extent of the debt, over real estate on Look-out Mountain. The valuation, confirmed by the Bank, was several times greater than required. The mortgage would carry interest at the current rate which, unbelievably to Andrew's ears, stood at eighteen per cent. This would be paid half yearly, the firm's ability to do so being covered by a good and dependable bankers' opinion. It seemed too good to be true – a very worthwhile investment indeed. Andrew had the mortgage and accompanying Title Deeds copied and certified by an Attorney at law. He lodged the copies with the bank in Chattanooga and sent the originals through the mail to Vic Zoller in Philadelphia.

Unlike Richmond and Atlanta, Chattanooga had had time to recover; for it was as early as the fall of 1863 that Sherman had passed this way, defeating the Confederates up on the mountain at what had become known as the Battle above the Clouds. Consequently, Andrew was in no hurry to move on and he spent the best part of a day inspecting the property he had taken in security. A marvellous swathe of land it was, high on the terraced slopes of the mountain and containing three fine houses and a number of smaller properties.

From Chattanooga, Andrew moved on to Memphis, where he crossed the mighty Mississippi and headed west into the state of Arkansas.

Over a thousand miles south-west of Richmond, on the edge of the untamed wilderness, the flag of the United States of America flapped sluggishly in the October breeze from the tower of the military outpost of Fort Smith. Andrew had ridden up from Little Rock following the course of the Arkansas River as it wound its way down from the hills – on one side the deep pine forests of the Ouachitas and, on the other, the bluffs and stark scenic beauty of the Ozarks where all the trees wore the brilliantly coloured mantle of the fall. Here, at Fort Smith, Andrew felt he was indeed at the very limits of civilisation; for beyond, lay wild and largely untamed country whose very name, Oklahoma, is a Choctaw Indian one meaning "red people".

And Indian country it was in very truth, for it was to this "Ultima Thule" that the tribes from the eastern forests – Cherokee, Choctaw, Creek, Chickasaw and Seminole – came after the Indian-hating President, Andrew Jackson, had them banished west of the Mississippi, upon that which became known as the "trail of tears". Nor did they have much peace once they attained journey's end, for westwards, beyond the Arkansas River, were the endless plains stretching out towards the Rockies nearly nine hundred miles away; and there, following the wandering herds of bison, roamed other tribes but, unlike those from the Appalachian valleys, the plains Indians were savage and bloodthirsty. By and large however, with the exception of tough hardy frontiersmen, a few intrepid settlers and the ultimate outpost of the United States at Fort Gibson – a few miles west of the Cherokee capital, Tahlequah – the red man had Oklahoma to himself.

Fort Smith was a typical town of the western frontier, brash and rowdy, centred upon the military post on the far side of the river. In Fort Smith as in many similar locations throughout the west, the law, or what passed for the law, was maintained by the power of the gun. Andrew had been warned of this by the banker he had dealt with in Little Rock. It was power, so the banker said, that owed its being to what he called an unholy trinity.

"Why!" he said when asked for an explanation, "I guess that first and foremost, it is the long established practice – no, right – of the frontiersman to carry a gun. It was a vital necessity to protect himself and his family from wild animals and Indians, and to bring down game for the pot. Secondly, you can blame the war. War cheapens life – if you don't believe me, you've only got to look around and see what goes on!" Andrew nodded agreement. "Moreover," the banker went on. "The ebbing tide of war has left behind a kind of human flotsam – homeless, broken men who see in the west a land unconstrained by established behavioural conventions where they can give full rein to their disillusionment and despair!"

"And the third factor?" Andrew had asked.

"Well now! The third and last is probably the most significant of all. I guess you can define it in three words – Colonel Sam's revolver!"

Andrew smiled grimly. The revolving pistol, invented some ten years prior to the war by Colonel Samuel Colt of the United States army, had created a revolution in small arms and, in Britain, had led to the establishment in 1855 of the armament factory at Enfield in Middlesex.

The memory of this conversation came back to Andrew as he looked out from his hotel window overlooking the courthouse square. From what he had heard from his banker friend in Little Rock, this name was most probably more than a trifle euphemistic. He suspected that the justiciary was not particularly learned and that wrong doers and miscreants – and many an innocent man as well – who escaped the bullet, or the lynch mob, lived only to find themselves condemned by a hastily convened, and short in the law, court and hanged anyway. Andrew had no illusions as to the stark reality of life – and death – here on the frontier in this year of grace 1865.

The tinkling of a badly tuned piano drifted up to him from the saloon below and vied with the metallic clanging of the blacksmith's hammer from the livery stable further down the dusty street. Having tidied himself up, Andrew went downstairs. Although it was still early in the evening, the saloon was busy. There was a number of men at the bar and at least two tables where a poker game was in progress. The bartender nodded to Andrew and placed a glass and bottle of Bourbon beside him. Andrew poured himself a measure and engaged the man in small talk until he was called away to deal with two newcomers who had just come in through the swing doors.

"Y'all English or something?"

Andrew looked round. The speaker was an elderly man who bore a startling resemblance to the Reverend Mr. Black back home in Pitbuddo and it was as much as Andrew could do to refrain from laughing out loud at the thought of that narrow and perjink old Presbyterian frequenting any bar, far less this saloon up on the American frontier.

"Something!" Andrew replied.

"Gee! I thought so: where y'all from?"

"Scotland!"

"Scotland! Gee! I gotten a far-out cousin over there; guy called McGregor – Ewan McGregor – lives in a town call Glass-gow; d'y'all know him?"

Andrew had to admit he did not.

"What y'all doin' here?"

"Well!" said Andrew, "I've been visiting a few southern cities where I have a bit of business to transact."

"You don't sound like it but – you a salesman or something?"

"You could call it that: last call at Little Rock, next in Austin, Texas."

"You ain't aimin' to go all the way to Texas from here?" ·

"Why not? From the map, it seems I'm going in the right direction."

"Oh mister! You don't want to even think of doin' that! No sir! That's Injun country out there in Oklahoma Territory. You'd end up with a tomahawk in your neck and scalping knife at your head. Look, mister! That's the wilderness out there and no goddam American would be crazy enough to go out there alone unless he had been raised on the frontier, Even then he might think twice about it – 'specially seein' the winter's comin' on! Jesus! If they wouldn't do it, what chance for you, mister, a bloody limey! Now! Y'all go back east – d'you hear me – back to Memphis. Get a river boat down to New Orleans. There's plenty coastal streamers there'll take you on to Texas."

The Reverend Mr. Black's double stopped for breath. He looked closely at Andrew.

"You got your mind made up – haven't you?"

"Yes: I suppose I have," said Andrew slowly. He had not really thought about it before but perhaps the old fellow was right. Maybe he was crazy to contemplate venturing into the wilderness on the threshold of winter – but he had come thus far and it would be losing faith in himself were he to turn back now! Mr. Black's double sighed.

"You're crazy, man! But – if you're real set on it – you're sure goin' to need a guide and a good one at that!"

"Where might that be found?"

"Well I reckon you might find what you are looking for right here in this saloon – only, he ain't sober right now, nor is he likely to be for a couple of days yet! Yessir! If you're lookin' for a guide, you're never likely to find a better one than Zeke Harrison. Why! Zeke's been around the frontier ever since he was a kid. He was a Confederate Army scout during the war and knows the country better'n the back of his hand. There's no better shot with a rifle from here to the Texas pan-handle and, what's more, Zeke has a way with the Injuns. He married one – leastways she's more a Cherokee than a white woman. If anyone can survive out there among the Injuns and all the creatures of the wilderness – cats and bears and rattlers – Zeke can, when he's sober which, as I've said before, he ain't right now!"

Andrew was intrigued. He refilled his glass and that of the man at his side.

"Which?" he asked. "Which is Zeke?"

"Why! That's him! Leaning against the bar beside the guy with the cigar!" He indicated the couple that had come in while Andrew had been talking to the bartender. Andrew had a closer look. He saw a man of about his own height and build, a shade older, probably rising forty, dressed in a checked shirt and buckskin trousers. Under a mop of fair curly hair, his forehead was deeply tanned, as were his hands and also his face, or what could be seen of it under an immense growth of whiskers and beard. His blue eyes had a glazed look to them. As the man said, he was certainly not stone cold sober. Even as Andrew watched, he and his companion, a small stout elderly man, picked up their glasses and a bottle and, walking somewhat determinedly, they made their way to a couple of vacant seats at a table set near the far end of the bar.

"Reckon Zeke'll be here all night!" Andrew's new-found friend and fount of all wisdom looked with pained expression at his empty glass. Andrew filled it and pushed the bottle from him.

"Does he live here?" he asked.

"Zeke! No way! He don't live nowhere, mister! They say he's gotten himself a cabin down in Texas but he ain't never there! Spends his time huntin' and doin' odd scoutin' jobs when he can get them – and most all of the time that Injun wife of his goes along too!"

"Is she here in Fort Smith?"

"No! Reckon he'll have left her back with her own people in Tahlequah. He's here to sell skins or something – and for a blow out. He'll not touch a drop of liquor for months on end and then, when he hits town – wow! Where y'all stayin', man!''

"Me? Right here in this hotel!''

"Well! Dang me if I won't bring Zeke to see you once he's slept this off. Reckon you and Zeke will get on together – just fine!''

4. United States
1865-1866

Zeke Harrison, frontiersman, hunter, scout and guide, was a man inured to the west; a man rugged as the bluffs and scarps of the Ozarks Andrew had glimpsed on his way up through Arkansas. He had spent the greater part of his life on the frontier where survival depended so strongly upon a number of inter-related factors – knowledge of the wild, and of the Indians whose hunting ground it was, skill in tracking and in hunting, a keen eye, a steady hand and a quick draw with both rifle and gun.

Although a shade sceptical about Andrew's fitness for the journey he had in mind, Zeke liked this young man from Scotland and, after only brief hesitation, he had decided to accept the commission. Never before had he been asked to accompany anyone who was such a greenhorn. For instance, he had never held a gun in his hand and he barely knew one end of a rifle from the other. Nevertheless, he had an honest face, a direct gaze and was tall and well built. No doubt he would give a good account of himself if the chips were down.

And his money was good. Zeke had checked this out with the local banker as Andrew had suggested he might. He would be able to pay all right once they got him to Austin. Anyway, Zeke had had his blow out and could not afford to remain anything but sober until such time as he should be in the money again.

"You got yourself a guide, mister!" he said, shaking hands with his prospective employer, "But first, we gotta pick up my li'l 'Gail. Guess she knows better'n to ride into town with me: stopped up among the Cherokees at Tahlequah while I came down to hit the liquor! But she goes everywhere with me – you understand, mister? Engage Zeke, and you engage 'Gail Harrison as well!"

Before leaving town, Andrew was taken to the gunsmith's store where, after thorough inspection and examination of the merchandise on display, Zeke finally selected a long-barrelled rifle with a stock of wavy grained maple, smooth as a pebble out of a creek. He hefted it in one hand and balanced it, assessing it carefully for the beautifully proportioned weapon it was. Unlike many the gunsmith had on offer – early breech loading, bolt action German rifles by Dreyse, such as were introduced into the Prussian army some twenty years or so previously, French carbines and British rifle muskets similar to those that had seen service in the Crimea – the rifle picked out by Zeke was not imported but home produced by Spencer, a lovely, modern, magazine repeater. He pulled back the bolt, ensured that both breech and magazine were empty, and pushed it forward again.

"Here!" he cried, tossing the rifle to Andrew, who was just quick enough to catch it. "Try that!"

Andrew lifted the weapon to the firing position. The stock was smooth as silk against his right cheek, the weight perfectly balanced in his arms. He squinted along the barrel, aligning the sights and he moved the little knurled screw that adjusted the rearmost to take account of the range. He curled his forefinger round the trigger, squeezed gently as Zeke instructed, and heard the spring-loaded firing pin shoot forward with a sharp "click".

"That," said Zeke, "is one hell of a good gun – take it!"

With the rifle now in the saddle holster at his side, his blanket roll behind him, and his valise strapped to the back of the mule plodding along on a leading rein immediately at the back of Zeke's tall black stallion, they set out from Fort Smith on a dull grey day – not unlike many a November one Andrew had known in the past. Andrew rode a big chestnut gelding with a white star on his forehead and this too had been selected for him by Zeke – again after much deliberation and many derogatory remarks about the general standard of horses available at livery stables. According to Zeke, who had looked closely into the poor beast's mouth and ears, and had run knowing fingers about its forelegs and hocks, the chestnut was sound in wind and limb, which was more than could be said for the rest of the collection that, in his opinion, were nothing better than a bunch of old mustangs.

They crossed the Arkansas River and headed north through hilly country where settler's cabins were few and far between. At noon, they passed through the pioneer settlement of Stillwell beyond which they met with no further evidence of civilisation. It was as if the forest had completely swallowed them up. The trail they followed was that marking the end of the forced migration of the eastern tribes, a matter about which Zeke – as he told Andrew – held strong views.

"Man!" he said, "it kinda makes a guy mad to think how Jackson treated the Cherokee, after one o' them savin' his life and all at Horseshoe Bend. You know, my li'l 'Gail' s three parts Injun. Her ma's grandpappy was the chief Yonaguska – Drowning Bear. I guess he spent most of his life doin' his darndest to keep his people back where they belonged in North Carolina. Didn't do him much good neither! By the time he died, up there in the Smokies, there were only a few score Cherokee left hiding up in the mountains with him. Yes sir! He was some guy, old Drowning Bear. Can't say I would have cared for him though!" He shook his head.

"Why not?" asked Andrew.

"Why? He outlawed whiskey – that's why! Right across the Cherokee nation; and if some poor guy disobeyed and was caught, old Drowning Bear had him bound to a whipping post and flogged!"

"So Drowning Bear never moved west. What about his family?"

"Seems they were rounded up with the rest. 'Gail's ma was born along the trail on the very day the old chief White Path died – somewhere in Kentucky I guess, just short of the Ohio."

"Gail's mother was born on the trail!"

"Sure was! Her ma was real tough: soon as the baby was born she had to get up and move on. They covered ten miles a day – no more, often less. Hundreds fell sick; hundreds lay dying; hundreds were already dead – they buried fourteen or fifteen at each night's halt."

"'The Trail of Tears'," said Andrew softly.

"Yeah! And they hadn't done nothin' to deserve it – 'cept being Injuns, poor devils!" Zeke shifted the quid of tobacco he was chewing from one side of his mouth to the other, and spat out a long stream of yellow nicotine juice. They fell silent and nothing broke the stillness but the creak of the saddle leather, the jingle of harness and the muted sound of the horses' hoofs as they picked their way along the woodland trail.

It was early evening when they entered the village. One minute they had been riding quietly through thickets of yellow locust and silver birch, interspersed with sourwood and sassafras – the next they were in the midst of a scatter of huts with the trees behind them. Many were the curious glances cast at Andrew, especially by the girls and younger squaws, but before he had even begun to get his bearings, there was a great shriek and a small woman came running, skirts flying and hair streaming out behind her.

Zeke, already on the ground, caught her in his arms, kissing her hair, her neck, her mouth. Abigail Harrison was a comely woman, a number of years younger than her husband. When she greeted Andrew she flashed a smile and her teeth gleamed white and even. It was a considerable while since Andrew had seen such an eminently attractive woman. Her mouth was small, her chin rounded and her eyes were green as the water of a mossy pool in some mountain creek. Only about the nose and the eyelids did she display any trace – and it was only a trace – of her Indian ancestry.

Walking between her husband and Andrew and holding each by the hand, she took them, as courtesy demanded, to meet chief Running Deer. The chief was in the Council House, a large hut of woven oak splints, seven sided to represent each of the individual clans. A ceremonial fire burned in the centre of the floor area, its smoke curling up to escape through a hole in the peak of the high conical roof. The door was wide and all three entered in line abreast. Once inside, Abigail halted and lowered her head. She spoke quietly, but as the language she used was that of the Cherokee, Andrew could understand nothing of what was said. The fire was burning low and the interior of the chamber was dark, doubly so to those coming in from the broad light of day. Once his eyes grew accustomed to the gloom, Andrew saw that the Council House was empty but for themselves and a number of people, probably not more than a dozen, who were seated on benches directly across from the door. These, he assumed, were the elders of the tribe and the one in the centre, who now appeared to be responding to whatever Abigail had to say, would no doubt be the chief, Running Deer. At all events, he was a very old man, gaunt and frail. A cape of feathers was slung around his thin bony shoulders and on his head he wore a skull cap decorated with plumes of what appeared to be woven horsehair. He raised his arm and, miraculously, his magnificent cape stayed in place.

"Chief Running Deer asks us to approach nearer where he can see us the better." As she spoke, Abigail unhanded the two men and, signing to them to accompany her, she moved round the Council House, keeping to the outside of the poles supporting the roof. There were seven in all and Andrew could see that from each one there hung a number of strange-looking artefacts – rattles made from long-stemmed gourds; and weird and wonderful head-dresses. They stopped some two paces away from the chief.

"The husband of this daughter of ours is ever welcome inTahlequah." Chief Running Deer, speaking slowly in English, inclined his head in Zeke's direction. Zeke looked the old man steadily in the eye and nodded. The chief went on.

"White stranger!" he acknowledged Andrew's presence. "This is the land the white man said would be ours. From our homes in the mountains where the sky, golden in the sunrise, bends down to touch the earth, he drove us here. At that time I was in the prime of life, even as you are now, and I suffered with my people wherever we spread our blankets on that terrible journey.

"Therefore, it is not pleasing in my sight to see one of your race ride into my village; for the red man knows to his cost that, where one white man goes, six will follow."

Out of the corner of his eye, Andrew saw that the Harrisons were looking at him. Clearly they expected him to speak – a task all the more difficult in the absence of a welcome.

"Chief Running Deer!" Andrew said, "I should be proud to be a guest in your village if you will have me. I do not think that six of my race will follow on my heels."

"You come as the friend of the white man who took our kinswoman for squaw; therefore, white stranger, you may remain here among us as guest. You say six will not follow," the chief's thin-lipped mouth curled in a sardonic grimace. "When I was a boy in the mountains, I heard a government soldier say much the same thing to my father's brother, Yonaguska. He did not believe him. 'I can remember,' said Yonaguska, 'when the white man had not seen the smoke of our cabins westward of the Blue Ridge. It is foolish in you to tell me that the white man will not trouble the poor Cherokee in western country and, as to his promises of protection, they have too often been broken; they are like the reeds in the river, they are all lies!'"

Andrew lowered his eyes and, as he did so, he heard Running Deer speak again – this time in Cherokee.

"It's the pipe," said Abigail. "He is about to pass the pipe round; we must all share in the smoking of it."

Running Deer, having made sure that the pipe was drawing cleanly, handed it to the elder at his side. His face inscrutable, the elder inhaled deeply of the tobacco smoke before passing the pipe to the next in line. When the last of the elders had blown out a long plume of smoke, he rose from his seat and handed the pipe to Zeke, who in turn passed it to Abigail, and she to Andrew. The smoke had an aromatic scent to it and was quite remarkably cool. Carefully, carrying the pipe as if it were the most delicate of instruments, Andrew stepped forward and returned it to the chief's safe keeping. Then he bowed, and returned to his place beside the Harrisons.

"Go in peace!" said Running Deer.

Outside the Council House, the light was positively blinding. Andrew was allocated a hut close by that to which Zeke was led by Abigail and, having deposited his gear upon the earthen floor, he went to see to the horses.

Andrew lay on a bed of buffalo skins spread out on the floor of beaten earth. There were no windows in the hut. Windows can let in the cold winter air as well as light, so it was dim inside and warm, very warm in comparison with the cool air of early November in the Oklahoma hill country, where chill mists hung over every lake, sending wisps to curl here, there and everywhere amid the trees. It was the trees which had supplied the material for the cabin and scores of others like it – roughly hewn logs of poplar or pine, notched at the corners and chinked with mud. A canopy supported on two poles formed a frontal continuation of the roof, which was steeply pitched and covered with overlapping shingles of white oak. The chimney was built against one of the gables. From the ground to beyond throat level, the stack was constructed of rocks from the creek and mud mortar after which the rest of the structure was of wooden slats chinked with clay.

Andrew felt comfortable and relaxed. Earlier, he had wakened feeling hot and clammy. It must have been just on day break for, nearby, a cockerel was serenading the morning. He had thrown off his blankets and dozed off again. Now he lay on his back listening to the sounds of morning in Tahlequah, the village founded quarter of a century previously by the sorry remnant who had survived the terrible "Trail of Tears". Andrew had been here for a week now and the sights and sounds were growing familiar although he did from time to time wonder what he, Andrew Gray, raised at Pitbuddo at the gates of the glens of Angus, was doing here in the American wilderness surrounded by a tribe of red Indians.

The horses were corralled in a makeshift stable close to the hut and Andrew could hear them now as he lay listening while the village stirred and folk set about their daily chores. It was high time he, too, was up and about. He pulled on his trousers and looked out the door. A scurrying of feet and a high-pitched giggle or two let him know that his awakening had not gone unobserved. It was a cold, grey morning and the sharp wind carried more than a hint of rain as it whipped the colour to his face. Outside the hut, a tub of water, newly drawn from the nearby creek, stood ready for his ablutions and the thought flashed through his mind that a bevy of Indian maidens was a very unusual form for Aquarius to take. Smiling to himself, he stripped off his shirt and splashed the ice cold water over his naked torso, an act greeted by a fresh burst of giggling from somewhere among the nearby trees. A vigorous towelling and he was ready to dress.

After he had seen to the horses, Andrew presented himself at the Harrisons' hut where the tantalising smell of frying bacon told him that Abigail had their breakfast well in hand. Andrew had been ravenous ever since setting foot in the wilderness and he ate all that was placed before him. This morning it was bacon and eggs with Indian bean bread, while to drink there was Indian tea – a somewhat scented black infusion made from the leaves of the yaupon, the wild holly. Abigail said that the yaupon, commonplace in the southern Appalachians, was not to be found so frequently here in Oklahoma, so the Cherokee had to obtain their supplies of the leaf from the trading post at Fort Gibson. Andrew rather wished it had proved unobtainable, but Zeke appeared to relish it and he belched loudly before handing his mug to Abigail to be refilled.

"Well!" said Andrew, "there will not be another breakfast like that for a while!"

"Sure won't!" agreed Zeke. "That's to say if we do hit the trail at sun-up tomorrow. Y'all still aimin' to go?"

"Yes!"

"Well! I guess that's O.K. by me. Reckon we've been here long enough!"

For the past two days they had had the company of Abigail's half brother, Lone Eagle, who had newly returned to the village after leading a scouting party deep into the wilderness. To the west of the Arkansas River, the character of the country – so Zeke said – began to change as the wooded hills and the lakes gradually gave way to rolling grassy wastes, the home of the bison herds and of the nomadic tribes who depended upon them to sustain the normal pattern of their lives. For the Cherokee – and for the other "civilised" tribes from the east – the savage Indians of the plains represented a danger, menacing and constant. Hence the need for regular reconnaissance, and Lone Eagle's patrol.

He had been out for the better part of six weeks, sweeping the vast territory between the Arkansas and Cimarron Rivers, and southwards to the Canadian River, and the broken country beyond as far as the Texas border. What he had to report was not altogether reassuring. The bison were on the move; and the tribes with them. Several bands of Comanche were out on the war path; and in the area south of the Canadian River, Lone Eagle and his braves had narrowly avoided a full scale raiding party of Arapaho. By no stretch of the imagination could this be considered other than bad news; for the route Zeke proposed to take passed directly that way.

On the other hand, Lone Eagle did not think this need concern them unduly for the Arapaho were very far to the east of their usual stamping ground and, from the look of them, Lone Eagle felt that they had been out for quite some time. No doubt they would be well on their way back to their home lodges. Nevertheless, Zeke, although he did not say so, remained a degree anxious. Clearly, more than ordinary care was needed.

On this their last night atTahlequah,the chief had commanded that the age-old Eagle Dance of the Cherokee should be performed in their honour on the sacred ground – in reality a dusty square – where all the great ceremonies and ritual were staged. The arena lit by torches flaring against the night sky, the gyrating dancers, and the incessant beat of rattle and water drum created a spectacle the like of which Andrew found beyond his wildest imaginings, and the excitement and thrill of which would remain with him for all time to come.

Zeke had said they must leave at dawn and Andrew was up and ready long before the first streamers of the new day had spread over the eastern sky. The Harrisons too were up betimes; the horses were saddled – Zeke's black stallion, Andrew's chestnut gelding and a lovely little grey mare called "Mist" who belonged to Abigail. The mule, rather more heavily laden than when Andrew and Zeke had ridden up from Fort Smith, hung its head in dejected fashion.

Lone Eagle came to bid them farewell.

"Running Deer bade me give you this, white man who is grey!" he said, smiling and handing Andrew a small leather bag. "Do not open it until you can no longer see the smoke of our cabins," he added as Andrew started to loosen the drawstring at the neck of the bag. "It is a gift which, when you return to your own land where the morning sun shoots up from the rim of the Great Water, will remind you, so Running Deer hopes, of the Cherokee nation that even yet may vanish from this land like spring snow in the sun. Go in peace, and may the white man's god go with you!''

Often before, Andrew had marvelled at how these people could suddenly disappear from view as if they were able to melt into the background. So it was now with Lone Eagle. Before Andrew, who was in any case taken aback, could muster a reply, Lone Eagle was gone. Out of courtesy, of course, Andrew, on the previous afternoon, had gone to pay his respects to Running Deer and bid him farewell. Running Deer had received him in his usual dignified fashion and had wished him well. It was strange he should now send Lone Eagle bearing a gift, but then – the ways of the red man and the white were seldom alike and, as a newcomer to this land, Andrew knew he had a long way to go before he even began to understand them.

"Let's go!" cried Zeke, urging the black stallion forward. The trailing rein in his left hand went taut and, with a jerk, the mule at its other end was dragged into a walk. Abigail flashed Andrew a smile and, together, they followed – Abigail dressed in a cut-down pair of Zeke's breeches, sitting astraddle on "Mist", the grey. Later that morning, they forded the wide and muddy Arkansas within sight of the United States soldiers on the walls of Fort Gibson. There appeared to be a ceremony of some sort going on in the fort for they could hear the sound of a military band and, in addition to the flag flapping lazily on its tall pole above the entrance gate, there was a profusion of banners in red, white and blue strung all around the walls.

"Listen!" said Andrew, "it's a church service." They stood the dripping horses on the far bank of the river and clearly from the fort about a quarter of a mile behind them they heard men's voices raised in Martin Rinkart's glorious hymn *"Nun danket alle Gott"*.

"Christ!" said Zeke, irreverently. "Wouldn't y'all know – it's Thanksgiving!"

"Ezekiel!" Abigail rounded upon him.

"Well! Isn't it, woman?"

"Yes," said Abigail, "I guess it must be so."

Andrew looked from one to the other. "Thanksgiving?" he asked.

"Yeah! I guess it goes back to the Pilgrim Fathers in Massachusetts giving thanks for their survival in the wilderness!"

"That's right!" Abigail nodded. "They say the first settlers shot down a turkey, and cooked it along with a stew of berries they found growing among the rocks – so nowadays, on Thanksgiving Day at the end of November, everyone eats turkey with cranberry sauce and follows it up with pumpkin pie and cream."

"Shut up, woman!" growled Zeke. "I'll be danged if I ain't hungry already!"

While they stood there, Andrew undid the string of the bag Lone Eagle had given him. Inside were two stones about the size of sparrow's eggs and roughly the same shape.

"Guess these'll look real pretty if you can get them polished up once you get back home." Abigail was most enthusiastic.

"What are they?" Andrew was puzzled.

"Why! – turquoise. They make real pretty jewels – sort of greenish blue. Many Indians have them."

"You must have gone down real big with Running Deer!" Zeke shook his head, "Ain't never happened to me!"

"You got me, didn't you?" Abigail snorted.

"Come on!" said Zeke. "We're wasting time – let's go!"

That night they camped on the edge of the trees and next day they were out on the rolling grasslands which seemed to stretch into the distance, limitless, immense and somewhat awe inspiring to one used to the confined landscape of Scotland. For four days they travelled without seeing any sign of human presence. At night, they camped wherever they could find shelter from the wind – in the lee of a rocky outcrop, under an isolated clump of bushes, anywhere that offered the merest hint of protection. The mesquite bushes were best, for their wood, when thrown on the fire, gave off a marvellous aromatic scent which, Zeke swore, kept the mosquitos off in summer time. One night it snowed and, when they awoke in the morning, they had to shake their blankets clear. They passed a number of rivers all flowing northwards to the Arkansas until, on the fifth day, they found themselves in broken hilly country which, according to Zeke, constituted the watershed between the Arkansas and Red River systems. The Texas border was not now so very far away. Once among the hills, Zeke exercised rather more caution than hitherto for, although they had seen no sign whatsoever of any Indians, he considered it much more likely that they could be surprised in this sort of country than on the relatively flat and open prairie. Late that afternoon they saw smoke coming from a fold of ground a mile or so distant over on their left flank.

"Reckon that must be the Donovans' place!" Zeke had been talking all day of the possibility of their reaching Joe Donovan's cabin before nightfall. Now, a wide grin spread over his rugged features, "There'll be a roof over your pretty head tonight, 'Gail my sweetheart!" he cried, "Here! Grab a hold of this goddam mule and let me go warn them that we're a'comin'!" He threw the mule's rein to Abigail who laughed and caught it, while Zeke cantered off up the hill towards the lip of the little valley.

Joe Donovan's cabin stood in a sheltered spot, in a lightly wooded depression close by a bubbling creek of pure spring water. Around it, he had carved out of the wilderness a small farm consisting of several fenced fields where he grew a few crops and grazed a small herd of longhorn cattle. As Andrew and Abigail rode down they could hear the distant barking of dogs and the faint sound of Zeke's voice which was probably raised in a mighty bellow. When they came closer they could see Zeke standing outside the cabin with a man and woman. A couple of dogs were prancing about their legs and three shy children were peeping round the cabin door.

Joe Donovan greeted them civilly. He was a man of indeterminate age but was, Andrew decided, considerably younger than he looked. Doubtless the harsh life of the frontier had taken its toll. His back was stooped from working in the fields and his hair and beard were snowy white: but his eyes were bright and alert and there was latent power in his broad shoulders and heavily muscled arms. Moira, his wife, was a raw-boned woman with a flat, expressionless face and straight black hair parted in the middle and plaited into a thick pigtail that hung down the back of her blue and white striped gingham dress as far as her waist. While the men talked, Moira Donovan, shooing the children away, led Abigail indoors. The middle child, a boy of about twelve, looked at Andrew curiously.

"Hello!" said Andrew. "What's your name?"

"Patrick," said the boy.

"Well, Patrick," said Andrew, "my name is Andrew and I am very pleased to meet you."

"We ain't used to strangers, mister," said the boy. "Where y'all from?"

"I'm from far away," said Andrew, "far away across the sea from a country called Scotland."

"Scotland? That's near Ireland, ain't it? My ma and pa were born in Ireland. I'd like to go there some day!"

"Do you go to school, Patrick?"

"No: ain't no school this side of the Red River. Ma and Pa teach us a bit but they ain't much good: not like real teachers, that is: they can't even read nor write: Pa says learnin' is of no account anyway out here in the wilderness. It ain't what a man knows that counts, it's what he does! D'you know how to look after cattle?"

"No," admitted Andrew, feeling rather inadequate. "I'm afraid not. How old are you, Patrick?"

"I dunno: I guess I'm older than my kid sister, Kathleen there –" he pointed to the smallest child, a little girl of about eight who was hanging on to Joe Donovan's legs and trying to hide herself behind him, " – And I'm a mite younger than Jessie. Pa says she's a woman grown."

Right enough, Andrew could see that the eldest of the family was no longer a child. She was standing in the cabin door watching Zeke in conversation with her father. She had her mother's featureless looks and dull expression and her dress was made of the same material as that of the older woman.

"My mother's name is Jessie," said Andrew, but Patrick was no longer listening nor interested. He had run off down to the creek and was wandering aimlessly along the bank, scattering a family of ducks that went squawking off into the water.

For all their isolation, the Donovans were hospitable enough and insisted that Zeke and Abigail should sleep in the small back room the children normally shared. They would sleep the night with their parents and Andrew could lay his blanket before the living room fire. That morning, Zeke had shot a young deer and, although Moira Donovan protested that she had plenty to offer them, Zeke managed to persuade her that a roast of venison would be just the very thing to feed a party such as she would have at her table that night and, this decided, the two women, aided by Jessie, got down to the matter of preparation.

The kitchen/living room was sparsely furnished. Apart from the plain wooden table, five chairs and a small dresser, there was nothing else in the room. Two rifles hung on pegs along one wall and above the fireplace there was a picture of the Madonna and child. In one corner, a wall cupboard provided the only storage accommodation for food and household effects. When, at last, the meal was ready, they all sat down by candlelight, the five adults on the chairs, and the children and Jessie sitting on the floor.

"Holy Mary, Mother of God – bless this food provided for us," said Joe: all the Donovans crossed themselves and the others bowed their heads in silence. The meat was succulent and surprisingly tender and to go with it there were freshly dug potatoes and wholesome cobs of home-grown, white Indian corn. And there was tea, real tea, black as coal and thick with tannin – much too strong for Andrew's taste. Joe Donovan spiked a potato on his fork and waved it in front of Andrew's nose.

"There now, young fellow," he said, "the potato! The cause of Moira and me being out here on the frontier and not back home in Ireland. Have you ever been in Ireland now?"

"Now Joe! Don't you be troubling our guest wit' your questions and him in the middle of eating!"

"Ach, woman! Am I not at my supper as well?"

"It's all right, Mistress Donovan," said Andrew, "I can do a bit of talking while I eat. Been in Ireland? No, I'm sorry, I have never been to Ireland – but I hope to go some day."

"Ah! 'Tis a small piece of heaven – green fields and hedges, the Shannon shining like a silver ribbon, and the light o' the sun falling across the blue line of the mountains – "

"Huh!" Moira Donovan was not impressed, "Turf cabins, black sticky bog, and empty bellies more like! Take no notice o' him! We're better off here – even in the wilderness!"

But Joe Donovan was not to be so easily put off.

"We lived in County Roscommon, not far from Athlone – " he

pronounced it, "At'alohn". "– The crop failed all over Ireland in 'forty-six: we had to leave, Moira and me, aye and hundreds like us – we couldn't pay the rent. Wrapped our things in a shirt and walked all the way to Cork. There might have been a ship nearer to hand in Galway but, mostly, the emigrant ships were sailing from Queenstown. Landed at the end at Galveston. 'Twas a queer place, Texas, in them days – just coming to terms wit' being ruled from Washington instead of Austin and the United States at war wit' Mexico over it all. Me and Moira settled by the Colorado in the frontier country north of Austin. Good land it was too – better than we have here!"

"Why did you leave?"

"Wasn't safe any more! Comanche on the prowl: too many raids. We headed east. Stayed for a while up by the Red River, then moved on here – water sweet and plentiful and soil not bad at all."

Zeke, who had been eating steadily, pushed away his empty plate and wiped his mouth with the side of his hand.

"No trouble with Injuns?" he asked.

"Sure we've seen some from time to time but – no raiding parties like we had in Texas."

"Heard there were some Arapaho on the war path – not far from here. South of the Canadian River – or so they said."

Moira Donovan's weather-beaten face paled and, involuntarily, she put a hand to her mouth to stifle a gasp.

"Arapaho?" Joe scratched his head. "You wouldn't be trying to scare me now, would you?"

Zeke said no more and the subject was dropped. Joe was right. What was the use in scaring them? This country was big enough to hide any number of Indian raiding parties and the odds against any of them stumbling across this isolated cabin were fairly high. Nevertheless, after the women had cleared away the supper things and the children had gone to bed, Joe lifted the rifles down from the pegs on the wall and, while Andrew and Zeke watched, he cleaned and oiled them before they all turned in for the night.

Andrew was awakened by the hoarse crowing of one of Joe's roosters and he got up and tidied away his sleeping things before the Donovans should come into the kitchen to set about their morning chores. It was cold outside with a touch of frost but the clear sky augured well and the sun when it came up would quickly warm the ground again. There were eggs for breakfast and thick slices of homemade bread liberally spread with butter. In some ways it all reminded Andrew of his childhood days in Pitbuddo. Young Patrick was out in the yard breaking sticks, Jessie was shaking out sheets and little Kathleen was helping her mother in the kitchen. It was all so reminiscent of how Meg and Jemima – and of course he himself – had been organised by his own mother.

When the time came for them to go, the entire family stood outside the cabin to bid them God speed and wish them farewell.

"So long, Joe! So long, Moira – say, will you cook me another roast next time I stop by?"

"Sure I will, Zeke – God willing!" said Moira. "Always supposing you bring in the meat – that is!"

Abigail kissed the children, one by one, and embraced the older woman.

"Y'all take good care of yourselves!" she called.

Andrew waved to the girls and, solemnly, took young Patrick's hand in his.

"Goodbye, Patrick," he said, then – lowering his voice so that no one else could hear – "if I were you, I'd ask your pa to take you, one of these days, down to Texas where you could learn to read and write! But – that's a secret, Patrick, just between you and me."

Patrick grinned and nodded.

"Thank you, Joe, Moira!" So saying, Andrew leapt up on to the chestnut's back and cantered after the others, who had forded the creek and were already half way up the side of the valley. When he caught up with them, Andrew turned and looked back. The Donovans were still standing where he had left them and they continued to wave until a fold of ground hid them from sight.

That morning their progress was a shade slower than usual. The trail they were following twisted and turned as it wound this way and that through a maze of rocky boulders interspersed with mesquite and tumbleweed. About an hour out from the Donovan cabin, with the horses still picking their way through the rock and scrub, they found themselves on a long ascent facing a peculiarly shaped knob of a hill glinting steely blue in the morning sunlight. Zeke, on his black stallion up in front, Abigail in the centre leading the mule and Andrew at the rear – they travelled strung out in an extended line to avoid, as far as possible, the constant stream of stones and gravel dislodged by the horses' hoofs.

Zeke was wary and alert. Not for one moment since they left the cover of the trees had he relaxed his air of constant vigilance. He had found Lone Eagle's report altogether disturbing and, like the good and efficient scout he was, he scanned the trail ahead for any tell-tale signs; and the countryside around them, so far as could be seen, for any untoward movement. Consequently, Andrew's heart leapt with excitement when, up ahead, he saw Zeke rein in and raise his hand, signalling them to stop. Zeke beckoned them forward and they closed up beside him.

"What is it?" Andrew hoped he did not sound as anxious as he felt.

"We got more than one trail."

Andrew breathed a sigh of relief.

"We sure do," said Abigail. "Quite a junction – in fact, I'd call it a crossroads!"

It was too. On their left a narrow trail converged on the broader one they had been following, and almost immediately, split up again.

"Seems there are two ways round that dome up there," said Zeke.

"Which way then?" Andrew asked. "Left or right?"

The scrub was thicker here – in fact only the rocky dome up at the summit stood out and it was like a bald pate above the dense mass of bushes clothing the hillside.

"What d'you think?" Zeke passed the question back again.

"Right!" said Andrew. "Easier on the horses: looks less of a climb."

"Well – I dunno!" Zeke scratched his head. "I guess I'd rather have the advantage of height. We'll go left! Anyways – the other looks like it runs out too far to the west. Let's go!"

They went on up the hill. It was a slow and arduous climb and after half an hour or so Zeke called a halt to rest the animals. They knee-haltered the horses and hitched the mule's rein to a stout sapling growing at the side of the track. On their right, the ground rose steeply to what appeared to be the spine of the hill but the bushes hemmed them around and they could see very little.

"Come on!" said Zeke. "Can't see anything for these goddam bushes. Let's have a look from up there!" He pointed up to the right.

Leaving Abigail with the horses, the men scrambled up through the bushes. As they neared the crest, Zeke went down on all fours and signalled to Andrew to do likewise and to remain silent. They crawled the last remaining yards to the top of the ridge. There was nothing to see but a continuation of the thick scrub running down on the far side. They lay there on their stomachs for several minutes, silent and unmoving. Zeke could not have said why, but he felt more uneasy than at any time since leaving Tahlequah.Andrew could sense the tension in the man at his side and it came as no shock when he felt Zeke's hand grip his elbow. At the same moment he heard the sound of horses, many horses – doubtless the noise had been muffled until now by some configuration of the ground. Zeke pointed to a spot away downhill to their left and Andrew realised that what he had assumed to be a patch of lighter coloured scrub was in fact a clearing behind which ran the other branch of the trail – that bearing to the right back at the crossroads. As he watched, a horse and rider appeared in the gap, followed by another and another. They were riding nose to tail in single file and Andrew's blood ran cold. Never in his life before had he seen a Plains Indian but he knew, beyond any manner of doubt, that – right now – he was looking at not one but at a complete war party, at least thirty strong. It was mesmerising watching them and Andrew soon lost count of their numbers. Even at that distance it was not hard to see that they were armed to the teeth – bows, tomahawks and feathered lances. Towards the tail of the column several of the horses carried more than one rider. They were about half a mile away, riding westwards at a much faster pace than Andrew and his companions had achieved and it required little imagination to realise what would have happened had Zeke allowed Andrew to take the right-hand fork at the junction. As it was, Zeke was in a lather of sweat lest any should have followed them and, although there was no sound from behind, he cursed himself for leaving Abigail all by herself down on the trail. In his view, it was inconceivable that the Indians could have failed to pick up their tracks. Whichever trail the war party had used before reaching the crossroads, they must surely have read the signs and they must know that three horses and a mule had, within the hour, taken the other fork.

If they were quick about it they might just possibly get back to 'Gail in time. It seemed that an age had passed since they had first heard the sound of the horses but the speed at which the Indians were travelling was such that they did in fact pass by in only a few minutes. When the last of the party had cleared the gap, Zeke rolled over and put his mouth to Andrew's ear.

"Keep down," he whispered, "they will know we are here and have probably sent scouts out. Must warn 'Gail! We gotta split company. You go on down – keep to the right: I'll go the other way: shoot if you have to – war party may be far enough away not to hear! With that, he was off, running down the hill, half crouching, dodging in and out among the bushes. His heart pounding, Andrew followed, veering off to the right. The bushes lashed at his face and hands and several times he all but tripped but he reached the foot of the slope at last and paused behind a screen of mesquite at the edge of the trail. There appeared to be nothing amiss. Over to his left, some two hundred yards away, he could see the horses and the mule standing quietly in the warm sunshine. Close by, Abigail was sitting with her back against a rock. There was no sound but the jingle of the horses' bridles as they moved about.

Andrew very nearly failed to see the Indian. It was the glint of the sun on the blade of his knife that gave him away, and in the nick of time too, for the Indian was crouched in the bushes only a few yards from where Abigail was seated on the opposite side of the trail. Andrew raised his rifle and fired just as the man leapt to his feet – knife poised for the attack. Then – everything happened at once.

The Indian crumpled and fell; another two shots rang out from the direction Zeke had taken, and Abigail screamed in terror as yet another Indian whom Andrew had not seen jumped upon her from behind. Andrew ran. He covered the distance between them like a sprinter going for the finishing tape, and leapt upon the Indian with such force that the man was knocked aside leaving Abigail free to pick herself up and back away. Andrew's arms closed around the Indian's, pinioning them to his sides. He wriggled and squirmed under Andrew's relentless grip and the smell of his sweat was rank and sour. Andrew himself was breathing heavily with exertion and his shirt was sopping wet.

With a mighty heave, the Indian twisted clear and, like a flash, had thrown himself upon Andrew, rolling him over, knees in the pit of his stomach, long strong fingers round his throat. The man's face, contorted with rage, was within an inch of Andrew's and, as he choked and gasped for breath, Andrew could see, through a maze of shooting stars, the lank black hair held back by a broad band of buckskin, the broad nose, the folded eyelid, and the vivid daubs of war-paint all glistening with sweat. His foul-smelling breath came out in great gasps and the teeth in his open mouth were broken and yellow. Afterwards Andrew remembered thinking that if this was to be his last moment on earth, it could scarce have been a more unpleasant one. As it was, the Indian very nearly succeeded in squeezing the life out of him but, just as Andrew felt he was whirling off into blessed unconsciousness, the Indian's fingers slackened their grip and the man's body went limp above him. With the last remaining ounce of his strength, Andrew wriggled over to one side just as a stream of bright red blood poured from the Indian's slack-jawed mouth and soaked his shirt. As he fought to regain his breath, Andrew saw what had happened. It was Abigail who stood there, staring down in horror at the half-naked Indian and, as he dragged himself to his knees, Andrew could see the handle of her bowie knife sticking up between the dead man's shoulder blades. Then Zeke was upon them, bursting through the bushes and gathering Abigail in his strong embrace.

"You all right?" He looked anxiously at Andrew now struggling to his feet.

"Yes," Andrew's voice was thick and distorted. "Throat hurts – but I'll be all right in a minute or two."

"There were six of them," said Zeke. "I got three; you've dealt with these two, and the last vamoosed; must have left their ponies back at the fork; heard him gallop off!"

Abigail was shivering with pent-up excitement and emotion. However, she too insisted that she was perfectly all right, but Zeke made her sit down – just for a moment, he said. He pulled Abigail's knife out from the Indian's back and cleaned the long curved blade. What a girl, he thought; imagine a woman having strength enough to plunge a big knife like this into a man's back and drive it home! The same thought had occurred to Andrew. No doubt both the will power and the strength had been the products of fear.

Zeke turned the Indian's body over.

"Arapaho!" he said. "Same goddam war party that Lone Eagle saw. Lord only knows what damage they've done!"

The man had some hairy looking objects hanging from his belt.

"What are these?" Andrew asked, although he guessed the answer.

"Scalps!" Zeke did not add that, but for Abigail's prompt action, Andrew's might very well have been taken to join them.

"Abigail," said Andrew quietly, taking her right hand in his, "thank you!"

Abigail smiled – a wan, tentative smile, but this vanished as quickly as it came when she heard what Zeke had to say next.

"Now that we're all recovered," he said, "I guess you'd better have the bad news. When I was back down the trail there, I could see a bit of the country behind us. I guess there's a goddam column of smoke going up from the direction of the Donovans' place. These bastards must have got there soon after we left. Reckon we better go back: Lord knows there's not likely to be much we can do but say a prayer and do some diggin'. Come on!" He unhaltered the stallion and swung himself up into the saddle.

"What about the mule?" asked Andrew, as he clambered on to the chestnut's back.

"Mule can stay here till we return."

Abigail was deathly white, but she loosed Mist and mounted.

Zeke led the way at a cracking pace. They paused only twice. Once at a bend in the track where they passed the bodies of the three Indians despatched by Zeke, two of them shot, and the third garrotted with a leather thong – a little trick Zeke had learned from an old Mexican bandit he had once met somewhere down near San Antonio. And they halted briefly at the junction of the trails. Four of the Indian ponies were still there, quietly grazing. The man that had escaped had presumably taken one on a leading rein as well as his own. All along the trail they had come up in the morning they saw evidence that many horses had passed this way after them and they realised all too clearly how very fortunate they had been. It really beggared thought. There they were in the morning, riding up that twisting trail quite oblivious of the fact that a strong war-party of Arapaho was right on their tail.

Some forty minutes hard riding brought them to the Donovans' little valley. The smoke which, from a distance had been billowing upwards in a thick black cloud, had thinned considerably. When they reached a point from which they could look down upon the farm they could see that there was nothing left of the cabin but a blackened smouldering ruin. A few nearby trees had also been alight and were now smoking like tall chimney stacks. At fifty paces or so they reined up and walked the horses slowly forward. There were three bodies lying well spaced out between the heap of charred timbers and the creek – those of Joe and Moira and young Patrick, recognisable by their clothing rather than by their faces, which the removal of their scalps had contorted into gruesome death masks. Before they died the Donovans had given a good account of themselves for the bodies of several Indians were lying sprawled along the side of the creek. Of Jessie and little Kathleen there was no sign. While Zeke and Andrew dug three shallow graves and laid the Donovans gently to rest, Abigail searched the fields and the creek without finding any trace of the girls. Over the graves, for headstones, they placed roughly made crosses of wood and they knelt and recited together the metrical version of the twenty-third psalm, and the Lord's Prayer.

"Goodness and mercy all my life, shall surely
follow me,
And in God's house, for evermore,
My dwelling place shall be."

They had just risen and were moving towards the horses when, once again, they heard the sound of approaching hoofbeats and in considerable numbers.

"The goddam Injuns!" exclaimed Zeke. "Bastards have come back for us, damn them!"

Whoever was coming was riding up at a gallop and kicking up a cloud of yellowish dust that drifted over the lip of the valley. There was nothing for it but to stand their ground, rifles at the ready. The oncoming riders stopped at the crest of the hill and, when the dust cleared, Andrew and his companions saw to their great relief that this was no Arapaho war-party but a posse of white men to the number of about a score. Their leader, a thick-set man with long drooping moustache, rode down alone, his rifle in one hand.

"Well! Lookee here!" he cried. "If it ain't old Zeke Harrison! Howdy, Zeke! Howdy, ma'am!" He nodded to Andrew. "We been trackin' these murderin' savages for the best part of a week: called out when the bastards crossed the Red River and did some raidin' up Clarksville way!" The man dismounted, shook hands with Zeke and lifted his large broad-brimmed hat to Abigail.

"Steve!" said Zeke, "Steve! This here is Mr. Andrew Gray who's makin' for Austin. Andrew! Meet Steve Lacy of the Texas Rangers."

Andrew had heard of the Texas Rangers and of their somewhat chequered history: originally a loose-knit band of armed backwoodsmen, some genuine pioneers who sought to push the American frontier down into the Mexican province of Texas, others little better than bandits and desperadoes. They had continued to flourish during the time of the Lone Star republic, sometimes assisting President Sam Houston, sometimes proving a real thorn in his flesh, and then – after Texas had joined the Union and seceded from it – providing a useful source of semi-trained manpower for the Confederate Army. Now that the war was over, they had reverted to their official role of a policing and peace-keeping force.

"Howdy, Mr.Gray!" Steve Lacy held out his hand. "Saw the smoke," he continued. "Same as you, I guess; had to be the Donovans' place – ain't no other in this God forsaken territory. Poor critturs! Got 'em all, did they?" He probably could not see the three mounds of newly dug earth and the crosses partially hidden as they were by Andrew and the Harrisons.

"No," said Zeke. "Girls missin'! We've had a good look around – they ain't here!"

"Bastards! They'll have taken them for squaws: we gotta get 'em, Zeke!"

"Yeah! Sure thing! We saw 'em; 'bout two hours ago, some forty minutes

west of here; war-party of around thirty, give or take a few; Arapaho, ridin'
west – fast!''

"That rate they got one hell of a lead! We best get goin'! Y'all comin' along?''

"Sure!'' said Zeke, looking at Andrew who nodded vigorously, we're
comin'!''

They were picking their way along the trail in the semi-darkness, strung
out over a distance of more than a mile. Steve Lacy and his men were up
front, following in the steps of one of the Indian guides the rangers had in
their party; while Andrew and the Harrisons brought up the rear, dragging
along the reluctant mule they had collected when they returned past the spot
of their first encounter with the Arapaho. The rangers were confident that
the war-party would have halted at nightfall – a view in which Zeke con-
curred. Accordingly Steve Lacy was anxious to make up the lost ground
between them. Fortunately, the moon, which had a day or two to go before
reaching the last quarter, had risen and was shedding sufficient light, even
when obscured by cloud, to let them make out the trail ahead.

The Arapaho would have look-outs posted. Everyone was in agreement on
that score, and anxiously, they awaited the return of the other Indian guides
who had been sent on ahead to reconnoitre. Just about midnight, the setting
moon and the rapidly deepening darkness effectively inhibited any further
progress. Steve Lacy halted and the column closed up. As luck would have it
they found themselves in a shallow bowl in the hills, a place wide enough to
let them spread their blankets within a circle formed by the haltered horses.
They posted sentries all around and Steve Lacy made arrangements for these
to be relieved at regular intervals. Everyone else tried to snatch such sleep as
they could. It was a cold night and Andrew fell into a fitful doze, his ears
filled with the eerie wailing of a coyote near enough at hand to make the
horses restless.

It was still pitch dark when he was awakened by Zeke's hand on his
shoulder.

"Dawn in fifteen minutes,'' said Zeke. "Arapaho are only about two miles
ahead – so Steve's Injuns say – lying in a depression much like this; they ain't
likely to move before sun-up, so we'll get goin' at first light and try to sur-
round them. Mule stays here.''

"What about their sentries?''

"Steve's seein' to that! Remember the one I got yesterday – the one that
didn't get shot?''

Andrew nodded. Doubtless the rangers were well practised in the use of
the garrotte. He had no time for further speculation. It was already light
enough to see the look of set determination on Abigail's face. Word was
passed down the line and they were off, rifles loaded and held in one hand.

After a mile or so – fortunately on grass and not on the boulder-strewn ground to which they had grown accustomed – they reached the foot of a short incline. Zeke held up his hand and they halted. The rider immediately ahead had stopped some fifty paces to their left and, beyond him, in the strengthening light, they could see his neighbour standing his horse about the same distance further left. They stood in silence for several minutes until Andrew heard a sound that set the blood pounding in his veins. It was the sound of a horseman away over on the right – Arapaho surely! What fools they were to think they could surprise these savages who were, after all, part and parcel of this land. But Zeke, who had also heard the noise, appeared quite unconcerned. Small wonder, for round the side of the hill came Steve Lacy and the head of the column. Steve halted well over to their right and signalled to Zeke.

"O.K." said Zeke, "Abigail! You go fifty paces to my right; Andrew! – one hundred; that will complete the circle. Fire only after you hear Steve's first shot – and make sure y'all keep your sights down or you'll shoot the guys on the far side of the circle! Seems the goddam Arapaho haven't heard us!"

Once Abigal and Andrew – the last links in the chain – were in position, Steve signalled and they advanced up the hill. After a few paces, Andrew's chestnut shied violently and Andrew had his work cut out to hold him steady. The body of an Arapaho was lying at the beast's feet. The first sentry would, of course, be posted where he had a clear view back along the trail. Andrew was now in little doubt as to the fate of the other Indian look-outs. At the crest of the hill they were able to look down upon the camping ground and, of course, they were, for the first time, visible to the Arapaho. For a second – almost as if time stood still – Andrew saw the waiting ponies and men moving about as they prepared to strike camp. There were no fires burning whatsoever. And then, as if someone had thrown a lever actuating machinery, they were running to the ponies even as the rangers, themselves whooping like the very savages before them, set off down the hill with the velocity of a cavalry charge. Over to his right, Andrew heard Steve Lacy fire and even as he himself, gripping the chestnut for dear life with his knees, raised his barrel, found an Arapaho in his sights and fired, there was a blaze of fire from all around, constant and sustained. Away over on his left, Andrew could see Abigail taking aim and calmly firing, again and again.

Nothing seemed to have any cohesion after that; Andrew felt like a detached observer watching a stage on which a series of cameos was being enacted. He saw long-shafted arrows landing around them, sticking up out of the grass at an angle of forty-five degrees and quivering from the force of impact. An occasional bullet whinged past his ear, presumably fired by an Arapaho with a gun stolen during the raid. He saw Indians going down like ninepins, riderless terror-stricken ponies milling around adding to the confusion. Then they were in among them and there was no more shooting, only hand to hand combat with whatever weapon came most readily to hand. The rangers' fire had taken a severe toll of the Arapaho but those left, including a tall, well-built man with a couple of feathers in his head band who was probably the leader, fought like demons. One of these – a snarling, wolf-like man – lunged at Andrew with a long, wicked-looking knife. In the nick of time, Andrew brought the butt end of his rifle down on the man's head cracking his skull. He heard Zeke shout and turned just in time to avoid a swinging tomahawk. He countered with his boot, a mighty kick catching his attacker on the chin and spinning him round. The horses were having difficulty maintaining their foothold on ground becoming slippery with blood, and just as Andrew was wondering how much longer he would be able to avoid these murderous attacks, it was all over. The few remaining Arapaho – four or five at the most – leapt on to ponies and fled. Of these, three were brought down by rifle fire and the others were hotly pursued by half a dozen yelling rangers.

Zeke and Abigail had already dismounted and, along with Steve and a number of rangers, were searching the camp area, no easy task with the numbers of dead – men and ponies – lying around. No sooner had Andrew joined them than they heard Abigail cry out. She had moved towards the perimeter of the camp and was standing on the edge of a small, crater-like depression alongside the roots of a fallen tree. Huddled together in the base of the crater were some six or seven dishevelled wild-eyed creatures. Only from their long dirty hair and from the torn scraps of what had once been dresses flapping around them could it be seen that here were the female captives – women and girls. They shied away from Abigail when she jumped down beside them. Cowering under the tree roots, they stared at her with haunted eyes. Among them, Andrew recognised little Kathleen Donovan but, of her elder sister, there was no sign.

Meantime, Steve mustered his troops. Their casualties amounted to four dead, including one of the Indian scouts, and nine wounded. Of these, two had injuries of such severity that it would only be a matter of time before they succumbed. The remainder had flesh wounds of one kind or another and, once these had been staunched and bound up as well as possible, they all declared that they were perfectly capable of riding. Just then, the rangers who had gone after the fleeing Arapaho returned.

"Get 'em?" Steve asked.

"Hell, no! These Injun ponies sure are fast – got clean away!"

One of the rangers led Andrew and the Harrisons to where he had found Jessie. The man kept muttering, "Ain't never seen anything like it. Ain't never seen anything like it."

Jessie was quite dead. She was sprawled alongside an Indian. In her right hand was a tomahawk, its blade embedded in the man's neck.

"I see'd her!" said the ranger. "Goin' about like crazy, lookin' for wounded Indians, and killin' 'em with that axe! One after another – slash! slash! slash! I called to her but she wouldn't stop. Reckon she never heard me. This here varmint must have got her as she got him!"

Abigail, who a few minutes earlier had done her own share of killing, buried her face on Zeke's shoulder and sobbed. Andrew, crouching over the dead girl, pulled the Indian's knife out from under her left breast and, as the bright crimson blood began to flow, he gently closed the crazed and reddened eyes. They buried Jessie alongside the dead rangers – the four killed in battle and the two who had subsequently died from their wounds. Thankfully then, they moved out. It was just on high noon.

Taking the freed women and the girls with them, the rangers set out at once for their home base, a frontier post on the Texas side of the border, a few miles north of the little settlement of Denison. Provided they maintained a good pace they should be there by nightfall. Zeke indicated that his party would follow them in since their direct route ran through Denison and Fort Worth, and on down to Austin. However, with the mule to hinder them, they would have to spend a night on the trail before crossing into Texas.

"Tomorrow night, then, Zeke," said Steve Lacy. "We gotten a good supply of Kentucky liquor – guess we deserve to blow it!"

"Sure thing!" grunted Zeke. Abigail said nothing but she shook her head in disgust.

They found the long-suffering mule and set out in the wake of the rangers. By mid-afternoon they reached a crest beyond which the land fell away gently to a flat featureless plain. They made camp early at a stand of trees beside a narrow creek. Still watchful and alert, Zeke insisted that he and Andrew should take it in turns to stand guard but they each slept well when relieved, as did Abigail. The night passed without incident and, when morning came, they felt much refreshed. An hour short of noon, they saw a wide river winding across the plain a mile or so ahead. This, said Zeke, was the Red River, here forming the boundary between Oklahoma and the state of Texas. They swam the horses and the mule across and rode up to the frontier post. Two flags flew in the breeze from the tall white pole over the entrance gate. One bore the single star of Texas and the other the starred saltire of the Confederacy.

Steve Lacy came to the gate to welcome them. He and his party had ridden in just after sundown the previous evening and this morning he had sent the women and girls on under escort to Denison, where they would stay until it could be ascertained whether they still had homes to return to or whether they would have to find new ones.

"What will happen to little Kathleen?" asked Andrew. There was none other quite so young and helpless.

"Reckon the best place for her is one of the convents down in San

Anton'," said Abigail. "Why don't we take her along, Zeke? As far as Austin anyway."

"If you'd do that, ma'am," said Steve, "I guess the sheriff down at Denison would be mighty grateful."

The accommodation at the frontier post was spartan in the extreme, but they found a room for Zeke and Abigail and another for Andrew. It was so long since Andrew had slept anywhere other than on the ground that had the simple bed been a four-poster it could hardly have looked more luxurious. They ate round a long trestle table – a stew of beef with onions and beans – and, true to his word, Steve produced a large two-handled jar of bourbon.

"Plenty more where that came from!" he announced.

Andrew could see Abigail wince but she forced herself to smile and watched while Zeke picked the jar up with one hand and upended it over his open mouth. The raw spirit gurgled down his throat in a steady stream. Andrew reckoned he must have swallowed close on a pint before he set the jar down again, belched loudly, and wiped his mouth with the back of his hand. The jar went round the table and when it was empty a full one was set in its place. Steve and the rangers grew more and more rowdy and then, quieter and quieter as the soporific effect of the alcohol began to take hold. All the while Zeke drank steadily and only his eyes, expressionless as a couple of marbles, showed the growing extent of his drunkenness. Andrew, although seeming to take his fill, managed to swallow very little of the fiery spirit, and as for Abigail, she had long since retired to bed.

One by one, the rangers fell by the wayside. Some merely slumped over the table; others got up and did their best to stagger out into the yard. Some did not quite make it and fell senseless before they got there; others completed the course and, when the night air hit them, were promptly sick. Once Andrew had freed himself from a neighbour who had fallen half across his chest, he got up and made his way outside to cleanse his lungs from the all pervading smell of whiskey and tobacco. Zeke could drink no more. He was no longer conscious but half lying, his head on the table. When Andrew came back in, he found he was the only man remaining on his feet. He pulled Zeke clear of the table and laid him full length on the floor.

Back in the small bedroom, Andrew stripped for the first time in days. He folded his shirt and trousers and laid them on the wooden floor. When he blew out the candle there was sufficient light coming in from the cracks in the door to enable him to see reasonably clearly. He pulled back the blanket and drew back in astonishment. Abigail was lying there. She had snuggled in under the blankets and she was stark naked.

"I thought you were never coming," she said.

Andrew opened his mouth but, before he could speak, Abigail had leapt to her feet and, placing her two hands on his shoulders, she covered his mouth with hers. Andrew responded as she knew he would. The scent of her was in his nostrils and her hair brushed against his chest. He put his arms round her waist and drew her to him. Her hands went round his neck and they stood in a close embrace until the need to gasp for breath forced them apart. Without a word, they lay down together on the bed and made love. Eventually, their passion spent, Andrew rolled over and regarded Abigail in some awe.

"We shouldn't have done that," he whispered.

"Why not?"

"Well ... Zeke!"

"What about him? He won't trouble us for quite a while – nor anybody else for that matter!"

"But ... it's ... it's like taking advantage of a child!"

"He's not unlike a kid – crazy old fool that he is!"

"But – supposing ...."

"Something comes along to remind me of this night's work you mean?"

"Yes."

"Then I'll be mighty glad – and so will Zeke! Zeke will think it's his own!"

"And would you let him think that?"

"Sure! It's the only way he'll ever father a kid. Poor old Zeke! He don't know it, but he had a kind of accident a while back. Not been the same man since. I asked a medical man I know about it. He said there would never be any little Harrisons. Maybe we'll prove him wrong!"

Andrew stared at her.

"Oh, Andrew! I'm sorry!" Abigail saw the expression in his eyes and was filled with remorse. "Dear Andrew," she whispered. Gently she kissed him on the forehead, slipped out of bed, and was gone.

"Look at that, Mr. Gray, sir! A mighty fine slice of real estate – y'all have come a long way to see it but I'll be dog-goned if you can find better. That's real good cattle country, Mr. Gray – could make y'all a powerful sum of money one day. Ask Zeke here if you don't believe me: Zeke knows good territory when he sees it – that right, Zeke?"

The real estate agent from Austin – a man highly commended by the Texan banker who carried Vic Zoller's mark of approval – took off his large wide-brimmed hat and wiped the sweat off his forehead. For his part, Zeke, seated like a statue upon his great black stallion, scratched his head and nodded.

"Yeah!" he drawled. "Reckon it's good land right enough: ain't worth much right now but things could change if the railroad comes out west. I guess the Texan longhorns could fetch good prices in the stockyards at Chicago if we could only get 'em there!"

"Yes, sir!" The real estate agent settled his enormous hat back on his head. "Zeke's right, Mr. Gray! Railroad's the key!"

Andrew looked from one to the other.

"But surely," he said, "the line of the railroad's already decided and Texas is far off that line."

"Sure thing," said Zeke. "Railroad's not likely to come to Texas, leastways not in the beginning, but it will come a whole lot nearer than it is right now and when that day comes there'll be no shortage of cowboys to drive the longhorns north to meet it – you'll see. You gotten yourself a good deal, Andrew. Y'all see and take it now!"

As they said, the land gave every appearance of excellence – a vast undulating slice of Texas running to some 60,000 acres and lying 150 miles or so northwest of Austin. The Lone Star Trading Post had been unable to settle with Andrew. Instead they had offered a mortgage for $50,000 secured over the land which Andrew, accompanied by Zeke and the real estate agent, had ridden out to see. The grass was good and plentiful as was only to be expected in mid-winter, but the summer situation was likely to be almost as good, seeing that the land was well watered by a number of creeks and by a major tributary of the Brazos River. In addition, the entire property was sufficiently wooded to provide a reasonable amount of shelter from the worst of the summer sun. As security for $50,000, it was probably thin enough but the interest rate was unbelievably good at thirteen per cent and the banker's opinion on the Lone Star Trading Post was unqualified for such a commitment.

Andrew decided that he would take it but, to the agent, he was non-committal.

"I'll think it over," he said. "You'll have my answer when we get back to Austin."

He was as good as his word, and after they had returned to town three days later, he shook hands on the deal and, once the documentation had been completed, he rode out again with Zeke to the little property he and Abigail owned in Bastrop County ten miles or so to the southeast.

Abigail had said little to Andrew since that night up at the frontier post. Once Zeke had sobered up, they had saddled up immediately and had reached journey's end in Austin without further incident. After the harshness of the ruined cities of the south, the miles of desolation in Oklahoma, and the raw, thinly populated lands of up-state Texas, Andrew felt that, at last, he had returned to the sanity of civilisation. The new and growing city of Austin was an interesting and exciting place, beautifully situated on a bend of the Colorado River in a rolling, well-wooded countryside. He and the Harrisons found rooms in an establishment with considerably greater pretensions to the title of "hotel" than anything Andrew had come across since leaving Tennessee.

Andrew's first port of call had been the bank, where he picked up sufficient cash to settle with Zeke and – more importantly so far as he was concerned – mail from home, the first he had received since he had collected a letter from Meg that had awaited him at Little Rock.

Back at the hotel, Andrew toyed with the idea of handing Zeke's fee to Abigail, a move which he believed might prevent a large proportion of it being squandered on another almighty drinking spree, but he rejected the notion and paid the money to Zeke. When all was said and done, the contract had been between him and Zeke; he had shaken hands on it at Fort Smith and any other action would have been tantamount to breaking his bond. To Andrew's astonishment, Zeke gave the money to Abigail and, although he did indulge himself fairly freely at the long bar in the hotel, he was perfectly steady on his feet when he and Abigail retired to their room at the end of the evening.

As for Andrew, he burned his candle long into the night while he caught up with the news from home. There were half a dozen letters from Henry Caldwell and business-wise the news was good. The mill was working to capacity and Henry Caldwell was well pleased with the manner in which remittances were coming in against the American debt. His letter dated 31st October was full of the news of Lord Palmerston's death. Apparently the old man had died on 18th October and had been buried in Westminster Abbey on the 27th. Palmerston had been involved for so long in the affairs of the nation that it was difficult to imagine the political scene without his rumbustious and controversial presence. Earl Russell, who had taken over as Premier, was a staid and sober-sided character by comparison, but Henry Caldwell had a great deal of time for Russell – probably more than he had had for old "Pam" and consequently was well enough pleased.

On a personal note, however, he was gloomy in the extreme. It seemed that Vicky had not picked up again following her aunt's death and Henry Caldwell expressed himself as very glad that Andrew's sojourn in America was nearing an end. Maybe his return home would supply the tonic so sorely needed. The poor girl was always ailing and spent most of her time in bed. It would be some comfort if they could only find out what was wrong and start treatment of one kind or another, but the family physician, Dr. Tannahill, could find nothing the matter. Henry Caldwell had decided that it was time they consulted a specialist and he was putting the necessary arrangements in hand.

Despite the fact that Vicky was lying abed idle, she had found time to write Andrew only two letters. In fact he had received only four from her all the time he had been away. The latest ones were no different from those which had gone before, each being a catalogue of the writer's wretchedness — sick in body, deserted by an unfeeling husband and quite without any purpose in life, all of which – she wrote – could be laid fairly and squarely at Andrew's door.

Jessie, in her latest letter, confirmed the view expressed by Dr. Tannahill. Knowing that Andrew had been worried, she had pocketed her pride and had paid her daughter-in-law a visit at Riga Lodge. In her opinion, there was nothing the matter with the girl other than a great fit of depression and, once Andrew got her home to Strawberry Hill, she would probably pull out of it. Andrew would require to be firm with her or he might be faced with a wife who was a permanent invalid. Even Andrew could read between the lines of his mother's letter her firm conviction that Vicky was nothing but a completely spoiled little brat who, years ago, should have been laid over somebody's knee and soundly spanked.

And the awful truth was that Andrew had begun to realise it. He had been trying to evade the issue for quite some time but as he read his wife's letters for the second time he could not help wondering what on earth had possessed him to fall for her in the first place. But that, of course, was beside the point; he had made her his wife and there was nothing he, nor anyone else, could do about it now. "Whom God hath joined together, let no man put asunder." The more he thought of it, the more he wondered at his stupidity. To say he had been caught on the rebound was not strictly accurate. But that he should have chosen someone like Vicky – the very antithesis of all he had previously looked for in a girl – now seemed beyond belief. Abigail, for instance, and Mary – oh, how he longed for Mary! Mary – the unattainable! There had never been anyone like her and never would be. Life for Andrew – domestic life at any rate – was like to be a dismal existence.

In the morning, half slept and with an incipient headache Andrew called at the Lone Star Trading Post and – apart from visits to the bank, to a lawyer and to the real estate office – he remained there for most of the day. Early on the following morning he rode northwards out of town in the company of Zeke and the real estate man, Dick Passingham. On this occasion Abigail stayed behind to see to little Kathleen Donovan. As luck would have it, a party of nuns from the convent of Santa Gertrudis, down San Antonio way, had been up in Austin delivering some petition or other at the state capitol and they readily agreed to take Kathleen back with them. Much relieved, Abigail had left for home and was there to welcome Zeke and Andrew when they got back from the north.

The Harrison's place reminded Andrew rather forcibly of that of the ill-fated Donovans. The situation was remarkably similar, a narrow creek of gurgling spring water, well-grouped trees, and a cabin identical in every respect, even to the rifles slung from pegs against the living room wall. However, unlike the Donovans' which had nestled in a little valley, the Harrisons' place stood on the crest of a open ridge with panoramic views on all sides. Also – they had neighbours; not close, but scattered around them. Within a radius of five miles, Zeke said, there was a round dozen similar holdings to theirs, but their neighbours were farmers who worked their land and made a reasonable living from it. With Zeke and Abigail constantly away on one ploy or another, their land lay fallow, given over to grass and daisies and a spreading carpet of Texas blue-bonnets waving and dipping in the breeze. They did, however, keep poultry and a few hogs, looked after in their absence by their nearest neighbour, Luis Rosalis, whose family had been in Texas for generations and who was a decent, law-abiding citizen although, as Zeke said, when they sat talking after their meal on that first evening, "he had never quite gotten over the shock of having to live on his own land, under a foreign flag, ruled by a bunch of gringos."

"Gringos?" Andrew was puzzled.

"Yeah! Reckon it comes from the Spanish word for Greek." Zeke frequently displayed a surprising degree of erudition. "It means 'gibberish', son, that's what! You, me and Abigail – all of us in these United States – I guess we speak gibberish that sounds mighty harsh to these guys, even though their Spanish may be a long way off true blue Castilian!"

"Where did you pick up all that knowledge of yours, Zeke?" Andrew was intrigued.

"Zeke!" snorted Abigail. "Never did have any learnin'!"

Zeke merely smiled; but Andrew persisted in his questioning. After all, he realised, he had never heard anything whatsoever of Zeke's background.

"Where do you belong, Zeke?"

"Well, now," said Zeke, "I dunno if I can rightly tell. Guess I've knocked around some since I was a kid. Raised in the Old Dominion down in the lower Tidewater."

"The Tidewater!" Andrew was more surprised than ever. Only the highest pedigreed of blue-blooded Virginians hailed from the old plantation country in the lower reaches of the James and York rivers.

Zeke smiled. "You bet!" he said. "Harrisons've been around there since the days of Pocohontas! Me? Why! There was a round dozen of us and me, the youngest! Big place we had too, in New Kent County..." his eyes grew misty, "... raisin' tobacco and corn on slave labour but 'tweren't big enough, I guess, for all of us. My brothers were through college at 'William and Mary' and I had 'bout six months there myself until they threw me out."

Andrew could see that Abigail was listening intently and it was clear from her expression that she had heard nothing of this before.

"Threw you out!" she exclaimed. "Why?"

"Guess 'twere the whiskey, 'Gail, even then! Seems they found me senseless and sprawled on the college steps, with an empty magnum beside me, on the morning the State Governor was due to pay an official call!"

Abigail shook her head in a gesture of despair.

"And, after that?" Andrew remained intrigued.

"I lit out west!"

"Didn't you never go back home?" Abigail wanted to know.

"Hell, no! They none of 'em wanted to know me!"

"What about your ma?"

"Died when I was a kid. Guess I was raised by my eldest sister; never really cared for sister Martha – nor she for me!"

After that Zeke would say no more. It was growing late and, mumbling something about having a look at the night, he rose abruptly and went outside.

Andrew stayed with the Harrisons for several weeks. So much had happened in the immediately preceding past, so many experiences had crowded in on him, one after another, that he had quite lost count of time. It came as a great shock, therefore, when – on the second Sunday of his visit – Abigail announced that, seeing it was Christmas Eve, she proposed they should all go into San Tomas the following morning for the Christmas Day service. Where the main turnpike crossed the Colorado River, there was a small town boasting a telegraph office, a general store, a school and a church – just sufficient amenity to serve the rural community around it.

Unlike many of the towns further up state and those on the wild frontier where the only recognised law was that applied by the man with the quickest draw – San Tomas was normally a peaceful place, quiet and law abiding, where the only excitement was the twice-daily arrival of the stage operating between Austin and Galveston. On Christmas Day, however, the little town was packed to capacity with horses, wagons and people everywhere. Abigail had insisted that Zeke should drive them over in their farm wagon. She had dressed in her very best bonnet and gown and there was to be no question of her riding to church. She, Abigail Harrison, would be driven, just like any lady in the Virginian Tidewater – and that was that! Even Zeke donned a suit that was a shade too tight for him and he grumbled mightily as he got out the wagon and hitched up. He had trimmed his beard and whiskers so that Andrew scarce recognised him.

The roads and trails were athrong with folk, country folk like themselves heading for town,

"Happy Christmas, Zeke!" they called. "Happy Christmas, Abigail!"

The little church was bursting at the seams by the time they arrived and they had to stand behind the rearmost pew. But they were among the fortunate ones – many who came later could not get in at all. The preacher, a native Texan, middle aged and balding, offered up prayers of thankfulness for the birth of the Christ child and for God's goodness to the great state in which they lived. After their experience with the Arapaho, neither Andrew nor either of the Harrisons required any prompting in their own unspoken prayers.

The preacher read from the second chapter of St. Luke, the marvellous tidings of the nativity:

> "For unto you is born this day in the city of David, a Saviour which is Christ the Lord ... And suddenly there was with the

angel a multitude of the heavenly host praising God and saying, Glory to God in the highest, and on earth peace, good will toward men ... "

Andrew thought of the Arapaho – how he had killed them without a thought of what he was about. Of course he knew it had been a matter of survival – he and his friends, or the heathen Arapaho – nevertheless when he bowed his head at the preacher's prayer "for others", he sought God's forgiveness that he should have been the instrument whereby the life blood of fellow human beings had been spilled. What a crazy, mixed-up world it is, he thought, as inwardly he prayed for the souls of the Donovans, Joe and Moira and little Patrick, who had never been to school, butchered by the self-same Arapaho; and poor Jessie, used by them – God alone knew how – and finally running amok, and dying half crazed under an Indian's knife.

Then, they were all on their feet singing, unaccompanied, the Christmas hymn, "Angels from the realms of Glory". The sermon was long, longer even than those of the Reverend Mr. Black, but the preacher was able and he kept his hearers wide awake. When, at last, he reached his conclusion, and they stood to sing the one hundred and twenty first psalm to the old tune of "French", Andrew felt the hot tears stinging his eyes as his mind was filled with the vision of the hills that crowd about the Angus glens beyond the wide and fertile plain of Strathmore.

"The Lord thee keeps," they sang,
"The Lord thy shade
On thy right hand doth stay;
The moon by night thee shall not smite,
Nor yet the sun by day."

"Go in peace!" said the preacher, in benediction. "May the peace of our Lord Jesus Christ, born this day, go with you and remain with you wherever you may be – Amen."

As they drove home, the sun came out and lit up the pleasant undulating grasslands with a golden light.

"I to the hills," said Andrew,

"Will lift mine eyes," added Zeke,

"From whence doth come mine aid." Abigail, sitting between Andrew and Zeke, took Zeke's free hand in one of hers and Andrew's in the other.

"Happy Christmas!" she cried, and they all laughed with the sheer joy of it.

On a Thursday morning, early in February 1866, Andrew boarded the Galveston stage at San Tomas. The Harrisons had driven him over in the wagon and they stood together on the dusty side walk waiting until the driver should crack his whip and set his team into motion. Abigail had kissed

Andrew and she had squeezed his hand – a little intimate gesture which Andrew, with Zeke's kindly eye upon him, did his poor best to disregard.

"Y'all come back and see us, now!" Zeke cried. "See how that property's doin'! Meantime – I'll keep an eye on it for you!" He gripped Andrew's hand in a vice-like handshake.

"Goodbye, Abigail! Goodbye, Zeke! Thanks for everything! Sure – I'll be back – someday!"

With a sound reminiscent of the rebel yell, the driver flicked the reins and set the horses going. As the coach lurched forward, Abigail brushed a tear from the corner of her eye and did her best to smile. She stood by Zeke's side and they both waved. Andrew leant out the window and he too waved until the dust cloud hid them from view. There was no doubt in Andrew's mind that this was the hardest parting he had endured since leaving home.

He spent a couple of days at Galveston before securing passage on a small coastal steamer which the shipping agent said would take him as far as New Orleans, where he should have no difficulty picking up a vessel bound for Philadelphia or New York. The important seaport of Galveston – a place which had figured prominently during the war – lies on a long narrow sand bar created by the Brazos and Trinity rivers as they pour their floods into the Gulf of Mexico. The harbour was thronged with shipping of all sorts and conditions and the docks were humming with activity. Beyond the harbour area at both ends the beach on the Gulf side was lined with wooden piers, where men and boys stood with rod and line vying with the brown pelicans for fish, some quite sizeable, swimming close inshore. Andrew walked along the beach, watching the incoming tide and the plummeting pelicans, screwing up his eyes against the glare of strong sunlight upon the water. Down here at sea level it was very much warmer than it had been up country – in fact, these February days were every bit as warm as many a summer day at home in Pitbuddo. Andrew turned, long before the end of the beach, and retraced his steps. He had had little exercise over a period of months and was sadly out of condition, a situation not likely to be improved by the enforced inactivity of his forthcoming homeward voyage.

New Orleans was gay, vivid and exciting; a delightful town, singularly un-American in appearance with a colourful population in which the Creole and Negro elements greatly outweighed all others. A flourishing seaport of very long standing, it was by far the largest town, although not the state capital of Louisiana. Originally a huge chunk of the American west, and latterly a vast empire comprising the greater part of the Mississippi basin northwards to the Dakotas and the Canadian border, and westwards as far as the Rockies, Louisiana – named for *le roi soleil* – bore ample evidence of its chequered past, first under the royal banner of France and then, for thirty-seven years, under that of Spain. France took over once more, albeit briefly, in the last year of the eighteenth century but, in 1803, Jefferson purchased the territory from Napoleon and, at a stroke, spread the influence of Washington far beyond the bounds of anything dreamt of by his predecessors in the Presidency. Now, of course, Louisiana had shrunk into a relatively compact area centred upon the Mississippi delta. Admitted to the Union in 1812, if the state was now in a like situation to those it had followed into the ill-starred Confederacy, this was not immediately apparent in New Orleans as it prepared for the festival of *Mardi Gras*.

Andrew explored the streets and the alleyways of the *Vieux Carré*, many of which advertised their French origin in names like *"Chartres"*, *"Bourbon"*, *"Orleans"*, *"Toulouse"*, *"Dauphine"*. Many of the houses, reconstructed following the fires which largely destroyed the city towards the end of the Spanish period, boasted wrought iron balconies of exquisite grill-work while, behind the brightly painted facades, were shady patios which, so Andrew was assured, were similar to those that were commonplace from the Pyrenees to Andalusia.

Andrew stood on the levee watching beyond the mass of funnels, spars and rigging, the lazy swirl of the Mississippi slipping down to meet the sea. He had arranged a passage to Philadelphia on a coastal steamer named *Beauregard*; the vessel was due to sail at six o'clock that evening and Andrew had already been aboard to find his cabin and stow away his valise, but as it still wanted a couple of hours before sailing time he had come ashore again to stretch his legs. He walked up Canal Street past the infamous Monkey Wrench Corner and turned right into Bourbon. At the corner of Bourbon and St. Ann, he found a small café with tables and chairs set out at the side of the pavement. Andrew seated himself at a vacant table and ordered a coffee which was brought to him by a flat-footed negress, who was so plump that she was practically bursting out of her candy-striped calico frock.

There had been only one letter awaiting collection at New Orleans – one from Henry Caldwell – and Andrew now slit the envelope and looked inside. It contained a cutting from the *Advertiser* dated Tuesday 14th November. Andrew unfolded the newsprint and spread it out on the table beside his coffee cup. He found he was looking at mutilated front page columns reporting upon sales at Perth Auction Mart the previous Friday. He turned the paper over and his interest quickened.

"PRIVATEER SURRENDERS," he read,
"from our special correspondent: Liverpool 9th November:

> "The privateer, *Shenandoah*, sailing under the flag of the Confederate States of North America, entered the Mersey under escort on Tuesday of last week. Her master, Captain Waddell, surrendered both vessel and crew to Her Majesty's Government stating that he had not heard of the end of the war until the beginning of August. He and his crew were given

parole on November 8th and, on the following day, with due and proper ceremony, representatives of the Royal Navy turned the vessel over to the United States Consul.

DUNDEE MAN'S ORDEAL RECALLED

"It will be recalled that Dundee business man, Mr. Andrew Gray, of R. J. Caldwell & Son, Baltic Mills, suffered at the hands of this Captain Waddell in July last when the *City of Baltimore*, the vessel upon which he was voyaging to the United States, was intercepted by *Shenandoah* off the American coast. Despite the fact that Captain Waddell was advised by the *City of Baltimore*'s skipper that the war had been over for some two months, Waddell set the passengers and crew afloat in the ship's boats before turning *Shenandoah*'s guns upon the luckless *City of Baltimore*, sinking her before their very eyes. With this in mind we cannot but deem it highly unsatisfactory that Waddell should now contend he knew nothing about the end of hostilities until August. While Mr. Gray was one of those fortunate enough to be rescued by the local fishing fleet, one of *City of Baltimore*'s boats was never seen again and it must be accepted that all aboard her perished at sea."

Henry Caldwell would no doubt now be redoubling his efforts to claim compensation! Andrew sipped his coffee and watched the passers-by. When he had finished, he paid the bill and pressed a nickel into the serving woman's pink outstretched palm.

When he returned to *Beauregard*, Captain Reeve was awaiting him at the head of the gangway. Jack Reeve had been raised in the Bayou country right here in Louisiana, but he had sailed the seas for a quarter of a century in the ocean-going ships of the New Orleans Blue Star Packet Company before retiring to the less onerous duties demanded of a skipper in the coastal trade. But, despite all his years at sea, there was no trace of grey in the fringe of black whiskers round his chin. Right now, he was puffing away at a pipe filled with very pungent smelling tobacco. As Andrew came up the plank, the Captain took the pipe from his mouth,

"Reckon y'all could have stayed ashore a mite longer!" he said, the black eyes in his dark complexion glowing like coals. "We ain't sailing at six after all."

"No?"

"No. Gotta wait for the stern wheeler comin' down from Baton Rouge. She's due around a half past six. Has a fellow country woman of yours aboard – English dame who's come down from Natchez and is looking for a passage east. Owners had the message over the telegraph and as we've gotten a berth available, I guess we wait!"

"I see."

"Yeah! Seems there's been some kind of accident. Guy she was travellin ' with – husband I guess – was playin' poker and got himself shot! Killed stone dead, so they say! These card sharps are a bad lot – 'specially those on the river boats. Don't y'all ever go and get mixed up with them!"

"Well!" said Andrew. "The poor chap has certainly learnt the hard way!"

"You bet!"

"What happened to the card sharp?"

"Ain't never said: but I guess he'd light out pretty damn quick! He'd slip over the edge more'n likely!"

"And what about the man who was shot – English, I suppose?"

"Oh! They buried the poor guy at Baton Rouge."

"Poor devil!"

"Yeah! Well! If you'll excuse me, Mr. Gray, here comes the pilot!" The Captain pointed to a man making his way to the foot of the gangplank.

Andrew turned away and, climbing the companionway to the upper deck where, he took up a position from which he had an uninterrupted view of the quayside. The sun was nearly down now but it was still pleasantly warm. *Beauregard* was, of course, loaded, cleared and ready to sail. There was little activity going on and the dock below was deserted but for the seaman on duty at the foot of the gangway and a couple of stevedores who were hanging around ready to cast off the mooring ropes. Andrew heard the clock of a nearby church striking six. Some twenty minutes later, he was just about to go to fetch his greatcoat when he heard the pounding paddle wheel of a river steamer as it approached the ferry landing 200 yards or so upstream from where *Beauregard* was tied. Surely this would be the boat from Natchez and Baton Rouge bearing the tragically widowed Englishwoman. Unless the poor woman kept to her cabin throughout, the voyage to Philadelphia was not likely to prove very stimulating. The sun had sunk down in the west and the light was beginning to fade. The river boat's horn blew – a single long strident note – and Andrew could see the wake from the wheel at her stern creaming down towards them. Despite the increasing chill of the evening air, Andrew stayed where he was. It was nearly seven on his watch when he heard footsteps. Several people were approaching; it was not easy to see how many, or even to make them out properly, for lamps had been lit along the gangplank and this made it even more difficult to look beyond into the gathering dusk.

Below him, Captain Reeve came to stand at the head of the gangway. The shadowy figures resolved into sharper focus as they stepped into the pool of light thrown by the lamps. A woman wearing a cloak and bonnet stepped onto the gangway and walked smartly up. Clearly she was not old. Behind her came two negro porters carrying her baggage which, so far as Andrew could see, consisted of a valise and a large tin trunk.

Captain Reeve was holding out his hand to help the woman down to the deck from the end of the plank. Andrew could hear him greeting her and then instructing the porters to set down their loads.

"Welcome aboard the *Beauregard*, ma'am," the Captain said, and then added, "I sure would like to offer you – er – condolences – ma'am!"

"Thank you, Captain Reeve," said the woman, and her voice was soft as the caress of mist on the hill and gentle as thistledown carried on a summer breeze – and it had a lilt to it far removed from the southern drawl of Louisiana.

"Thank you, Captain Reeve. You are most kind . . ."

Andrew heard no more of what she had to say. His heart had missed a beat and his mind was whirling. He would recognise that voice anywhere and he knew now that which, in his heart of hearts, he had always known. But then – circumstances being what they were – he had never thought it possible they could meet again, certainly not thousands of miles from home on the deck of a small American coastal steamer lying in the flood tide of the mighty Mississippi.

Like a bullet from a gun, he dashed along the deck and almost fell down the companionway.

"Mary!" he shouted – then stopped in his tracks a few feet away.

The woman gave a sharp, startled cry, picked up her skirts and – to Captain Reeve's utter astonishment – threw herself into Andrew's outstretched arms.

Andrew spent a sleepless night. In the cramped space of the small bunk he occupied on the vessel's starboard side, he tossed and turned, banging his elbows against the bulkhead and his head on the ceiling when he forgot where he was and tried to rise. To say that his mind was reeling would be a massive understatement. It was gyrating back and forward, round and about and back again, in an endless intricate pattern, but a pattern without shape or substance. Was it not Byron, he thought, who coined the phrase regarding the incredible strangeness of truth. Nothing that could ever be imagined in a work of fiction could surely be stranger than the extraordinary coincidence that had thrown him and Mary together in such an unlikely setting. And yet, when he thought about it, was it really so unlikely? It would have been presumptuous in the extreme to imagine that R. J. Caldwell and Son could be the only Scottish – or English for that matter – concern to be anxious in regard to monies owing to them by debtors in the former Confederacy.

From what Mary had told him, it seemed that the legal firm in Edinburgh, of which her late husband had been a partner, had several clients with business interests in the southern states. What could be more natural than to send out a partner to represent these clients and to attend to such legal formalities as might arise? And as in their case there were no inhibiting family ties, was it not to be expected that the partner should take his wife along with him on the trip?

Captain Reeve, once recovered from the astonishment of discovering that his two passengers were well known to each other, had left them to their own devices. Neither Mary nor Andrew felt like eating and when they asked the captain to excuse them from joining him over the evening meal, he readily acquiesced and made no attempt to persuade them otherwise. In fact he insisted that the pair of them should have the use of his day cabin – normally pressed into service as a mess room for the passengers' meals – and he ejected his fellow officers and the remaining two passengers saying that, for this evening only, dinner would be served in the seamen's mess.

For Mary, the emotional strain of her unexpected meeting with Andrew, coming as it did right on top of the dreadful stress of the past few days, was almost more than she could bear. But they sat together at the captain's table until well after midnight – talking.

Mary and Robin Cargill had sailed from Liverpool in early October and, much as Andrew had done, they had visited clients in several states, success-fully for the most part. Robin's last call had been at Jackson and they had travelled from there by coach to Natchez where, when his business was done, they had embarked upon the ill-fated voyage down the Mississippi. Andrew could not be expected to know, of course, but Robin – so Mary said – was an inveterate gambler. Her eyes filled with tears as she recalled how he loved to sit down with his friends round the table, wagering far more than he could afford upon the mere drop of a card. He had played at Lagganeinich the very first time she had met him, just as he had been playing when he was killed. If she remonstrated – as she often did – his answer was always the same.

"'Tis but a moment's relaxation, Mary my girl! Indulge me, I pray, for this brief, ephemeral moment and we shall be rich, girl – richer than we have ever dreamed! One more hand – at double the stake! The very pulse quickens within me! Don't look so glum! It's... it's the way I am. I...'drink and swear and play at cartes...' just like the man Hamiltion in 'Holy Willie's Prayer'."

"The devil's books!" said Andrew

Mary nodded.

"He must have been a great character," Andrew added. "I should like to have known him."

The voyage across the gulf, round the Florida keys and up the Atlantic coast was smooth and uneventful. The weather remained calm and fair, enabling Andrew and Mary to spend much of their time on the upper deck and, gradually, the colour began to return to Mary's cheeks. She told Andrew of Robin's dislike of sailing. Poor man, he had spent most of the voyage across the Atlantic sick on his bunk and even on that awful river steamer he had complained of feeling queasy. Mary did not condescend in any way upon the circumstances surrounding the fatal shooting – nor, of course, did Andrew enquire. It was quite possible that she did not know – Andrew sincerely hoped that this was so and that she had been in their cabin at the time and not in the saloon.

They stopped for two days and nights at the busy port of Mobile where there was cargo to pick up and three more passengers, all male. As there were only four cabins in all and one of these was occupied by Mary, it meant that the men had to double up. This, of course, produced conditions even more cramped than previously. Andrew's bunk-mate was a fat, heavily perspiring man of about fifty. He hung his sweat-sodden shirt on the hook at the back of the door and the rank unpleasant smell of it mingled with that of his breath, which stank of onions and chewing tobacco. He loosened the bulging waistband of his trousers and, without removing his boots which looked as if they had come straight from mucking out a stable, he lay down on the bunk and belched loudly.

Andrew excused himself and shut the door behind him. Mary's cabin, by comparison, was cool, airy and fragrant as a bunch of roses. From that moment on, Andrew did not return to his former bunk. If the fat man thought anything of it, which was doubtful, he kept the matter to himself. When their paths crossed, he greeted Andrew with, "Hi there, bud!" and passed on. At meal times he was much too busy to speak as he stuffed himself with food, wiped his plate clean with a crust of bread and picked his yellowing teeth with the point of a vicious-looking knife. At night, when Andrew lay with Mary enfolded in his arms, the thoughts continued to buzz around in his head until after the first streamers of the dawn had penetrated through the slatted shutter drawn over the thick glass of the port hole.

When they reached Philadelphia, Captain Reeve stood at the head of the gangplank and shook hands with them.

"Goodbye, Mistress Cargill! Goodbye, Mr. Gray! I trust you'all will have a smooth passage home to England."

They let that one go – after all, they would most probably be routed via Liverpool! They had to wait for a cab, there being none on the rank as they walked up from Penn's Landing. When one did come along, Andrew heaved the baggage aboard and clambered in beside Mary.

"Keystone Hotel, please!"

"Yes, sir!"

The clerk at the reception desk was very helpful.

"Good afternoon, sir!" he beamed a wide and welcoming smile, "Double room? How many nights, sir?"

Andrew, conscious of Mary's eyes upon him, swallowed.

"No," he said, endeavouring to suppress what might be regarded as a sigh. "Two single rooms please, one for Mistress Cargill and one for me, Andrew

Gray. I don't know yet how many nights: why don't we say two to begin with and we'll let you know our plans as soon as possible?"

"Of course, Mr. Gray! I'm sorry, sir! Will you sign the register please, ma'am?"

Mary did as she was bidden, Andrew following suit. The clerk, with a flourish, banged the bell on his desk and held up two keys to the smartly uniformed boy who answered the summons.

"Rooms 216 and 218, please, Larry!"

"Sure thing! This way, ma'am ... sir!" Carrying a valise in each hand and leaving the tin trunk under the eagle eye of the ebony-faced bell captain, the boy led the way across the lobby and up the wide carpeted staircase. At the first landing they turned into the corridor and stopped outside room 216. Andrew had never quite got used to the American system of treating the ground floor as the first. The rooms were adjacent, each having a small window looking out on to Arch Street. It was a dull afternoon, cold with a smirr of rain that felt as if it might well turn to snow – vastly different from the hothouse atmosphere Andrew had encountered on his first visit to Philadelphia. There was a small German restaurant just round the corner on 2nd Street where they found a quiet table near the door. The food was simple but good: steaming hot soup straight from the stock pot, followed by a rich stew of pork served with spatzle and a salad of cucumber and onion with diced beetroot in one corner and shredded radish in the other. They had very little room left for dessert, which was a mouth-watering strudel, bursting at the seams with apple and raisins, laced with sugar and cinnamon and smothered all over in whipped cream. They sat for a long time over their coffee, so long in fact that, when Andrew paid the bill and they rose to go, they were the last customers left.

In the morning Mary stayed at the hotel writing letters while Andrew went out, first to Isaacs & Zoller to tie up any loose ends, business wise, and then to see Vic at Ledger, Marks & Lindenbaum. Robin Cargill's American law agents were the New York firm of Lynch & Balfour with whom his partners in Colville, Carrington & Cargill had dealt over many years and Mary had said that she wished to visit them before sailing for home. In fact, she was writing to them from Philadelphia, notifying them as to what had happened and saying that she would call in the course of the next few days. There was, of course, no question of Andrew letting her go on to New York on her own, and for her part, Mary had been perfectly content to stay on in Philadelphia until Andrew should be free to leave.

Vic Zoller was his usual debonair self – delighted to learn how well Andrew had got along and how successful had been all the arrangements they had made together in the first place. He was incredulous to learn of Andrew's adventures in the wilderness. Whatever had possessed him to go off like that into the blue? He might have been killed – and scalped. It was,

Andrew said, a good deal safer than certain rather more conventional forms of transport. At least he had emerged, alive and kicking, which was more than could be said for a fellow countryman of his who had been shot dead in the course of a poker game in the saloon of a stern wheeler on the Mississippi. Vic was horrified.

"What the hell happened?" he asked.

"I don't know." said Andrew. "Seems he had got involved in a game with one of those card sharp characters that plague the river steamers. I've no idea as to what he had done, if anything. All I know is that the card sharp pulled a gun on him and shot him dead."

"Was it reported to the authorities?"

"I imagine so; in fact they must have done so for they buried the poor devil at Baton Rouge – his widow has all the papers."

"Well – they'll be on the look out for the villain, if that's any consolation. Unlikely to find him, though."

They said no more but, if it did nothing else, it confirmed Andrew's fears that Mary would be pressed by the New York solicitors for the whole story, whether she liked it or not. Andrew asked Vic to join them that evening for dinner at the City Tavern. He readily agreed and, as on the previous occasion, he called for them at the "Keystone" at six o'clock. He bowed to Mary and took her hand in his.

"How do you do, Mistress Cargill! Please accept my sincere sympathy upon the dreadful calamity you have suffered in my country."

Mary murmured acknowledgement and, from that moment on, neither Vic, nor any of the others, made any further reference to the matter. Indeed, as Mary walked between the two men from the "Keystone" to the "Tavern" she felt almost carefree – an extraordinary sensation and quite unaccountable. The joy of meeting Andrew, and there was no other word for it – it was a joy – had helped to distract her mind from the shock of Robin's violent death. Even although she knew that Andrew was a married man, and could never be hers, maybe in a peculiar way because of that knowledge, she had revelled in his company. But this feeling of carefree detachment was somehow different. The evening promised to be a good one and she would enjoy every minute of it. There would be plenty time for the unhappy thoughts, the ache of memories, first during the interview in New York to which she was not looking forward and then, after she got home and Andrew had left her to be re-united with the wife she tried not to think about.

Two days later they checked out of the "Keystone" and took the train for New York. As their carriage, with a hollow rumble of wheels, jolted across the bridge over the Delaware into New Jersey, Andrew could not help thinking of all that had happened to him since last he left Philadelphia by train. Hopefully, he was now on the last lap of the journey but, no sooner had this thought entered his mind than he was assailed by the miserable realisation that once they got home he would require to leave Mary all by herself, while he returned to Dundee to pick up the threads of life once more with Vicky at Strawberry Hill. Mary was quite sure she knew the trend of Andrew's thoughts and she took his hand in hers and held it fast as the train ran swiftly up through Trenton to the sprawl of metropolitan New York and the boat that would take them across the Hudson to the ferry terminal near Battery Park at the southernmost tip of Manhattan.

They hailed a cab and asked to be taken to the Stuyvesant Hotel in Washington Square – one recommended by Vic Zoller.

"This your first time in New York?" The cabby was muffled against the biting wind and his breath was like a puff of steam in the chill atmosphere. His accent was clipped and sounded strange to ears that had become attuned to the southern drawl. It was also difficult to follow, sounding like "foist time in Noo Yoick".

"Yes," said Andrew. "What a big city it is!"

"Over 800,000 people," said the cabby. "Many of 'em came in right here!" He pointed with his whip to a small round brownstone building standing at the edge of the park. "That's the Immigration Depot where the United States authorities screen 'em when they get off the ships from Europe!"

"Looks more like a fort," said Andrew.

"Sure! It was a fort. Built to keep the British out in 1812. After that they used it as the theatre but, for the past ten years, I guess, it's been the Immigration Depot. Now – it's too small. They'll sure have to find somewhere else and pretty soon too.

"Now, d'you see that church over at the corner of Wall Street?" He pointed to a building with a tall spire. "That's Trinity – building's been there – oh, twenty years, I guess – but the church is a whole lot older. Reckon Trinity Church must be close on two hundred years old. If you've time you should see the old graveyard. Gee! Some of these stones go back to the 1600s."

Although Andrew had not previously heard of Trinity Church, the name, Wall Street, was well enough known to him as being the American equivalent to the City of London – the financial hub of the nation.

"Yep," said the cabby, "that's Wall Street where fortunes are made and lost in a day. They say it's named after the original wall the Dutch settlers built across the northern boundary of their colony. New Amsterdam they called it. I guess there's a city of that name back in Holland where they came from. Would you believe they bought the whole of Manhattan from the Injuns for a handful of beads, for Christ's sake! Gee! That was some bargain!"

New York was big and brash. The sidewalks were crowded with people and the streets thronged with horse-drawn traffic of all sorts and descriptions from cabs, carriages and omnibuses to delivery vans and carts. Through it all, boys pushing handcarts darted to and fro, narrowly escaping being trampled underfoot by the horses' hoofs, or crushed under the wheels. The noise was quite incredible and the air was heavy with the scent of horses intermingled with a smell of cooking compounded of hot oil, vinegar and spices.

As they passed the busy intersection with Fulton Street, their self-appointed guide was hard at it pointing out the large and ornate City Hall.

"There it is!" he cried. "Over half a million dollars worth of public money went to build that – even though they couldn't afford to do the job properly – look! The front there, and the sides – Gee! ain't that beautiful marble! But look there – at the back! What do you see?"

"Ah yes!" said Andrew. "No marble."

"That's right! Back's faced in brownstone. Reckon some day they'll maybe finish the job but I don't think it will be in my time!"

The Stuyvesant Hotel occupied a prominent site among elegant red brick houses, trimmed with white, lining the north side of Washington Square. Andrew asked the cabby to wait while he ascertained whether the hotel could accommodate them. The lobby was busy and there were several people waiting at the reception desk. Mary was sure the hotel was full – there were far too many people around for what should be a quiet time of the day. Luckily she was proved wrong. There were two rooms available and, what was more, they each looked out to the front. Andrew paid off the cabby and saw to their baggage. Then, after washing off the stains of travel, they went down to the dining room for a late lunch. In the afternoon they walked a bit. The streets around the hotel were full of students, understandable looking to the fact that the University of New York occupied a large part of Washington Square itself. It was still cold; in fact, the snow that had threatened off and on for several days now, finally, started to fall. By the time Andrew and Mary found their way back to the square and the welcoming warmth of the lobby at the "Stuyvesant", the snow was lying on the streets and on the sidewalks, and the bare branches of the trees in the square were laced with white. The night was frosty and cold but there was no further snowfall.

Next day was Sunday. The city authorities had worked all Saturday evening clearing the snow and movement along the sidewalks proved relatively easy. On enquiry at the reception desk, Andrew was directed to a small Presbyterian Church down on Canal Street near the intersection with Lafayette. On their way back to the hotel, they walked up the Bowery, a thoroughfare which, less than a decade previously, had been vibrant with life – given over to the theatre and all the elements of fashionable society that went with it. Recently, however, the high life of the city had tended to move northwards – up town – and the Bowery was beginning to decline as a steady stream of immigrants from all over the old world, having newly been cleared by the authorities at Castle Clinton down at Battery Park, poured into the area, rapidly turning it into a multi-racial slum. Back at the hotel, Andrew and Mary spent the rest of the day quietly – perfectly content in each other's company. Tomorrow would have to take care of itself but, of course, tomorrow had to be faced and it came along all too soon.

The firm of Lynch & Balfour, Solicitors and Attorneys, occupied a small suite of offices in William Street and, when Andrew and Mary got there on Monday morning, they were immediately ushered into a low-ceilinged but well-furnished room where a tall and elderly gentleman in knee breeches and cut-away tail coat rose from his desk and came forward to greet them.

"Archibald Balfour, Mistress Cargill," he said, shaking Mary by the hand. "I am distressed and shocked to hear of your husband's ... er ... demise. Pray accept my deepest condolences, ma'am." Archibald Balfour was a man of nearly eighty but, although he had lived nearly all his life here in New York – having arrived from Scotland when Thomas Jefferson was President – he had never lost the accent of his native Linlithgow. Somehow or other, it put them both at their ease.

"Thank you, Mr. Balfour, you are very kind. May I introduce Mr. Andrew Gray. We were friends years ago in Forfarshire and, by great good fortune – and incredible coincidence really – Mr. Gray was a fellow passenger on the coastal steamer upon which I took passage from New Orleans to Philadelphia."

"Yes," said Archibald Balfour, "you did mention that in your letter, Mistress Cargill. How do you do, Mr. Gray?"

"Mr Balfour!" said Andrew, inclining his head.

Archibald Balfour, having made sure that his visitors were comfortably seated, resumed his own chair behind the desk. He lay back in his seat and placed his hands together fingertip to fingertip.

"Mistress Cargill," he said, "I regret very much having to ask you to cast your mind back to that melancholy day aboard the river steamer but I am afraid it is necessary that I be put in full possession of all the facts. I trust I shall not cause you overmuch distress."

"I realise that there are many questions you will wish to ask, Mr. Balfour," said Mary. "And I shall try to answer as best I can."

"Capital! Capital!" Archibald Balfour was greatly relieved and he spoke rather more heartily than he had intended or would have wished.

"On the day of his death, Mistress Cargill, your husband was, I think, playing a game of cards. Is that correct?"

"Yes."

"What was the date, Mistress Cargill?"

"February 7th – three weeks past on Wednesday."

"And the name of the vessel?"

"*Memphis Queen* – Captain Theodore Gerard."

"Thank you." Archibald Balfour was writing everything down in neat copperplate. "Did the game take place in the ship's saloon?"

"Yes."

"Were you present, Mistress Cargill?"

"Yes." Andrew looked up sharply. He had so hoped Mary had been spared that.

"Playing?"

"Oh no!"

"Who were the players?"

"My husband, a fellow passenger – Mr. Harold Delahunt – I have his card here..." Mary handed over a small visiting card. "...and...and...the other man. They were playing poker."

"Who was the other man?"

"I don't know. I had never seen him before."

"Never mind. Villains of that nature seldom stay any time aboard: they work from one boat to the next, often staying on for only one stage.

"Your husband was a good player, was he not?"

"Yes, very good,"

"Was he winning?"

"Yes: to begin with he had his share of wins, and then... the luck seemed to change and the other man won time after time."

"Did Mr... er... Delahunt win at all?"

"Yes. He was like Robin: occasional wins, then – nothing."

"Did this upset your husband?"

"Not at first; but after a while I saw him beginning to look very closely at the cards – and at his fellow players."

"What happened then?"

"Well..." Mary hesitated.

"I'm sorry, Mistress Cargill; please continue."

"Robin suddenly pushed the table aside and jumped to his feet. He was very angry indeed and I heard him shout, 'Cheat! – marked cards by God!'" Mary stopped abruptly and shuddered. Andrew placed a hand on her arm. She was as white as a sheet but Andrew saw her chin go up as she continued, speaking in a low voice, "That was all he said. I heard a shot and saw two things – the man standing with a smoking pistol in his hand, and Robin collapsing with blood welling out over his shirt."

There was a long silence broken only by the slow ticking of a long case clock standing in one corner of the room.

"I don't quite know what happened after that," said Mary, "I rushed to help Robin but there was nothing I nor anyone else could do: he had been killed outright. There was a scuffle near the door of the saloon and the man with the gun had gone. I remember seeing that he had taken with him the cards and the money that had been lying on the table."

"Can you describe the man?"

"Yes. Thirty-five or so – short – not much more than five feet six. Heavy featured, thickly lidded eyes – light blue, I think. Long darkish hair, clean shaven, cleft chin and protruding ears. Oh yes, and on his left hand he wore a gold ring with a heavy square signet that had markings of sorts on it in black – I couldn't make out the design."

"This was all reported at the time?"

"Yes – to the Louisiana State Police at Baton Rouge and to the registrar there. It was necessary to register the death so that arrangements could be made for burial."

"Of course. Mr Cargill was buried at Baton Rouge?"

"Yes. In the old cemetery there. I have the papers."

"Perhaps you will allow me to make a copy of these."

"Yes – certainly."

"The report filed with the police – did it contain statements by Mr . . . Delahunt and by the master of the ship, Captain . . . er . . . Gerard?"

"Yes."

"Good. Well, I think we have covered everything, Mistress Cargill. May I thank you most sincerely for your cooperation. You have been clear and concise in what must be very trying circumstances – very trying indeed. It is, however, essential that we, as your husband's agents in America, should be fully informed. If I should require anything further, which I doubt, I shall refer to the authorities at Baton Rouge. And now, there is really nothing more. Your husband was quite meticulous and he passed on to us all the documents and papers covering each item of business as it was attended to. His last letter was written from Jackson, Mississippi and you say, Mistress Cargill, in the letter you wrote us from Philadelphia, that he had undertaken no further business calls. As you can see, we are therefore in the position of being able to report and account fully to Messrs Colville, Carrington & Cargill in Edinburgh."

"Thank you, Mr Balfour. I shall let my husband's partners know how very helpful you have been throughout our stay in America."

"A great pleasure, Mistress Cargill – in fact it is a rare treat to hear Scottish voices again!"

"Well, good-day then, Mr. Balfour. Perhaps you would be kind enough to leave the death certificate and the burial papers for us to pick up tomorrow morning."

"Certainly, Mistress Cargill! Have you arranged your passage home?"

" Not yet." Andrew spoke for the first time. "We are going to seek a shipping agency now."

"Capital! Capital! Why don't you try Johnstone & Barrie – have a place near here on Water Street. Ask for Bob Johnstone and mention my name. His grandfather came out with me from Scotland in '09! Goodbye, Mistress Cargill! Mr Gray!"

When they got out into William Street Mary sighed with relief. She was shivering – not from cold but from pent-up emotion. There and then, in the busy narrow street, Andrew put his arms round her and held her close.

5. Dundee
1866

Andrew and Mary arrived back in Liverpool on a breezy blustery day at the beginning of March. The air was clear – certainly in the lee of the crowded shipping in the docks. Windward too, the smoke from the scores of steamers was plucked away in long trailing banners over the white-flecked waters of the Mersey. It was just after breakfast when they landed and, within the hour, they were aboard a train bound for Edinburgh. After some delay at Carlisle, they crossed the western border and came up into Annandale where on the low ground by the river teams of horses were engaged at the ploughing. Overhead, the gulls were wheeling against the blue of the sky and the green slopes of the hills where the cloud shadows chased. It was a day when the dullest of dull people could hardly help but feel exuberant and, with Mary at his side, and the beauty of an early spring afternoon in Scotland unfolding before them, mile after mile, Andrew's spirit should have exulted within him. The reality, however, was very different. They were both gloomy and despondent – prisoners of their thoughts, silent and withdrawn.

They reached Edinburgh in the early evening and took a cab down to Heriot Row. The colour of the sky had faded with the sinking sun and ahead, as the cab went down Dundas Street, the river was a steely grey framed in the bare branches of the trees in Queen Street gardens. A smudge of smoke against the hills of Fife showed that the good folk of Kinghorn and Burntisland were cooking their evening meals. The cab turned left and drew up at a closed door.

For Mary, entering the house, packed as it was with memories of Robin – tangible and otherwise – was as traumatic an experience as any she had endured since the day of the shooting. The house smelled musty and stale – and it was cold. Andrew busied himself setting and lighting fires while

Mary did her best to set the place to rights after her long absence. There was, of course, no food in the larder so they went out to a nearby restaurant for a bite to eat. There was so much to say and so little time in which to say it. Nevertheless, they ate in silence, much as they had sat in the train. When they got back to the house, they found the cold air off it and warmth gradually beginning to steal in. Mary made up a bed for Andrew in the spare room and took herself off to the bed she had shared with Robin for the past six years. She undressed slowly, climbed between the cold sheets and cried herself to sleep.

In the morning, Andrew wrote and posted letters to Vicky and to Henry Caldwell, advising them that he would be arriving in Broughty Ferry off the Edinburgh train at midday on Friday 9th March. He also wrote a brief note to his mother telling her that he was safely back in Scotland and that he would be home in Dundee on Friday. This gave him today and tomorrow to spend in Edinburgh with Mary, who still had to face the ordeal of calling upon Robin's partners. She thought it best to go there alone while Andrew was busy with his correspondence. For his part, Andrew, once he got back from the post box, was in a lather of sweat awaiting Mary's return. It was nearly one o'clock when she came in carrying bread and a heavy bag of groceries which she dumped on the kitchen table. By this time Andrew was beside himself with anxiety.

"All right?" He placed an arm round her shoulder. Mary turned to face him and placed her forehead on his chest.

"Yes: but let's not talk about it any more – not just now at any rate."

Andrew gathered her in his arms.

When Friday morning came, they embraced again like a pair of young lovers.

"I suppose it's goodbye, then." Andrew's voice was thick and his words sounded choked.

"Andrew dear," said Mary. "Farewell I'll allow – but never goodbye."

"What else can I do?" Andrew spoke gruffly and crushed her to him even more tightly. Mary gasped and he slackened his grip.

"Dundee is not so very far away," she said. "You can always come to Edinburgh to see me. Everybody has to come to Edinburgh at some time!"

"Are you going to stay on here?"

"Yes – I think so, meantime at any rate, although I would not wish to remain long. I shall have to know how I am going to be placed financially but – this part of my life is finished; I would prefer to sell out and go back north."

"What? Back to Lagganeinich?"

"Oh no! I don't get on at all well with my sisters. My brother, Alasdair, the one you saw me with at Craigbeg, is a dear, but he has his own life to lead and certainly has no need of yet another sister hanging on his coat tails.

No – I might go back and live with Uncle John at Craigbeg. But I shall write and let you know what I am doing." She tried to sound matter of fact and normal.

"Best write care of the Bank," said Andrew. "Better than risking a letter to the mill."

It was then that the cab came and Andrew was gone, leaving Mary forlorn and utterly dejected.

There was quite a reception party waiting on the platform at the Broughty Ferry railway depot when Andrew stepped from the train that had carried him up from the railhead at the pier. He saw Henry Caldwell's square figure right away, the face under his tall hat looking redder than ever. Henry Caldwell was waving his cane in the air and shouting something or other which Andrew could not quite catch. Beside him was a youngish woman in a crinoline dress of bottle green and a short outdoor coat. She wore a furred and be-ribboned bonnet of the same shade as her dress and her hair, done in a mass of ringlets like those of some woman in a painting by Van Dyck, escaped at the back and sides. One gloved hand held a small beaded reticule and the other, to Andrew's utter astonishment, was tucked in under Henry Caldwell's free arm.

There was yet another surprise in store, for before Andrew could take it all in, another female figure hidden until then behind Henry Caldwell's broad back, came scampering along the platform with a flouncing of petticoats and threw herself upon him.

"Vicky!" he said in amazement. "You are better then? How...how good to see you." He had little time to wonder whether that sounded as lame as he imagined for Henry Caldwell was bearing down on them, hand out-stretched.

"Andrew, my boy! Welcome home! You look well – in fact I'd swear you've grown while you've been away!"

"Good to be back, sir," said Andrew. "How are you?"

"Fine! Just fine – and all the better for seeing you home again!"

"So this is the paragon of all the virtues – bronzed, I swear, and muscular as a Greek god." Andrew spun round to find the woman with Henry Caldwell looking at him. She smiled sweetly, but her eyes – china blue like Vicky's – were cold.

"Pappa! Pappa!" cried Vicky, jumping up and down clapping her hands, an animated performance quite unlike anything Andrew had seen her do in the past, and certainly quite out of tune with the gloomy reports he had been receiving in America as to her chronic indisposition. "You haven't intro-duced 'Cilla!"

"Dear, dear – neither I have!" Henry Caldwell tut-tutted and took the woman's gloved hand in one of his. "Andrew, my boy!" he said, "I should like you to meet Miss Priscilla Swankie who has done me the honour of consenting to be my bride!"

Andrew was aghast – but he smiled and made suitable responses while Vicky once more clapped her hands and then clasped them firmly upon Andrew's forearm.

"Isn't it marvellous?" she cried. "Pappa's getting married again and I'm to be matron of honour at the wedding!"

A porter had hold of Andrew's luggage and they all turned to follow him out of the depot to where Joseph was waiting with the carriage.

"Gude day to ye, Mr. Andra, sir! Man ye're looking richt braw! Thae foreign pairts maun hae 'greed wi' ye fine!"

Joseph helped the ladies into the carriage and lifted up Andrew's bags.

"When is the wedding to take place?" Andrew asked as the carriage jolted out from the yard and set off towards West Ferry.

"In June!" Vicky answered, "in Arbroath Parish Church."

All the way to Riga Lodge, Vicky kept up an endless stream of chatter about the forthcoming wedding, to all of which Andrew and her father made non-committal comments while the bride-to-be regarded them with a languid and bored expression.

It was almost dark before Joseph brought the carriage round to take Andrew and Vicky home to Strawberry Hill. As they drove through the darkened streets under the guttering gas lamps, Vicky prattled on and on about the wedding. Once or twice she made some pouting comment upon how unfeeling Andrew had been to leave her languishing for so long all on her own while he went gallivanting abroad; but she neither pressed the point nor did she in any way hint that she had missed Andrew's presence for his own sake. She had, of course, been very unwell; Aunt Tina's sudden death had been a great shock and Vicky had taken a very long time to recover. In fact, it was only in the past three weeks that she had begun to feel well again. Who wouldn't be stimulated at the thought of a wedding? It was just the tonic she had been needing and both the specialist from Edinburgh whom Pappa had engaged and Dr. Tannahill had been amazed at the change in their patient.

It seemed that Henry Caldwell had met his bride-to-be at a reception in Dundee at New Year hosted by the Lord Provost. Vicky had been unable accompany her father, although she had been included on the invitation. Among the guests that evening were Sir Robert and Lady Dargie. Did Andrew not know them? He did: the Dargies were prominent mill owners in the county and they lived in considerable style at St. Vigeans on the outskirts of Arbroath. What he did not know until Vicky told him, was the fact that Priscilla Swankie was Lady Dargie's niece. Priscilla's parents had died when she was little more than a baby and she had been brought up by the Dargies along with their own progeny, which numbered a round dozen. Priscilla had accompanied her aunt and uncle to the Lord Provost's reception which she had found boring in the extreme until she chanced to be introduced to the wealthy widower who owned the Baltic Mill. Vicky assumed she must have set her cap at Pappa – why should she not? She would certainly not see thirty again, Vicky remarked cattishly, and her father was a better catch than any she was likely to come across at this stage in her life! At all events she had succeeded in knocking Henry Caldwell off his feet: he was absolutely infatuated with her and for days afterwards could talk of little else.

Vicky was, of course, delighted, for poor Pappa had had a terrible time with Aunt Tina's death and all the cares of the business on his hands while Andrew was gadding about all over America. What was the Mississippi like? She hoped he had not looked at the much vaunted southern belles and had he ever been on one of those river boats with the big wheel at the back? How glamorous life must be sailing down the Mississippi on such a floating palace. Andrew winced inwardly. That was hardly the description Mary would have used – floating hell more likely! But Vicky was chattering on. June would be here soon enough and there was so much to do in the interval. Andrew would help her draw up a list of guests from the Caldwell side .... She was still talking breathlessly when Joseph pulled up at No. 2 Strawberry Hill, where the girl, Moira, opened the door to them and bobbed a curtsey as Andrew and Vicky came in. To her intense surprise, Moira saw that her mistress had the master firmly by the hand. After supper – a snack taken on a tray by the fire in the parlour – Vicky announced that she was tired and sleepy and, without another word, went off to bed. It was just ten minutes past eight.

Sarah Robertson was pleased with herself. The dining room table was looking its best – just like the picture in the late Mistress Isabella Beeton's *Book of Household Management* which David had given her as a present soon after its publication some five years ago. So far as she knew there was no other copy in Pitbuddo – not even up at the big house – and she was inordinately proud of it and anxious to manage her own household accordingly. She looked at the white tablecloth. Beautifully laundered and starched, its crisp folds fell evenly upon all sides. Sarah had especially asked David to refrain from making any caustic comment. She knew from past experience how apt he was to voice his objections to what he called "a' thae new fangled notions."

"Gudesakes, lass," he would say, "where's the sense in having good furniture gin ye canna see it!"

In the space between the settings of knives and forks, Sarah had placed linen serviettes, each folded in the shape of a fan and each with a sprig of lily of the valley tucked into one of the folds. The Robertson's dining room did not have a central light fitment such as advocated in Mistress Beeton's book but the candles in the three sconces set at intervals down the length of the table would provide more than sufficient light, and would set off quite admirably the arrangement of lilac blossom lovingly set in the middle of the table. Gas fittings borne upon wall brackets affixed to either side of the fireplace illuminated the sideboard from which, in accordance with Mistress Beeton's strong recommendation, the food would be served and the joint carved.

Kate the housemaid would help to serve. Sarah was fairly sure Kate would rise to the occasion; she could comport herself with dignity when required. Dochie, however, was a completely different kettle of fish. Sarah was not quite sure that she agreed with David who had insisted that his coachman could double, for this evening, as a butler. Sarah did so hope that Dochie would not let them down. He and Kate were in the kitchen when she returned there to see that all was in order. Kate's uniform was clean and fresh, her apron spotless and her cap set demurely upon her rather unruly mop of hair. Dochie, on the other hand, was dressed in one of their son Stewart's discarded suits. It fitted him where it touched and tended to make him appear smaller and more lugubrious than ever. Still, there was nothing much more Sarah could do about it at this late stage so she betook herself upstairs to dress.

When David suggested that they might arrange a dinner party to celebrate young Andrew Gray's homecoming after all those months in America, Sarah had jumped at the opportunity and had lost no time in talking the matter over with Jessie. As she had expected, Jessie immediately tried to discourage her. If there was to be any formal gathering on Andrew's behalf – of the necessity or desirability of which she was by no means convinced – then she, Jessie, should be doing the arranging and bearing the cost. In the end, however, but only after the doctor himself had intervened, they won her round and, after the invitations had gone out and all the acceptances had been counted, they were left with a final tally of eighteen which included the two of them and young Stewart, whom his father had taken into partnership after he had graduated from medical school.

Sarah so hoped the party would be a happy one. It ought to be; for most of the guests were well known to each other. She was not too sure, though, of Andrew's wife whom she had met only once and that on the day of the wedding; and, of course, there was the young couple from Pitbuddo House whom David had insisted upon adding to the list.

Up at Pitbuddo House, the Honorable Mrs. Maud Ramsay, dressed in a crinoline gown of midnight blue, the décolletage caused by its exceptionally low cut over the neckline and bust modestly veiled by a matching silken stole draped carelessly over her shoulders, stooped to kiss her father-in-law upon the slack, wrinkled skin of his highly coloured cheek.

"Goodnight, Pappa!" she said, "I do wish we didn't have to go out but Havelock says it would not be politic to turn down an invitation from the doctor."

"He's quite right, my dear." Following the death of Lady Ramsay a couple of years earlier, Sir George had aged considerably and his voice no longer carried the authoritative ring so familiar of yore. He was fond of this daughter-in-law and he was confident she would make a first class lady of Pitbuddo once he had been laid to rest and Havelock had inherited the estate and title. "Robertson is an influential man in the town and it is as well to keep in with him. I'll be interested to hear what you think of Mistress Gray – senior that is. They are an estimable family, the Grays. I knew the boy's father – grocer fellow; used to deliver up the glen once a week the way Mathers does now. He was killed you know – Gray. I spoke to him that very afternoon. Ran into a swarm of bees at the top of Cadger's Brae; horse bolted – Gray was thrown against a tree – killed stone dead! Widow's an admirable woman and son seems to have fallen on his feet! Married into money in Dundee – daughter of a fellow name of Caldwell – a manufacturer – Indian grass – jute, you know!"

Just then, Maud's husband made his appearance. Percival Havelock Ramsay was a man of thirty-eight, lean and spare. He had his father's eyes of piercing blue but, unlike Sir George, his hair, eyebrows and beard were black, now flecked with grey, and his complexion was to match. Educated at Eton and Sandhurst he had been commissioned into the 42nd (Royal Highland) Regiment and had seen active service at the Alma during the Crimean War and at Lucknow in the terrible time of the Indian Mutiny. In fact, he had been severely wounded in the groin during the latter campaign and had been so gravely ill that he had been invalided out of the service before the end of hostilities. Although left with a severe limp, he managed well enough and in recent years he had been spending more and more of his time at Pitbuddo and had virtually taken over from his father the duties of laird. The previous autumn, at Peterborough Cathedral, he had married the Honorable Maud Tinsley, the second daughter of an English earl with wide estates in the east midlands. Now, he offered his left arm to his wife and escorted her across the hall to the front door.

"Goodnight, sir!" he called, and his father inclined his head. Mr. Cloake, the butler, opened the door for them and they walked down the steps to the coach waiting below.

Jessie was in her element. It had been a long time since Andrew had stayed under her roof and now that he was here she intended making the most of it. The only cloud on the horizon was that wife of his. Try how she might, Jessie could not bring herself to like the girl. Admittedly, on this occasion, she appeared livelier and displayed more animation than she had ever previously

done in Jessie's presence, but still the doubt persisted. What was worse –
much worse in Jessie's view – was the fact that, for the first time, she now had
a niggling feeling that Andrew was thinking much the same way. She
couldn't be sure, of course, but the feeling wouldn't go away. Jessie had
never discussed the matter with either Jemima or Meg but she had the feeling
that Meg knew something that she didn't and the thought did nothing to
reassure her.

Thank goodness Henry Caldwell and his new lady love had declined the
invitation. It would have been ten times more difficult with them around. She
had quizzed Andrew regarding this but, so far as could be seen, there was no
ulterior motive behind it. Apparently there was some function or other at
Lintmill this weekend, which they had been unable to get out of, much as
Henry Caldwell at least would have wished to be in Pitbuddo. Jessie had not
met this Swankie woman but she was in no doubt as to her motives in setting
her cap at Mr. Caldwell! If she, Jessie, were any judge the advent of this
woman upon the stage did not auger well for Vicky's future inheritance.
Much as she disliked the girl, she could not help feeling sorry for her. Maybe
it was a measure of Vicky's stupidity but this aspect did not seem to have
dawned upon her. She was still as excited as a child at the thought of the
wedding and her own role in it. By the time she came to her senses, if ever
she would, the deed would be done and it would be too late!

Andrew was looking well! He told her very little about his American
experiences apart from the fact that he had enjoyed his time in Philadelphia
and that he had travelled across Texas on horseback. As she said to Meg,
getting any information out of him was harder than drawing teeth. Andrew
had come up for the day, shortly after his arrival home, but as there was a
considerable amount of work to be done following his American trip, it had
been arranged that he would delay another visit until such time as he had
sorted things out at the office. When the Robertsons had made their
suggestion of a welcoming dinner, Jessie had succeeded in getting Andrew to
specify a firm date in accordance with which he and Vicky had arrived from
Dundee yesterday afternoon. It was, of course, the first occasion upon
which Vicky had stayed with her mother-in-law at the Meal Wynd and, to
everyone's surprise, the girl had settled down without comment or complaint.

"Just let me hear her say anything nasty!" said Jemima, "and she'll know
about it, I promise you!"

"That will do, Jemima," said Jessie. "Remember that she is a guest in my
home – and your brother's wife."

"Worse luck!" said Jemima.

And now, the hour of the dinner party was approaching fast and Jemima
was first ready. She had on a very flattering gown – a product of her mother's
deft and capable fingers – and was dressed most becomingly; in fact, when

Andrew caught sight of her when he and Vicky came through into the kitchen, dressed and ready to go, he was in no doubt at all that this young sister of his would turn a few male heads before she was very much older. Vicky, in a full-skirted dress of crimson taffeta, looked dowdy by comparison but Jessie, when she appeared dressed for the occasion, looked positively regal and quite outdid them all. Although now somewhat fuller of figure, with silver streaks muting the lovely russet colours of her hair, she was still a fine-looking woman, although care lines around her mouth and at the corners of her eyes bore mute testimony to the fact that she was not far off her half century.

"Mother!" said Andrew, "I do declare you more and more beautiful with the passage of the years!"

"Rubbish!" Jessie snapped, but she could not entirely disguise the colour that mounted unbidden to her cheeks. To cover her embarrassment, she peered at the clock, "I thought they would have been here by now!" she said.

"They" were the Shirress family, elder and younger. The Robertson home, a detached modern villa, stood in its own grounds at the top of the High Street and as the Shirresses, on their way up, had to pass the top of Meal Wynd, it had been arranged that the Grays would wait till they came so that they might all walk up together. Almost as if Jessie, like a kind of Aladdin, had conjured him up, Joe Shirress – having knocked loudly – opened the door and walked in.

The rest were waiting on the High Street at the head of the Wynd – Sandy and Jean and Meg; Meg was now far advanced in pregnancy and the arrival of yet another young Shirress was imminent, so imminent that her mother had expressed some doubt as to whether in fact she ought to be attending the dinner party at all. Meg, however, had no qualms. Where better could she be – she had asked – than at the home of her medical adviser? Anyway, the other bairns were all bedded down and under the watchful eye of Lizzie Kidd, who had kindly agreed to look after them while their parents went out. Slowly then, the Gray and Shirress families walked up the High Street.

It was not long before all the guests were assembled in Sarah Robertson's pleasant drawing room – a delectable place where chintz-covered chairs and brocade curtains acted as a backcloth to ornaments of Meissen china and Benares brassware. Looking about him, Andrew felt a rare sense of to-getherness that he had not known for a very long time. Strangely enough, the sensation was rendered all the more vibrant by the fact that the one thing uppermost in his mind had nothing whatsoever to do with the men and women around him, or with their idle chatter. A triple question it was that bothered him – the unanswered and ever remaining one – "Where is Mary tonight? How is she? And what is she doing?" He had not yet had a letter from her and he had enquired regularly at the Bank ever since he came home. Small wonder that he was growing anxious. He caught Meg's eye and they both started guiltily and looked away.

Charlie and Ellen Tait had come up that afternoon from Dundee. Sitting awkwardly and side by side on the edge of their chairs, they were trying to look as if it were perfectly natural that they should be hob-nobbing with the laird's son and his wife, who happened to be sitting alongside them.

The only other guests were the Gardynes – Jim looking old and worn and his wife thinner and more acidulated than ever – and the Bells. Andrew was delighted to see Simon Bell again and to be introduced to his wife, Ruth. Andrew knew, of course, that Sam Coutts had died some five years ago and that the Bank had appointed Simon to succeed him as agent in Pitbuddo. He and Simon had much in common and they were still talking when a miserable-looking Dochie appeared in the drawing room doorway and, having knocked to obtain a modicum of silence, announced in sepulchral tones, "Leddies and gentlemen! Yer denner's served."

"Capital, Dochie! Capital!" cried Dr. Robertson, "Jessie, lass – here! Tak' an arm! And Vicky! Tak' the ither ane! Let me, mesdames, escort you to *la salle à manger!*"

After everyone was seated, Dr. Robertson rose to say grace. He chose the beautiful stanzas composed by Robert Burns:-

> "O thou, who kindly dost provide,
> For every creature's want,
> We bless thee, God of Nature wide,
> For all thy goodness lent:
> And, if it please thee, Heavenly Guide,
> May never worse be sent;
> But whether granted or denied
> Lord, Bless us with content!
>   Amen."

Kate and Dochie served as if to the manner born. First there was soup, made from good beef stock, thick and rich; followed by baked lemon sole with tartare sauce. Meanwhile, Dochie was putting up a fine performance with a decanter of a light dry wine from the Moselle. He had fished this out from a bucket of ice standing in the sideboard recess and was busily filling glasses with an élan which even Mr. Cloake might have found difficult to emulate. Then, while Kate cleared away the fish plates and cutlery, he was already hard at work, standing at the sideboard carving away at the most succulent-looking leg of lamb Andrew had seen in a very long time. Seeing his discerning look, Dr. Robertson called down the length of the table, "Home grown! One from the Mains. Geordie Milne may be getting on like the rest of us but naebody in Strathmore has better sheep."

Sarah frowned. She wished David would behave with a shade more decorum. Apart from his not infrequent outbursts, she was really very pleased with the way the evening was shaping. The two servants had quite surpassed themselves and now, with Dochie carving – he was much more expert than she had dared to hope – and Kate serving, the main course was being distributed with the minimum of delay. There would be no question of congealing fat round this table. Kate was now rushing around with the vegetables – spring cabbage which young Stewart commended to all and sundry as brim full of health-giving nutrients, and fluffy mealy potatoes liberally sprinkled with chopped parsley. All the while, having finished carving for the time being, Dochie was going round with decanters of a most excellent claret.

At length the table was cleared and after Kate and Dochie had reset it for dessert, they withdrew, leaving each guest to make a choice from a delectable selection of crystallised fruit, walnuts and dates to which could be added, if desired, portions of charlotte russe or lemon sponge. When eventually Sarah and the other ladies withdrew, and the men lit their cigars, and filled their glasses from one or other of the decanters of port and armagnac passed round by their host, the conversation ranged far and wide.

"How did you find things in America, Gray?" Out of the blue, Andrew found himself addressed by Havelock Ramsay.

"Much as I had anticipated," Andrew answered, looking at the bright blue eyes that seemed to bore into his very soul. "Business-like and efficient in the north; shattered, distressed and disillusioned in the south."

"Aftermath of war, what! Damned unpleasant business at any time. I saw some of it out in the Crimea, you know. The devil of it is, Gray, many of those whose policies make war would never do so could they but see for themselves the devastation and human degradation that follows inevitably in its wake! Not been to America myself. Would like to go. They tell me you travelled a bit in Texas and that you have even come home with the deeds of some land there!" Havelock Ramsay was remarkably well informed.

"Yes – well, my firm has, anyway."

"Good show! Quite a sound investment I should imagine."

"Yes. I believe it is."

"And likely to get better?"

"Yes. It is marvellous country to run cattle on – great rolling plains, empty under the sun but for the herds of bison, now rapidly diminishing, and the Indian tribes who live off them and, what many here fail to appreciate, plenty water."

"Go on. I'm interested. I have a bit of cash to invest. I wonder – would Texas be the place to put it?"

"Maybe not yet," said Andrew, "but – give it ten years or so and it could be that we'll see an investment in Texas doubling in value overnight. It all depends on the railroad and the ease, or otherwise, of getting Texan longhorn cattle into the stockyards at Chicago where they'll fetch high prices!"

"Mm...." Havelock Ramsay wrinkled his brow and still he gazed at Andrew with those disconcerting eyes. Meantime, the dining room door had opened and Dochie, looking like an undertaker coming to interview a client, came and spoke quietly to Dr. Robertson.

"Right, gentlemen!" said the doctor, "Dochie here tells me that tea and coffee are being served in the drawing room where the ladies await us! Shall we go?" He rose and, with a scuffling of chairs, his guests followed suit.

"Baltic Mill, isn't it?" Havelock Ramsay gripped Andrew by the elbow and spoke into his ear. "I may call in and see you sometime I'm in Dundee – what?"

"By all means," Andrew said, "I should be very pleased to see you."

It was well past eleven o'clock when the time came to go. The Ramsays, who of course had a mile or two to drive back to Pitbuddo House, went first.

"Goodbye, Gray!" Havelock Ramsay gripped Andrew's hand. "*À bientôt* as the Frogs say!.... Goodnight, Mistress Robertson – a memorable evening! Thank you so much for inviting us!"

"You know," Sarah's husband whispered in her ear as the coachman busied himself helping the Honorable Maud into the coach, "I really believe he means it." He had not time to say more for, one by one, the rest of the guests were coming up to say goodnight. The Gray and Shirress families were last to go.

"Thank you, doctor," said Jessie. "And thank you, Mistress Robertson, for a lovely party. It is as I have always said – whenever something essentially good happens in Pitbuddo, you may be sure a Robertson is behind it!"

"Ach! Awa' wi' ye, Jessie," cried the doctor. "This was our pleasure, woman!"

Jessie looked around. There was no sign of Jemima, although she had been standing close by a few minutes ago.

"Jemima!" she called, a trifle sharply perhaps.

"Yes, mother!" There was a rustling of skirts and Jemima, looking a shade pink and the smallest bit untidy about the hair, materialised from inside the house. Behind her, Jessie saw the tall figure of the Robertsons' eldest son. Dr. Robertson himself had his arm round Meg.

"Goodnight, lass!" he said. "Leastways – let's hope it is but remember, Joe, if I do have to see her again this night, you're not to hesitate to send for me!"

"Thank you, doctor," said Joe while Meg, reaching up, pulled Dr. Robertson's head to her level and kissed him fully on the lips.

Vicky was quiet and mournful of face. She had been complaining to Andrew for the past hour of feeling sleepy.

"Get that wife o' yours hame to her bed, Andrew Gray!" Dr. Robertson, disentangling himself from Meg, clapped Andrew on the shoulder.

"Yes, sir!" said Andrew. "Goodnight – and thank you!"

There was no moon that night; the street lamps had long since been extinguished but the summer night held a luminous quality and it was not really dark in the High Street of Pitbuddo as they made their way, slowly, home.

The following day was the Sabbath and they all went to sit under the now aging Mr. Black at the United Presbyterian Church. When the service was over, first one member of the congregation, then another, came up to shake Andrew's hand and be introduced to the whey-faced lass he had married down in Dundee. It was the same in the street as they walked back to the Meal Wynd and met many folk walking home from the other churches. When they got home, they had to wait for Jemima, who taught at the Sabbath School and would get back later. Meg, it appeared, had had a good night and the waiting – a situation to which she was by now well inured – continued.

Dr. Robertson had kindly arranged to send Dochie to take Andrew and Vicky to Brechin to catch the afternoon train. This would get them into Dundee around seven in the evening and, provided they got a cab right away, they would be in good time to have a tray supper in the parlour before Vicky would get sleepy and want to be off to bed. Jessie had arranged with the doctor that Dochie would go by way of the old Brechin road so that she and Jemima could get a lift out to Old Pitbuddo. After they had paid their respects at the little patch of green where Tom had lain for so long now, they parted. Jessie and Jemima to walk back to the Meal Wynd; Andrew and Vicky to go on with Dochie in the gig to Brechin. It was a fine sunny day and with the wind in the west – a rare treat for May – it was warm, too warm in fact to be sitting in a stuffy train jolting along on its way to Dundee. As they waited at Broughty Ferry for the Edinburgh connection to come up the line from the pier, the evening sun was flooding the platforms with glorious golden light. It was only three weeks now until the 16th June, the day fixed for the wedding, and Vicky did so hope that this lovely summer weather would continue.

"Wouldn't it be perfectly awful," she had said, as they were approaching Arbroath. "If the wedding day should turn out to be one of those dismal ones, when nobody can see because of an east coast haar and everyone is suffocated by an overpowering smell of smokies – you know what Arbroath can be like!"

Andrew had laughed, but he had to concede that Vicky had a point. A cold misty day would be bad enough, especially for the ladies in their summer dresses, but the additional hazard would be far worse. Andrew knew well enough how the haar was apt to trap all the odours of fish and smoke, an altogether unpleasant combination that could be expected to linger upon one's clothes for weeks afterwards!

The sunshine dimmed momentarily as the smoke from the engine bringing the connecting train up from the pier drifted overhead. There was a clanking of couplings, and a jolting, as the connecting carriages were hitched on to the Dundee-bound train. Then, with a mighty jerk and a loud blast on the whistle, they were moving again out past neatly kept back gardens to the shore line at West Ferry. They passed underneath the terraces at Riga Lodge but there was no sign of Henry Caldwell, or of Joseph, or anyone. Vicky was quite sure, however, that her father would be home long ere this, especially as he was to be on his own, Priscilla having announced that she would be staying at Lintmill now until the wedding as there was so much to do in preparation.

At the Stannergate, a number of folk, dressed in their Sunday best, joined the train and the carriage, which Andrew and Vicky had had to themselves since leaving Arbroath, filled up. However, when the train finally pulled in to the depot at Dundee they secured a cab readily enough.

"Strawberry Hill, please!" Andrew called, "Number two!"

"Aye, aye, sir!"

The cab lurched a bit as most tended to do on the Dock Street cobbles, and Vicky clutched at Andrew for support. If, as Andrew suspected, the cabby was an old sailor, he would, Andrew felt, be quite in his element from the way they rocked slowly from side to side as the cab took the short incline at the head of the Seagate. After that, however, it was plain sailing along the Nethergate and out the Perth Road. At the Sinderins, they passed the end of the Hawkhill and the cabby turned left and clamped on his brakes at the top of Strawberry Hill. Andrew had his purse out to pay the fare when the house door flew open and the girl, Moira, came running down the path, her hands twisting and turning in the folds of her apron.

"Oh sir!" she cried, "I'm richt glad to see ye! It's the mill, sir! A fire! And the police roond speirin' for ye and a'!"

Vicky shrieked.

"When was this, Moira?"

"No hauf an hour syne, sir! I said I didna think ye'd be lang in comin', and the policeman says 'Tell him to get there', he says, 'jist as quick as he can!'"

"All right, Moira, thank you! Help Mistress Gray in with the bags if you please!"

"I'm coming with you!"

"No, Vicky! You stay here! There won't be much any of us can do. I expect the Fire Brigade will have everything in hand."

"I'm coming: maybe father will be there!"

Andrew had never seen his wife in more determined mood – anyway, argument would only waste valuable time.

"Very well, then," he said, "Moira! Will you please take the bags in. We shall be home as soon as we can! Cabby! Baltic Mill – as fast as you can!"

Whenever their cab turned into Dens Road, Andrew could see that the fire at the mill was a very serious one. Although they were still too far away to make anything out in detail, it was obvious that a large part of the mill was well and truly alight. In fact, all they could see was one huge wall of fire which lit all the surrounding area as brightly as the midday sun. The nearer buildings were etched black against the lurid glare and acrid clouds of smoke were billowing upwards into the evening sky. Police, reinforced by soldiers from the barracks, were endeavouring to keep the roadway clear and to hold back the excited crowds of onlookers thronging the pavement on either side. The cabby had not got very far up the road when he was stopped by a police constable who, stepping out, blocked the way, arm upraised.

"What is it, constable?" Andrew put his head out of the window.

"Sorry, sir!" said the policeman. "Road's closed to all traffic! Ye'll have to turn aboot and gang back whaur ye cam' frae."

"But – I must get through," said Andrew, "I'm Andrew Gray of R. J. Caldwell & Son and this lady is Mr. Henry Caldwell's daughter."

"Sorry, sir! Eh couldna care gin the leddy wis Queen Victoria hersel' – ye're no gaun through!"

"But – this is ridiculous!" said Andrew. "One of your officers called at my residence at Strawberry Hill about an hour ago requesting my immediate presence at the Baltic Mill. Suppose we leave the cab and go on by foot. Would that satisfy you?"

"Ye can walk gin ye wish – but ye'll no walk up the road. Naebody passes – ither than the Fire Brigade, police or soldiery! Noo sir! Are ye gaun back or will Eh hae to get a few mair constables to persuade ye like!"

"Andrew!" cried Vicky. "We must get through. Don't let this stupid constable keep us back!"

"Constable!" said Andrew, "I appreciate that you have your orders and I do not ask you to overturn them. I do ask, however, that you seek guidance from your sergeant or someone else in authority. I promise you, we shall not attempt to advance any further until you return."

The constable removed his helmet and scratched the back of his neck. However, before he had to bring his wits to bear upon this proposition, another uniformed figure appeared at his side.

"What's going on here, Farrell?" The newcomer had an authoritative voice.

"Good evening, Superintendent!" said Andrew. "The constable has been doing his duty." Briefly, Andrew outlined the reason for their presence in the middle of Dens Road at such a time and the police officer accepted his assurances.

"Farrell!" he said, "ride with the cabby! See that Mr. and Mrs. Gray get as close to the mill as is consistent with safety!"

And so, escorted by the constable of police, they made rapid progress but were stopped, eventually, some two hundred yards short of the blazing building. Andrew could see now that it was the new mill that was ablaze and afterwards he remembered thinking what a blessing it would be if the Fire

Brigade could contain the conflagration there and prevent it spreading to the older building. The Fire Brigade appeared to be here, there and everywhere. Men in helmets and goggles were scurrying about all over the place dragging hoses, playing jets of water over the flames and working on the hand pumps. Their leader, Captain Fyffe, was very much in command and was co-ordinating the whole operation. The heat was intense and Andrew could feel the hair of his head, eyebrows and beard singeing. Great tongues of flame were spurting down the walls of the mill like lava flowing from the crater of a volcano and the stench of burning yarn and blazing whale oil was well nigh stupefying. Every now and then, as a beam or rafter, or part of a containing wall, fell in on top of the flames, bursts of fire dust shot into the air like exploding shells. Part of the furnace room was now alight and flames were flickering all round the outside brickwork of the single tall chimney.

Just then Vicky, who was standing with one hand clutching Andrew's arm and the other shielding her face from the pulsating heat, caught sight of her father's square figure over at the corner of the furnace room. Andrew saw him at the same moment. What Henry Caldwell was doing there Andrew had no idea. He only knew that he was much too close to the fire for his own personal safety.

"Pappa!" Vicky screamed and, before Andrew could stop her, she rushed forward.

It was then there occurred a phenomenon that had been experienced before at the height of severe mill fires in Dundee and would doubtless be seen again in the future. It had to do with the massive build-up in temperature which caused the tightly packed bales of codilla, tow and jute to expand to such an extent that the mill walls could no longer resist the pressure. The building quite literally exploded in a hellish cascade of tumbling brick and, as Andrew looked on aghast, Henry Caldwell and Vicky with him vanished from sight, buried under tons of debris and rubble. A flying brick fetched Andrew a sharp blow on the shoulder and another actually felled and killed a fireman standing close beside him. To some extent, the collapse of the building acted as a damper upon the flames and, very gradually, the fire began to give way under the sustained assault of the fire fighters' hoses. Andrew stood as if rooted to the spot.

"I don't think there can be much hope, Mr. Gray!"

Andrew turned to find Captain Fyffe at his elbow, his face streaked with a mixture of blood and ashes. "We'll start digging just as soon as we may. The trouble is the heat. Right now we can't even get near the rubble."

The short summer night was over before the flames were entirely extinguished. The cold light of dawn revealed the full extent of the damage which was quite horrifying. But considerable as this was, the physical damage was in no way comparable to the immense loss they had all suffered through the double tragedy that had overtaken Henry Caldwell and his daughter. That they were both dead was scarcely in doubt although, human nature being what it is, they all steadfastly refused to believe it until – about seven o'clock in the morning, and after hard and sustained digging – they uncovered the bodies, first that of Vicky and then her father. Both must have been killed instantly when the burning building collapsed on top of them.

"I am very sorry, Mr. Gray." Captain Fyffe held out his hand and Andrew took it mechanically. "If it can be of any consolation, they would know nothing about it – nothing at all."

"Thank you, Captain Fyffe – you, and all who have worked under you this terrible night." Andrew was still standing in the same spot – quite literally numb with shock. At least it was not cold. The sun had been up for three hours and the day was obviously going to be another warm one.

"Mr. Gray, sir! There is little you can do here." It was Captain Fyffe again. "Could I suggest that you move down to your office?"

Andrew started and looked about him as if for the first time.

"Oh!" he said. "Yes – very well."

He was there, in his own office, four hours later, when a horrified Charlie Tait arrived, having come straight off the early morning train from Brechin. Charlie and Ellen had spent Saturday night with the Gardynes and had taken the opportunity of going up the glen on Sunday to visit Ellen's mother, who had not seen them for quite some time. Somehow or other, Andrew felt a great sense of relief with Charlie beside him and from then on his confidence began to return. Charlie insisted that first he must go home, get himself tidied up and get some sleep. Andrew demurred. There was too much to be done. Quietly, however, Charlie took charge and Joseph – who the previous evening had driven his master up to the mill and who had also been up all night – drove Andrew home to Strawberry Hill where they found a distraught and frightened Moira. The poor girl had waited up expecting Andrew and Vicky to come home at any minute and she broke down completely when they told her what had happened. Andrew suggested that they might try to get her mother down from the mill – provided she had turned up for work that morning and had not been among those that had to be sent home – but this only served to make Moira shriek and sob all the more and it took the combined efforts of Andrew and Joseph to quieten her and to persuade her to go to bed and try to get some sleep. Joseph too was exhausted and in dire need of sleep but he knew that his wife, along with the rest of the household at West Ferry, would be on tenterhooks awaiting news. No doubt they had already had a surfeit of rumour. Unfortunately, they – and everyone else – would get news and to spare in the columns of tomorrow's *Advertiser*.

Andrew did not know what he would have done without Charlie Tait. It was Charlie who arranged for a messenger to go to Lintmill to break the news of the tragedy to Miss Swankie and it was he who co-ordinated the task of effecting some sort of clearing up. It would, of course, take weeks before everything was finally sorted out but at least they could make a start at assessing the damage and ascertaining whether or not they could continue in production at any level. When Joseph brought Andrew back to the smoke-filled offices at the mill in the early evening, Charlie was able to give him a report which in many ways cleared the air and allowed Andrew to spend most of Tuesday morning making arrangements for the double funeral.

Dundee had been stunned by the news. Although there were few who could have failed to see the blaze throughout Sunday evening and far into the wee small hours, many did not know the full extent of the tragedy and all day on Monday rumour and distorted versions of the calamity had been rife in the town. But the full story was there for all to read when the *Advertiser* came out on Tuesday morning.

The tragedy – so the reporter wrote – could be compared with the fearsome conflagration which occurred eleven years ago, almost to the day, when nearly all the buildings on the east side of Trades Lane were destroyed. On that occasion, the blaze was so intense that it had been visible as far away as Edinburgh. The *Advertiser* did not condescend upon the extent of the loss in pounds, shillings and pence, except to comment that the Baltic Mill would clearly be very severely crippled. The loss to the business community by the tragic death of Mr. Caldwell was, they said, incalculable. Since the death of his grandfather, Mr. Caldwell had controlled the family business with a firm and capable hand. Astute and perspicacious in every way, he had kept the Baltic Mill right in the forefront of modern development. Quick to spot the increasing importance of jute, he had hastened to increase the capacity of the works, having finished the new mill, now sadly burned down, in time to meet the increased demand brought about by the American Civil War.

A widower for many years, Mr. Caldwell had been about to marry again – indeed the *Advertiser* understood that the wedding invitations were already out, the ceremony having been planned to take place in Arbroath in three weeks time. To his affianced, Miss Priscilla Swankie, niece of Sir Robert and Lady Dargie of Lintmill, St. Vigeans, the *Advertiser* expressed deepest sympathy. Heartfelt condolences were also extended to Mr. Andrew Gray of R. J. Caldwell & Son, whose young wife Victoria, the late Mr. Caldwell's daughter, had also perished in the fire. To these deaths, the paper continued, must be added a further two – Mr. Patrick Lenihan (fifty-six) furnaceman, and Mr. James Phillips (twenty-two) a part-time member of the Fire Brigade – killed as they tried to subdue the flames. The reporter understood that a memorial service to Mr. Caldwell and Mrs. Gray would be held on Thursday 31st May in St. Roque's parish church in the Seagate at eleven o'clock in the morning – the funeral, which would take place immediately afterwards to the Western Necropolis, Arbroath Road, being a private family affair.

The *Advertiser* went on to praise the work of Captain Fyffe of the

Fire Brigade – once again called upon to take charge of a very serious conflagration – and of the troops from Dudhope, a detachment of the 93rd (Highland) Regiment, whose contribution in assisting the police in the maintenance of law and order had been quite invaluable. No tribute, however, could, in the reporter's view, be great enough to honour the valiant effort made by Mr. Henry Caldwell to rescue one of his employees, Patrick Lenihan, who it appeared had been trapped by a falling beam as he tried to clear the space between the blazing mill and the detached furnace room to prevent the fire spreading. Alas, it was all in vain, both Mr. Caldwell and Mr. Lenihan, having perished when the mill wall had collapsed.

On the Thursday, Andrew had the support of the Taits and of a large contingent from Pitbuddo, including his mother, the Robertsons, and Bells and Mr. Havelock Ramsay. Aunt Eliza, who according to Jessie "must be nearly a hundred" also came to the church, despite the fact that she always insisted she couldn't abide the Reverend Mr. Whamond. Priscilla Swankie was there – all in black and heavily veiled. Andrew had a difficult interview with her, her haggard, tear-stained face presenting a vastly different appearance from the haughty visage she had turned upon him at their first meeting at Broughty Ferry station. The Shirress family were not present. Meg's baby – another little girl – had been born on the Monday. Both mother and child were doing well but the family were naturally occupied with domestic matters and remained at home in Pitbuddo, whither, Andrew betook himself over the weekend – going up on Friday and returning to Dundee with the morning train on Monday.

The meeting to discuss Mr. Caldwell's will and to consider the financial implications upon the business following the death, and the destruction of the new mill, took place at noon that day in the chambers of Messrs Morton, Sime & Horsburgh in Meadowside. Mr. Horsburgh, lawyer and personal friend of Henry Caldwell over many years, presided with Mr. Petrie from the Bank also in attendance. There was a short silence while Mr. Horsburgh, having completed the reading of the will, refolded the heavy sheets of parchment.

"Quite straight forward, really," he said. "Apart from these small bequests and the lump sum to the Royal Infirmary, the whole of the residue of the estate, including Henry's interest in R. J. Caldwell & Son, which amounts to the whole of the capital of the firm, is divided equally between Victoria and Mr. Gray. Poor Victoria died intestate and accordingly her share will also fall to you, Mr. Gray, as her husband. Clearly, Mr. Gray, you have come into a considerable inheritance – Mr. Petrie will know more about values – eh, Petrie?"

"Yes," said Mr. Petrie, "Mr. Caldwell had a very worthwhile portfolio of shares – all soundly based – worth at the very least something in the region of

£50,000. As Mr. Gray will know, the expense of the new mill, erected in 1860 at a cost of £15,000, and now sadly destroyed, was carried by the Bank on an overdraft in the firm's name entitled "Building Account". In security we hold from Mr. Caldwell some £8,000 in Consols and a Bond of Credit and Disposition in Security over Riga Lodge. There will, of course, be a valid insurance claim in respect of the fire damage but I suspect that, adequate though this may be if settled in full, the proceeds may not be sufficient to cover the full cost of replacement. In addition, I must warn you, Andrew, that in my experience there is frequently quite an inordinate delay before the insurance company is finally persuaded to pay out."

"The claim is in already," said Andrew, "I saw the N.B. & Merc. people last week."

"Good!"

"We can carry on to a certain extent as we are," Andrew continued. "As you know the old mill is intact and we still have both spinning and weaving capacity. We had intended to concentrate all the manufacturing process in the new mill, leaving the original for yarn production alone. Fortunately we had not got round to it and there are still a number of looms – albeit not modern – in the old mill. We shall, of course, have difficulty until we get the chimney replaced and the furnace room sorted out. The damage there is not extensive – the worst affected being the chimney stack. Another trouble is that we lost a considerable quantity of finished goods, and, of course, we shall not be able to fulfill our contracts. With the best will in the world we cannot expect our customers to do anything other than turn to alternative suppliers. If and when we regain our former capacity it may take us a long time to build up our order book again."

"Oh, surely your customers will be loyal!" said Mr. Horsburgh. "Many will have dealt with R. J. Caldwell & Son for years – they will come back."

"With respect, Mr. Horsburgh, I don't think it will be as simple as that. The competition in the industry – in Dundee itself – is very keen. There is also the question of our raw material. We shall require only a small part of our customary order and the brokers, both here and in India, will be looking to replace this business. No! The next few years look like being very lean ones so far as R. J. Caldwell & Son are concerned and we may have to lean on the Bank, Mr. Petrie, from time to time. My first inclination is to consider the immediate sale of Riga Lodge to cut the indebtedness on the Building Account and save the upkeep which must be considerable. There is also the question of interest!"

Mr. Petrie smiled sourly. "Well," he said, "that is certainly for consideration unless, of course, you feel you might wish to retain Riga Lodge for your own use either now or in the future."

"No, Mr. Petrie, I have no wish whatsoever to reside at Riga. I think I have really made up my mind but I shall confirm or otherwise within the course of the next few days. If we are going to sell there is no sense in delaying the matter!"

Mr. Petrie nodded. "As for the necessity to lean more heavily on the Bank," he said, pursing his lips, "I think you may be assured that the Bank will be...ah...supportive: yes, supportive! Let us cross that bridge when the time comes, shall we?"

Andrew smiled. "Oh, by all means, Mr. Petrie." Then, turning to the lawyer, "Mr. Horsburgh!" he said, "I would like you to draw up a contract of co-partnery: I wish to take my office manager, Charlie Tait, into partnership with me in the firm of R. J. Caldwell & Son. His full name is Charles Ogilvie Tait, and he resides at number twenty four Albert Street in this city."

"Before you reply, Horsburgh," said Mr. Petrie, "I think I have completed my business with you both so, if you will be so kind as to excuse me, I must get back to the Bank. Oh! I nearly forgot: here is letter for you, Andrew – received on Saturday morning." He handed Andrew an envelope and rose to go. "Don't worry, Horsburgh – I'll see myself out! Good afternoon, gentlemen!"

Andrew shoved the letter into his breast pocket and endeavoured to remain calm and business-like, nothwithstanding the pounding of his heart at the sight of Mary's handwriting on the envelope. He forced himself to concentrate and to answer the questions Mr. Horsburgh was firing at him in regard to the terms in which he wished the partnership agreement to be drawn up. While they talked, a clerk came in carrying a tray on which were set a teapot, cups and saucers, milk and sugar, and a plate of hot mutton pies. Behind him was one of Mr. Horsburgh's partners. The clerk set the tray down upon a small table and withdrew.

"I think you've met my partner, Mr. Brough," said Mr. Horsburgh.

"No! How do you do, Mr. Brough?"

"Good afternoon, Mr. Gray. You will take a cup of tea, I hope, and a bite to eat. It is long past dinner time!"

"Why, thank you, Mr. Brough," said Andrew. "It is in fact a long time since I broke my fast this morning in my mother's house in Pitbuddo!"

"Pitbuddo!" Mr. Brough exclaimed, "Pitbuddo, near Brechin?"

"Yes."

"Oh! I have a friend in Pitbuddo," Mr. Brough went on, "one whom I haven't seen for years. We were at college together – I in the law faculty, and he – a medic. David Robertson is his name. A brilliant doctor – could have gone to the top of his profession, but all he ever wished for was a country practice!"

"Well," said Andrew, "Dr. Robertson is a very good friend of ours. He is fit and well. As a matter of fact he was here last Thursday at the service in St. Roques."

"Ah yes," said Mr. Brough, "that was a sorry business. What a tragedy! Who would have believed it?"

They munched their pies in silence for a while. Andrew could hear his stomach rumbling loudly.

"This is very kind of you," he said to cover his embarrassment.

"We shall concentrate all the better now," Mr. Horsburgh smiled and wiped his fingers on the serviette which had come in with the tray.

"Glad to have met you, Mr. Gray," said Mr. Brough, rising and brushing the crumbs off his trousers. "Please give David Robertson my warmest regards when next you see him."

"I certainly shall," said Andrew.

When, some ten minutes later, Andrew walked out of the building on to Meadowside he found Joseph awaiting with the carriage.

"Mr. Tait said you'd be needing me, Mr. Andra! Back to the mill, is it?"

"Yes, please, Joseph!"

The coachman felt Henry Caldwell's death very keenly and it was clear to Andrew that the only thing keeping him going was the knowledge that he could be of assistance to the new chief. Should the old man ever be made to feel that he was no longer needed, he would no doubt just curl up and die. Andrew had to see to it that this did not happen. Joseph and his wife occupied the room and kitchen tagged on to the coach-house at Riga Lodge and they would have to be found alternative accommodation should the place be sold.

As the coach went slowly up Victoria Road, Andrew wondered whether he should read Mary's letter now, but he decided to keep that pleasure until he got back to Strawberry Hill at the end of the day. Meantime, he had to keep his mind clear and concentrate upon business matters.

At the mill he found Charlie Tait closeted with two men from Edinburgh who proved to be insurance adjusters come to inspect the damage. The sooner they did their job the quicker Caldwells would be able to get started on the immense task of clearing the site, so both Charlie and Andrew bent over backwards to ensure that their visitors could see everything they wished to see. When they left, they indicated that they had sufficient upon which to formulate their official report and that the site could now be cleared at the firm's convenience.

Charlie was quite taken aback when Andrew asked him to join the firm as a partner.

"Andrew, man," he said, "ye ken there's naething I'd like better but I've nae siller to my name and ye canna be a partner wantin' siller."

"Charlie! Charlie! The money doesn't matter a damn. It's you I want – no, need – not your money even if you had it. In any case, if you and I work hard, as I for one am determined to do, we'll get the profit moving again and Charlie Tait's share will soon begin to build up his capital base! You will join me, Charlie – please!"

"Yes, Andrew. I'll join you, and I'll stick with you, come hell or high water! Ye ken fine it's you and yours alone that have ever given me a chance in life. I'll work with you, Andrew Gray – by God I will!"

Standing there amid the charred embers of Henry Caldwell's once proud new extension, they solemnly shook hands like a couple of strangers!

Andrew walked down the Hawkhill with a very slightly unsteady gait. After asking Joseph to call for him at Strawberry Hill on the following morning at eight, Andrew had sent Joseph home for the night. Then, after he and Charlie had finished and locked up, they walked together in the evening sunshine down the hill. Close by the Wellgate steps was a small bar run by an Irishman by the same of Roonie. Andrew had heard of Mick Roonie's establishment, but had never visited it before. Charlie had been once and said it was reasonably respectable. At all events, the new Gray/Tait partnership of R. J. Caldwell & Son required to be properly toasted and this seemed as good a place as any in which to do the job. If the bar proved to be full of Baltic Mill workers – that would be just too bad! They would have to take the chance. As it happened, the bar was quiet.

"Sure – it's normal for a Monday night," the proprietor, a small man with a walrus moustache, hastened to assure them.

They both had rather more to drink than was good for them. So far as Charlie was concerned, he felt it would do Andrew no harm after all he had been through in the past week and consequently he did not demur when Andrew repeated their order for the fifth time. When at length, they surfaced, and continued down the steps, the sunshine had gone and the sky had clouded over. At the foot of the Wellgate they parted and Andrew, walking with exaggerated care, made his lone way westwards. At the end of Hawkhill he crossed over the Perth Road and turned down Strawberry Hill. He was quite glad to reach the haven of number two where Moira had his supper ready for him. He felt better after he had eaten. It had been a long and difficult day. Small wonder the whisky had had such effect! Compared with what Zeke use to put away it was just a drop to wet the bottom of the glass! He smiled when he thought of Zeke and he wondered how he and Abigail were and what they were doing.

But now for Mary's letter. He lit the reading lamp, pulled the envelope from his breast pocket and broke the seal.

The letter was superscribed: "Edinburgh – 26th May 1866."

That was the day before the fire – the day of the dinner party at the Robertsons – a week past on Saturday! Where on earth had it been in the interval? He turned the envelope over and looked at the postmark. It had not been affixed clearly and was difficult to decipher but it seemed to read – although Andrew could scarcely credit it – "Southampton 1-6-66" With a sinking feeling in the pit of his stomach he started to read:-

"Dearest Andrew," Mary wrote, "By the time you get this, I shall be on board ship bound for Cape Town. After you left me, all those weeks ago, I thought long and deeply about the situation in which we are placed. I know when last we spoke I said I would always be around should you have need of me, and it was me who countered your 'goodbye', tempering it to a mere 'farewell'.

"On deeper reflection, however, I realise it would be a selfish act on my part to allow you to continue to see me when we both know that your place is beside your wife. All I would be doing would be to weaken your resolve to remain faithful to her whom you have vowed to love and cherish. It breaks my heart, my darling, to put you from me – for you are all I have ever wanted – but, truly, there is no other way that would not place an undue strain upon a marriage which would never have been contracted had it not been for my own stupidity.

"I went up to Lagganeinich and had a long talk with Alasdair. I have always been able to speak my mind with him and he, of course, was a great friend of Robin's. He helped me to reach a decision. Speyside was perfectly lovely with the birches all coming into leaf and wild hyacinths like a blue tide surging among the trees. How I shall miss it all! There have been great changes since I was home last, with a railway line running all the way from Perth to Kingussie. In fact, you can now go the whole length of the journey from Perth to Inverness by rail! The folk today don't know how lucky they are!

"Well. Having made up my mind, I was left wondering just what to do, when it occurred to me that I might go out to the Cape Province where I have an aunt and uncle. Two of my mother's sisters married brothers. Aunt Kate, as you know, married John Pattullo and my mother's youngest sister married John's brother, Willie. Willie Pattullo was never really robust: they said he had a weak chest, and soon after they were married he sold up his farm – he had a place down near Inverkeillour – and emigrated to South Africa. He seems to have benefited by the change of climate and he now farms in a big way near a place called Stellenbosch where he rears cattle and grows vines. I wrote and asked whether I might come out to visit them. They said 'yes' – so I'm on my way.

"I have booked a passage on the mail steamer, *False Bay*, sailing from Southampton on 3rd June. When you read this, I shall be at sea!

"Goodbye, my dearest. When you think of me, as I hope you

sometimes will, remember that I shall always wear – pinned on my dress or blouse, close to my heart – a certain cameo brooch.
With all my love.
Yours always . . . . "

The salt tears stung his eyes and Andrew could see no more. Moira found him when she came down in the morning, sleeping in his chair, a crumpled letter lying at his side.

"Oh, sir!" cried Moira, "ye're fair worn oot! Did ye no get to your bed at a'!"

Andrew woke with a start and saw the girl standing at the door. He had a splitting headache and a stiff neck.

"Have you nothing better to do than stand about staring!" he snapped.

Moira took to her heels. She need not have worried unduly. She may have been the first, but she was by no means the last to get the rough end of Andrew's tongue that day. He snarled at Joseph and he growled at Charlie and he went about the mill scowling at everyone unfortunate enough to come up against him. It was the same the next day – and the next. Andrew remained grim faced and morose.

Mary had gone. That was the sum of it – gone – probably forever, just at the very moment when it would have been possible for them to consider a future together. She must have left Edinburgh on the weekend of the fire and so would not have had the opportunity of reading about it or of learning of the tragic deaths of both Henry Caldwell and Vicky. She would probably settle down in the Cape Province, marry some Dutch-speaking farmer and go trekking off into the interior. Even if he wrote right away, he could hardly expect her to come hot-tailing it back to Scotland. And what would he say anyway? "Dear Mary – It's all right now: Vicky's dead and you can move in to take her place." As it had done over and over again since reading Mary's letter, deep and hopeless depression welled up and engulfed him.

By Saturday morning Charlie Tait had had more than he could bear. He had no idea what had got into Andrew – he had been all right when they parted that evening after visiting Mick Roonie's bar. Charlie could only assume that the terrible events of the past weeks had unhinged his mind – temporarily, he hoped.

"Look, Andrew!" he said, "I dinna ken what's come ower ye, but whatever it is ye'll no be muckle use till it's bye wi'! Ye're waur that a bear wi' a sair heid. Get awa' to Pitbuddo for a few days and see if a breath o' country air can clear that heid o' yours o' whatever it is that fleein' aboot inside. If your mother canna mak' heid nor tail o' ye – maybe Dr. Robertson'll ken what to dae!"

To Charlie's amazement, Andrew did not demur.

"I'm sorry, Charlie," he said. "There is something wrong. Someday, I'll tell you. Right now I think maybe you have the rights of it. Could you manage on your own for a week till I see whether the good air of the glens can chase away the black shadow on my back?"

Andrew caught the afternoon train which got him into Brechin just after five o'clock. The rain which had fallen steadily since early morning had cleared away and the clouds were breaking, allowing a blink or two of sunlight to filter through. Andrew decided to walk home – the exercise would do him good – or so he hoped. On impulse he took the old road and headed along Clerk Street, past the shop where he had bought that cameo brooch of Mary's and up the long hill to Trinity. The road was unusually busy with carts and waggons coming and going, their wheels splashing through the puddles and gouging deep muddy furrows at the narrow parts when forced on to the verge as they tried to pass. Every now and then, Andrew had to jump out of the way to avoid being run over and before long he had been liberally splashed with mud. It was only when he reached the crest of the brae and saw the activity going on there that he realised that Wednesday of the following week would be the date of the June Fair. Already there were tinker encampments on the edge of the moor and folk were swarming all over the place, struggling with wet canvas and standing precariously perched on orange boxes while they hammered nails into boards and battens. A number of stands and most of the livestock pens were already in place. Dirty-faced urchins were running around getting under the feet of the men putting up the stands and a group of tinker loons was cantering around on wild-eyed ponies whose hoofs cut up the turf and sent divots and stones flying in all directions, to the fury of those who happened to be at the receiving end. Understandably the air was loud with imprecations.

Andrew veered away as soon as he could along the familiar road to Craigbeg. The red sandstone of the farmhouse glowed a dusky pink in the evening sunshine and he heard dogs barking in the steading. There was no-one about, however, as he came down past the cottar houses heading for the wood at the corner. His heart turned over as he passed their trysting place at the field gate. Apart from half a dozen half-bred stirks standing at the fence looking inquisitively at him, their moist noses covered with flies, the place was deserted. Andrew walked on and turned off on to the path leading through the birch scrub into the beechwood. Mary's favourite place was, alas, unrecognisable – a tangle of elm and hawthorn, overgrown and well nigh impregnable. Beyond the hedge, however, the smiling farmlands stretching away to the high hills were as bonny as ever and gave an almost imperceptible lift to Andrew's spirits, so that he found himself wondering what it is that persuades a man to slave away in the city when he might just as readily live out his life in glorious surroundings such as this beautiful and favoured countryside.

A mavis, perched on the gate post at Old Pitbuddo, was pouring out her evensong, a tumbling cascade of notes, full of joy and vibrant with life. She flew off as Andrew undid the latch and walked in among the grave stones. This was a more suitable setting for his mood and he stood looking down upon the little plot where his father lay. The headstone which old Dod Watson had put up at his mother's behest was covered at the edges with lichen. At the base there were flowers in a pot of water – a bunch of lupins, faded and wilting. Tomorrow afternoon there would be fresh blooms to replace them. As if seeing them for the first time Andrew looked at the dates under his father's name – "1815-1850". Gracious goodness! He was only five years away from the age his father had been when he was killed! On top of his misery and feeling of utter dejection, there was now an added sense of the transitory and ephemeral nature of human existence. Weighed down by his thoughts he closed the cemetery gate behind him and walked on.

Jessie was surprised to see him but she made no comment and refrained from plying him with questions. In any event she was busy getting the supper ready. Jemima, it seemed, was out. When she came in she made some comment regarding the increasing frequency of her brother's visits back home which caused Andrew to snap back at her.

"My! My!" she taunted, "we're a bit short tempered tonight, are we not?"

"Jemima!" exclaimed Jessie. "That will do! You know quite well what Andrew has had to endure over the past few weeks. It ill becomes you to treat him in such fashion!"

Jemima was immediately crestfallen.

"No, mamma," said Andrew, "I should not have spoken so rudely! I'm sorry, 'Mima – I fear I am not very good company these days!"

Next day, Sunday, Andrew once more accompanied Jessie to the church. The Old Testament reading was the well-known passage telling how Elim- lech, his wife Naomi and their two sons, seeing there was a famine in Bethlehem-Judah, journeyed into the land of Moab where, after ten years, the three men died, each leaving behind a widow – Naomi who now desired to return home, and her two daughters-in-law who were women of Moab. Mr. Black's high-pitched voice cracked as he read how Naomi put the younger women from her saying – "Go, return each to her mother's house." And while one eventually did as Naomi bade her, the other – Ruth – would not be moved and did in fact return with Naomi to Bethlehem in the time of the barley harvest.

Poor Andrew! This did nothing whatsoever to soothe his jarred and shattered feelings. It was quite bad enough listening to the infinitely moving plea with which Ruth successfully beseeches her mother-in-law to change her mind – but it turned out to be these stanzas upon which Mr. Black had elected to preach.

"Our text this morning," he intoned, "is to be found in the passage we have already read; in the Book of Ruth, Chapter 1, at verses 16 and 17.

> "And Ruth said, Entreat me not to leave thee,
> or to return from following after thee;
> for whither thou goest, I will go;
> and where thou lodgest, I will lodge;
> thy people shall be my people,
> and thy God my God;
> where thou diest, will I die,
> and there will I be buried;
> the Lord do so to me, and more also,
> if aught but death part thee and me."

Andrew took out his handkerchief and did his utmost to make it appear that he was dabbing at his nose. But Jessie saw his red-rimmed eyes and her heart was heavy for him. Lord knows she had never taken to Vicky, but Jessie of all people knew only too well what it was to lose the darling of one's heart; and she assumed that Andrew mourned Vicky's death as she had Tom's – over all the years.

In the afternoon, they walked out as usual to Old Pitbuddo and, after supper, Andrew asked to be excused and took himself off to bed where he did, in fact, sleep better than he had done since the night of the fire.

Next day, Andrew chanced to meet Havelock Ramsay in the High Street – a meeting which afforded the latter an opportunity to revert to the question of investment in land in a developing state such as Texas. It was apparent that he had been giving a great deal of thought to the matter and that – even in the short time since they had last talked of it – he had advanced his ideas quite considerably.

"You know, Gray," he said, "I have been thinking of what you said regarding the inter-relationship of land values, railroads and cattle. It seems fairly certain that the east-west rail link will have spanned the north American continent before the present decade is out. The ideal would be a slice of land lying athwart the cattle trails leading north to the transcontinental line. Now you – or R. J. Caldwell & Son – have the very thing. I should like to invest in such a project. Should we not consider putting together a company which could buy up the titles to land of this nature – either the land itself, or mortgages over the land – and hold it as an investment for the future? If the cattle trade builds up, as you think it will, it could prove a lucrative one. If the track does not materialise – or should the line go elsewhere – we can withdraw, or switch location. Meantime, if interest rates in America maintain their present level we are hardly likely to lose. Worth the gamble?"

"Yes," said Andrew, "I think it would be."

"Well! Let us talk further. I still have to make that visit to the Baltic Mill, you know. Perhaps in a month or two, once you've had time to sort yourselves out after the recent calamity, don't be surprised if I come knocking on your door!" He smiled broadly and Andrew could not help smiling too; certainly he felt a great deal cheerier than for many days past.

By the time he got home, it had started to rain – a bad omen for the following day which was of course that of Trinity Fair. Andrew had a notion to go to the fair. He was not likely to have a similar chance again unless he were to come up specially from Dundee and the present seemed too good a chance to miss. If he were indeed to head for the fair in the morning, he would have to be up and about early. Accordingly, Jessie saw to it that he had a light supper and turned in before ten o'clock.

In the morning, Andrew got a lift into Brechin from Jock Lundie and he joined the crowds making their way up Trinity Road towards the moor. The rain had played itself out overnight and the morning was bright enough under patchy cloud, although still on the cool side for June. Underfoot it was wet with muddy stretches in the busier parts where folk tended to slip and slide, some indeed – especially those who had already been visiting the refreshment tents – to fall. Andrew walked around avoiding the more densely packed areas, listening to the patter of the hucksters and showmen and watching the country folk enjoying what, for most of them, was their one and only "day out" in the year. Girls dressed in their Sunday best clustered at the corner of the stands, laughing and making eyes at the young men trying their hands at the coconut shies and shooting galleries.

Down at the livestock pens the auctioneers were busy, their sing-song mumbo-jumbo rising and falling monotonously. Andrew took great care not to scratch his ear nor brush a fly from his jacket lest he found himself the unwitting owner of a penful of sheep.

He left the sheep ring and wandered over to the cattle lines – home-bred blacks mainly, with some shorthorns and a few shaggy Highlanders with wide curving horns standing as if looking for Edwin Landseer to come and paint them. Farther over there were brown and white dairy cows from Ayrshire with horns that swept outwards at the tips. Andrew leant an arm against the wooden rail of a pen where half a dozen stirks, their coats like black velvet, stood bunched together looking woebegone and thoroughly dejected. He was miserable too but it came to him the that in truth these poor beasts, did they but know it, unlike himself really did have cause for dejection. He was about to move away when he felt a hand on his shoulder and a voice, well known although not heard for many a long year, saying, "Gudesakes, if it's no Andra Gray! Man, Andra, it's lang ere I clapped eyes on ye, and ye've had a sorry time o't – so I hear. I'm richt sorry, lad!"

Mary's uncle, John Pattullo, was standing there, hand outstretched. They shook hands.

"Thank you, Mr. Pattullo," said Andrew, "I'm up in Pitbuddo for a day or two and I thought I might as well pay a visit to the fair while I'm here. How is everything with you, sir?"

John Pattullo certainly looked well and, so far as Andrew could see, the passing years had marked him but little.

"Nae sae bad, Andra! Prices are haudin' up and the crops are daein' awa'! Mind ye – the land at Craigbeg's better nor maist!"

"That's true," Andrew nodded, "I passed by on Saturday afternoon on my way home from Brechin. There didn't seem to be anyone about."

"Maybe no! I was awa' up at my sister's place at Edzell but Willie and Bessie Smith would be there. They bide in noo!" he smiled, "Bessie keeps the hoose and sees to my meals. I had to get some help after Mary left! Man! I aye thoucht it wad hae been you she married – no yon lawyer lad frae Edinburgh! A nice eneuch lad, Robin Cargill, but – talk? He'd talk the hind legs off a cuddy! Trouble was – I could never understand the hauf o' what he was on aboot!"

"I never met him."

"Weel! Ye'll no hae a chance noo! The puir lad was shot deid in America by ane o' yon caird shairpers. He was aye the gambling kind. Mary came to see me after she got hame. The puir wee lassie was gey upset but noo – she's awa' to my brother, Will, and his wife in the Cape Province, that's to say if she ever gets off! I had a letter frae her this morning, just, saying that the mail boat she was booked oot on – *False Bay* I think it was cried – never left Southampton. It seems she developed some trouble wi' her boilers and they had to tak' her oot o' service! It maun hae cost a pretty penny since the company put a' the passengers up in hotels until they could get a replacement. Mary says this is noo on its way – sister ship *Mossel Bay* – they're haein' to sail her roond frae Tilbury. She'll probably be awa' noo! She was writing on the seventh – that was last Thursday – and she said they had been told they would sail in one week's time. That wad be . . . er . . . the fourteenth! That's the morn, is it no?"

To John Pattullo's astonishment, Andrew seized him by the hand and pumped it up and down.

"Mr. Pattullo!" he said, "I must go! I shall come and see you at Easter Craigbeg very soon. I promise you . . ." and he was off, at a run, dodging through the crowds, slipping in the mud, but, by a miracle, managing to keep his feet. He reached the highway and ran down the hill. By the time he reached Clerk Street, he was sweating profusely and considerably winded, but he carried on at a half trot all the way to the railway depot.

"Losh keep's!" exclaimed the booking clerk who knew him well by sight. "What's your hurry, man?"

Mopping his face and forehead on his handkerchief. Andrew straightened the neck cloth he was wearing and smoothed down his jacket.

"What is my quickest way to London?" he asked in rather an unsteady voice.

"Well! Let's hae a look," the booking clerk consulted a sheaf of papers hanging on a hook alongside the rows of cardboard tickets, "...it's gone half past twelve. The route ye tak' mak's nae difference – ye'll no get there ony sooner than the morn's morn and that only gin ye travel though the nicht!"

"Well! Give me a return ticket if you please."

"First class?"

"Yes."

The booking clerk date stamped the ticket, handed it to Andrew and gave him the change from a five pound note.

"Tak' the 2.30!" he said. "That will connect wi' the express frae Aberdeen to Perth. Ye'll hae a lang wait in Perth, but there's a connection for the south at eight o'clock and ye'll be in London by eight in the morning. Gey uncomfortable, mind! Hae ye ever tried to sleep in a railway carriage?"

Andrew left it at that. He had time to get something to eat before the train was due out and he found a little place at the corner of the High Street. There was no choice – mutton broth, mince and potatoes, baked rice pudding – take it, or leave it! He ate the lot – it could be long enough before his next meal whenever that might be. His mind was in a turmoil and he wasn't quite sure whether he was coming or going. What was it John Pattullo had said? This other boat – this *Mossel Bay* – would sail on the fourteenth. That could mean anytime after midnight tonight, depending on the tide. And hadn't he heard somewhere, probably at school, that Southampton had not two but *four* tides a day! He was quite possibly away on a wild goose chase. But then – there was just a chance that he might be in time. One minute he was all keyed up and hopeful, the next he was once again plumbing the depths of despair, for was it not much more likely that, while he was rattling through the length of England during the hours of darkness, *Mossel Bay* would be slipping down the Solent bearing Mary away from him to the far ends of the earth and life in another continent and another hemisphere, where even the stars in the night sky would be alien? And yet – it was a gamble he must take.

Before he rose from the table he tore a leaf from the notebook he carried in his breast pocket and scribbled a pencil note to his mother.

"Mamma," he wrote, " – a matter of extreme urgency has arisen requiring my immediate and personal attention. As a consequence I shall not be back in Pitbuddo tonight, nor for a number of days, how many I cannot say. I shall, however, write you again just as soon as I may. Please do not concern yourself over this change of plan on my part, nor worry regarding my well being. I am, I assure you, fit and well and I send you my best love and respects. Your affectionate son, Andrew."

Having folded the paper and written Jessie's name on the outside, he left the restaurant and walked smartly to the yard beside the railway depot which acted as the town terminus for the country carriers. It was a busy place, packed with horses and waggons, loading and unloading but, to Andrew's great relief he spotted Matt Lundie in the crowd. Matt readily agreed to take his note and have it delivered to Jessie that evening. When Andrew re-entered the railway depot, he was just in time to catch the 2.30 train.

The booking clerk at Brechin had been quite right. Andrew found it difficult to imagine anything less conducive to sleep than a railway carriage. The first class seats, three to a side and divided by arm-rests, were well enough cushioned but the combination of rigid couplings, and three fixed and unyielding axles on a short-wheel base, made for a rough ride and when the train reached London at eight o'clock in the morning and Andrew alighted on the platform at Euston, he felt he had had no sleep at all. From Carlisle on there had been no empty seats in the carriage, with the result that all six travellers were required to sit bolt upright every inch of the way, much to the annoyance of one who had boarded at Lockerbie. He was clearly an experienced night rider for, before placing his bags in the overhead rack, he got out two stout sticks which he placed across the gap between the seats. With a cushion over the sticks he was able to lie full length across the breadth of the carriage and he fell soundly asleep until folk came in at Carlisle when, with bad grace, he had to remove his improvised couch.

It was pouring rain when Andrew, having secured a cab, was driven through the magnificent arch at the station exit and out into Euston Road. The traffic was thicker than anything he had seen in the other big cities he had visited either in Britain or America and he found it frustrating in the extreme when, as frequently happened, the pressure and sheer volume of the traffic brought everything to a standstill. On the pavements, the crowds, under a sea of umbrellas and behind upturned coat collars, hurried along with only one thought in mind – that of seeking shelter as quickly as possible from the relentless driving rain. The cabby, sitting hunched on the driving box, turned left off Marylebone Road into Baker Street. The journey seemed interminable and the motion of the cab soporific. When next he opened his eyes, the cab was rolling out over the leaden water of the river on Vauxhall Bridge.

Andrew was fortunate. He arrived at the Nine Elms depot five minutes before the train was due to depart for Southampton and he just had time to pay the cabby, buy his ticket and get himself on to the platform where the guard was already blowing his whistle. Andrew found a carriage to himself and, thankfully, threw himself down in a window seat. The train jerked and clattered out of the station into the rain-swept southern suburbs – row after row of little red brick houses with back greens criss-crossed with drying lines. On this occasion the jolting of the train proved no deterrent and Andrew fell sound asleep. He was awakened when three people, two men and a woman, pushed past him as they boarded the train at some stop or other. Andrew looked out the window and read the name – "Eastleigh".

"Next stop So't'on! Next stop So't'on!" A porter was walking up the length of the train making sure the doors were closed.

"Is it far to Southampton?" Andrew enquired from his travelling companions.

"No! We are very close: we'll be there in ten minutes!"

It was just after eleven o'clock, not quite twenty-four hours after his conversation with John Pattullo at Trinity Fair. But – would he be in time? Andrew's heart was pounding as the train pulled into the platform at Southampton docks.

"*Mossel Bay*? Never 'eard of 'er! What line is that?"

Andrew's heart sank. He had no idea as to which shipping line Mary had booked on. The uniformed man at the gates was looking closely at him. Clearly he did not rate Andrew's intelligence too highly.

"Not much use if you don't know the line! Now – stand aside, sir, if you please! There's others waiting to pass!"

The rain had stopped but heavy clouds were still scudding across the sky and the wind was plucking at anything that was not securely tied down. Andrew approached the gateman once again.

"Look!" he said, "I'm sorry I've no idea as to the shipping line but – *Mossel Bay* is bound for Cape Town and is due to sail today if she has not already done so!"

"Oh – the Cape! That'll be number six wharf. 'Ang on! I'll see if I've got 'er on my list! *Mossel Bay*...eh? Mm...."

Andrew's impatience knew no bounds. Why could the man not hurry? He had said the number of the wharf – why could he not leave it at that?

"'Ere we are!" The gateman stabbed a finger at a grubby sheet of paper pinned up inside the little box he occupied, "*Mossel Bay* – Wharf 6, due out at noon!"

So there was still a chance! Or was there? Andrew pulled out his watch. Eleven fifty-five! He had no time to lose.

"Thank you," he said. "How do I get to Wharf 6?"

"Turn left and keep going: it's not far – 400 yards maybe!"

But Andrew had already gone, racing along the dock like a sprinter coming up to the tape. He had to duck under the jibs of cranes, swerve round groups of dockers and lascars and leap like a hurdler over the piles of cargo they were busy shifting. When, at last, he reached Wharf 6, he found the quayside crowded with people who had come to see their friends and relatives off on their long voyage to South Africa. These last were lining the rail of a long, lithe-looking steamer waving and shouting last minute messages. On the ship's stern, under the long pole where the red ensign streamed out in the wind, there was painted the legend.

"*MOSSEL BAY*, LONDON"

"Excuse me! Excuse me!" Andrew, more frustrated than ever, was making absolutely no progress. It was as though he had never spoken. No-one moved aside; no-one let him through. Being somewhat taller than most of those around him, Andrew could see dockers moving towards the vessel's mooring hawsers to cast them off and, even as he watched, two seamen started untying the ropes securing the gangway in place. Up on the bridge, the captain seized the lanyard dangling from the ship's hooter and blew a long loud blast which was shredded by the wind to echo in a score of places.

"All visitors ashore! All visitors ashore!" From where he stood, Andrew could hear the ship's officer's voice and the clanging of the handbell he was ringing. If he didn't move now it would be too late! It was almost too late as it was! He tried again, flexing his muscles and pushing with all his force, but it was no use; he was a prisoner of the crowd and unable to move. Once again the captain tugged at the hooter cord – this time a shorter, more urgent blast.

Mary had found a space at the rail, at the corner, not far from the head of the gangway, and was idly watching the anxious upturned faces of the folk on the quay. She was glad there was nobody there to see her off to the other side of the world; she could not, she thought, have borne it to stand in either place and see a loved one for what might well prove to be the last time. She was glad too that the interminable waiting was at an end and that she would soon be at sea and away. Ever since selling up the house in Heriot Row and coming to a decision regarding her future, Mary had been in some agitation to get away lest she should weaken and change her mind. When the mail steamer, *False Bay*, had broken down, after they had all boarded and before casting off, all the passengers had been put up at the shipping line's expense in one of the local hotels and Mary had spent a week of sheer frustration not knowing what to do. Thank goodness all that was now behind her and she was on her way.

She nearly jumped out of her skin when the hooter went off behind her but she scolded herself for being so nervous and flattened herself against the rail as the Third Officer went past ringing his bell and calling upon all visitors to leave the ship. What it was that drew her eye to the particular section of the crowd she did not know but, suddenly, she saw Andrew. He was, of course, prominent enough in view of his height and, even from a distance, it was apparent to Mary that he was trying unsuccessfully to force his way forward towards the gangway. She had no idea why Andrew Gray would be here at Wharf 6 on Southampton dock, but the mere fact of his presence was quite sufficient so far as she was concerned. The ship's hooter blew again – a much more compelling note – and Mary, elbowing her way through the pack of passengers crowding the deck, moved as quickly as she could towards the head of the gangway.

They had already cast off and the captain was holding the ship steady on her engines. The gangway had been untied and as Mary set foot on the top-most tread, the duty officer standing by lunged to grab her arm and pull her back. But Mary side-stepped as much as it was possible so to do in that confined space and – avoided him. She ran down and jumped on to the quay. Behind her the gangplank was pulled away and R.M.S. *Mossel Bay* edged away from the dock and headed out into Southampton Water.

Andrew saw her as she came down the gangway and his spirit lifted. He gave one almighty heave and the solid wall of humanity before him parted like the waters of the Red Sea. He was through and Mary, his own darling Mary, was in his arms at last.

Andrew Gray and Mary Cargill, born Grant, were married in Kingussie on Friday 17th August 1866 before these witnesses – Charles Ogilvie Tait, Jute Spinner, Dundee, and Margaret Shirress, born Gray, Pitbuddo, Forfarshire.